Mage World

Matti Silver

This is a work of fiction. Names, characters, businesses, places, events and incidents are either the products of the author's imagination or used in a fictitious manner. Any resemblance to actual persons, living or dead, or actual events is purely coincidental.

Copyright © 2016 eVw Press, Ottawa & London Ontario, Canada

All rights reserved. No part of this publication may be reproduced, stored in a retrieval system, or transmitted in any form, or by any means, electronic, mechanical, photocopying, recording, or otherwise, without the written permission of the publisher.

eVw Press
www.evwpress.com
E-mail: publish@evwpress.com

978-0-9950351-0-2
First Edition
AOE2-141414-090616

Cover illustration by Serene Lucyk of Shooting Star Press

*Special thanks are due to my best friends and brothers,
my baby cousin Rin
and
Ruth R. Crocker, the best and most patient editor in the world.*

CHAPTER 1

Silvanus wiggled his toes over the edge of the expanse, the columns of clouds far beyond his vision. Each time he did this it felt like it was further than the last, inching closer to the moment when he'd have to back off before he fell. The pace of his heart was only outdone by the thunderous momentum of the storm the city brewed beneath him.

He looked back one last time to make sure the other children were gone and would not be there to tell the elders. He was in this moment alone, this rare opportunity to push the limits far past what was deemed responsible.

How far is it really? Silvanus thought. *If I fell, would the drop kill me? Would I be strong enough to survive it? Could anyone be that strong?*

He spent the majority of his childhood hearing the tales of the Winged Ones, the elders that developed the ability to fly freely amongst the clouds. He wondered if he could do it without wings, just by manipulating air currents. Although, history had no record of such a thing being possible. That would make him the first and only Aerial being to do so; the very notion sending shivers down his svelte body.

He took another look over the edge, peering down to where all of his reality stopped and the unknown began. Beneath the nation of the clouds he lived in was the forbidden world below, a world that no one could ever witness and return from to tell the tale. It was vaguely described in legend but he was never satisfied with what the teachers taught him. *If the elders are so powerful and have full control of flight, why couldn't they go down there and then come back to tell us all about it?* He often wondered, increasingly skeptical of their true abilities.

Although this day was dark and the clouds dense, he recalled other days where the view straight down was clear and the coloured visuals left an imprint in his mind. The intoxicating greens and browns below tantalized his imagination, not being able to exactly picture what sort of environment would earn those spectacular hues that were foreign to his homeland.

His ambition and wonder were quickly overruled when he realized how late for class he'd actually be. Looking down one last time, he turned around and towards the school, following the familiar trail he and his classmates had used so many times. *I've been down this path in both directions, over and over. Where else is there to go between breaks? I bet they don't bother with school down below because there are more important things to do than learn about useless subjects...*

He watched hundreds of town folk work on reconstructing the meeting hall right beside the school. Construction and maintenance were a constant priority in the Realm Empyrean. The shifting cloud forms, gathering moisture, required continuous action on the part of the populace. Should the moisture accumulate too densely, the domain would be rained away.

Watching his father working from a distance reminded Silvanus of how much he dreaded becoming an adult where the only options were becoming a builder or an elder, dedicating his life to preserving the culture or enlightening others. Neither option sounded appealing to him. He was convinced that the universe had to have more than those two professions. He wondered about the mysterious world below the clouds.

"Late again, Silvanus?" his teacher asked, looking quite annoyed at his hold up.

Silvanus quickly looked around to see the mocking reaction of the other students. "Sorry, Lady Livfya."

The spot assigned to him was still vacant and inflated, clearly pointing out his absence. He took his seat, filling the gap in the circle around the teacher.

"It's one thing for *you* to be late," Lady Livfya said, "but don't forget that today is about the little ones. They count on us to learn the basics and help integrate them into society, just as it was done for all of you."

Silvanus felt embarrassed and hoped everyone would stop looking at him and get on with the morning announcements. He daydreamed about the upcoming cloud-hopping races and how he would dominate, just like the week before. His train of thought was interrupted when the lineup of young Aerial children were led into the class. He didn't recognize any of them, realizing this was a new group. His teacher told each child who they were to be paired up with and he awaited his partner.

Moving shyly towards Silvanus was a little girl, not quite four feet in height. Her slender frame was covered by her dark vest and kilt, just like all the other children. Her blinding white hair partially covered her angelic face, but her big green eyes were sharp and focused on Silvanus as she approached him. She politely introduced herself and awaited him to do the same. She reached out to perform the traditional salutation of gripping the forearm, but she could not get her tiny hand all the way around his arm.

"Nice to meet you, Clarea. My name is Silvanus, but everyone calls me Sil."

Sil recalled the formal discussion topics they were given to begin the proper discourse. To him, it felt like going through the motions. He remembered that he interrupted his student mentor at the first chance he got to ask the burning questions he had.

Clarea remained silent and polite until it was her assigned time to make conversation. She hesitated to express herself, but Silvanus encouraged her to ask whatever was on her mind.

She finally spoke up. "If we live in the clouds, and all that's around us is sunshine and clouds, then what are our clothes made out of? What is the inside of the school made out of?"

Silvanus took a second to formulate the perfect response. He wanted to make the explanation simple without talking down to her, giving her some credit.

"When the clouds are at their darkest and densest, they contain the most energy and substance. An experienced Aerial with an ability for alchemy can use their powers on those clouds to shape and forge them into different things. Depending on what you want to craft, you can turn those clouds into different materials. Some are soft, which are what our clothes are made of, and some are strong, like what holds our school together."

Clarea's little face lit up, now imagining all the different things they could make, most of which weren't actually possible.

"That's also how our food is made," Silvanus continued. "If you don't process it too much, the stuff that's made is actually edible! That's how *manna* is made."

The mentoring visit continued for most of the hour, but Silvanus was distracted. Clarea opened up and began to get comfortable, showing her curiosity and talking like a child trying to impress someone older. He tried his best to answer her questions (and in fact, try to even understand what she meant by half of them), but he was more interested in continuing his class afterwards.

He looked around, but Lady Livfya was gone. It was out of character for her because she always stayed in the room, even if she was on break. She returned to send the young ones away, looking a little concerned and made several glances at Silvanus. The regular lecture began until school time was over.

"Silvanus, please come over here," Lady Livfya said discreetly, not wanting to make a scene.

He floated over to her. "Yes?"

She looked around one last time to make sure no one else was around to listen in on them.

"Headmaster Janus wants to speak with you. Please go see him now."

Silvanus nodded, not wanting to question her further.

Going down the hall to the Headmaster's office was the longest route known to anyone his age. It involved traversing many floors upwards, a combination of makeshift staircases and cloud-hopping. It was a rare event, only saved for the most serious of misbehaviours. He reached the end, took a deep breath, composed himself, and slowly drifted in.

Headmaster Janus was relieved to see Silvanus, briefly convinced that he wouldn't show up. His relief quickly turned stoic as he greeted him and prepared his speech. Silvanus stood straight and tall, arms folded behind his back and head slightly bowed, showing the traditional posture of respect towards an elder.

"Silvanus, it has come to my attention that you were late for class again."

Silvanus looked up and made direct eye contact, silently admitting his guilt.

The Headmaster continued. "While your lateness needs to be dealt with, the reason for it concerns me."

Silvanus now put his head straight, making a point of looking less guilty, not wanting to admit to anything until he heard that facts.

"I know where you've been spending your time. I know you were at the edge looking down at the world beyond."

Silvanus now nervously listened for what came next.

"I don't tell many people this, but when I was your age, I, too, spent a lot of time looking down. As I got older, I actually planned to petition the elders and perhaps lead an expedition. I have mastered almost every ability in harnessing the power of air currents, studied all the techniques and history of our people, and I have to tell you… it's impossible. Even if we made it down without dying, there would be absolutely no way to return."

Silvanus immediately sprang into enthusiasm. "What were some of your ideas to get down?"

"What do you think you're going to find down there?" the

Headmaster asked. "Don't forget that we, as a people, actually came from there over a thousand years ago. There's nothing down there and nothing has followed us up here. Your curiosity is misguided. Try channeling your efforts and imagination into *actually* helping your nation."

Sil nodded, saddened by what he just heard.

"Silvanus, please go home now. I won't mention your excursion to your parents, but I will notify them if you're late once more. This has to stop. You're a bright student. Leave the idea of the world beyond alone, for it's no world at all."

Sil politely nodded and exited the headmasters chamber, now picking up the pace as soon as he was out of view. He made haste and started jumping down between floors, using his athletic abilities to nearly glide down gracefully.

*****

It was dinnertime at Silvanus' house and both his parents were hard at work on preparing the biggest meal of the week: the last night before the day of rest. All week, the highest elders used their abilities and techniques to manipulate the air currents to keep the entire dominion of clouds moving in the sun. However, on the last day of the week, they stopped. The natural cycle would bring with it hours of pitch-black night that allowed the territory a restful sleep. No one worked, and due to the danger of the darkness, no one flew or posted watch. It was then that Silvanus realized something very important: when the domain's shape and path is not being manipulated, there are a lot of stray clouds, and more importantly -- there are many layers and columns of clouds that extend in various directions. *If they break off and go into different directions, who's to say that they don't also go down?* Silvanus pondered, now getting excited at the notion.

He did his best to maintain composure over the course of the evening, waiting for his tired parents to finally turn in and get some sleep. Sil paced around his room until the silence of his house granted him the opportunity to make his move: Travelling to the edge of the Realm Empyrean.

Blinded by the darkness and only guided by instinct and the touch of familiar landmarks, Silvanus made his way to the edge. Now that the air currents were untamed, the cold nighttime winds rushed against him and gave him full-body chills. It became obvious he was at the edge, for the sounds of the wind were no longer muffled by the clouds in front of him. He lay down on his front and shimmied forward until his head and arms were dangling over the threshold.

There's nothing to see! he thought, surprised at the experience of looking down at an infinite expanse. It was nothing like the greens and browns he was used to seeing, and there was no way to gauge how far it was. As his eyes struggled to adjust to the darkness, Sil could make out faint outlines of stray clouds palely illuminated by moonlight.

I can see clouds below me! They've never been there before!

Now teeming with adrenaline, he pushed himself away from the edge and stood up. Like last time, he stood with his toes hanging off the edge.

Whether this works or not, I'll never be in trouble again!

He looked down one last time.

*****

Looking up for the last time, Sil came to the realization that the moon light faintly revealed the position of broken cloud formations. *Next week there will be a full moon on the Sabbath and I'll be able to completely see all the clouds!* Excited about the new revelation, he retreated from the premises and made his way home through the darkness, gently glided through a window into his room. As fatigue began to overpower his senses, Sil lay in his bed plotting the course of events that would take place in a week.

*****

During classes, Sil slid into the room quickly, hoping to avoid attention while he spent most of the day scheming, trying to imagine the best possible scenario for his arrival in the world below. His obsessive daydreaming made him more absentminded than usual, prompting a reminder from his teacher.

"Silvanus, are you paying attention back there?"

All heads turned and stared in his direction. He stood up unaffected while responding, "Miss, we all come here every day to hear you talk about history and eldership and the way our society functions. Every person in here would rather be out *there* racing right now."

Taken aback by his affront response, Lady Livfya retained her reposed demeanor.

"Silvanus, don't you want to have the right instruction for when you grow up?" she quizzed.

"When we grow up we become elders, clothing makers, engineers, or teachers. Why can't we just learn on the spot? It's not like we have much to choose from."

The other children sat in a daze, excited about the debate and nervous for their classmate. None ever questioned authority the way Sil did.

"Here, I have a solution for this problem," stated Sil earnestly. "Let us go out and race early and we can learn all this stuff in the future when we need it."

The children stared at the teacher with great anticipation, hoping that Sil's logic would be accepted and an early release from lessons would be allowed.

"*No*," said the teacher half-smiling, amused by his rhetoric and frustrated by his disturbance. "These lessons have been passed down for hundreds of years and you will need them for proper growth."

His hopes, and those of his classmates, were shattered as the lesson continued. Soon after the interruption, a gust of wind effortlessly tore through the room. The gaseous clouds forming their school enclosure lightly collapsed, signalling the end of the day. Lady Livfya gave a dismissal, sending an onrushing flood of fledgling mages flying through the realm.

Aerials never truly walked, but lightly floated, and the young ones were always delighted to rush at top speed over the wind currents.

"Alright, we race by teams," exclaimed Sil as he led a small group of his friends into the contest. "Whoever reaches the end first with most of their guys wins. No hitting this time."

The rules were set and the match named. They dashed through almost the entire kingdom passing others who joined in along the way. Upon reaching the end, they settled at the edge, waiting for a mass of others to join them. No one was sure what team made it first, so a draw was decreed.

"How far down do you think it is, really?" asked Erastus, one of his cousins, whom most called Era for short.

"I don't know," Sil replied.

"Look! Shadow beasts! Try to hit them," shouted someone from the crowd.

All of the classmates started spitting over the edge, in attempt to hit the winged creatures that flew closest to the realm. The creatures passed by, and with the excitement gone, they all reclined at the edge.

"The engineers didn't leave us any jump spots this time," complained Sil, "Erastus, did you tell them we were doing this?"

Erastus looked up clearing his white hair from his face; surprised by the charge of wrongdoing. He quickly defended himself, "No, Sil, honest."

He would have said more but Sil cut him off. "We only have so many years of freedom until we make a decision to work for the rest of our lives. Why are there so few choices? The Realm of the Unlimited Empyrean and we get *three* jobs to choose from."

"What would you do Sil?"

"I'm not sure," said Sil. He thought for a moment and before he could respond, one of the girls from his class broke in. "You know what? You sit there talking badly about our way of life, when at one time we lived in war and starvation. Our elders saved us by bringing us up here. Show some respect and appreciation for the sacrifice of our ancestors."

Sil, bothered by such a brazen interruption, regained his train of thought and shot back, "I really just think we should have more to do then keep a city pasted together."

"Yeah?" she harshly responded, "Like what?"

Silence... Sil sorted his thoughts. Everyone was watching. "Well?" she insisted. *Damn*, he had nothing...

"I don't know," he stated.

"Exactly! *This* is the world, *our* world and if we don't work to keep it together, it falls back into hell!" Her statement slightly crushed him, leaving him wishing he had more clever thoughts.

Most of his classmates began to depart for home. Era and Sil moved together slowly. Era looked at his friend who had been so proud of his independence and was now confronted with the depressing concept of inevitable conformity.

Era decided to change the subject as they floated towards their homes. "Will you be at the calling? There is one coming up for high-elder Onkelos."

Sil broke from his deep reflection as his trademark smile slowly returned to his face, "Oh yes, of course. He will be missed; he was good, really good to us."

Era's home was close by. Before parting from his friend, Era turned back. "You're okay, right?"

Sil smiled widely, "Of course. How can I not be?"

Era, pleased with the report, went off to eat with his family. Sil continued floating slowly through the landscape.

He passed by the outfitters, stopping for a moment to watch them in their crafting, using the special alchemical methods to transform heavy clouds into a clothing material. The practice had been passed on for centuries, making pants and long coats, which was the style for every Aerial to wear. He remembered learning in school that weapons were also crafted in this way, but since there had been no fighting for over a thousand years, such procedures were deemed unnecessary.

Sil noticed some of the engineers coming from the lower levels of the realm. Most of the men in the kingdom aided in expanding and maintaining the domain. If the clouds began to attract too much moisture and turn black, they needed to be shed and replaced. *This is what keeps our nation from melting away,* Sil thought, hearing lady Livfya's voice in his head.

He also began to think that the whole reason for school was to keep the children in one spot so the adults could work.

It seems so regimental. Is life really supposed to be prepared in advance like this? We all wear the same clothes, have white hair, and are shaped the same way.

Sil drifted on slowly as he contemplated the structure of reality. Elders flew overhead. They were preparing for the calling.

The elders were the most prominent of the race and, unlike the others in the kingdom, had large wings. Following close behind were the Sylphs. Powerful air currents imbued with life, they could only be created by elders. Once created, Sylphs would be loyal forever to their maker. This training was only ever passed to those who advanced into the higher studies.

Arriving at home, Sil's mother greeted her belated son. "Food has been ready for some time now. Have you been racing again?"

Sil looked up smiling gleefully. "*Me?* Of course not! Racing isn't something useful Aerials would do."

Sil's mother, rolling her eyes, ushered her son in and the family sat together. There were big smiles all around as a blessing was invoked and dinner began.

Even the food, Sil thought to himself, *manna… the same thing every day and always. Why does every day look so much like the one before it?*

He ate quietly while his parents made light conversation and deliberated over the day's events.

Nothing here is ever permanent, but then nothing ever seems to change.

*****

The next day went by quickly and lessons were postponed. The entire nation would be assembled for the calling of High Elder Onkelos. Rarely on a weekday was night allowed to overtake the city. This assembly was one of those rare exceptions. The gathering happened at night.

Sil found Erastus in a group with many other classmates whom welcomed him gladly. The elders were all standing at the base of a high stand-alone stairway constructed exclusively for this event.

Sil tapped his father on the arm. "What is going to happen to him?"

His father knelt on one knee to keep his voice from rising. "Well, the calling is a great honour. Only the greatest and most powerful elders of our people can endure it."

Sil and his classmates leaned in with him to hear the explanation properly.

"After achieving the highest levels of proficiency and control among the air currents, a calling from the Eternal One is placed in his heart. It lets the elder know that his work here is finished and that he must ascend to the source where Aerials come from."

"But doesn't that happen when we die?" asked Sil.

"Of course. All Aerials are a breath of life; breathing includes inhaling and exhaling so we all have the same destination. But for some like the great elder there, they are able to return perfected, body *and* soul."

Sil and his friends stood edified by the speech, observing the elder standing. He wore no coat, unlike the rest of the Aerials. Instead, his wings draped across his body like a nobleman's cape. Climbing the staircase slowly with his Sylph following, he stood toward the night sky, with the shining stars ready to guide his way back to the ancient eternal home. His wings spread, summoning the air to gently lift him off. He made a pass over those assembled: one last display for the nation, and one last glimpse of the realm for himself. He then flew higher and higher, summoning a greater concentration of air under his wings, propelling him faster until he cleared the atmosphere; a feat no normal Aerial could produce.

Then, he was out of sight. Like all others who took heed of the calling, High Elder Onkelos would never be heard from in this world again. A long vigil followed, with singing and praying for his safe journey and for his intercession that blessings be showered down on his home world. Eulogies were spoken of his deeds while all stood in silent appreciation. Some cried quietly, others stared into the sky, while Sil, filled with wonder, could not help but wish he could hear a calling and see what the elder was seeing.

The realm was then shifted back into place. The sun's beams overtook the Aerial habitation once more and its golden brilliance overshadowed any trace of the night's sky that stood before them. The Sylph remained hovering alone, loyal to a master no longer present.

"Father," asked Sil, "what will happen to the Sylph?"

"He will stand his final vigil alone and be reunited soon with his creator," replied Sil's father.

"Why not just go with him?" Sil continued inquisitively.

"The atmosphere above does not have the same strength of current necessary to fly alongside him. Sylphs are made of currents from our realm. They cannot move on currents in the upper world," his father responded.

Sil stared silently. Many of his people were gliding up, giving prayer requests to the Sylph in hopes that they reach their elder. Sil could not help but feel a deep sadness for the loyal Sylph. Silvanus drifted away soon afterwards with a heavy heart.

The day was decreed a holy day and all people were ordered a cessation from work and study. Hours later, the Sylph, floating alone during the nationwide day of rest, eventually dissipated into a vaporous mist.

CHAPTER 2

Days later, Silvanus was playing by the edge of the city, racing with the other children. When they became exhausted, they rested, staring over the edge and guessing what was happening in the 'hellish' realm below the group.

"What do you suppose the green means?" asked Erastus. "And the brown." Why is there more of it?"

"You know something? I was wondering why don't we have those colours up here," Sil responded.

The children stared for hours. All of the friends took turns describing their own version of the happenings on the surface. They argued and laughed. As time passed, many departed leaving Sil and Era with two other children.

"You know, Sil," Erastus started, "the elders say if we drop to the surface-lands, the air currents are not strong enough to raise us up to the realm again. Would it be worth it to go down there if it meant never seeing family or friends again?"

Sil thought silently, knowing that he would never want to lose his family but unwilling to accept defeat.

"I don't know," Sil replied. "The elders also say the fall would kill you, so the currents really would not matter after that."

"I think the elders would *know*," stated one of the remaining classmates. "The reason why our enemies are unable to reach us is because the currents are weak. If we fall and the currents are not strong enough to bring us back, our souls might get stuck down there too."

"Acacius, nothing *but* us has ever come up here. How can we be sure of any enemies or *'souls'* being stuck underneath us?"

"Even if some sort of enemy did manage to reach us, the thunder force clouds at the bottom of the realm would fry them," Acacius responded.

Sil was no spiritual master but could already see some holes in

Acacius' reasoning. Afterward, the group left together and headed for home.

*****

The next day's school lessons passed quickly and during break, Sil, thinking about his upcoming endeavour, started getting nervous. He wondered about the fall, the world below, and if he was great enough to survive. He wondered why elders like Onkelos, who commanded the great power to fly into the universe, wouldn't just float down and take a look below.

Sil's thinking was interrupted when one of the younger Aerials from another class hall approached in a hurry.

"Sil, they're jumping…" He stopped for a moment to catch his breath, "by the edge! The engineers left some!"

Sil, Erastus and his classmates rushed off as fast as they could and found the engineers, who were restructuring the city, left remnants of individual floating clouds all in a row. Almost immediately, Sil and the others began hopping from one cloud to the other, going as far out past the edge as they could and returning. The game continued for many rounds. Erastus then spoke up.

"Sil, we should get back to class. The teacher will tell our parents and then we will be in big trouble."

"Just a couple more!" Sil shouted, as he continued jumping.

As they raced, Silvanus took forceful leaps, trying to gain ground by jumping over two at once. Seeing the land below, he began to resent his elders.

Why would we be born above a world we can't reach? How can it be that our realm is constantly rearranged but our lives stay the same? Who would not want to see a new world? Why am I the only one who thinks this way!?

In his anger, Sil had unwittingly depleted himself of energy and when he returned from his pondering, found himself far from the edge. Seeing his position, he made a hard leap to get back to safe ground. The remnant clouds loosened under the sporadic racing and the step on which he trusted gave way.

*****

The fall was the worst feeling he ever experienced. His lack of energy combined with gravity's force allied against him. Sil desperately tried to harness the air currents only to have them fling him into a spiraled frenzy. His unstable rotation left him helpless. Unable to restrain the currents or hold his bearings, Sil was now in a free fall. A chaotic blur permeated his mind as his body heated up under the pressure of his increased decline. Silvanus attempted again to gather the currents for support, only to have his native energies turn against him. With his body plummeting with great speed, the air syphoning around him only served to crush his slender frame. With his final thoughts turning to prayer, Sil plunged into the water.

The sensation of drowning was almost a release from the previous fall. Instinctively, he resisted the tide's pull and rose to the surface gasping for air. His efforts were thwarted by violent waves, submerging the young Aerial against his will. At the mercy of the tides, Sil was eventually thrust to the shore. Terrified, cold and soaked, he dragged himself further inland and lay trying to breathe.

Weakened severely and half-conscious, Sil eventually sat up. The sun was setting. It would be dark and he was in *hell*. When he rose to his feet, his knees gave way as the gravity and hard ground beneath him was another reminder of the mistake he made. Gathering his strength, Sil flew as high as he could. The conditions of his new environment proved too strong and he was forced back down. He tried twice more and each time gravity's burden sent him back to the ground even harder.

"*Ima!*" cried Sil, yelling for his mother in the Aerial language. Only cascading waves and a darkening sky responded to his shouts. Exhausted and mentally crushed, Silvanus passed out.

*****

The Aerial children stood in a row starring over the edge. The thunderous lightning miles below now obscured the path of Sils fall. As one, they turned toward Erastus, whose face fell into a contorted, pale expression. They all remained silent. No one moved from their places. An unthinkable act had occurred and many of the children began to lightly sob.

"I'm going to get an elder!" Erastus turned to see a girl rush away toward the city.

The border shifted. Now a large wall of cloud, that normally would have prevented this from happening, rose into place. Once the construction was completed, Erastus felt faint. The others around him supported their friend Era as he became lightheaded.

Sil... What do we do now?

CHAPTER 3

The elders of the nation held a gathering in great haste. The assembly sat in a circular tiered chamber with the high elders in the center. The high elder raised his hand, calming the cohort and began the inquest.

"How were their no adults in the area?"

"Due to our cities expansion, the maintenance has become more involved. Adults were in the region, but we just don't have the workforce to cover all the area. There are times when the engineers must focus their attention together and, as such, sections are left temporarily unattended," responded an elder.

"Do we have a bearing on the boy?" asked the high elder.

"Not exactly. We haven't channeled the lower air currents in centuries. Even if we did, the natural imprint of the air flow prevents any adult mage from naturally falling. Only children can fall over the edge."

Another elder from the crowd rose and added to his response. "In order for an adult to actively enter the lower realm, we would have to use considerable power to negate their abilities *and* we would have to create a stable wind tunnel for safe passage. We may have to accept that this risk is too much."

The room became silent and all present turned their attention toward the high elder.

"If one of our own is lost and even if the likelihood of his survival is slim, we *must* do what we can. Bring forward the children who witnessed the fall."

*****

Sil woke to the sounds of waves striking the shore. The darkness made it impossible to see. He wiped his face spreading sand across his drenched brow.

He had learned in school that during dreams you could not feel pain. If pain was an indication of life, Sil was living to the fullest.

The night's draft gripped his skin as Sil wrapped his tattered coat around him for what little warmth it offered. His exhaustion outweighed his fear as he drifted into a light sleep.

He lay unconscious for what seemed like moments… then something struck him on the head. Sil's fatigue compelled him to ignore the disturbance. Then it struck again.

"Ow! Dammit! What the hell!?"

Small drops of water began falling from the sky. Now awake and panicking, the water came down like a flood from the sky, each drop striking his body in cruel torture.

Silvanus quickly pulled his long coat over his head and rose feebly to his feet. His knees, having never held him up under an increased gravitational pressure, tightened to offer support. The resulting pain shot through his legs leaving him limp. Sil quickly fell bracing himself against the ground. Continual pain coursed through his body as the rain picked up. Sil struggled to his feet. He began to trek uphill. His skin felt as if it would peel off his body as the rain poured harder.

Still unable to perceive his surroundings, Sil staggered into a grouping of trees and collided against the bark. His hands were beset with an army of lesions.

Sil partly collapsed against a large tree's trunk. He tried to get his bearings but the night's darkness added the sensation of an overwhelmingly enhanced vertigo. He wiped the rain water from his face, digging the grains of sand into his skin like small claws.

Despite all of his painful experiences, Sil's erratic movements incidentally provided shelter against the rain. With his clothing now almost completely torn, he prayed that this would all end and somehow his family would rescue him. As he continued to pray, Sil fell under the burden of his surroundings into a coma-like sleep.

*****

Silvanus slept for hours, awakening only to the sounds of birds chirping. Night still held the world in its grasp keeping Sil in darkness. The rain had ceased. Sounds of mild thumping against the ground spread out all around him. Afraid to move, he lay still, hearing the noises erupting from around him. The wind brushed through the trees creating a serene calm that eased the young Aerial's mind.

Currents… they have air currents in hell!

*****

The elders' gathering had become far more intense. A fierce dispute about whether travelling to the surface world was possible had engulfed the assembly.

"How is it even possible to expect any of our people to risk their lives? The boy's demise is assured. Trying to reclaim his body exposes our people to serious danger."

Another elder stood. "Above this, what do we know about the lower world? What lives there now? Our ancestors battled the *gargaroi* and settled our nation here. What will we stir up if we step into that territory again?"

The high elder raised his hand to indicate silence. The bombardment of negative bickering overwhelmed his judgment.

It will be relatively easy to send a search party. Even though it will take great strength, we can withdraw them also. This, however, has not been done for over a thousand years.

What about the surface? What lives there now? There has been no sign of anything worth pursuing. If Silvanus has not survived and we send a rescue and they end up dying also…

Maybe I should take the jump myself?

He considered all of the possible outcomes and listened intently to his cohorts. He thought in silence for a long time pondering the consequences of his actions. In the end his compatriots' opinions weighed down upon him. He rose to announce that following after Silvanus would be too much of a risk.

"Brothers, I must agree with…"

The high elder's speech was cut off by the approach from an exhausted looking Aerial slowly moving towards the high elder. At first there were protests, and as some moved in to intercede against his advance they quickly ceased, realizing who he was.

"Send me," he spoke, obviously disheartened.

His eyes had dark circles underneath them. He looked exhausted and as he flowed into the room, it seemed he would collapse at any moment.

"I'll go. I'll take all the risk. Even if it's just for his body...... Please…"

One sitting close to the high elder leaned in to address the situation.

"This is the father of…"

"I know this man," responded the elder spreading his wings and flying towards him he folded the tired aerial into the elders arms as they met, "and I know his family."

The tired Aerial looked up into the eyes of the elder silently begging for relief. Leaning close he spoke to the father personally. "Hanael, we *will* find your son."

The broken father's eyes widened in appreciation and those within earshot gasped at the statement. The high elder allowed an aid to escort Hanael away before addressing the entire eldership.

"As of this moment, as high elder I decree a state of emergency. One of our own is lost in the world below. We are going to devise a plan of action and send three select mages from our nation to engage in a rescue. No more warnings or protests. From now onward, we only focus on proposals for retrieval."

*****

Sensing the air at his fingertips, Silvanus' hope began to rise. Air on the surface-land was more abundant then he was taught to believe. With enough rest, maybe there was a way for him to return to his home.

Sil had awoken to a nice breeze and was now thinking clearer. Still in the dark, he refused to move. Though he was still fearful, his hope had somewhat returned with the feeling of the wind at his palms.

All I need to do is be able to see...

As if in answer to his silent prayer, lucent rays began to extend past the horizon. A reddish spectrum of colours filled the sky. Sil unsteadily rose to his feet, hypnotized as the world around him illuminated. Transfixed by its beauty, he noticed the ocean, the beach, the forest, and the tree that sheltered him. He saw birds flying in the sky and waves striking the shore. He became light-headed from processing the majestic visual.

My god... Hell is beautiful...

The familiar thumping sound interrupted his morning reflections. Turning, he noticed his nighttime shelter dropped round, oval-like objects from its branches. Sil picked one up and studied it. As he did, a small rodent rushed up and abruptly stopped at Sil's feet. The young Aerial was so startled he forgot his fears and fixed his attention upon the small creature.

It chirped softly as Silvanus looked at it in total awe. Unsure of what to do, the two stared at one another. The rodent chirped more lively, now seemingly waiting for Sils' response.

Silvanus, now fascinated by the small animal, moved closer, watching it jump somewhat excitedly.

"Oh! You want this."

Sil opened his hand as an offering and the small creature snatched the round object from his hand and began eating it in front of him. Sil followed the small creature's lead. After sinking his teeth into the soft outer skin, Sil's eyes lit up and he began to wildly consume the small fruit. Prompted by starvation and the discovery of a new taste, Sil began to consume as many as he could. He had not realized how hungry he was and now, finding many littered on the ground, he and his rodent friend shared a modest feast.

"Well, that was actually really good! Sooo... What's your name?"

His new friend's small eyes shifted from his own half eaten meal and starred at Sil. His head turned slightly as if trying to make sense of his question.

"Can you maybe tell me about the air currents? You don't understand anything I'm saying, do you?"

Silvanus sighed and looked into his hands which had become stained purple due to the fruit.

I definitely feel them. But I may not be strong enough to…

A large shadow cast over Silvanus, interrupting his thoughts. Sil's heart almost stopped as he remembered exactly where he was. As the shadow loomed, he could feel the presence of something large close behind. His little animal friend scurried away.

You're leaving me, too! Oh god, please help…

With his heart beating rapidly, Sil's body froze as the giant drew nearer.

*****

Three young Aerials stood before the high elder. The assembly had been dismissed as the elder prepared his final instructions.

"Do you understand why you have been chosen and what we are prepared to do? If you have any questions, ask them now."

The three Aerials looked up at him. Erastus looked visibly nervous.

"Wouldn't it make more sense to send elders down?"

Era slightly lowered his gaze to hide his fear and embarrassment.

"We need the power of all the elders as one to create a funnel for setting Aerials down on the surface and for retrieval. We will be in constant supervision of the currents and follow you from above," explained the high elder.

Lanea spoke next. She brushed aside her flowing white hair, long even by Aerial standards. The elders had selected her to oversee the rescue. "What are the chances of finding him alive?"

"I will not lie to you," responded the High elder. "The chances are slim, but we owe it to the family to try. If that is all, stay close by. I will summon the elders and make our preparations for descent."

The three chosen Aerials exited and floated away from the building. All of them were anxious. They remained quiet for a while and then the eldest, Salus, broke the silence.

"We shouldn't worry so much. We will be making history."

"But if this has never been done, how will we know what will happen? Can't an elder at least be on the journey with the three of us?" Erastus asked.

Lanea turned to him. Placing her hands on his shoulders, she gently reassured her companion.

"Elders have harnessed the currents to their strongest levels and naturally bonded with them. Even adults have this bonding. The only ones free of this adhesion are young ones and children like us. If they were to try to dive, the high end currents would simply pull them into an unbalanced orbit. They are working on negating this, but it could take months to undo years of conditioning."

Salus turned to interject and add to the explanation. "Silvanus' father also wanted to volunteer, but as an adult mage his bonding would be too strong. We have been selected by the elders for this task and only *we* can do this."

Era thought hard about what the two were saying. They floated close together waiting for the inevitable time when the elders would call on them for the task at hand.

*****

Silvanus was now totally overshadowed by the shade brought on by the size of the monolithic monster. It slid through the earth without treading, seemingly a part of the surroundings. Large, stiff tendril-like protrusions extended from its body, as if to suddenly strike at any moment.

Sil backed away slowly, still on the ground. He could feel his hands becoming sweaty as his breath quickened. He wanted so badly to jump up and race away but his whole body was shaking.

As if on cue, his rodent friend rushed to the scene. He leapt passed Sil, climbed the body of the threatening giant, dashed over its boney arms and plucked a small oval fruit from the tree. The critter gracefully returned to the ground by Sil where he began to consume his newly acquired prize.

Sil looked at his friend. Then at the large *being* slowly advancing toward him.

"Okay, that's enough! What the hell is wrong with you people?!"

Silvanus was quickly distracted by a new thought. *Oh hey! My legs? They don't hurt anymore. Have I adjusted to this place so soon?*

Silvanus was driven from his inner thoughts by the sound of the thumping that he heard all night. The fruit fell in abundance and Sil realized this "thing" was trying to help him.

At first Sil was cautious, but his curiosity overwhelmed him. He leaned toward the tree for a closer inspection. The large tree leaned right back, imitating his motions. Sil, startled by the unexpected action, fell backwards only to be caught by a root that elevated upwards from behind, bracing him from the fall.

The rodent made another appearance, scurrying over the root to Sils' side. Silvanus sighed deeply, then, handed over the fruit he was holding.

"You know, I'm starting to think you only like me because of my ability to gather stuff."

Sil steadied himself and began to take a calmer approach to his whole situation.

"Sooo… How does this world work? You feed me," he said aloud while pointing to the tree, "he eats and… Oh damn, there was nothing in class about things like this. Hey… Hey! Wait! Where are you going?"

As if beckoning for Sil to follow, the tree paused, patiently waiting for Sil to catch up. Silvanus began to pick up as much food as he could hold and ran towards his escort, not noticing his pain had lessened significantly.

"Wait, wait, wait… Hold up! Hey! You don't even have legs!"

As Sil trailed after his newfound companion, he realized the depth of the world he had fallen onto. Emerging from a small patch of woodland, he saw a huge forest surrounding a great plain. He stopped to look back and could see the shore and hear the waves still brimming in the distance.

Despite all of this, Sil stood awash in wonderment as his large friend carried itself with a nest of tendril-like roots that slithered through the ground, mobilizing the large trunk atop. At once, a branch swung and hoisted Sil onto an upper stalk.

    Together, they left the forest. Silvanus noticed large fields of golden grain and rivers of bright blue curving through the landscape. In the distance, he saw rows of trees like the one he was riding. The exhilaration of the moment was broken when he looked up, seeing the clouds. His eyes raced through the firmament trying to pick out from where he fell. As they traveled, the sadness that place had started to overtake him quickly faded.

CHAPTER 4

The two continued to travel through green fields that stretched onwards into the horizon. Silvanus began to focus on the world around him and ate the produce he collected from one of his friend's branches. Sil began to notice a gradual change in the landscape; where once the area seemed more diverse, now, there became definite patterns and an arranged structure to the settings around him. A yellow flower caught Sil's eye and he instinctively glided down to get a closer look. The large tree patiently halted his progress waiting as Sil investigated the find.

Silvanus moved close to the flower whose yellow colouration enticed the young Aerial. Sil ran his hand up the stem and gently palmed the broad, oval leaves arranged in a disc formation. In response the flower widened into a full blossom. Sil jumped back as its stem straightened and the plant stretched tightly out towards the sky and then slowly leaned towards Sil. He stared deeply into the flower's head, not sure where the eyes were or how it sensed his presence at all.

This is amazing. I have never seen this colour before. Sil reached toward the flower slowly only to have it affectionately caress his hand. He smiled as the seeds on the head tickled his sensitive skin. He slowly lifted his hand away. *I wonder how far you can reach?*

As if in response to his mental calling, the entire field awoke in-bloom covering the expanse in a blanket of gold. Sil stood astonished at the feat. The large flowers leaned towards him as one. Sil was amazed at having the attention of the entire field. His hand remained in its frozen position at eye level and when he realized what directed the plant's attention, Sil slowly moved his arm from side to side with the yellow flowers flowing with unified smooth motions. Waves of gold, stretching out for leagues, softly danced as his motions became more complex.

Silvanus continued to conduct the golden orchestra with great delight and as his movements became more intense he caught a glimpse of his friend still waiting for him.

"Oh. Hey sorry, I totally forgot." Silvanus turned to the field before him. "Nice to meet you guys." Sil waved as he was swooped up by a large branch and the Aerial and the tree took off toward an unknown destination. The flowers tried to reach out for Sil, but unable to surpass their vegetative limitations, gradually gave up their struggle and settled back into their permanent dwelling. They closed their buds in a sporadic sequence gradually returning the countryside to a deep green hue.

As they travelled further down a dirt path, Sil stared at his companion's roots coiling through the ground. He became mesmerized by the motions, watching the soil turn underneath the tree's fluid movement. Histhoughts broke at the sound of a young boy's voice.

"Pop, I found Gus!"

Sil looked down and saw a boy about his age. The boy spoke some commands to the large tree, who promptly set Sil down before him.

"What were you doing riding Gus?" he asked. "And why are you eating prune berries? How can you even take the taste of them?"

Sil looked bewildered as the boy spoke to him. Between the fulfillment of his childhood curiosity and his inability to understand anything that the boy was saying, Sil found no words to respond.

"Here, have these." The boy handed him a bowl of red berries. "These ones are for the festival. My name is Victor. You can come play with us, if you'd like."

Silvanus followed Victor. Victor began to talk endlessly. Sil could only listen in awe as he followed, not understanding anything the young boy was saying.

Sooo… Who is this person? Are these lost souls of mages who died in the ages past? Did he expect me? Maybe he saw me fall?

As Victor lead him onward, the makings of structures and civilization came into view and with them, strange and marvelous sounds filled the air; a great celebration was underway.

Brushing his hair back, Sil's eyes widened. He gazed at the commotion. This was not a land of enemies from an ancient past or a hellish prison that entrapped wayward souls. This was a nation of mages. Sil could hardly believe what he was seeing. The music from mandolins, trumpets and violins were sounds he had never heard.

The mages wore long pants and button-front shirts of various styles topped with a sea of hair colours, ranging from dark brown to dirty blonde, creating the appearance of a chromatic river flowing before him. Sil lingered as the sight of the festival overwhelmed his mind and his perception blurred, melding reality into a kaleidoscope of colouration.

Sil, remembering the small fruit in his hands, filled his mouth with the bowl's contents. Very quickly, he felt strength return to his bones and a huge smile spread over his face. The influx of enlivenment sent him into the crowd of dancers. Some of the women took notice of him.

"Boy, why are your clothes torn?"
"Where are you from?"
"From which family are you from?"

Sil, not wanting to be rude, responded in the only language he knew.

"Sh'ell niev,e he'EEE,el SHHtarlin vastroria,n EE ssa" [I fell from home and ended up here.]

Catrina, a lady from the crowd, stepped forward and spoke. Silvanus spoke back. The women decided it would be easier to just change his clothes and send him back to the party.

Now re-entering the scene, Sil was clothed in a more indigenous fashion: pantaloons held with suspenders, braced over a long sleeved shirt. His thin white hair brightly contrasted the swarm of bushy tops.

The party continued and many of the women began to inquire about the white-haired boy's origin.

"We found him following one of the healing trees that wondered off. He must have gotten caught in the storm," Victor explained.

"Oh my god, the poor thing… He must have been terrified," said one of the women.

"He seems well enough. I can't believe he was eating those prune berries! Normally, only old people without feeling in their lips can handle them," replied Victor.

Catrina laughed.

"Where do you suppose he comes from? He has a head of thin white hair. From which town is that a strong trait?"

"It does not matter now. His parents are probably at the other side of the village. Just give him a bowl with some berries…"

Sil listened in, understanding nothing. However, one word perked his interest; something he would come to remember: "Berries!" He shouted gleefully as an older mage refilled his bowl, smiling. These berries were like nothing he ever dreamed of. He danced and ate as the celebration went on into the evening.

CHAPTER 5

The fields were endlessly lined with trees, rivers were irrigated and artificial ponds had been created for the trees to drink from. It was a fantastical world that Sil would never have believed existed. Music, sounds and smells that he had never known before filled his awareness.

Along with this, he had picked up some of the language in his brief stay: *Berries, please and thank you.* However, with his accent, they sounded more like, '*Bewiesss*', "*Pleash*,' and 'Sank yu.' The "th" sound being something he never encountered before, but as a work-in-progress, there was definitely room for improvement.

The celebrations continued until early morning. The families began to return to their respective villages and homesteads. All except, of course, for one youthful, thin, white-haired boy.

As everyone exited the town, the population dropped from over 1,800 to a small group of families and acres of trees, rivers and ponds. Trying to find the white-haired boy's parents was becoming a huge ordeal. His language was so foreign that the adults had to conclude that his 'roots were soft' and the fact that all he did was eat berries and show gratitude made him seem more simpleminded. Everyone was notified and messengers were sent. No one had heard of the child.

"I thought we knew all the families from the region? Patros, how can parents just forget their child?" inquired Victor's mother.

"I don't know," responded Victor's father, Patros. "We haven't been able to reach the friends from Nebat yet and we are still waiting on word from the Megaros as well. Catrina should be returning shortly…" he halted his discourse as he saw, through a window, Sil skipping through the air and snatching a kite that had been stuck in one of the trees.

"Honey… you all right in there? What is it?" she asked, turning her head toward the now vacant window. "What is it?" she repeated.

Without a word, he raced outside to find the children also looking on in awe at their new friend.

"Victor," he said, calling his son. "How did that happen?"

The children all remained silent, unsure, confounded by Sil's natural abilities.

Victor's father took the kite and released it to Gus, the prune berry tree, who gently caught it in his branches. As if on cue, Sil took off and brought back the sail with a big smile, presenting it to Victor's father as if to insist he join the game with them.

"I guess he can step on air," announced Victor, excitedly.

"*Sil*," addressed Patros, realizing he never actually learned the youngling's name. He stood dumbfounded, with all his children, nieces and nephews. Gus arched up ready for another catch, Patros turned to see his wife also stunned by the recent events.

Good, he thought. *She sees this too. I'm not delusional.*

He brought the smiling child closer to him, placing both hands on his shoulders.

"Uh… *Sil*, right?"

Sil nodded responding, *"Be'wisss."*

"Not right now, Sil! My name is Patros," gesturing to himself. "Patros."

"PahTroSss."

"Yes, that's right! Sil, where are you from? Your home. Do you understand?"

Sil looked quizzically at him.

"Okay, look… home. This is *my* home," said Patros gesturing to the house and farmland.

"Ohmm," responded Sil doing the same.

"No, Sil, my *home*. *Our* home. Where is *your* home? Where are you from?"

Sil stopped a moment and thought before he answered.

Home… he looked up at Patros, then at his new friends and pointed up to the sky.

"Home."

The next moments were a sort of blur for Sil as they began to talk fast in their native speak and he was rushed into the house.

"He is an angel sent from the Giver."

"Pop," responded one of Victor's older brothers. "Don't get hysterical. We barely understand him at this point."

"The boy can fly! If that does not prove that in some way he is supernatural, then I don't know what does."

They argued for a while and then it was decided to summon someone from Nebat, the capital city.

*****

Back home in the Realm Empyrean, the elders prepared their final calculations for the surface landing.

"Moving to the surface can definitely be achieved," the high elder began his instruction, "if we hold our force as one to create a funnel to touch down on a specific drop point. However, we must not exert too much strength. Should this experiment become uncontrollable we need our team to be able to stabilize without our aid."

"Have we really considered the environment below?" interjected another elder. "We could crumble under gravity's weight and what about the old legends? The Gargaroi? Our ancient enemies? We only ever escaped by remaining at this altitude. Is it wise to send younger Aerials to risk their lives against dangers we cannot perceive?"

"There has been no evidence of attack from below for over a thousand years. We use those narratives in the schools to keep this from happening," another elder returned.

They began to argue for a short time until the high elder raised his hands and calmed the gathering. They discussed the final point of the strategy and then moved their meeting to the edge of the realm in order to pin point a location.

Watching the elders depart, the three Aerials selected for the service held council of their own.

"The elders will be returning shortly," stated Salus. "They are discussing the plans for the cycling of the currents. Era, how is your family holding up?"

"Sil's father wanted to go himself. His mother nearly died of grief. I hope at the very least we can bring his body back."

"Did they explain how we are to come back up?" asked Lanea.

"I think that's what they are discussing," replied Salus.

The elders returned and the three were given instruction on how to conduct themselves while within the current and how to signal for retrieval.

*****

Back on land, Sil had become a spectacle and many people were trying to communicate with him. He just stood confused, realizing that his abilities may have really drawn him the kind of attention he was not looking for. Representatives of the queen, from Nebat, filled the house. Amidst the commotion, Victor came to his side.

"Here, Sil… have some berries."

Sil desperately wanted to sneak out with Victor and that chance came at night. The adults began a heated debate on what the presence of such a talented boy could mean.

"Okay Dimitri, we know the boy possesses incredible abilities beyond that of our own people, and his origin, though questionable, leads me against the theory that his is a divine being. Instead, and most definitely, this boy is a mage from another realm."

"And which realm is this?" one of the townsfolk asked Patros.

"Not sure, exactly," responded Patros.

"How come this has not happened before?" Dimitri interjected.

"No clue. There could be others like him, you know, and if they…"

"Then why have we not ever seen them? You think a flying mage would be easy to spot," another senior interrupted.

"Well I don't know, now do I? I have to tell you, the chance of him being the only one seems slim. We have all heard the legend that says the original families broke off in groups and settled in different locations. It is possible that this mage is a settler descendent from one of those original clans."

The arguments continued. Tea was poured as the debate sprawled over into the night.

Many people passed by to hear the *'angel mage'* speak. Some of the older women brought gifts as offerings.

This is getting really weird, thought Sil. *This whole nation must be crazy. Still… the food is awesome.*

CHAPTER 6

That morning, a thin tornado descended onto the surface. Spiraling within, the three mages used all their power to stabilize themselves to keep from being torn apart. Between the elders' powerful control and their united efforts, the landing was untroubled. Severely fatigued from the drop, the Aerials rested at the edge of the forest.

"Keep aware of your surroundings. We have food to regenerate ourselves," Salus said, passing rationed manna out to his friends. "We rest for a while, then sweep the area. We do not want to get caught out here during nightfall."

"My knees really hurt," stated Erastus.

"The elders warned of this," Lanea replied. "Just rest awhile. We cannot be too far from where your cousin fell."

Salus sat quietly and drew his comrades' attention to the landscape surrounding. "Brothers, look!"

The waves striking the beach mixed with the sounds of the sea. The birds overhead and the breeze, partially created by the Aerial's interruption of the air currents, provided a serene setting, transfixing the trio. After immersing themselves in the soothing ambiance, Era spoke up.

"Why haven't we been down here before?"

The Aerials were silent, allowing the harmonious compilation of natural forces surrounding them to reply. None came.

They rested for over an hour, then readied for the search. They all felt a great deal of pain as they stood up. The trio cautiously crossed the forest, carefully observing everything around them.

"Do you think that our enemies are down here?" asked Lanea.

"I have not seen any yet," answered Salus.

The Aerials carried on with their search, all the while overawed by the world they had been transported upon. Approaching the edge of the forest, the commotion within a homestead drew their attention. Looking at one another, Salus gestured forward for the trio to discreetly inspect the source of the clamor.

Sil, playing outside with Victor, was one of the first to notice his compatriots' approach. Their long, dark coats and white hair fluttered in the wind.

Victor stayed close to Sil, unsure of the outcome of the following events. Sil addressed the trio and before they could respond, the surface-dwelling mages took notice and poured forth as one. No words were exchanged. Only a silent expression of shock possessed the clustered mages.

The trio halted their advance as the mass of surface mages gathered before them. Both sides remained quiet, each uncertain of how to address the other. Sil ran forward warmly, greeting his rescuers.

"You survived!" confirmed Era. "Please tell me you did not do this on purpose."

"No, I *had* planned to," admitted Sil, halting himself mid-sentence realizing that the other Aerials now looked vexed at his admission of guilt. "But I fell when I lost my footing on some free clouds."

Salus and Lanea were both amused at the fact that an Aerial, who was born floating in air, could actually drop from his native environment unintentionally. Salus drew the party's attention to the crowd before them. The crowd stood silently observing their new guests. The obvious disparity between them was not only physical, but their apparel contrasted so starkly, making the Aerials look like impoverished beggars and the observing throng affluent nobility. Breaking the silence, Sil suddenly recalled his own landing.

"Oh, that's right! Wait here!"

Silvanus ran back into the house and returned with a bowl of prune berries. "These will help you adjust."

"What is this substance?" asked Salus.

"Oh," replied Sil. "Food."

Taking a bite, the sweet, sugary taste immediately brought a smile to their faces. Patros was the first to approach. Standing before the trio, Patros daringly greeted them with an outstretched arm. The Aerials stared, not knowing how to respond the other. Looking at Patros, not sure what to do, Salus tilted his head slightly sideways, confused by the whole ordeal. Sil jumped between them, grabbing his Salus arm, fastening his hand with that of Patros.

"It's how they hail one another. Don't be so rude!" Sil informed.

The welcome didn't last long. At that moment, a large dire wolf jumped out from the woods. A look of terror overran the face of Patros as he ran toward the house where they kept the spears.

"Get the children inside!" he shouted, to his oldest son, who grabbed Victor and Sil, pulling them from the predator's path. The three Aerials remained perplexed by the uproar around them. Having never been in mortal danger or seeing animals of any kind, they were unaccustomed to the distress around them.

The three Aerials watched the wolf slowly approach. It snarled and growled at them, bearing its teeth. Salus stepped forward, assured he could handle the situation without problem.

Extending his arm to toward the fearsome intruder, Era gave an excited *"Hallo!"*

The dire wolf, trying to frighten its prey, roared loudly. The force of its breath blew the Aerial's white hair back and its smell filled his nostrils causing instant repulsion. Staring at the wild hound, Era simply leaned frontwards and to the on-looking crowd, blew gently in the direction of the wolf.

In reality, Erastus orally propelled the air currents violently towards the attacker, sending it flying deep into the background. The beast let out a yelp as it was propelled by unseen currents. The villagers were both amazed and frightened. All was silent as Era held onto the bowl, proudly munching on some prune berries.

This strange event, with all its accidents and imperfections, marked the beginning of the gathering of all the mages that had once been separated. There they stood, amidst water and land, reunited after a millennium.

*****

Shortly afterwards, the four Aerials were confronted by the entire village, as well as those who gathered from the township. The four Aerials faced down the crowd, many of which were carrying spears in response to the previous threat of the dire wolf.

Patros was the first to turn his weapon downward and kneel before the Aerial children. The throng alongside him did the same.

"Dad, I really don't think these are angels…" protested Victor.

"Enough son," returned his father, who lightly encouraged the boy to kneel.

Now, with the whole township kneeling towards the Aerials, the rescue team turned to Sil for an explanation.

"What? They never did this with me," Silvanus replied, unsure of this new behaviour.

Salus quickly refocussed and turned aside, casting his hands upwards to feel for minor currents let down by the elders. He sent a signal that only an Aerial would detect. Shortly after a small wind funnel dropped from the sky ending the rescue mission.

Sil adamantly protested, but Salus insisted on his immediate return.

"Your father has not slept and your mother is ready to throw herself off the Realm to look for you. Do you think she would survive the fall?"

No, thought Sil. He turned to look at Victor once more as he and his kin moved away from the kneeling masses. Sil noticed the air tunnel and before he could say his farewells, he was sucked through and sped back to his home world above.

Below, the people again stood in wonder at how quickly the alien visitors had vanished from their view. As the crowd slowly returned to their feet, vague speculation began to surface as to where the visitors had gone and why they had made themselves known. Victor jumped up and ran towards the place where he saw Sil last.

He investigated the area as thoroughly as he could. Finding no sign of his new friend, Victor looked upward, scanning the sky for any irregular movement.

Well friend, I will set aside a bowl for you. Come back anytime you like... please.

*****

In the Realm, Silvanus was quickly escorted into the assembly of the elders. They all quietly stared. A boy in ill-fitting pants held up by suspenders stood before the council, alive. The silence was palatable. Nothing like this had ever happened and there was no precedence. As the high elder approached, Sil swallowed hard. He was not sure as to the possible punishment he might have to endure.

"Where did you acquire this clothing?" the High elder asked while circling Sil.

Sil paused, not sure how to respond to the high elder.

"Well, you see, mages on the surface gave them to me as a gift."

The entire assembly gasped and began to murmur among themselves. Sil's head turned toward them, now distracted by their worried tones.

"Silvanus," the high elder lightly commanded, drawing his attention back to him. "Tell me about the surface-dwelling mages."

Light shone through Sil's eyes as a big smile creased his face. "Well! Down there is awesome!"

The assembly let out a bewildered shout, baffled as to how any Aerial in his right mind could say such a thing. Years of entrenched tradition thundered forth as the elders began to question Sil all at once.

"What about the demons? Do the gargaroi still abound?"

"Did you battle them at all?"

Before things turned disorderly, the High Elder raised his hand. "Silvanus, tell us more."

Sil spent hours relating his adventure to the council. Most of his time was consumed with description, since there was almost no counterpart for anything that existed below. The elders all sat in silence at the end of Sils' report.

The high elder approached and question Sil one last time. "Tell me, is there a good reason for us to return?"

Sil thought for a moment as his mind raced with a barrage of answers. "Oh… These!" He held out his hand after retrieving some small berries from his pocket. The elder inspected the objects, not sure what to make of their presence.

"Taste one," encouraged Sil.

The elder Aerial took a small bite and as the sugary substance was absorbed by his tongue, he smiled. "Do you have more?"

Sil grinned, pulling more from his pockets.

"Pass these around to the assembly."

As the berries were consumed, a new uproar was stirred and the high elder called some of his council into a private meeting. Sil now stood alone totally ignored by the elders surrounding him. He listened as they commented on the new discovery he brought to light.

"How do you even define this?"

"Can we make this up here?"

The conversation continued and forgotten were the threat of devils and gargaroi.

Nice, thought Sil. *They sound like they went down and picked those themselves.*

The high elder returned and a hush fell over the Aerial leaders.

"It has been decided," the high elder declared. "We will make a second drop into the world below."

No one could believe the announcement. A gentle breeze from a loose current passed through the room. The stillness was deafening.

"And who would lead this expedition, my lord?" asked an elder.

"Him." Responded their leader, pointing at Silvanus.

"Me? But… why me?"

"As you know, our laws state that the one with most experience leads. The one with the experience is you. I name you, in the hearing of your brethren, our first ambassador to the surface world."

Sil, now thoroughly confused, attempted to make sense of the situation. "Umm… what?"

"You will return to this surface world. Learn of their language and open up communication between our nations. You will teach them about us and select a representative so that we may dialogue."

"No... umm... what *is* an ambassador?"

There was a sudden commotion in the assembly hall. An Aerial broke into the conference and needed to be restrained. Sil turned and his eyes brightened as he saw a most familiar face.

"Dad! Nice you made it."

The elders restraining Hanael were silently ordered by the high elder's gesture to allow him passage. Hanael embraced his son. For a moment Sil could not breathe and started to struggle against his father's grip. His struggle quickly ended and Hanael, now holding his son's arms, drew back and shouted at his wayward son.

"Are you insane!? Do you know what we have been through here? How did you survive? Your mother has been driven into grief!"

"Dad, I know what this looks like, but I've been promoted."

"Are you even... what!?!"

"I'm an ambassador now."

His father, now caught off guard, looked quizzically at his son.

"What the hell is that?"

Sil, not sure how to answer his father, turned to the high elder.

*****

Hanael was calmed by the elders. After the meeting was finished, father and son made their way back to their home where Sil's mother would be waiting.

Along the way, Silvanus talked eagerly about his findings. Despite not understanding most of what Sil was talking about, Hanael was entirely relieved to see his son alive and well. Once they neared their home, Sil's father stepped aside to let his son walk in first knowing full well what waited for him.

As soon as Sil passed through the door, his mother was waiting and forcefully embraced her son. Again overtaken by parental concern, Sil found himself struggling to breathe and speak.

"What the hell is wrong with you!?" she said as tears streamed down her face. "Do you know how worried we both were?!"

"Oh, hi mom." Completely taken aback by the state of his mother, Sil felt incredible guilt for having caused her such anguish.

"How could you do something like this?!"

Sil thought briefly about the question, not sure what to say. His silence only fuelled his mother's anguish. "I am so thankful you are okay," she said as she started to cry even more. She hugged her son again.

Why are you so sad, Sil thought, *I am right here... I know what will cheer her up!*

Thinking he could undo the results of his actions, "Mom, I got a job. I'm going to be an ambassador."

Sil's father, standing in the background, looked away wishing he could have stopped his son from saying that.

Just smile and nod, Hanael thought. *You used to be really good at this.*

"Job? You are lucky to be alive and this is what you say?! You're not leaving this house for the next three years!"

"Mom, calm down."

Bad choice of words, son.

"Clam down? I didn't give birth to you to see you fall off the edge of reality! You are restricted to *this* area!"

"Restricted?! You think giving birth is painful? Try plummeting off the edge of the world!"

Ooh, I'm not staying for this.

Sil's father silently retreated in hopes the situation would settle on its own.

"You are *never* getting out of here now. Your whole life will be making manna. You will do *nothing* else. No racing. No dreaming. No friends. Nothing."

Sil's mother thundered on about how much torment she was in. As she went on, Sil's eyes glazed over and his internal monologue blocked her incessant yelling.

If I could get back to the edge, I wonder if surviving a second fall would be easier.

Hanael resurfaced and interceded on behalf of his helpless son.

"Sernea, listen, it's not so bad. He's back. Why don't we all just get something to eat. You sit down. I'll set us some food."

"Are you taking his side in this?" she shrieked, scolding her husband. "Am I the only sane person left in this household?"

Now Hanael became slightly indignant. He argued back and the two of them contended with one another while Sil stood by.

"Our son almost died! Am I the only one who cares?!"

"He ended up unharmed and our nation is actually better as a result. Just for now, let it rest"

"Yeah mom," Sil interrupted. "This whole thing worked according to my plan."

Sil's belligerent statement caught her off guard, as he usually did when he was in trouble. She stopped midsentence:

"Ugh!" She hugged him again tightly as her final tears ran down her face. "Don't *ever* do this again."

They all smiled as she brushed back his hair, grateful to see him again.

"…what are you dressed as?"

*****

Victor left early in the morning to the same spot where Sil had been evacuated. He stared up at the sky and waited. More and more people from Nebat had arrived too late to see Silvanus. As such, they had been housed in the farmsteads along the trade way.

"C'mon Victor. We need you at the river," called out Catrina from a distance. Victor delayed in his return.

If I wait a little longer, I know you will come back and I want to be here to welcome you.

*****

Large roots stretched out from the riverbanks. They tangled about one another, thickening as they coiled about and connected to the other side of the shore creating a wide, bridge-like dam.

"Okay boys! You're up!" shouted one of the frontiersmen.

Victor jumped into action and ran for the mage-made crossing.

"Paulo, hurry! We only have so much time," he hollered. With wide smiles on their faces, the two boys darted over the temporary dam. Tangled within the root structure's system of heavy, vine-like stems were fish. The boys gently removed the fish from the snares and placed them in the bags they had brought. This activity went on for hours. When Victor and Paulo brought in full sacks, they exchanged them for empty ones and carried on in their undertaking. The women gutted and prepared the fish for canning on a table not far from the river. As the root structures collapsed, new bridges were built and more fish were caught.

*****

The ride down the funnel was much easier than Sil's fall. He silently wished he could have travelled this way the first time as he was able to analyze his surroundings on the way down.

Approaching the surface world was beautiful, but as they neared the bottom, the Aerials present would have to work together to prevent themselves from being thrown in every direction. Keeping stable would allow for a safe landing. Silvanus banished all of his musings in order to keep focused.

The moment they touched down, the currents cleared and daylight revealed the world Sil had recently departed from. He recalled the mission the high elder had charged him with.

Once you land, establish contact with a mage you deem suitable for a position of permanent ambassador alongside yourself. Then, learn their language and customs, ensuring that communication becomes easy. After this, send word back here and we will follow shortly after.

The Aerials lightly floated together following the shoreline. The villagers immediately took notice of their long coats and uniformly white hair and alerted the others. Eventually, the commotion found its way to the fishing party and as Victor and Paulo raced to the coastline with their catch, the party of Aerials stopped right in front of them.

Victor dropped off his sack and looking up, noticed his white-haired friend. No words were exchanged; the two immediately embraced and laughed happily at their reunion. Sil spoke to his friends in their home tongue and it was made very apparent that Victor would be the partnered emissary to aid the diplomatic effort.

Many days passed. An envoy from the capital city of Nebat arrived and greeted their foreign guests. It was agreed that the Aerials would be taken on a nationwide tour to be introduced to the surface world. Before anything could happen however, the Aerials needed to learn at least some of the language of the local populace.

Victor and Sil enrolled in an intensive program. Together, they spent days with teachers and scholars in order to engrain them with the speech of the surface world. Sil proved to be an apt student and quickly began to help the teachers with lessons for his Aerial brethren.

When the time came for their travels to begin, Silvanus made it clear that Victor was to accompany them. Together, they would travel to Nebat and hold an audience with the Queen.

Travelling by carriage, they spanned the countryside stopping at every village so citizens could engage with their skyward neighbours. People from the townships emerged in force and prepared great feasts. Every time they stopped, food, music, dancing and celebration were so frequent, it became the norm.

"Your world is so much fun!" said Sil to Victor. "We do this only on special days."

"Well, to be fair, all of *this* is happening really for you. It's a worldly welcoming," he responded.

"No. This is happening for *us*," corrected Sil.

They danced in a circle spinning wildly. Everywhere they went joyous greetings and mirthful parties awaited their arrival.

*****

After weeks of visiting the surrounding the cities and towns, the group arrived in Nebat. The entire city was larger than the entirety of the Realm. The structures were more densely placed and created a completely different atmosphere than what Sil and the Aerials were used to.

A vibrant procession led them through the main square and into the palace. Sil marvelled at the largest structure in the city. He could barely comprehend how an actual building stayed in one place, let alone one so large that it seemed he could climb to the top and leap back to his home world. It was something no Aerial would ever believe existed.

Inside the palace was no less magnificent. With marble stairways and floors, the entire royal domicile seemed to glisten. The Aerials could not keep their attention focused on any one particular portion for a very long time, nor could they immediately comprehend how the castle did not just collapse in on itself.

The Aerials flew around the ceilings, touching the artwork and getting lost in the colour scheme and the engraved designs. The Aerials were particularly stunned by the painted winged figures. This drew the Aerials attention for some time, having a certain resemblance to their elders. Their guides gently called them back to the floor as they prepared to enter the royal assembly.

It surprised Sil that the Queen was actually a young teenaged girl. As they approached, Victor told him that she would be raised to be a ruler of the kingdom.

They both kneeled before her until given the order to rise. The Queen sat before them, quietly at first, then she stood and made her address.

"Silvanus of the Aerial Nation, we welcome you to the Plainswalker Nation's capital city of Nebat to complete your training. In the future, we hope to establish permanent relations with your people to further the prosperity of both nations and bring a lasting unity to the world."

Those present clapped boisterously. Sil and Victor were taken around the room and introduced to every major and minor political figure. It was an exhausting event that ended with them being lodged in the royal guest rooms.

"This room is bigger than my house!" exclaimed Victor.

"Sooo, what comes next?" asked Sil. Victor smiled at his friend.

As an Aerial, whenever Sil would say 'Soo...,' it sounded like a minuscule gust of wind.

"Well, we will be learning here for a while. You and the others are going to be trained here to understand everything about us. Then, I think they hope to meet your leaders," explained Victor.

"Yes, that sounds like something the elders would want. You're going to be here too, right?" Sil questioned his friend.

"Of course. I'm going to help get you into top shape and then me and you are going to discover other worlds," replied Victor excitedly.

"You think there are more of them?" Silvanus inquired.

Victor posed an interesting idea. "If there are your people in the sky, then can mages not live anywhere else? We will find them together."

*****

As time passed, the elders also made their appearance. The entire capital suspended work and declared a permanent holiday. The winds that brought the elders forcefully brushed against the city. It almost became too much to endure, but after, in the stillness, the leaders of the Aerial nation stood before the entire city's population. The high elder, as well as some of the others, had wings, giving them a holy appearance. Silvanus flew out to greet his leader and behind him Victor followed.

"Hail Silvanus! Your stay on the surface looks to have treated you well."

"Yes sir! It certainly has. *This* is Victor," Sil said, motioning to the young Plainswalker who was desperately trying to draw his breath after catching up to his friend. Victor bowed respectfully and extended his hand. The high elder did the same and awkwardly grasped hold of the young mage's arm, giving an unorthodox handshake.

They turned towards the population behind them. To their surprise everyone, including the royals, were kneeling and muttering chants in unison. Sil and the high elder looked at each other.

"Is this normally how they greet guests?" he asked Sil.

Victor leaned towards Sil. "Have you told the assembly about your elders having wings?" he inquired of his friend.

"Oh… you know what? I forgot. Why does that matter?" responded Sil.

"We have a custom that says holy beings are normally winged. You know, divine messengers," explained Victor to a slightly bewildered Silvanus.

"Ohh yeah. Right, that I missed," stated Sil. Silvanus turned to his elder, *"Don't worry, they greeted me the same way when I came here first."*

"What did you tell him?" asked Victor.

"I told him this was normal behaviour for your people."

"What?! Why would you do that?" the Plainswalker retorted.

"Why don't we just go talk to the Queen?" he said as he glided towards her majesty.

*****

From this meeting, an inevitable strategy was formed and the two societies became trading partners. The Plainswalker and Aerial nations made use of each other in the most practical ways. With their ability to control clouds and wind currents, the Aerials ensured an amazing harvest, increasing output by over two hundred percent throughout the kingdom. In return for such services, the Plainswalkers provided food for the Realm Empyrean.

Silvanus and Victor became known as heroes. They grew up together, both with the dream of discovering nations that may exist in lands unknown.

CHAPTER 7

Seven years later

"I am telling you there has to be *something*!" Victor said fiercely.

After the encounter, the frontiersmen began travelling along the great river, which connected the kingdom from one side of the world to the other. However, finding new people became difficult as one left the boundaries of the Plainswalker territory.

"Where would you have me send you, exactly?" exclaimed the magistrate. "Have you seen the western deserts? During the day you're likely to dehydrate and at night freeze to death. Maybe, you get a little smart, comb the desert's border and end up in the south: a volcanic wasteland. The only discovery to be made there is the feeling of being roasted alive *if* the gasses don't kill you first."

"The northern reach is still uncharted," Victor responded.

The magistrate, now losing patience, tried to retain his composure while delineating common sense.

"What will you do to keep yourself warm? Wear coats? You will freeze to death faster than in the desert. Look, I appreciate the sentiment, I really do, but the Aerials can't even fly close without freezing."

Victor, now grasping at straws, trying to keep the debate going and to turn it to his favour, brought up a recent sighting.

"The centre of the desert…"

"Yes… What about it?" replied the magistrate, calming down.

"That anomaly?"

"Listen, you want to know what happened? The Queen sanctioned a huge expedition. An enormous caravan filled with survivalists, experts, militia and who knows what else. They headed towards this *thing* and on the way were attacked relentlessly by beasts that inhabit the area. No one escaped without being injured or killed."

"Did they find anything?" Victor persisted.

"They didn't even make it. Whatever it is, we can't reach it. The borders are closed to everyone and will remain closed until you can survive in scorching heat or bitter cold."

After a brief pause, Victor continued with his discourse,

"Who would have ever believed that mages could live in the sky? You must let us search again. I will set a course up the river and through the mountains. From there we may be able to find an opening into the..."

"Victor, this council has already made its decision. There will be no further endorsements from any of the frontier's guilds or municipalities."

As Victor departed the hall, he pondered what led to the discontent the authorities had with exploration:

It has been next to impossible for anyone to get questing permits anymore. A sort of religious fervency struck all the plains land after the Aerials were discovered. Travelling became the pastime that was preferred to working. The old maps were brought forth and people began to follow the ancient frontiersmen's way of life, migrating and surviving along the wild lands between the dominions.

The queen commissioned an Aerial group to fly over all the lands possible and search for any signs of other mage-life. Our mapping system was improved, however, they could not get close enough to the southern wasteland without volcanic smoke suffocating them. In the north, they could not even fly close enough for a proper survey because freezing to death became an issue.

The resting places and cabins were rebuilt and many more were constructed. The movement gained great momentum for about six years, then some Plainswalkers got lost in the mountains. Others, believing in the righteousness of the cause, ventured into the desert, hoping a higher power would guide them to mages lost to time. Instead, the sect died and by royal decree, no one was to go adventuring in the harsh lands without serious questing permits and magisterial approval.

The desert had some sort of beasts that inhabit the central area. The reports stated that they were big, strong and impossible to approach. Also, from the high level flight surveys mentioned, there was some sort of anomaly happening in the centre of the region. A large part of the surface was reflecting the sun to such an extent that it could be seen by the Aerial observers. Approaching such a very strong, bright and hot surface could not be risked. This left over half the world's surface undocumented.

Victor made the long walk back to one of the cabins along the trade way. Tomorrow, he would rise early and head home. With all that had happened, taken together with the great defeats sustained by the Crown, it was decreed that mage-life existed in two forms: *Plainswalkers* and *Aerials*.

CHAPTER 8

It had been Victor's life goal to explore the world and aid in finding other possible mage colonies. The probability of getting a questing permit to kill himself in the southern wastes or freeze in the north was looking next to impossible. As he returned from his audience with the magistrate, he noticed an Aerial gliding over the land towards him at top speed. The wind currents under his control swept leaves and foliage aside as he traversed the landscape.

"Hey, Sil. I have some bad news," Victor started.

"I know," Silvanus responded as he slowed his approach, coming to a complete stop beside his friend. "I wouldn't worry too much. I think our situation may turn around soon."

"What are you talking about? We have been through every magisterial and regional group. I even travelled to Engedi last week for a possible endorsement. There is nowhere else to turn," stated Victor.

"You know," Sil continued, "if you keep getting stressed over this crap, you're going to have a stroke. Then it will make no difference. Why not just me, you and whoever else go travelling anyway? We follow the great river and investigate as we like?"

"Already thought of that," Victor replied. "They post sentries at all the main watches and have ordered the settlements not to give aid to anyone suspected of exploration. I think it had something to do with the morons of the realm getting killed in environments they were not prepared for."

"You could just give up, you know," Sil said thoughtfully. "Maybe start a family, work on the farm. Your father does need the help. He's not young like when I first met him. He's old, like when I see him now."

"...You know, I think it was a good thing those morons died. There can only be so many and if you thin the herd, it's probably better for all of us. Wait a minute… *what?*" replied Victor absentmindedly.

Victor had continued without even thinking about Sil's suggestion for him to go home. The words finally hit him and Sil repeated himself.

"Go home for a while. See your family, feed the trees, play with Gus, relax and take it easy. In a few days, they're going to give us what we want," Sil remarked confidently.

"How can you be sure?"

"Trust me. I have called in the favour of a higher power."

Sil took off before Victor could inquire further. Taking his friend's advice, Victor went home. Surveying his homeland before sunset, he noticed the trees moving in for a night's rest around the ponds. Victor's family had farmed these lands for generations in the dominion of Miano: a large rural community, spread out hundreds of miles.

He loved it, but after meeting Sil, his perspective changed. Could there be more than this? Even though Plainswalkers could not ascend into the Aerial realm, they all know what exists up there. Perhaps other places are similar. That night, he slept peacefully, dreaming of what tomorrow would bring.

CHAPTER 9

During the early hours of the morning, Silvanus crept through the farmlands, making sure not to disturb the trees in their frolic. He softly glided through an open window into one of the cabins, knowing Victor was sleeping. Snatching an open jar of berries while casting a soft breeze behind him, Sil floated directly above his sleeping friend.

He waited a moment.

"Hey!" he shouted.

Victor jumped from his bed, his heart racing as he dropped to the floor.

"Honestly, I don't know how you Plainswalkers ever get tired of eating these things," Sil paused as Victor regained his composure. "If I owned a farm, I would have the biggest berry belly. Eh! Walkabout! Wake up!"

How does he always get in without making any noise? Victor thought as he rubbed his eyes to force the sleep from his head. Coming to his senses, he made a failed lunge for Sil, who, in midair, backed off and used the wall to lightly propel himself out the window.

"I'll be back when you're dressed. Hurry up!" shouted Sil.

Victor put on clothes and set the table for a morning meal. Soon after the two sat together and Sil laid out the plan.

"Alright, here it is. We did things your way and that just sucked old roots. Now, have a look at this," declared Sil.

He presented a rolled-up scroll with the royal emblem embedded in the wax seal. It was a permit—a questing permit stamped by the ambassador.

"Sil, how did you get this?" Victor asked, astounded.

"Alright, you ready? Your people are completely satisfied with the current mapping system. They have their frontiersmen. We have fly-around patrols that cannot see the ground. *The current administration*," he said with a refined voice, "would like some of their own people to have a firsthand experience and report back to the elders privately. In short, our leaders told your queen this would aid in the trading process. Soo... in other words, we're in."

They set to work right away gathering supplies, packing the essential tools, and charting a course. Being overjoyed was an understatement as the two mages prepared for the journey ahead.

"Oh, I almost forgot," added Sil. "As part of the bargain, we will be accompanied by two elites along our journey."

Victor remained silent waiting for further explanation.

"No worries. They're good. One is my cousin Erastus and the other one you haven't met is Erasmus. He's training to be an elder, so I suppose this helps."

"Your people need to work on some diversity with naming your children," commented Victor. "Also, I would like to bring Paulo. He would be really useful as his father was a frontiersman."

"Done."

*****

The journey was set to follow the great river through the forest and into the mountains. The team were directed to look for evidence of mage civilizations and report back. Their first meeting was slightly awkward since Erasmus could barely communicate in plains speak. As the night passed, they all became acquainted with one another.

"How did you guys manage to spread? It must have taken hundreds of years and loads of breeding," Erastus stated, totally perplexed as to how the Plainswalkers population actually outnumbered his own without overcrowding.

"Look at how long it took us and how much energy we had to use just to make it here. We have barely begun the journey and your language..." added Sil.

Victor cut him off instantly. "Hold on air breather; we already looked this over. Your people have a language of 35,000 words where we have almost 62,000. Most of which, you've never heard of before. Concepts such as chairs, tables, and solid ground."

Victor then turned his attention to the other two Aerials sitting alongside them.

"So, *Erastus* and *Erasmus*. See, you don't only look alike, you're *named* alike. You sure the two of you aren't twins?"

Sil interjected to bring Paulo into the conversation.

"If you get confused, that's Era One and that's Era Two.

They all laughed.

The troupe stayed at different cabins along the way. When people saw them, they greeted them and offered food. Finding out the travellers were Victor and Sil made them even more excited. Being the first to bring about the meeting between the mages gave them celebrity status. Everything was so perfect, there could not have been a better cohort-aside from the unusual complaints from the two Eras. Sil would translate just to see Victor's reaction.

"They say we can do this journey in jumps. Walking feels unnatural and takes too long."

Victor became annoyed at first, but then found it amusing that walking could cause such discontent. *Whatever, live with it. Besides, you don't really walk, you kind of awkwardly float. If the Aerial big bosses want a ground up perspective, tough shit. This is real ground up perspective. At the next stop, I will tease them about it,* thought Victor happily.

They came to the great forest after two weeks of travelling.

"Now remember," Paulo informed, "most of the trees here are wild, so they do not move or grow anything edible."

As they passed through, the air mages became more impressed with the scenery.

"See?" said Victor. "If you flew, you would miss this."

"Guys, I am going to scout ahead to get a look for some camp grounds," said Paulo.

Among the beautiful sights, there were other creatures: Dire wolves and bush hounds claimed territory here. Victor's family and others like his had no trouble keeping them from invading the farmlands, but here in the forest, there were many places where the animals hid in ambush for prey. Fortunately, as it was late in the year, the migration of stag, wild trotters and antifers were still in effect, dire wolves and bush hounds generally returned to the forest during winter when mating ceased.

The team found a great setting ground by the river where two waterfalls poured down.

"It's going to be warm tonight; we won't need fire. We'll eat the dried foods," Paulo assured his friends.

All of them admired the waterfall and nearby wildlife, entirely entranced by the sound of the flowing river. The Aerials especially loved seeing the forest as they had none in their home world. Rocks protruded from the riverbed, tempting the Aerials to try to hop them as they would clouds. The surrounding dense green leaves seemed to surrender their hold at the rivers banks, allowing the team to set up a decent campsite.

"Hey," Victor motioned to Sil, "do you guys even have words in your language to describe places like this?"

The team lingered as long as they could before setting off. Upon reaching the mountains, ahead of schedule, the team began heavily scouting and studying the area. After another month and a half of devotion, they found nothing.

Victor kept a journal, recording their findings:

A great trip with no success. We managed to set up maps and journals for our benefactors, the elder Aerials. Other than that, no other mage nations to be discovered.

Erastus began talking of future settlements for Aerial families on the surface. The mountaintops were unclaimed. Part of the reason for the trip was to assess the possibility of free land and the surrounding environment.

"Are you guys really going to start settling here?" Victor asked.

"Yes, we have plans to take the mountains and some infertile land awarded to us by the crown," replied Sil. "We will be closer to our allies. The elders are trying to be proactive in establishing friendship and closeness with your nation. I'm hoping to see the colonies develop within my lifetime. Your world is so beautiful."

"Well, no worries. There is lots of room. Just remember, the Aerials who live here are going to grow up with heavier food. I think we may see the first fat air child," Victor joked.

Ending their excursion, the team followed their trail down the mountainside and when they re-entered the forest, the Eras requested to see the waterfalls for one last time before they departed. Paulo led the way and the team arrived, once again, standing by the waterfalls in the afternoon sun. Victor and Sil set up camp, while Paulo caught some fish from the river for a meal. As they ate, Paulo raised a question to Sil.

"How is it more of you haven't fallen from the sky? What are the odds that in all the years only *you* accidentally end up in our world?"

Sil grinned at the chance to educate his companion.

"Well, actually, as an Aerial matures it becomes impossible for him to *accidentally* fall. You see, a thin layer of air coats our skin as we age, giving us a sort of permanent buoyancy. However, if a child should somehow reach the edge of the nation during the moment a breach in the three-leveled barricade that surrounds the edge while it's being repaired, *then* in theory, he could fall."

Later, as evening settled in, Victor and Paulo were skipping rocks – a common river pastime for young Plainswalkers. Even Sil got in on the action. Era and Erasmus looked on puzzled.

Erastus spoke up.

"How do you make hard things jump through water?"

"Oh yeah, you guys are really foreign. Here, try it out," Sil proposed while laughing.

Eventually, they got the hang of it. Then, it became a game that ended with Erastus using the air currents to float a load of stones and send them skipping over the water's surface.

"You know, you could seriously damage the forest with your breeze powers," Victor said, inciting Era. Era grinned and used a gust of wind to shoot water at him.

Sil took Victor's side and shortly afterwards, the two Eras were firing stones at their opponents while floating over the water's surface. Paulo and Victor looked on, soaked from the previous event, waiting for one of them to lose an eye. At one point, as the match became heated, Sil's attention was diverted.

"Ow, dammit, Era, stop a second," he cried while floating closer to the higher waterfall.

"Hey, Sil what the hell? You were doing so well," shouted Victor, not understanding why Sil, of all mages, would turn away from a winning game.

"Shush," Sil responded.

Silvanus moved closer and passed through the downpour. He remained missing for a matter of minutes. His friends stared on for moments… waiting…

Abruptly, Sil emerged.

"Guys, in here! Come see this!"

The Aerials took off leaving the Plainswalkers. Paulo spoke up.

"Umm, mage friends, we may have some difficulty crossing such a deep river."

The Eras looked at one another, floated backwards toward their compatriots, picked them up beneath their arms and flew them towards the rushing waters.

CHAPTER 10

Behind the waterfall, the explorers stood inside a cave, completely soaked.
Paulo broke the silence as he looked into the darkness.
"Where are we? How deep is this cave?"
"I flew through pretty far already. I say we explore," responded Silvanus.
Victor agreed and sent Erastus to retrieve their provisions. The team used small torches as lights, walking and investigating everything as they passed. They progressed deeper into the cavern.
"How far down does this go?" questioned Paulo again.
"Maybe to the centre of the world," Sil exclaimed.
The team laughed. Eventually, the cavern broke off and the torches needed to be re-lit.
"We have enough supplies for at least eight more torches. Should we split up?" Paulo asked, noticing the cave had started to slope downwards.
"No splitting," Victor replied. "We take this together. How much further down do you think this goes?"
The team continued for hours, stopping once to eat. The cave became more labyrinthine as they journeyed. Not knowing which way to turn, they began placing markers to guide them back. Sil, excited about the new adventure, became overtly confident, proceeding forward as his torch died. Unable to view the ground before him, he fell into a hidden opening.
"Ahhh shit," he said striking the ground beneath
"Sil, are you alright? Bring a torch. Era, here!" shouted Victor.
"Yeah, boys. I'm okay. Nothing broken, only bruised." He flew up and began sweating visibly.
"Woo! I didn't think that would take so much energy out of me," he said sitting on the ground.
"Listen," Victor stated, "the air is thinner down here. There is

more moisture making it harder to breathe and in your case, harness. Use your abilities sparingly."

"That's what that is," Erastus added. "I have felt lightheaded for some time now."

"Are you alright, Sil," Victor repeated.

"I'm okay, just surprised."

The team ventured on, passing the crevasse. It was easy enough to walk around.

"Guys, look," Paulo called. "As we go deeper, the walls seem to be more fractured. When we started, everything was densely structured. Now it seems..."

The ground shook lightly.

"Hey, Victor, was that you?" asked Sil jokingly.

The ground shook again.

"I think we found our reason for the fractures and shifts in the walls," added Victor. "Everyone stay close and move slowly."

Paulo stopped the team, warning them of the reality of their situation. "Okay guys, we have to stop here. We're out of markers and we have been descending for hours now. Torches are running low and we need more food. We have to go back. I mean, this is crazy. We don't even know where we're going."

Victor spoke up, "Paulo, we have found something that isn't on the maps. This is new ground and we could be seriously discovering ..."

A more violent shaking of the floor and walls interrupted Victors lecture.

"Victor, look around you!" Paulo exclaimed. "We are dangerously low of supplies, our Aerial friends are suffering from the air shortage and that shaking has become more violent the deeper we travel. So please, listen to reason. We can go to the elders, show them our progress and you know they will fund a more developed team. Victor, seriously, we can do this— but not now."

The Aerials looked sick and even though Victor wanted to continue, it would never be at the expense of his friends.

"You're right. How far down do you think we travelled?" Victor inquired.

"Well, it's been at least more than half a day's time, but it's hard to be precise." Paulo replied. "Look, it's getting too steep to continue without ropes, or some kind of equipment."

A great tremor shook the cavern; a vibration pulsed below their feet like waves at sea. The force was more violent than the ones before. Caught off guard, Sil was thrust away from the group and fell down the opening.

"Shit, Sil!" Victor yelled as he jumped for him. The force of the reverberating earth matched Victors momentum, throwing him forward. After the shifting ceased, Sil and Victor found themselves somewhere dark.

"Hey! Throw me a torch," Victor shouted.

"Ow!" *Dammit,* Victor thought rubbing his head. F*orgot still dark, should have seen that coming.*

Victor lit the torch and examined their situation.

We fell a lot further than I thought, or rather, we slid — why is the ground suddenly so smooth?

Paulo, inquiring of their wellbeing, interrupted Victor's thoughts.

"We're alright! Sil can you fly us up?" asked Victor.

"Of course. I still have some air strength in me."

In the torch light, the deep cave began to look like a well-formed tunnel.

"Sil, look, you noticed this, right? This ground is smooth, meaning *something* is causing this. Hey Paulo, bring the others, come down here now!"

Cautiously, the others slid down to meet their fallen companions.

"Before we go I want one sweep. The area we fell from was cavernous, but now this area is definitely engineered or created. The formation of these tunnels below caused our level above to collapse within. I'm sure this leads somewhere. We should investigate. One sweep and we stay together," Victor ordered.

The team's inspection brought them into an underground world of tunnels that weaved together producing an artificial maze.

"Okay," Victor asked, "any ideas on which way to go?"

"We keep it simple," suggested Sil. "Move straight, or as straight as possible. Everything seems to be kind of curved and melded together."

The team began their sweep. Unlike the upper caverns they came from, the floors here were slippery. The walls were somewhat moist, but it was not water. It felt like a silk residue, forcing the team to tread slowly. After a while, they found it easier to slide as if they were on ice.

"Hold on, steady yourselves. If we go down this upcoming slope, we may find it hard getting back up. The floors are slick and there is no grip. Let's go back. We have enough information," Victor directed.

They all silently agreed and as they turned, a violent quake took hold of the cave causing the floor to shift. With only a filmy ground to support them, they all began sliding. They gained momentum and, with no way to grab the walls, started to accelerate dangerously. The tunnel narrowed and the mages jammed their bodies together, crowding the tunnel and halting their descent. The team found themselves staring into a large, dark abyss.

"Sil, where are we?" Victor enquired nervously.

Sil looked at him, his face now pale. His breathing had become labored.

"Well… we were in a slick tunnel, of all things, and now we are inside the centre of the earth… or maybe close to it. Yeah, the upper centre of the earth. See, the tunnels were the gateway and now we are umm… here, I guess."

"Will you two stop playing around? This is bad, really bad," Paulo said. "We don't know where we are and we have no way of getting back. We still don't know what made those damn tunnels."

"Easy, brother," Victor said, stopping Paulo mid panic. "We have lots of water and our Aerial friends, though weakened, with a little rest, can take us back to where we fell. From there, we go up and follow the markers. This enormous inner earth valley is something we have to try and document to some degree."

"Well in that case, you better do it fast," said Paulo. "Our torch is burning down, and the next one is our last."

CHAPTER 11

Victor stood with his brethren for a moment and looked into the darkened underworld they had just stepped into. They lit the last torch and the group set off.

"Hey, wind drifters," Victor spoke light-heartedly, "you alright?"

The Aerials looked pale. With the air levels thinned underground, they were suffering, but they endured for the mission. Victor supported Silvanus and Paulo did the same for the other two. Victor took charge.

"Alright, this is how it will be. We will have a look at the ground floor, collect some samples and let Paulo do some calculating. Then, we head back the way we came, rest awhile, then continue upward and head home. I know it's annoying, but this is what we came for."

Sil looked at Victor. "How do you mean?"

"Look at your feet. There is a way down and it's been worked. We are standing on ancient stairs. This must be the ruins of an ancient mage civilization."

They all smiled and began to descend. Though it was a long way down, the team's eagerness made the passage quick. Upon reaching the ground, they set to work. Paulo did some running, Victor took samples and the Aerials sat against the earthen wall of the canyon fighting exhaustion.

"Alright, I think we're good for now," announced Victor.

Suddenly, sounds of scuttling were heard. Victor waved the torch toward the noise.

Nothing.

Silence.

Then, rapid movements in all directions, more defined and closer.

Silence again.

"On your feet! We move back up now!" commanded Victor.

The scattered movements became more intense as the team attempted to move back up the stairs.

Too late!

Something or some *things* were already on the stairs. Paulo aimed the torch to illuminate the stairway in front of him. A terrifying horde of giant insect-like creatures had overrun the stairway and sealed off their only escape. Victor could tell by the noises that the creatures were also surrounding them. They had walked into a trap.

Flinching at the light, many of the insects scurried out of the way, making it hard to get a clear look at them. From within the darkness, the team could hear the sounds of hissing and slithering throughout the canyon. Judging by the variety of sounds they made as they scurried around, they seemed to be of different breeds.

The friends clustered tightly together, moving away from the already infested stairway. They were all sweating and horrified at what would be their untimely end. Victor's thoughts raced as the creatures began to advance. The five mages huddled together with torchlight for protection. The gigantic insects were everywhere, staying just outside the light, but also being drawn towards it.

While waiting for them to attack, Paulo spoke.

"I think it's the light. They're not used to it. We have to get out of here!"

Without warning, one insect attacked using a spidery leg to strike at Paulo's torch.

How could this be happening to us? thought Victor as they edged back towards the canyon wall.

Paulo aggressively brandished the torch at their attackers, which seemed to only momentarily deter them. The creatures approached cautiously now. The sounds of thousands of them filled the canyon. The team found themselves cornered. With nowhere to go, Victor grasped Sil's forearm.

At least we will go down together.

Something caught Victor's attention from behind. He noticed a pair of dim glowing lights. He and Sil looked toward the source that quickly vanished.

"You see that?" Sil asked Victor.

The insects unexpectedly ceased their advance. A loud commanding shout and lights exploded forth from behind them. A projectile exploded from the flank, pushing the creatures back. Amidst the greater darkness, it was difficult to catch sight of what was happening. Victor steered his friends out of the way and into a more sheltered area.

The fighting was ferocious. Strange pairs of glowing lights were invading the area, making it hard to focus. Between the battle cries, explosions and commotion, the team found it hard to understand what was going on. A pair of lights approached them, taking shape as it drew near. Victor was the first to realize.

The glowing lights! It's their eyes!

The mysterious new mage spoke in a language none of the team could understand.

We did it. We found our brethren. Now, how will we escape to tell everyone?

CHAPTER 12

The insects interest in the team faded as the battle continued. The skirmish became more intense as larger creatures entered the valley. A mixed horde of gigantic spiders, millipedes, cockroaches and dragonflies overwhelmed the area.

Sentient beings with glowing eyes stood defiant. They were clothed in dark brown, hooded cloaks and armed with spears, swords, cross bows and poleaxes. From a distance, explosive projectiles were launched into the bulk of the swarm. The resulting fires broke the insects' ranks and illuminated the surroundings.

There appeared to be as many mages as there were the creatures that were fighting. Victor watched a group of mages with spears lure one of the larger, slithering creatures while another pair of the mages, holding strange half-moon scythes, clamped the insect in at each side and ran adjacent to each other, severing the body in half. These mages were clever and organized. They attacked in rows as a phalanx, while others gave cover with long-range weapons.

Victor noticed the mage leaders wearing bright, heavy armour. Each one was positioned behind three rows of grey soldiers, observing the battle. They looked like small tanks and seeing them engage the enemy became all the more impressive. Every strike was directed at the weakest possible point, inflicting crippling damage to much larger enemies. With two swords, one bright silver-armoured mage hacked his way right through a dense cluster of creatures. The legs and mandibles he left in his wake continued to twitch on the ground as the creatures cried out in agony. The grey clad soldiers followed quickly, ending their suffering.

Tremors began coursing through the valley. Both masses immediately ceased fighting and made a hasty retreat. Some of the cloaked soldiers came toward the team. Sil and the Eras were now beyond exhausted and needed aids to carry them off the battlefield. Victor supported Silvanus with the help of one of the grey cloaked soldiers.

We must not be separated, Victor thought, as he retreated with their liberators.

The brightly armoured mages were the last to leave the battlefield. The tremors became increasingly violent and looking back, Victor saw the cause of the tunnels, the earthquakes and the retreat.

A giant worm, big enough to easily swallow the team whole, broke through the canyon side. Another noise came from in front of them. Two huge doors made entirely of stone, illuminated by the eyes of their protectors, swung open. Upon entering, it became apparent that this civilization was entirely crafted from the underground landscape. The large doors slammed behind them and the team was forcefully led to a solitary dark room.

The Aerials breathed heavily and lay on the floor. Victor knelt by Sil, trying to give him support while Paulo investigated the small room they had been stored in.

"Alright guys," Paulo asked. "What now?"

CHAPTER 13

It has been like this for days. We have not been able to make any progress. The captain walked ahead to his quarters, frustrated with the recent events. His bright red armour that adorned his body was proof he was a master of combat. It was his tactic to use the brightness of his armor to attract the creatures, giving an opportunity for his soldiers to attack undetected. For years now, they systematically drew them out. Normally, they could exterminate thousands of them, but things had changed and they needed a new strategy.

"Captain," said one of his soldiers, "they want your report, sir."

The captain readied himself, putting on in his lighter armour and long red cape. He exited his room and moved through the city. The people bowed as he passed.

The streets were crowded and most of the citizens wore the same grey cloaks. But he, a captain, displayed his rank and clan position with colour and raiment. Like most of the upper class and distinguished members of society, their bodies were fused with the earth of their homeland: jade, obsidian, quartz, onyx, ruby and all other manner of fine stones. This gave mages of this realm abilities beyond what their natural build could accommodate.

The captain entered through a large portico and into a chamber where the nobles were waiting for him. Large bloodstones fixed into the walls gave a slight illumination to the dark room by absorbing the mages' excess optical glow naturally given off by their eyes and spreading it evenly. It dimmed the brightness, but not its potency.

The captain and others of his rank met and took their seats in an oval chamber. The nobles sat above the captains. They were physically joined with the stone itself, giving them greater power, longer lifespan and greater insight of their world. These nobles strictly ruled the nation, dictating and enforcing its traditions. Now the captain would have to answer for the misfortune that befell the day's battle.

A noble with onyx-coloured skin and armour and a deep aristocratic accent addressed the captain.

"Captain Navious, this council has been gathered to discuss the extension of our borders into the outward beyond. We have given you the necessary time limit and would like to hear of your progress or in this case, the lack of it."

Navious rose, holding a stoic gaze that masked his inner fury.

"My lords, you know we are not losing battles. In fact, we have less fatalities now than any previous generation. In this last battle, only fifteen of my men were injured. As far as our military competence is concerned, my brethren and I are among the best in the stone nation. I make no reservation when I speak for the bravery and proficiency of our comrades. We have not lost a battle in almost ten years and have been involved in rescue, defence, expansion, assault and siege missions. We are the most experienced and successful of all the elite divisions. The fault in our current situation is not linked to our prowess but to uncontrollable, outstanding circumstances."

One of the nobles responded.

"We were well aware of the wyrm in our generation. We fought against this threat as well. That does not excuse your word to this council that within ten cycle's time we would have new claim. Our borders are stacked with massive over-population. What are we supposed to tell our people? That their nobles failed them? Maybe they should be limited to one child per household, as we have nowhere left to go."

The noble paused, letting the full effect of his speech penetrate the captain.

"Now, our scouts and gutter runners have gathered samples from the outside. The land across is resource rich and perfect for what we need to settle all of our habitation issues. You and the captains in your unit promised to deliver a starting range for our expansion project, regardless of the enemy. You insisted on taking this mission and now our situation is worse than before. Tell your lords and brothers exactly what we are to do, and please, spare us your valour and warrior hero speeches. No one is questioning the fact you know how to fight. It takes more than combat skills to serve your people."

Navious' face dropped, realizing the truth of the matter. He gave answer to the noble's response.

"In your day and in the days before, the situation was simple. We would mine in a direction to build up the nation. If we came across undesirables, we killed them and if wyrms found us, we petrified the area. In doing so, we kept the wyrms out of our living space, but as a result, we could not expand past the point of petrification."

"Our society and the world itself is a series of uneven living quarters and dying resource harvests. We have fenced ourselves in, and just as in the previous generations, we still have no weapons to pierce the wyrms' hide. To cross the valley and expand is necessary, but across the valley is the wyrms' lair. It is trapped between our shelled society and its empty home.

"I have no excuse for the lack of progress. We fought hard and our battles with the drone hordes have brought them to the point of extermination. It has been determined that the same must be done with the threat of the wyrm. It is the last of its kind and I believe it knows this. We have to kill it. The other captains and I will set a plan and use all the resources at our disposal. I have no estimation for completion time because this has never been done before. Our people will not starve or be forced to die in their own streets as if they were tombs. We have done enough running."

Silence blanketed the room. The nobles were clearly impressed.

"Do you have any developments in exploiting a weakness against the wyrm?" asked a noble at the far side of the room in a docile tone.

"None," responded the captain.

Silence again.

"I think we have covered this thoroughly," stated another noble whose dark lazerite skin made him blend into the far corner.

"Now, tell us captain, what of the reports of the five strangers who were rescued during the raid? This council has heard many different variations as to this groups' origin. In fact, it seems this group, though shaped like us, have some major differences. Some have said that they are alien to our universe. Could we bring in the scouts that first made contact with them?"

*****

"Victor, can you see anything?" Silvanus asked.

"I can see lots of blackness. Does that help?" he responded.

"Well, we need to figure out what…"

Victor was interrupted when one of their captors entered the room. His two glowing eyes brought an eerie dimness to their surroundings, allowing the team to slightly see one another. He brought water and spoke in his underworld language. Victor reached up and held him by the chin, pointing him at Paulo saying, "Have you learned their language yet?"

"Not exactly, but I think I'm close."

"Excellent. Sil," Victor added while pointing the patient messenger's face at the Aerials for illumination, "how are you holding up?"

"I've had better days. I think the Eras are worse though. They will need help."

Victor released the surprised and somewhat amused water bearer. He placed bloodstones in the room, which gave a soft glow to the area. Then, after saying something that no one understood, left.

"Well that solves one problem." Paulo moved over to Sil and let him lean against him. Victor looked after the other two.

"Looks like we did it. We found more of us. Now, all we have to do is find our way back up the canyon wall, try not to get eaten by insects the size of trees and keep us from suffocating. Then, we can be heroes," mused Sil.

"Oh and that tunnel worm may be a problem," Victor said, trying to make his friend laugh.

"You really are an ass, you know that?" Paulo commented, causing the whole cell to laugh. Erastus passed out and it looked like the other two Aerials were not far from doing the same. Victor fed Sil some water and silently prayed that something fortunate would happen soon.

CHAPTER 14

"They came from the roof of the universe! From where we all were said to have come, fearlessly they descended. They did not have eyes to see but still walked directly into the centre of the swarm. I have never seen such reckless courage," reported the scout.

"Did any of these beings kill or strike out at the enemy?" asked the blue-skinned noble.

"I saw no such thing. They seemed to be blind in their approach," the scout replied.

"Alright, that will be all for now. Are there more scouts who witnessed the event?" asked another noble.

"Yes sir, but these were the closest to the area where the encounter took place," remarked one of the aids.

"We will debate the interpretation of this omen. All are dismissed." signalled a dark stone-skinned mage.

The scouts and attendants exited, bowing toward the nobles at the entrance way. When the room was clear, the nobles began to discuss.

"Could these be from another world beyond our own?" proposed a noble with a crystal dermis.

"Brother, let us be logical," replied a shining ruby skinned mage from the far side of the room, "The last thing we need is religious fervency taking hold of the masses. The physician said that three of them looked sick and they have no illumination to their eyes. His concern was whether or not to treat such beings."

"Angels," said another noble shaking his head. "They seem more like invalids."

"This is not what we need now and with Navious, we may be sending some of our best to die in that valley. You know he will not stop. We are pushing him too hard," insisted an elderly mage, whose outer covering was of emerald green.

"Gorian," answered the onyx noble, "we have fought this war

for our entire lives and it is the only reason we have survived. Every generation has their obstacles, but if we do not act now, we may not have anything left to build on. Our population is surging and our mines are drying. The land across the valley is both rich and habitable. The space is almost five times the size of our own. We *need* this!"

"Everyone who directly stood against a wyrm has never succeeded. Our weaponry is not sufficient. Shouldn't this particular wyrm have starved to death already?" asked one noble.

"Our whole world is seemingly closing in on us from all sides, and if we cannot live in our world, perhaps those *'angels'* can offer us a place within their own," Gorian proposed. "As far as treatment, give them the full extent of care needed and feed them. Food is one commodity we have an abundance of. Let us give our alien guests some earthly hospitality."

"That is all for now. We will re-convene in four cycles to discuss strategy," declared the onyx noble, ending the council meeting.

*****

Gorian met up with Navious in the barracks. He and the other captains were preparing a strategy and preparing armaments for the attack.

"A word, Captain," spoke Gorian.

Navious dismissed his officers. Standing before the elder, the glowing outflow from his eyes gave Gorians' emerald skin a serene fulgent aura to match his demeanour.

"Perhaps rushing so quickly into battle without first allowing the engineering clans time to develop an edge for us is unwise," Gorian suggested.

"If we wait longer, the whole nation is pushed into jeopardy. None of us can afford that," Navious replied.

"Navious, the council is getting nervous. The wyrm has still not died. We just do not want to become sedentary. Everyone in the nation moves as one. If one part is weak, the whole of the nation feels the pain. Let engineering produce something."

"Sir, I will not stand for weakness. We are behind our position and the captains and I will not be the weak link," Navious retorted.

"Navious, please hold up for a short time. You and your men need rest. The wyrm is not going anywhere. You will kill it; just place logic before desire," Gorian countered.

"I was under the impression the council sees me in an unfavourable light and I must make amends," acknowledged the captain.

"I know and you will, but maybe there can be aid from something undetected. I hear your troop discovered some angels?" Gorian asked.

"Angels," spat Navious. *"Really?* Is that what they are called now? They're sickly, blind, and they can be of no use to us. We are on our own, as we have always been!"

Gorian sighed. "Perhaps, but everything exists for a reason and happens as a consequence. In a time of great need, their appearance is not coincidence. Don't you agree?"

Gorian had a way of seeing the deeper end of things, which made it impossible to argue with him. Navious had no reply for the noble, but gave a small bow as he took his leave and started back to work.

*****

With the addition of luminescence, things improved. The team was fed a strange, glowing, leafy substance that tasted good and filled them up. Victor's silent prayer was answered when a physician was sent in. He tended to the sickly Aerials and re-generated them using quartz crystals and citrine stones. Victor sat marvelling at the healer's ability.

"Did you know that stones could do that?" Paulo asked.

"I think this may be their natural ability," responded Victor.

After all the seeing, feeding and healing, the team was led on a tour. This nation's intricate artisanship was like nothing they ever encountered back home. Enormous tunnels went off in every direction, some full of people working. Other tunnels were walled with houses carved right into the rock. It was almost hard to believe that amidst their entire civilization, they had no freestanding structures. Everything either extended from the face of the rock or sunk deep within it. The entire society existed in a labyrinth of roads and mines. At times, they passed through a narrow alley from a deserted area and emerged into a densely populated marketplace bustling with activity.

Their guide pointed at different places as he acquainted the team with their surroundings. Even though they couldn't understand the language, his over-exaggerated hand gestures were a clear indication of what he was trying to convey. While touring, Victor noticed workers in a tunnel mining. The group paused to observe the operation in progress.

"Remember, always think of the next step. Your job exists only because you are part of a greater whole. Remember the person after you because how they receive the material determines their performance. Give them the best and most efficient output. Always keep in mind the survival of our people. Since our beginning was made possible only because of our process..."

The mage giving the instructions seemed to be a teacher or foreman, thought Victor.

"What do you think they're saying?" asked Victor.

"Not a clue," Paulo responded.

As they progressed through the metropolis amidst all the activity, mages would take notice and with their right hand placed on their chest, give a small bow.

"It seems they have a respect for us," said Erasmus. His comment surprised everyone. Normally his ineptitude with plains speak kept him silent.

"Hey Silvanus, does this remind you of anything?" asked Paulo. Sil smiled. He had now been an angel twice in his lifetime.

The tour lasted many hours, giving an exhibition of different aspects of the underworld nation: where they worked, trained for battle, produced their weapons, even gave a glance at how they grew those glowing roots fed to the team. A short stop was also made at a daycare area where they were introduced to children of different ages.

The entrance of almost every tunnel had a map carved onto the wall, outlining the standing location in contrast to the rest of the world.

"Hey," Victor motioned. "Get a look at this! We haven't seen even a fraction of their world."

At a large chamber, where many of their high officials were seated, the tour ended. The team was escorted within, given seats and then stared at for a short time.

"These must be their elders. I think they may be part rock or something," said Sil.

The different colours on their skin were the same as many of the stones they saw mined and used among the populace.

"How long do you think they will stare at us?" whispered Paulo. Victor shrugged in response.

One grey caped individual stepped forward, bowed toward the high-seated nobles and addressed the team in his own language.

"Ma aretz ateh bo?" ["From what land did you come from?"] he asked.

He then waited for a response.

"Sil, what did you do when this happened to you?" Paulo whispered.

"I pointed up and said, '*Ohmm*.'"

The grey mage seemed confused.

"Aretz?" he asked again. This time Victor responded.

"Aretz."

The mage nodded in approval

"Home," said Victor pointing up. "We have to get back home," Victor said pointing up again.

The chamber room filled with excited conversation. One of the nobles stood, elegantly addressed the assembly, and sat back down. The mages clapped and cheered.

Paulo then asked Victor. "What do you think?"

"I think I should have said *ohmm*."

The nobles debated for some time. Finally, one came forward and made a small speech. Everyone applauded, leaving Victor and his friends wondering what was going on. They were quickly ushered out of the room with everyone cheering.

"Paulo, have you learned their language yet?" Silvanus asked sarcastically.

"Almost. Still trying to get past *ohmm*."

After the meeting, the team found themselves moved to another chamber, this one obviously a barracks, full of armaments and mages. Some of the mages present had the same bright armour witnessed on the battleground.

"*Drnir*," said the guide introducing himself.

The team took turns introducing themselves.

You think this would have come first, Victor thought.

Drnir pointed to different soldiers and gave them their titles, ending at one very strong looking mage.

"*Navious.*"

CHAPTER 15

"How can this be the will of the council?" Navious spoke to Drnir.

"Well," Drnir replied, "there was debate, then applause and before you knew it, the nobles, as well as the clan leaders, instructed me to tell you that those *'beings'* are divine and therefore a good omen. They were insistent that they accompany us to war against the wyrm."

"Do these things know how to fight?" implored Navious.

"Not sure, sir. I have never seen them wield a weapon or do anything special," answered Drnir.

"Do they follow the process? Can they move in unison with the core?" Navious pried.

"I do not believe they understand our language," Drnir replied calmly.

Navious, now more perturbed than ever, began shouting at his subordinate. "Then what am I supposed to do with them?!"

Drnir, realizing they were drawing attention, moved closer to calm his captain down.

"Well, the nobles in their *wisdom,* have discerned that it would be most efficient for you to fight the war and choose a scout to aid them in finding their way back. Sort of a diplomatic mission. Placing them with the unit gives people hope and raises morale. Also, this allows us to make official ties with whatever heavenly realm they are from."

A look of disgust flushed over Navious' face.

"Do you truly believe they are angels? They are barely mages. Probably just some sort of colony we lost contact with a hundred years ago."

"Perhaps, but the men sir... they love them. In these hard times it is best to use all of our resources to the best advantage."

PREPARING FOR BATTLE

While the world's skies and grasslands remained peaceful, at the planet's heart, a timeless war raged on for its possession. In full battle armour, Captain Navious led his contingent to the doors where the team entered the city. There were fearless soldiers, prepared for a battle knowing they might not return. Some prayed for the last time, well aware the fate of their nation would be determined in the moments to come.

"Heavy artillery to closely follow the regiment. Remember, we have to make serious damage and we have to make it fast. We will flank in files of three, but I want the groups to divide further. This may be harder to direct, but at least the wyrm, should it strike, will take less of us down at a time," Navious instructed the captains.

He continued dictating to the captains as an unexpected visitor appeared with a gift for the burdened war hero.

"Captain Navious."

The captain turned.

"Lord Gorian," he said, surprised.

"Captain, in light of the recent events, I have convinced the council to hold session on granting emergency power of the eastern defence. Captain Navious, your mission has been deemed worthy of reinforcements. The eastern legions are at your command."

Navious exited the barracks to see large, well-organized groups of soldiers marching toward the main gate.

"Thank you, my lord," Navious said, bowing in their customary fashion.

"Also, to free up any reserves, you are to be granted your own personal stone guard."

The captain almost blushed with astonishment. The earth elementals are never released, to those deemed to be unworthy. He himself had not yet been taught how to summon them.

"The council is too kind," he whispered after a brief pause.

"The council trusts you with the future of our nation. You need to be properly equipped."

Navious smiled, regardless of knowing the full weight he had to carry. The summoned rock guard are answerable only to the nobles. The nobles, alone among the nation, are instructed in the sacred art of giving life to stone. This forges a bond between the world and themselves. Handing the rock guard to Navious displayed their sincere confidence.

Silvanus approached the earth elementals. They had a tank-like body made entirely of stone, supported by four pillar-like legs. They stood taller than their creators, with two small gemstone eyes fixed on the captain that they would be commanded to protect.

"Victor, look. They have familiars made of earth!"

He and his compatriots examined the rock guard with great interest.

"And as for our friends?" added Gorian, nodding towards the otherworldly beings.

"Sir, I have a man in mind. He is one of my best, a scout from a mining family," responded Navious.

"You have the full support of the council and of your people. I have done all that I can." The elder paused shortly before finishing his address. "Your father fought alongside me in my youth and I know that time with him was stolen from you. He would be proud of you."

Gorian gave instructions to the elementals before leaving. Captain Navious turned back towards his officers and began adjusting his strategy to include over 50,000 additional reinforcements.

CHAPTER 16

With everything in place, Navious readied himself. The wyrm was hungry and drawing it out would be easy: they just had to make a lot of noise.

"The elementals will follow me. I want a three-hundred-unit spread. Captains in charge of thirty. All heavy artillery, full forward."

There was silence at this last order and he knew exactly why.

"You all know what we are fighting here. Typical tactics will not work! We have to make an impact! I have freed up all captains from my end. The elementals will be my personal guard. Make sure that if I do not survive, the attack continues." Navious ordered rigidly. "Ophir!"

"Yes, sir," responded a grey clad, thinly built scout.

"You were with the angels. Do you remember the way they came in?" demanded the captain.

"That way has been corrupted. But I think I can make a crossing with the right materials," Ophir replied.

"Take what you need. The council has asked me to provide an escort for them. I have chosen you. You are my best scout. Keep them safe. Guide them well," charged Navious.

Raising his hand, Navious silenced all discussion as he addressed his men.

"You know if I had the talent for speeches I would already be a general."

Abundant laughter flooded the ranks, giving short ease in preparation for what was to come.

"Keep to the process. Do not deviate. We are strong so long as we stay united!"

"Strength through unity!" His men shouted in response as they began to march toward the beyond. Navious took a moment. He knew why the elementals were sent: it was going to be a reward should he succeed. This mission was his step up to becoming a noble; given high rights and greater training. His name would be remembered forever. All this if he succeeded. A lot was at stake. He readied himself, placed his helmet on his head and joined the march.

*****

"Sil, that is a lot of troops," Paulo said nervously.

The team had only heard of war in stories from home. The Plainswalkers had a small militia but purely as a defence against wild animals and things that steal livestock. This was something far more intense. Before any of them had time to collect their thoughts, they were directed into the centre of a certain group of heavily armed soldiers.

"Soo…," asked Sil, "you think they're taking us home?"

"Maybe, but they don't need an escort like this to do that," stated Victor. "Look, since we arrived, it has been very apparent the streets are overcrowded. I think they're trying to find a new area for settlement."

"That would make sense," considered Paulo. "You think they're going to make us fight?"

"Why? Are you *scared?*" teased Sil.

"Hey!" Victor interrupted. "What do you suppose those are for?" He pointed to what looked like heavy metal bells turned on their side.

*****

The army marched through the gates, entered the valley and took their positions. The regiments split up and heavy artillery was pushed to the front.

"Ophir," called Navious, "take them along the broken path. Fix what you can. Give them minor armaments. Move fast. We will be calling the wyrm. It is not far from here."

"Yes sir," responded Ophir.

A small metal spear was issued to each member of the team and, for sight, they were given active blood stones.

"Okay, so the sharp end goes into monster. I got this," said Sil.

The team was instructed mostly with simple gestures from Ophir. They moved in pairs. Ophir and Victor took the lead and began their ascent. Many of the steps that they had used were broken and unstable. However, Ophir had no trouble making repairs. Taking small stones from a pouch and using his natural talents, the earth expanded and closed over, not reforming the step, but definitely making it easier to cross.

When Ophir and the team had nearly made it to the top, Navious gave the command. His soldiers kneeled and placed their hands on the ground. Almost immediately, the earth began to vibrate.

Victor stopped to look back but Ophir urged him on. The tremors slowed and then came the response: the wyrm was enormous and the earth shook violently at its passing. Victor froze, seeing again the enormous snake-like creature moving toward the corps.

The soldiers were not hiding their eyes. This was a head-on confrontation. Mages with metal spikes and strange bells, though obviously well-trained and disciplined, showed astounding courage standing against the emerging behemoth. Its girth occupied almost the entire valley and the soldiers appeared smaller as it surfaced. The wyrm's ability to sense disturbances through its skin made up for its seemingly typhlotic appearance, making it look like a cylindrical eating machine.

Its mouth opened, revealing numerous rows of sharp teeth. As its head reared back ready to strike, an explosion from the artillery struck hard against its thick skin. The creature bellowed loudly as it fell toward the young mages ascending the canyon side.

"Shit! Sil!"

A screen of rock suddenly erupted before them…

How did this… Ophir… Thank you, Victor realized.

Ophir had saved the team by encasing them within layers of rock.

Paulo grabbed Victor. "Where are the Aerials?"

The wyrm slithered backwards and roared in anger. The artillery began to reload.

"Hit it again with more force. We have to damage it!" shouted Navious.

"Sil, Era One and Two, where are you guys?" shouted Victor as loud as he could, hoping to hear a response.

"There! Look!" pointed Paulo.

The Aerials were back down in the valley having been separated when the creature fell towards them. Somehow, between then and now, they had lost their position in an avalanche of rock.

"Ho la, *hikah ani ekabel atem!*" Ophir restrained Victor. [*Oh no, I'll get them. Wait here*].

"Damn it! Why can't you have a rock or some sort of stone that lets me understand you?!" protested Victor.

Just then, the wyrm noticed the arguing pair. With its senses evoked, it turned towards them. If it wasn't able to actually look at them, it was definitely aiming in the right direction. The wyrm opened its mouth as it dove forward. Paulo, without thinking, threw his spear, striking the wyrm within. Its body recoiled backward, making an excruciating sound that filled the valley. The wyrm's attention drew toward the Aerials. They were being moved back behind the regiment's position.

"Sil!" Victor yelled. "Inside the mouth! You have to make a hit when its mouth opens!"

If they could channel enough air to propel their spears, they could make it happen. As the creature moved again toward the army, Sil and his brethren, using their abilities, launched spears faster than anything the soldiers had ever seen. Striking true, the creature's agony doubled. After seeing its weakness, the army began to follow suit.

The wyrm drew back and closed its mouth. Jaw movement cast Navious out of a quick victory. The artillery and heavy weaponry were easily repelled and the beast struck back with a vengeance.

The wyrm attacked like a hammer, smashing itself into the left flank, destroying and crushing everything in its way. Then, opening its mouth, the monster sucked in at least thirty mages. Ophir cried out when he saw this happen. Slithering backwards, the wyrm's body started to pulse and vibrate as it digested the recently consumed meal.

"Paulo, look! It has to manually digest its food," observed Victor.

The sight was horrifying. Some of the mages who were crushed managed to use their abilities, hiding themselves under small shields of rock from the floor, sustaining only minor injuries. Many others were not so fortunate. While it digested their comrades, the army prepared for another strike.

*****

Sil, taking cover behind a crate of explosives, made a decisive plan.

"Erastus, listen! I will ready one of these exploding balls. You find something to light it with and together, we launch it into that thing." Era found a heated rod nearby as Sil harnessed the air currents to lift one of the mortars. Very quickly, he realized the weakness of his natural abilities in his current setting.

"Ah, damn!" Sil shouted as the mortar crashed to the ground. "Guys, give me some help."

The army began to regroup and aim heavy weapons at the wyrm. The injured were taken aside as the soldiers moved into position. Quietly and quickly, they assembled. The wyrm continued to pulsate, enjoying its recent meal.

One of the soldiers motioned to the Aerials to fall behind their position. Sil, not knowing what he was saying, simply waved and smiled then went back to positioning the mortar.

"Okay, Era, you light it when I say. I will lure it in. We will all have to lift it together. The air waves are weak here."

Even though the Eras were obviously tired from the spear toss, they followed orders.

Sil stood up. "Hey!" He meant to say something humorous, but the wyrm reared itself towards Sil and began to advance.

"Light! Light! Light!" Sil shouted.

The mortar was lit.

"Now, as one!"

With the Aerials' natural abilities, the mortar was raised from the ground. Navious and his men watched in amazement as it flew through the air and into the wyrm's open jaws. The explosion caused a sudden halt to the serpentine advance. The painful bellowing radiated throughout the valley, striking the ears of all who could hear with a painful discomfort. Sil and his brethren, now drained, watched on.

"Crap, I thought that would kill it. Okay, I'm out! We should run."

The Aerials, now covered in a waterfall of sweat, took off toward the line of soldiers who had renewed their attack, forcing the wyrm backwards and retaking most of their original terrain. The wyrm opened its mouth and began to draw in, like a whirlpool, everything around it.

"Ground yourselves!" shouted one of the captains.

Using the earth to their advantage, the army suctioned their feet and arms to the ground, preventing the wyrm to swallow them whole. Unfortunately, this meant the earth mages were vulnerable to attack. The beast lunged forward. Captain Navious, thinking quickly, ordered cannon fire on an ammunition crate causing multiple explosions and stopping the wyrms assault.

"Hold your positions, five front lines run forward. Tip the remaining ammo crates, elementals to me. One mortar unit to me, no more! The rest of you, concentrate your firepower. With all long range weapons, force the wyrm into my line of sight."

The captain's orders were followed unwaveringly. Navious, the elementals and a mortar support unit consisting of two soldiers pushing one small cannon moved with him directly in front of the wyrm's feeding path.

Navious raised his arm to hold the firing. The wyrm retracted, quickly recovered, then slowly moved toward Navious and his small detachment. The rest of the legion looked on as their commander faced off against the mage nation's greatest enemy. As the wyrm slithered forward, all watched fearfully, not knowing their captain's fate.

"Load the mortar!" ordered Navious.

The wyrm opened its mouth again and began to draw in everything in front of him; the spilled ammunition went first.

"Ground yourselves!"

The elemental giants crowded the captain to keep him stable. At that moment, the wyrm charged.

"Light... Fire!"

The blast shot the mortar into the creature's mouth, which exploded in its upper neck. The previously swallowed ammunition ignited, causing a huge expansion of the wyrm's body and its skin to briefly glow bright red with every discharge. The wyrm's head rose, giving one last outcry. Then, like a falling tower, the wyrm crashed down toward Navious, who was still grounded.

When the wyrm landed, the soldiers all gave an oppositional yell. Navious was crushed. The wyrm lay still and all were silent. The behemoth's body covered the captain and his elemental escort completely, lying motionless. The defeat of a terrifying threat had become the stage for a despairing aftermath.

None of the soldiers would never have dreamed that this strong willed fighter would be vanquished in such a way. Their preliminary cause for mourning was interrupted when movement from beneath the wyrm's body caught the attention of the legion.

The elementals had formed a shield of rock with the ground, creating a trench. Captain Navious, now covered in green fluid exiting from the wyrm's mouth, with the mortar team and the elementals, surfaced together. Breathing heavily, Navious, leaned on the dead wyrm. Removing his helmet, he looked at the army, then at the dead creature before him.

"I thought this would have taken longer."

Realizing what had happened and what had been achieved, the captain began to laugh and raising his arms he shouted in victory.

The surrounding legions, including Ophir, did the same. The Aerials were led to the steps and met with their friends at the top. The celebrating carried on and Navious shouted up at the team.

"You are angels! God is with us!" They cheered even more intensely when Sil raised his arms.

"They are angels!" spoke Navious to Drnir, who had run forward from the crowd to aid his captain. "Gorian was right. They were sent for a reason. God is with us."

His men held Navious up on their shoulders while the main gate received an overflow of citizens congratulating their heroes.

CHAPTER 17

It was obvious that Ophir wanted to remain and celebrate, but he was determined to fulfil his duty and return the team to their original realm. Many times even Paulo became lost, but Ophir was a great guide and seemed to know the way. The Aerials, though exhausted, made every effort to move at group speed. Finally, they arrived at the fissure where the upper cave connected to the lower tunnel that was made by the now deceased creature.

"Guys," Victor spoke, "the only reason we made it through is because that monster broke the boundary between these upper tunnels and its own."

The mages aided each other in climbing into the cavern. As they passed the markers, Victor pointed them out to Ophir. Ophir smiled, understanding their purpose.

It took a lot longer than any of them had imagined and they rested on the way. Ophir provided some rations during the break. The Aerials strength began to return when they felt the air currents become denser.

"Breath it in, bitches!" yelled Silvanus.

While travelling, Paulo heard something familiar, water.

"Boys, we're almost home, I can hear the water."

Anticipation ran high for the portal ahead. Everyone started to move faster to where their journey began. They stood before the waterfall.

"Well, here is one small step for mages… and up yours, Plainswalkers, we can fly again," spoke Silvanus more sarcastic and excited than usual.

Sil and the Aerials flew through the falls. Victor and Paulo looked at each other, grabbed Ophir by both arms and jumped through.

CHAPTER 18

It was such a relief to see the sun. Victor's eyes had to adjust because of the lighting difference, but the serene glow was a welcoming sight. Despite the carnage deep below, the surface world had retained its peace, which comforted the explorers as they emerged. Victor swam to shore, feeling blessed to be surrounded once again with a familiar landscape. His peace was shattered when he heard Ophir screaming in pain. Paulo swam over to give him support.

"Damn it! Get him to shore!" Paulo shouted.

Ophir was holding his face and shouting. Victor saw no visible injuries.

"What's wrong? Did he hit his head or something?" asked Sil.

"No, it's the sun," Paulo responded astutely. "He can't see. Era, give me your coat."

Both Aerials looked at each other.

"It doesn't matter which one!" Victor yelled.

Wrapping his coat around Ophir's head, Paulo calmed him with gentle words. After he settled down, the rest of the team, wet and exhausted, rested by the riverside.

Victor had to place food and water in Ophir's hands and physically guide him. The team restarted their travels hours later. It would be a two and half day journey before re-entering the Plains Walker kingdom.

"Do you think he is totally blind?" asked Erastus.

"Maybe, but I highly doubt it. His eyes emit light in the dark. All we have to do is wait until night settles in and we will see if he regains any of his sight," explained Paulo.

"It's going to be disappointing if these guys cannot even step into our realms without succumbing to blindness. What a start for diplomacy," grumbled Sil.

Paulo and Victor led the way as Silvanus floated along and the Eras walked on either side of Ophir.

"How is he?" Victor asked Sil.

"I don't know. He has been quiet, probably depressed. Think about it - imagine plunging into a whole world you never knew existed and being able to see none of it," said Sil grimly.

"It was dark at first, when we entered his realm," stated Paulo.

"Not like this," responded Sil. "I wonder what he is thinking."

Even though I have been in the heaven realm for many hours now, I have seen nothing and have to be led as a child. They speak in a language I cannot understand and feeding myself is impossible. I hear many sounds and smell new scents, but I do not know what any of this is.

Why have I been punished like this!?

Thankfully, the angels who I was a guide for have shown great mercy. I wonder if I will ever see again.

I very much miss my home and my family. I wonder if angels have families? Perhaps these have clans of their own that they wish to impress and have mothers and children. I highly doubt it. These beings are from the God-realm!

That light that took my eyesight must have been the Maker himself and I must not be worthy to look upon him. They should have sent a noble or someone of greater value then I. For whatever sins I have committed, please let this blindness settle on me alone and not my brethren. I am only a peasant scout and ignorant to things lofty. Please forgive me for entering your lands with unworthy hands and selfish thoughts...

"Hey, there is something wrong with Ophir," called Erastus.

"Let's rest. The sun sets soon and we should set up camp. Look at him," Victor said.

Tears were streaming down the earth mage's face as he quietly prayed. They settled him down and started a fire. After boiling some water, Paulo added some wild herbs and gave Ophir tea to drink.

"He's calming," spoke Silvanus. "How would you feel not being able to see?"

"I think this will take care of itself. His people see in a dark underworld and soon it will be dark here," reasoned Paulo.

The sun began to set. Dark red colours filled the sky as the team found a renewed appreciation for the beauty of their home world. The winds became cool as the sounds of insects and the breeze signalled the day's end. The moon and stars appeared as the night's grip took hold.

"Okay guys, I think we should try," Victor suggested, motioning to the Aerials to remove his coverings. Ophir resisted, but was easily calmed.

After the coat was untied from his face, Ophir rubbed his eyes, slowly opening them. The natural glow of his eyes lit up those sitting around him. His vision took focus and he could see. A huge smile burrowed into his face. Obviously overjoyed and excited, he began to speak rapidly. Nobody understood him, but the team could definitely share in his mirth. He was almost dancing around and when he looked up, his gaze became fixed. This was his first time seeing the stars. All present found themselves wondering what could be going through his mind....

My god, the roof of heaven has eyes...

CHAPTER 19

When the company arrived in the Plains Empire, it was daytime. Not only were the people happy to see them, but they were also happy to see the new blindfolded visitor.

The team had been missing for almost three weeks. They spent their second night in Nebat as royal guests. Ophir especially enjoyed the midnight banquet held in his honour. The plains food outmatched his homelands and as a soldier used to rations, the variety of tastes made every bite he took a new discovery. During the festivities, Ophir gave a great demonstration of his abilities: he used rose quartz to create a fog, a bloodstone to create light and even used jade to form protective armour around himself.

Their entire adventure was told while a scribe sat close by, chronicling the tale. Word travelled quickly about a new mage civilization and the next day, the palace was surrounded with subjects wanting to have a glimpse at the foreign guest.

"Well brothers," Victor said, "this is not over. If we can live under the earth and in the sky, there are other nations we will have to discover."

"We're all behind you, Victor. You have the support of the Aerial nation *and* me, too," added Silvanus.

"We have a lot ahead of us. There is much land unexplored," Victor began. The windows remained shaded so Ophir could see. Apparently trying to make up for his blind days, he was observing everything he possibly could.

"Before we start, let's make sure Ophir can understand our language," instructed Victor.

"I'm on it," said Paulo

So began the age of discovery, where mages disclosed the hidden nations scattered around their world. The chronicler termed the new nation discovered as *'Terrans'* and throughout the empire, that is how they came to be known.

Two years later

"It has been two years since we discovered your people buried inside the world," spoke Silvanus in his usual tone. "You think your technology would develop accordingly."

"I could almost agree with you," Ophir countered, "but when we try to drive heavy mortars or artillery into the deserts, they sink in the moving sands. The problem is not with development; the materials we used are too heavy. Why can't your people bombard them with some sort of flying assault? Oh yes, that's right. Your frail bodies heat up and dry out in the desert environment."

Sil loved teasing Ophir, probably because it was so easy. A lot changed since their first encounter. The Terrans had four settlements above ground and traded freely with the Plainswalkers. The Plains mages benefited much from the Terran inventions, including new stone heating generators that absorbed heat during the day and radiated it at night. They also provided advanced training to her majesty's blacksmiths, sculptors, metal and stoneworkers. The Plains nation introduced the Terrans to varieties of foods, fruits, and medicinal sciences. It had been a most profitable and prosperous time. The Terrans also developed specialized artifice machinery for Nebat's streets. Automated carriages conveyed the populace in an efficient manner, resigning the need for horses or donkeys.

Ophir, once a scout, became a mage of high position. He was given territory in his homeland rich in gold and was the first to start trading. He wore a golden cape and armour to denote the metal he was closest to. His eyes, once bright, had toned down. The team learned that it takes about a week for any Terran to adjust to the sunlight.

Many of Ophir's brethren followed him, now living in specially allotted lands that were infertile and useless for Plainswalkers. The Terran nation's initial problem of overcrowding was relieved with a new situation of having too much land and no threats. The world was going through a multi-layered revolution.

The legendary questing team was bestowed with diplomatic recognition as the '*Department of Mage Nation Relations*' and the full support of the three kingdoms.

"Alright boys, calm down. Let us gather what we know and we can make a decision from there. Now, there is definitely something in the desert's centre," Ophir said, pointing to a newly drawn map.

"Obviously, somehow light was drawn in as a shield in great extremes to keep those creatures out. The recent Aerial view from Erasmus says the light is so powerful, it can be seen in the dark from the heights of the Realm. That is more than enough evidence that *something* is there, possibly a small group of mages trying to protect themselves from those sentient monsters. We know our recent attempts have not been enough to slay the mysterious creatures. The weapons we use are too heavy, our people run out of water too quickly and navigating through the sands is becoming increasingly difficult."

He paused to let it all sink in. Taking a breath, he continued.

"The reports from Paulo say that we have injured the creatures, forcing them to retreat without making kills. To add even greater difficulty to the situation, the desert temperature changes. Some of our mages have frozen to death at night."

"I have not heard yet, but what of Paulo's report on the beasts that live in the deep deserts?" asked Victor.

Ophir addressed Victor's concern.

"I have encountered them many times; they have an odd shape to them and walk on four legs. However, when we engage them, they walk on two. Their feet are cloven and their heads have long horns. They stand and are shaped like mages, but more muscular and much larger. Long claws and sharp teeth are their main weapons. We encounter them not in groups, but one at a time and in distances apart from each other. This shows a certain degree of territorial behaviour. Even though we can fight them on even ground by combining our forces, we have not actually killed any of them.

"When the creatures sustain injury, they retreat faster than we can pursue. We can make it into the desert, but keeping ourselves alive and then giving chase to the threats becomes difficult. The soldiers are starving, overheating during the day and freezing during the night. Moving the necessary weaponry is almost impossible because the terrain is difficult to navigate."

"Isn't sand crushed up earth?" goaded Sil. "Can't your people petrify it for greater mobility?"

Ophir looked annoyed at the snide comment.

"Petrification only works on hard surfaces. Manipulation and harnessing of energies works on substances that have hard surfaces to begin with. Sand has no properties of this kind," snapped Ophir.

Sil grinned at causing minor irritation, then casually bit loudly into an apple he picked from a bowl of fruit. Victor stroked his forehead and took a deep breath in.

"Alright then. We are pulling out."

His compatriots gasped in surprise.

"We can renegotiate a strategy and give additional water supplies..." Cutting Ophir off in mid-sentence, Victor affirmed his position.

"No, we can't and I will not risk mage lives needlessly. We are pulling out. Send an Aerial dispatch to Paulo. Tell him to give the order for full retreat."

Victor stood up to leave while the others looked affronted at the drastic command shift. Victor left the main room for the study. Looking outside, the traffic of the capital city was at its peak for the day. He poured a drink for himself and his friend, whom he knew would follow up the discussion.

"Victor," Ophir began, "We have spent nearly seven months on reconnaissance. Mages have died fighting those monsters and even more have been scarred by the desert. We know something exists in the center of the desert. The Queen's men will expect a report and a more serious reason for an entire recall."

Handing the drink to Ophir, Victor replied.

"Listen, we have been wasting our time with these leads. We have become scattered and while we sit back here, even *with* greater resources, we accomplish nothing. Two years, no progress, just weak leads."

"The leads are not weak!" Ophir retorted.

"That's right!" Victor shouted. "We're weak! Don't you remember how we actually met? We walked into each other. Sil fell from the sky. It was mages meeting mages. It took guts and risk, and now, we send young boys into battle in unfamiliar territories and give long speeches to the aristo class about expanding trade with partners we don't even have."

Victor ceased his rant to take a drink. Then, after pouring some more, passed the bottle to Ophir.

"I have made arrangements to send an advanced team to the North Hold. Your people have been keeping me posted on their research. They have managed to live and remain in an environment we never could."

"Yes, it is true. There has been much more advancement in adapting to the cold than to the heat," replied Ophir. "But there is nothing there. Not even animal life is plentiful enough. The colony is not completely self-sufficient and the mountains are hazardous."

"I am ordering the immediate creation of an elite team to explore the frozen north and its territory, a team that I am going to lead myself. A scouting party made it over the mountains and has been documenting some interesting findings. With the mountain's composition, your people have found a way to drill through it successfully."

Ophir looked uneasy.

"I will need help if this is to be done," stated Victor.

"What do you have in mind?" Ophir asked.

"We will use Silvanus, the Eras, Paulo, you, myself and one other of your choice from the North Hold as a guide," Victor informed his friend.

"Is there any evidence of mage nations existing in those territories?" Ophir questioned.

"None. They finish drilling in a week. I am going to tell the officials I'm investigating our holdings in the northern base and while there, take a step over the border. It will look like a routine tour," Victor asserted.

"You know, we cannot survey the land properly at all. Aerials are completely grounded. We have nothing to aid us, no messengers or mapping. We have *proof* that mages live in the desert. How can you turn back on that?" Ophir probed.

"I leave in the morning. It will take about a week of hard moving to get there in time. Be ready," Victor affirmed.

"Wait, this is not right," continued Ophir. "It is reckless."

"No, it's not," Victor responded. "*This* is what we are supposed to do. We never had Aerials or mapping when we found each other! It was without technology or armies. We actually moved around, which is what we should have been doing from the beginning," Victor said, getting flustered. "Tell the boys we leave in the morning."

Ophir turned to leave, then stopped.

"What did the scouts discover?"

"We'll see it together when we arrive."

CHAPTER 20

Supplies were loaded into heavy mechanical carts powered by clear crystal engines. Perfected for above ground travel, the carts were an ingenious invention given to the Plains nation by their Terran allies. Before their departure, Victor made it very clear that there would be no stops but those necessary.

"Hey Victor, why can't the other air walkers and I just fly over to the base?" demanded Silvanus.

"Well first, you and your friends would freeze to death, and second, because I do not want our party split up. If any of us run into the Queen's officials at any stop point or are sighted by a royal post, we could be detoured and ordered to explain the desert retreat. The others in the two carts behind us, they have been instructed to do the same," Victor responded sternly.

"Ducking the officials. You sure that's a smart thing to do?" Sil asked.

"It doesn't matter. We cannot justify keeping the army in the desert anyway and if we look busy, they will be less likely to disturb us, at least for now," replied Victor.

Silvanus was silent for a while.

"Why the north? The area is totally experimental. The colony is stable but no one, except you of course, has anything substantial to report. Victor, what's the big secret?"

"The mountain range. It extends from the Western Lake to the ocean, covering the entire expanse," informed Victor.

"Yeah, the walled mountains. We all know them," interjected Sil.

"Well, the Terran scouts tried to climb them to no avail. Then they started to mine them. Of course, that was no trouble. Even in the cold they adapted. Whatever minerals they extracted, they would examine and use to aid the colony's development. You know what they found, Sil?" questioned Victor.

Sil leaned forward, anticipating an overlooked reference everyone had missed.

"Nothing. No minerals, no stones, no rocks, no earth. There is absolutely no value to be found and believe me, they made more than sixty dig zones. The mountain is entirely ice."

Sil leaned back, unimpressed with the conversation's outcome. The Aerial pondered for a while, then looked up at Victor puzzled.

"Soo… We are travelling almost a week, non-stop, to survey… nothing. Well, I did need the time off, but I would really rather vacation somewhere warm."

"Sil, listen. The scouts sent back another report, one which I never really let known to the officials. Many of the senior scouts have suggested that the geography is all wrong. Normally the earth is pushed upward by moving fault lines…"

"Wait, hold up," interrupted Silvanus. "Are you just reading the report? Do you even know what a fault line is?"

Victor sighed. Silvanus was right.

"The *point* is, the ice just simply stands like a wall. In fact, the consistency with the height and material, being only ice, suggest that the mountain may actually be an ancient mage structure."

"What mages could possibly be living in that wasteland?" asked Silvanus quizzically.

"What mages could live in the sky or under the earth?" Victor responded.

CHAPTER 21

The sun's rays evoked the morning epoch as three mechanized carriages sped through the lonely northern road. A perpetual chill enveloped the northland and despite being equipped with heavy fur coats, Silvanus was still lightly shaking. They had been stopped at a meeting point. The winds seemed to attack them as they stepped out of the chariot.

"We thought you would have been halted by the storm," spoke the scout who greeted the team excitedly. "Here, have these. They will warm you——they're hot stones."

He passed one to both Victor and Silvanus, who was obviously relived to grab anything warmer than his current condition. Sil arched slightly because of the weight of the coat and greedily grasped the hot stone given to him by the Terran.

"We will have to wait until noon to begin the assessment. The storm should die down by then. They happen periodically. Come this way, sirs. We have food and hot tea waiting for you."

As they left the cart, the Eras and Paulo emerged, each being greeted the same way. Terrans at the gate gave a welcoming smile to the team as they approached.

"Sil, you know slouching is bad for your posture," commented Victor on Sil's disposition.

"Shut up," he said shivering.

Settling inside, they were seated and fed a hot meal.

"Where is Ophir?" Victor asked.

"Oh yes. Sorry sir. He wanted to check out some of the posts on the outside and should be here any moment," added the Terran scout who led them in. "I am Avi, the base commander for the North Hold. I will be giving you the tour and showing you our progress."

"Thank you, Avi," replied Victor.

The team turned in unison when they heard the doors opening.

Ophir entered the room, clothed in light golden armour with red trim, obviously enhanced by Terran craft. His golden cape trailed behind, giving him a dignified authoritarian look. Victor immediately stood to greet his friend.

"How was the ride?"

"As good as yours, I think," Ophir remarked.

"Pleasure to see you, Captain Ophir," added the base commander.

The team sat united once again to accomplish their noble work.

"Paulo, you must feel special. You have been flown by Aerials and carted through the cold. You might as well be a royal package sent to everywhere in the kingdom," Sil joked. "Tell me, what do you prefer, the hot desert or the cold… this place?"

"I prefer results, which we better be able to produce for the royals before we leave here," replied Paulo.

"He's right. Commander, show us what you have mapped and give us all the information on the mountain breakthrough," Victor ordered.

Avi brought out an immense pile of scrolls and placed them on the table. Victor had not realized how large the table actually was until Avi unrolled a massive scale map of the mountain area.

"We have mapped from lake to the ocean. I have, for our purposes, only retrieved the ones that show our area. Now, the report we sent stated that we tried mining several different areas on the mountain range. The results and the tests are all documented for your inspection," Avi informed.

"I thought nothing was found?" asked Paulo.

"That's correct, but we kept documentation of the excursion for your reference," Avi replied.

"We will look at them later," Victor added. "Tell us about the surveys and the drilling."

"Of course," spoke Avi with a smile. "It has been getting interesting, as we have developed an entirely new artifice for the project. In fact, everything here has been the result of adaptation. We have not yet become self-sufficient, but I have to say, I doubt there is any other colony that has made as many advances as we have.

"The survey was interesting. We have managed to climb and even coordinate the heights of the mountain itself. Which, though difficult, is possible. We could not create a working pathway due to the treachery of the landscape and temperament of the weather. However, we discovered, through numerous dig sites, that the mountain is made entirely of ice. No minerals, no rock, nothing but ice. Now, we have tried to descend to the other side from above, but that was just too much of a journey and incredibly dangerous; So we developed a way to drill through the mountain itself."

What a mouthful, thought Victor.

The team stared at each other for a moment before Avi continued.

"We have made two drilling attempts and our second is the likely success. The first ended when we hit a large, sudden break. A canyon was found within the mountain. We could not manipulate any earth for a bridge, so we pulled out and started from a different location. As of now, we have been drilling for about seven weeks, if you count both attempts together," estimated Avi.

"Of this technology, do you have designs? Also, how do you estimate as to how long the drilling should take?" Ophir enquired.

"The designs are here my lord," Avi said, handing him a parchment from the pile of scrolls. "As for the estimation, we aimed for the shortest way possible and we believe that within the next two days, or sooner, we should break through. However, instead of telling you about the drill, I would rather show it to you on the tour," Avi asserted proudly.

"You also mentioned the theory you had about the mountain itself," Victor added.

"Yes! For that we will need these," he said shuffling through the scrolls to retrieve his intended document.

"Now the whole mountain being made of ice is strange enough. We do not see this phenomenon anywhere else. Its consistency is almost perfect from the sea gulf to the ocean. When we observe the opposite side, there is nothing similar to it. This would indeed suggest that this is possibly artificially built."

"Hold on," Victor said interrupting Avi, "What do you mean

nothing similar? What's at the other end of this thing?"

"Sir," another Terran interrupted. "We're ready."

"Well my lords, why not come and see for yourselves?"

CHAPTER 22

The storm had died down significantly. Since the winds calmed, noticing the enormous, mountain-like structure behind the fortress was much easier. Silvanus was the first to speak up.

"Soo... Did anyone else not notice this when we came? Seriously, I mean, I didn't even see it and it's huge," he exclaimed. "Ophir, did you see it?"

Victor noticed that the cold was not so much a problem, with the polished hot stones kept within their inner pockets.

"Here it is! The Northern Wall," remarked Avi. "As Lord Silvanus had said, it can be very difficult to see during the morning storms. Now that the noon calm has settled, we should have no trouble."

"Avi, you said you had climbed to the top?" Victor enquired.

"Yes sir, all the way up. However, going down to the other side proved too much of a hazard. The structure becomes steep throughout and too difficult to descend. Here, look toward the upper right," he said handing him a large cylindrical crystal used to enlarge images viewed from afar.

"There, you see them. The red markers glow in the dark and track the safest path, or at least the path we took. We marked our way every fifty or sixty paces, so we could find a trail back when the storms let loose. Where you see many of the markers clustered, they were former mining attempts," Avi pointed out.

Victor scanned the mountain thoroughly.

They've crossed this megalithic structure many times. I wonder what the other side looks like?

"Avi, what of the tunnelling?" he asked.

"Yes! Right this way, sir."

The team did not have to walk far before coming to the entrance of two huge tunnels. They passed the first one. The second one, further off, had a large machine that looked like a tank with a drill at its head.

"Commander, when you said you had been digging through the mountain, I was unaware of your capabilities being so advanced," declared Ophir.

"Thank you sir. We had to employ an entire engineering crew. The artifice is quite astonishing. The drilling mechanism does exactly that, but imbued around its edges is refined hot stone. It acts as a melting agent, so we soften the hillside to make drilling more manageable. This is done systematically, otherwise, the hole implodes. We dug it out three times before we learned that. The first tunnel led to a chasm and we could dig no further. Then, we did another survey and found this area sufficient. Luckily, we have borne almost twice the distance. I think today or tomorrow a breakthrough is expected. Come, I will take you through the first tunnel."

The moment the team entered, Victor slipped. Paulo caught hold of him on the way down. The entire tunnel was smooth and well rounded.

"Careful! The melting helps to keep it smooth as the drilling takes us through. It freezes rather quickly due to the temperature here," added Avi.

They held their bloodstones like torches to illuminate the way. Coming to the tunnel's end, the chasm lay like a cruel trap waiting for them.

"How deep is it?" asked Paulo.

"We are, as of yet, uncertain. I never gave clearance for a team to investigate. All our efforts are to open a path through the North Wall," Avi responded.

Sil stared almost transfixed by the deep darkness extending downward. His imagination led him to wonder if this mountain, possibly a structure created by mages, was really a tomb and below them lay the bones of thousands of their ancestors. He let his mind marvel at the possible horrors that the darkness concealed beneath them. The shouting of a Terran engineer interrupted Sil's thoughts.

"Commander, they have started up the drill. We have to ask you to clear the lords out."

"Well, we better go then," added Avi.

As they exited, Sil slid next to Paulo.

"I like being called 'Lord,'" Sil jokingly told Paulo.

CHAPTER 23

The team walked closely along the mountainside noticing the engineers ahead. Their quarrying seemed to shake the entire mountain. Avi described the process as they approached. The drilling commenced, sped up, then slowed and stopped, only to begin again on five-minute intervals. Every-so-often, someone would yell out in Terran speak and some of the engineers would run in. Then, gradually, they would return and the dig would resume.

After the engineers took a break, the team was invited to investigate the entrance of the second tunnel.

"Well, I know we have been *here* before," joked Silvanus once again. "I think the landmarks in this country are somewhat similar, wouldn't you say?"

Avi explained more about the engineering, how the tunnel became smooth after the drilling and melting. Victor found it somewhat interesting, but his focus on the tunnel put Avi's voice into the background. The engineers yelled in and the team moved out as the drilling advanced.

"The drill itself," Avi continued, "is powered by the Terrans who operate it. They manipulate the earthen energies from the stones and cause the melting and spinning of the engine to commence. This is why we need a full team because when one becomes tired, another takes his place..." Avi was cut off by Terrans shouting came from the tunnel.

"My lords, we have broken through!"

"This is much sooner than expected," Avi responded.

The engineers emerged dignified and contented.

 "My lords, we have completed the tunnel," repeated the Terran. "Please, come this way. It is fitting that you take the first steps into the new world."

*****

All of them entered the passageway. It was much longer than the last one. Everyone moved in total silence, followed closely by the Terrans. Gradually, after twenty minutes, they saw the ending: an opening with a snowy backdrop. Looking at one another and realizing how far they would have to walk, Silvanus took action.

"Okay, guys, form a line," said Sil. "Now, hold onto each other's arms and *do not* fall."

Sil, at the front, started to float with his Aerial brethren pulling the line of mages forward as one. The ice provided a perfect sliding surface. The team reached the end in quick time.

"So, who loves me more *now*?" Sil jested.

Sil began to exaggerate his usefulness, making it seem that the team would not have made it without his floating them forward. Victor zoned out, focusing on the snowy cascade. Sunlight reflecting from the frozen entranceway obscured his vision. Covering his eyes, he stepped through into the cold. As Victor's eyes came into focus, he beheld the new world.

Snow. No trees. No animals… not even any hills or variations in the land. Just… snow.

"Well, this is a really flat piece of property," said Sil looking around. "Waaay flatter than the desert."

Terrans from the North Hold had arrived and began surveying.

"Avi," Victor called. "Tell your teams to assemble and begin scouting. Leave markers every thirty or thirty-five paces. Make sure everyone keeps in close contact and reports on half cycle intervals."

"Yes, sir," responded Avi.

"Sil," Victor shouted, surprising his friend, "slide us back to the other side…"

CHAPTER 24

"Get some food and store some rations. The Terrans are efficient, so this won't take them a long time to finish. After they return with their report, we start in."

The team all looked at Victor in silent agreement and set to work.

"Ophir, choose one from among them. Someone highly recommended. We will need a guide more used to the terrain."

"Of course," Ophir responded.

There was an obvious commotion in the outpost. None expected high-ranking officers to be going through for exploration. Victor didn't have the heart to tell them they were just avoiding the councillors.

Talk to politicians, or risk our lives to discover mages that may not even be there. How can there be another choice?

"Sil, how is it coming?" Victor asked.

"Ready here."

"Us as well," spoke the Eras.

Paulo and Ophir stood in next and brought one of the North Holds' scouts.

"This is Danir."

"What's with all the *'ir's* on your names?" quipped Sil.

"I believe the phonetic pairing sounded by our home tongue is similar to the *'us'* sound mirrored by yours," replied Danir.

Ophir chimed in.

"Danir, Lord Silvanus was just joking—finding some small detail and exaggerating it for humorous result."

"Ah. Thank you, my lord," the scout replied.

"Oh, he's stiff," said Sil, half laughing.

"Enough of this," Victor added, bringing the light hearted banter to a halt. "Danir, listen, we need you to guide us as best you can. We all have markers and supplies so there is no shortage. You know these lands better than we do. You are in the lead and please, don't call us *lords* or *sirs*. You are a part of the team now."

Danir, elated by Victor's recent comment, smiled.

"Thank you, Sil. Thank you, Victor."

"You can call me 'Lord,' if you like. I actually prefer it," said Sil, smiling.

Danir proved to be a hardened scout and readied himself alongside them as if he had journeyed hundreds of times before. Victor nodded to Ophir in approval. With their resources gathered, the team received information. A path to the base was laid with markers and they were to continue from that point. A scout from the first dispatch gave a preliminary analysis.

"We have not seen anything of substance. The land becomes slightly hill-like, but not horrible. Use the snow shoes as they will allow for safe travelling. Now, it will probably become difficult to see when the storms come. Lay your markers in clusters. You have more than what you need to last you."

Sil spoke up. "If the land is flat and you have those seeing stones, why not just look across?"

"The snow and winds prevent us from seeing at a great distance. The markers will aid with finding and revisiting locations of interest. We will monitor your progress from the wall," explained the scout.

With the inquiries concluded, Sil's sarcasm ceased and supplies were loaded. Arriving back at the tunnel, the Terrans gathered to see them off and congratulate their young colleague. Danir began to walk in and Victor grabbed his shoulder to halt him.

"Hold on, grab my arm," as he held out his arm to the bewildered young mage.

"Um, sir? I do not understand."

"Just grab my arm, soldier," Victor insisted sharply. Danir quickly latched himself to Victor.

"Hey, Lord Silvanus," Victor shouted. "Give us a pull."

CHAPTER 25

They reached the end of the tunnel. Drawing their hoods, they set to work. The team passed the Terran crews doing surveys. The winds were strong and visibility was not ideal, but they kept on. Eventually, they passed all the markers and every thirty to thirty-five paces, they placed more. This was kept up until nightfall when Victor spoke up.

"Dan, where is a good place to camp?"

"Anywhere is good," he replied. "It seems to be one large plain."

The landscape was barren-unrestrained tundra with an unyielding snowfall. Victor looked back. Seeing the North Hold was impossible as the winds were strong and the snow it propelled seemed to cover every inch of visible reality. He could, however, see the markers, which was comforting. Backtracking would not be difficult.

"How will we set up a tent with this wind?" Victor asked.

The Eras stood at either end of the group and raised their arms. The winds did not stop but were somehow prevented from their directed assault. To the rest of the team, it was like standing within a clear dome.

"The smaller the space, the easier this will be," spoke Erastus.

"Sil, why not just use your abilities throughout the journey?" Victor asked.

"It takes loads of energy to keep focused for long periods of time, so we do it with breaks and rests. As the winds become harnessed, each of us can hold the currents by ourselves and take turns to let the others rest."

Ophir removed a large carnelian globe from a pouch, sat down in the middle of the group and placed his hand over top, closing his eyes. The stone heated up and created a greater degree of warmth throughout the camp.

"Well, if we are going to travel and sleep in the cold side of the planet, we should be able to do it comfortably," he added.

The snow around the mages melted allowing tents to be set up without issue. Everyone except for the Eras sat in a small circle around the heated globe.

"They will maintain the winds for a while before joining," said Sil.

The team took out their water canteens. Some, which had froze, were set over the globe to melt.

"The weather will not continue like this. Most likely it will settle. This is the spring season and storms normally hover closer to the mountain area," explained Danir. "It will become calm for days at a time, giving us the advantage for safer travel."

"Even still, if we had known before about the situation, I could have petitioned my elders to remove all high level clouds and currents. It would have made our way infinitely easier," stated Sil.

"No one will stop you if you want to fly up right now," added Ophir.

"Not a chance! I will freeze to death and so will any Aerial. We would have to get elders from above and a group of powerful Aerials standing near the North's entrance to aid from below. It takes some time to prepare," replied Sil.

The night around them had established itself. The glowing markers were set up throughout the camp and provided illumination. A comfortable silence settled around them. Victor broke the calm with the requirements tomorrow would bring.

"Alright, here it is. In the morning, whoever is on watch will wake the others. We will need full visibility, so the sun should be raised because we have to cover as much ground as possible. Paulo, you are on mark duty. I do not need to tell you that the locations we discover without mage activity may provide a strategic location for colonization and experimentation for future projects. Danir, you take point on all situations. You are scout leader on this mission. Please remember, we are in a strange land and we don't know what to expect, so keep close together."

They silently absorbed their leader's warnings. The team ate their first meal on mission and went to sleep. The night was peaceful and comfortably warm thanks to the efforts of the Terran and Aerial abilities.

This may be the last adventure we are on all together, thought Victor. *With land this size we will be 'surveying' for weeks, maybe even a month. The council will probably vote us off in our absence and replace us with newer, more obedient kiss asses that won't be so insistent on travel. Instead, they will give speeches in the capital classrooms about the importance of unity and other bullshit. This will give them high-paying jobs with little work and easy advancement into the upper end of the royal ranks.*

The idea made him sick. Nebatean politics were incredibly annoying-sitting at a desk, signing documents, giving speeches, drinking tea, and in the end, getting nothing done or having minimal result. Victor knew they wanted the team gone and their position filled by a more agreeable group of assets, which they could point in the public's direction. They would feed falsified stories of how the next mage world was going to be discovered and would yield unbridled advancements. It was a campaign promise for the senators and a past time for the royals, neither of which ever actually left the palace rooms.

The disconnect between the people and the officials is staggering. They do not even believe in our cause. Well, fine. For now, even if there is no result, just being with my friends is great enough.

Victor became tired. The very idea of the politicians actually exhausted him.

Tomorrow we will begin the search. I wonder what kind of mage, if any, could possibly live in this frozen land.

CHAPTER 26

One of the Eras roused the rest of the team in the morning, seeing that the storm had passed. A clear morning presented itself to the team. Danir's advice rang true like a prophetic declaration.

"You know, sleeping in would have been nice. It's not like we're stranded underground. We can follow back any time we want," complained Sil. He was about to continue his displeasure when he noticed the landscape. "Well, I have never been in a country where I can stand at one place and see its ending. Don't be disappointed if we find no mages here."

Ophir wanted so badly to knock him out. His Terran reserve prevented him from action.

"We move," Victor motioned to the others.

The campsite was packed, water readied, markers dropped and travelling begun. After walking for hours, the land slumped in, causing the team to sink into the snow. The Aerials simply lightened their bodies and walked softly over the top. The rest resorted to swearing and wishing they never packed their snowshoes away. The team traveled for hours more, talking, joking and reminiscing of older times. Victor took an interest in their newest compatriot.

"Danir, what about you? Why would you volunteer for working in the North Hold so far away from your family and the mainland?" Victor asked.

"Well, it's not that I wanted to work there. Originally, I was selected. After about a year, it became a second home. I have made many friends and the projects are rewarding. Back home, the most I could be is a miner. The necessary jobs are all filled up. Here, I am an engineer, a scout and a success. These would be almost impossible to accomplish in the homeland. Even still, to work with the great heroes who brought our worlds together, this is more of a dream then I would have ever expected for myself."

It was humbling having this much admiration from among the

mages. Victor was almost tempted to tell him that there was nothing heroic about it. Their fame was based more on accident then on skill.

"Danir, can you see the mountain with your crystal seer?" asked Sil.

Danir brought the cylinder to his eye and looked.

"I can, but it is very far away. I think in a day or two we should clear it."

He passed the crystal to Paulo who gave a look toward home base.

That night, they set up camp as they had the night before. The Aerials took a break from wind farming and got an early rest.

Tomorrow will be just like today, Victor thought to himself, *which means the team would have to be well rested and entertained. If the cold doesn't kill us, boredom will.*

*****

The team started later in the day. Rising without words, they packed up and continued their journey. The mages ate only dried foods, not wasting any time cooking. Even Silvanus was quiet as they moved onwards planting markers. The land began to slope downward again and for the first time, the explorers came to an area worthy of reference.

"How big do you think it is?" asked Victor.

"It looks pretty big," replied Paulo.

"I want markers placed along its coast line. Find out how far across it goes and see if there is an easy way to reach the other side," said Victor.

A lake with large pieces of broken ice splayed outwards, creating a boundary against their survey. Large pieces of ice lay scattered throughout the water. The Eras began to scout the shore and place markers along the way. Paulo and Dan checked the depth. Without warning, Sil began jumping from one piece to the next.

"Sil! Be careful! You know it is harder for the rest of the team to follow in case you fall in," Victor mentioned.

"That's fine. Just call one of the Eras to do it," he replied casually.

Sil skipped so far across he became lost to view. Victor yelled over to Paulo to keep an eye on him with the crystal seer. The Eras returned with reports:

"To the right, the land cuts off into the water and I cannot proceed. No way around from that end," stated Erasmus.

"To the left, the shoreline continues far. I could not find the end and ran out of markers and so I returned here," spoke Erastus.

Stopped by melting ice, thought Victor. *Definitely more irritating than it sounds.*

"Can you see Silvanus?" Victor asked Paulo.

"No, lost sight of him," Paulo replied.

"Erastus, if he does not return soon, you will locate him. Take a marker with you so we can see you in the distance..."

Victor was cut off by a familiar voice.

"Not needed, boss." Silvanus returned with a big smile on his face. "Well, there is another side to this. Unfortunately, we have to hop to get there."

They all stood in silence looking at him.

"Or, we could sail across," said Sil mischievously smiling.

"How do we actually perform this? We have no boats or oars," asked Danir.

"A fair question. Take out your tent pikes," replied Sil.

Sil led the team onto a large, floating flat of ice.

"Alright, everyone on board. Now, place your tent into the ice with the poles sharp end down. Hold onto each other and do not let go of the poles."

The team sat in silence waiting for what was to come next.

"So, what now?" asked Paulo.

Sil just looked straight at Victor.

"That is one large pole you're holding. I really don't remember yours being this big."

"Sil!" Victor shouted.

"Oh yeah, sorry Victor. Paulo grab the Era nearest you. Dan, you're with me."

Then Sil spoke in his native tongue to the Aerials. In unison and without warning, they began to fly forward, pulling the mages holding poles and, in turn, pulling the ice beneath them. The group *'sailed'* for almost half an hour before arriving at the other side. After placing markers around the landing area, they rested from their travels.

CHAPTER 27

The team advanced for weeks down the snowy plains. During their progress, they noticed the land taking on noticeable changes. Strange craters, in no apparent pattern, began to appear as they walked.

"Very interesting," remarked Danir.

"Yes, there are holes in the ground," added Sil.

"It may be a geological phenomenon," commented Paulo.

The team continued for hours and laid markers until the sun started to wane.

"Friends," Danir interrupted. "The days are narrow, even in the spring. We must set up camp before the darkness overtakes us."

They wanted to continue exploring the awkward terrain, but Danir's advice made sense. Since the winds were calm, the Aerials went to sleep with the rest of the team. During the night, a thunderous rumbling woke Paulo. He opened his eyes briefly, envisioning a storm forming. However, the hypnotic drumming eased him back to sleep without any trouble. The next day, the group packed up their tents and supplies and continued their journey.

"Victor, did you hear the thunder last night?" asked Paulo.

"Sorry, I was out."

"I heard it," Danir answered.

"We may be expecting a storm soon, so I think we should prepare accordingly," added Paulo.

"Paulo," replied Victor, "I don't see any clouds."

Looking up, Paulo found their leader's observation to be true and wished he had actually taken a glance before saying anything.

"It probably faded after sunrise," added Victor.

Paulo withdrew silently and continued to plant markers in the designated areas. The craters were now crowding the plains and the mages decided to rest within one.

"We have enough food to last us at least two months longer. I think it wise to eventually head back, or start a serious rationing if we want to extend our travels," Paulo insisted.

Most of the foods were of Terran origin and a small amount could feed a large group. This made for long travels and lighter packing.

"Victor?" asked Ophir, "I would like to run a full perimeter scanning of the area. We need to make a wider use of the markers."

"What do you suggest?" responded the leader.

"Send the Aerials in three directions: north, south and west. Danir and Paulo to the higher ground of the northwestward area. Me and you can do an earth layout study for mapping," Ophir proposed.

"Very well," said Victor approving.

"Sir, would I not be more capable of the layout?" asked Danir.

"Danir, go with Paulo into the northwest," interjected Victor.

"Yes sir," he answered back.

With everyone set to their tasks, Victor turned to Ophir.

"What did you want to ask me, old friend?"

"These craters are not a natural phenomenon," he affirmed.

"How did you determine that?" questioned Victor.

"Craters are formed by eruptions and there are no such things happening here," Ophir stated.

"Well then, what are they?" said Victor.

"Footprints."

"Are you sure? I mean what could have footprints big enough for six mages to sit within?" asked Victor shocked.

He sat remembering what it had been like underground in the Terran nation before the bugs had been wiped out. He hesitated to ask further questions, fearful of the answers they would provoke.

"Are you absolutely sure?" repeated Victor.

Ophir nodded silently.

"Then we have to tell the others."

CHAPTER 28

"So, do mages really grow that big?" asked Sil. "Because really, that's *big*."

"We are not technically sure about anything yet," responded Victor. "So, for the time being, we all stay close together."

Paulo added, "I have to say, if something this big were nearby, we would have seen or at least heard some indication of their presence."

"Even so, we stay close together," said Victor.

That night they slept in one of the "footprints." Sil made jokes about it and when everyone stopped listening, he fell asleep. Danir, however, was still somewhat awake and again he could hear thunder in the distance. He rose and looked around. The winds were calm, but the darkness was thick. Sitting back down, he was put on alert by a shadow blocking the marker's glow behind him. Danir turned quickly, startled by the disturbance.

"*Easy.* Just me," Paulo said.

"I did not even hear you," murmured Danir.

"You were focused on something else," stated Paulo.

Sitting beside Danir, Paulo motioned to the sound.

"I hear it, too," he said. "I originally thought it was thunder."

Danir thought about the earlier discussion.

"What do you think they are?" he asked Paulo.

"I don't know. From what I have gathered, they are well blended with the environment and nocturnal. These footprints are old, but I have a feeling that as we get closer to the noise, we will find fresh ones."

Danir thought about this for a short time in silence.

"Do you think they will be aggressive?" asked Danir.

"Not sure," answered Paulo. "If you think of creatures that live inland or in the desert, the most aggressive ones come from areas of scarcity. As of yet, I do not see many signs of any recognizable food sources."

Danir let it all sink in, again in silence. He wondered what they would do if they encountered whatever beasts may lurk in the frozen wilderness.

"I'm going to sleep," said Paulo casually.

"How can you sleep knowing there may be something out there whose footstep could crush three of us at a time?" asked Danir.

"To be fair, I don't actually know for sure," replied Paulo.

The night went on and continued with the sound of "*thunder-steps*" deep into the distance and the team slumbered calmly without interruption.

*****

The morning was like all others before it. The team arose quietly, gathered the supplies and started off toward an unknown destination. Paulo and Ophir were especially concerned with the *footprints*. The rest of the group stayed in close formation. That day, they covered a long distance and Victor halted the team.

"Ophir, do you see the lake from here?"

Ophir pulled out the crystal seer and looked toward the way they came.

"No sight of it," he responded.

"Boys, let's set up lunch," Victor requested.

After settling in and eating most of their rationed meal, Victor disclosed some bad news.

"I think it is time we headed home."

The group looked at each other in silence.

"We haven't found anything," responded Ophir.

"Our food supply is running low, our markers are almost all set, we have travelled further than *any* of us expected and have come across nothing but old footprints. We can set the last of the markers here so that the others will know that this is the place we finished our march."

"I have to admit, I think a change of scenery would be nice," added Sil.

"We have over-stretched ourselves as it is," affirmed Paulo.

"Tomorrow," said Victor, "we advance back toward the Hold."

The team placed all of the markers in a cluster close to the camp. Their presence thoroughly illuminated the campgrounds as night set in. Before everyone had settled, Paulo went over to Danir.

"Unhappy with the latest decision?" he asked.

"I was hoping to find new mage-life," responded Danir.

"We all were," admitted Paulo. "We could remain searching, but our food and marker supply are dropping dangerously low. We have a choice: lose our way or starve. If we return, we can at least survive."

Danir smiled.

"Also, if there were to be another journey attempted, I know of an experienced mage who would be endorsed for a leadership role," said Paulo.

Danir smiled proudly at the recommendation. He and Paulo continued talking for a while. Weariness eventually settled in on the team and despite their brightened surrounding, a serene peace overtook the mages as they rested for the journey back home.

CHAPTER 29

Nighttime's shadow gave a greater animation to the markers' red glow. Falling asleep around the carnelian, the team revelled in its warmth against the piercing cold surrounding them. At midnight, Danir awoke to strange sounds. As he came to his senses, he realized something was invading the camp. Afraid to move, he slowly raised himself to get a clear look. A hand, firmly planted on his shoulder, halted him.

"Paulo, damn it," Danir said quietly. "You scared the crap out of me."

"Shh," he motioned with his finger over his mouth. "The markers are attracting them. We have to wake the others."

The mages had chosen to sleep in the "craters" for the time being in order to go unnoticed by the beasts.

"What are they?" whispered Danir.

"I cannot see them very well. They're gigantic," Paulo replied.

Despite being reserved in speech, the pair suddenly drew attention away from the markers. A loud roaring filled the air and suddenly a large fist crushed the heating sphere. The markers were instantly trampled over and in complete darkness, the team awoke surrounded by attacking giants.

"Stay down!" yelled Paulo.

Ophir held up a bloodstone. A giant humanoid leg and hip were illuminated as it attempted to stomp Ophir and his conjured brightness. Then Erastus began yelling in his language and Victor was suddenly up and shouting orders. The giants, with every step and attack, sent tremors through the earth. It was complete chaos; the loud roaring overpowered any of the team's cries. Despite their attackers being gargantuan and their movements felt, seeing them was impossible. To most of the mages, it seemed as though the darkness around them had taken on a monstrous form.

"Run!" Paulo shouted.

"I can't see!" Danir responded.

"Keep running!" said Paulo.

Paulo instinctively grabbed Danir's arm as the two began to run aimlessly. The dark night created a perpetual blindness. The loud roaring of the giants blocked out all other sounds. A hand reached down toward Danir. Paulo panicked as he pulled his friend along, trying to evade the giant hand coming towards them. The two moved too slowly. The hand snatched Danir from Paulo's grip. Paulo stopped. He couldn't hear his friends and was too frightened to call out. He could feel the heavy breathing of the giants piercing through the cold. He calmed himself and used his abilities to sense his situation: they had him surrounded. Large footsteps shook the earth as an approaching giant made ready to strike.

This is the end, he thought.

What seemed like a strong wind rushed by his face, striking his attacker, thrusting the giant deeper into the surrounding night with an agonizing roar. With their attention drawn toward the new threat, a fierce battle broke out and Paulo ran back to find any of his comrades.

"Sil, Dan, Victor..." he called out.

He heard no response. With his sight obstructed, the sounds of the unseen battle overwhelmed his senses. Thunderous vibrations shook the earth and the giants' roaring split his ears. Paulo lost his composure as his breathing became heavy and felt himself lightheaded. His last cognisant thoughts about the friends drifted through his mind as he collapsed into unconsciousness.

*****

Paulo lay half-awake dreaming of a voice calling to him. His body ached and his head was spinning. He could see very little, but he was moving fast. It felt as though he were floating.

"Paulo." A voice sounded softly.

"Paulo..."

His name again followed by other words he could not make out.

"Paulo... nice! Hey Victor, he's up."

Sil... thought Paulo as he tried to rise, only to find he was too lightheaded to sustain himself.

"Victor," Paulo responded.

"Easy, just relax. You have been unconscious since the attack," said Victor.

"Wh-at... What attacked us?" questioned Paulo.

Victor leaned in close.

"We do not exactly know. But when they rescued us we were separated..."

Paulo cut him off.

"Separated by *who*? Who saved us from those things?"

"I don't know. I think we were carried away from the attack scene. I was half-out. When I woke, you and Sil were here with me. I hope the others fared just as well."

Paulo, feeling disturbed by the latest news, forced himself to get up. He was kept warm by heavy fur blankets piled on top of him. Noticing this, he began to stand. Both Sil and Victor placed their hands on his shoulders to hold him down.

"*Easy*, I told you relax. This platform is small, and we have not been on land for some time," added Victor.

Paulo, now somewhat less confused, held out his hand feeling the wind and quickly realized they were sailing through water.

That does explain the floating sensation, thought Paulo. "The others—have you heard from them?" He asked, anxious to hear news of his friends.

"There are other boats that we can't see and our stones and supplies were destroyed during the attack. I tried to yell but was silenced by our rescuers. Our friends were hopefully taken aboard other ships," responded Victor.

"Hey, *listen,*" Sil suddenly said.

Quieting down, Paulo could hear the voices of several beings. Oars from the small ships around them struck the waters. They were moving at a considerable pace.

"I have never heard this language," said Paulo.

"Neither have we," responded Victor. "It looks like we have been found by what we were seeking."

Paulo went silent. He prayed to the Giver that his friends were all safe. Midway, he began to feel the toll of exhaustion and fell back into a deep sleep.

"He's out again," said Sil. "What do you think they will do to us?"

"If they wanted to kill us, I am sure we would be dead already," attested Victor.

"Sunrise is coming. Nice. We should be able to see soon," said Sil.

As the light began to manifest in the east, a spectrum of deep red flowed over the ocean, mixing with the waters. Victor and Silvanus watched silently, then Victor's face changed. His eyes widened as if to horde the sun's revelation. Sil looked in awe at the sight of what was obviously their destination.

"Get Paulo up," Victor commanded.

Paulo, after noticing where they were headed, almost jumped to his feet in amazement.

This city… is made entirely of ice!

CHAPTER 30

The sun's rising divulged the secret kept by the northern night. Large buildings of ice refracted the light, creating a spectrum of colour, overwhelming the horizon. As they approached, the sun's position rose and the city became visible. Buildings constructed entirely of ice, some eight levels tall, loomed over the shore. Spellbound by the beauty of their surroundings revealed by the morning, the group looked on with childlike wonder at the city they were about to enter.

The mages working the boats shouted up to unseen watchers, who responded with a welcoming sequence of loud trumpeting horns. Victor looked over at Silvanus and Paulo.

"Well, it looks like this is mage world number four," remarked Sil.

"Look! The boats and oars— they're made of ice!" said Paulo.

Victor hit Paulo on the shoulder and pointed to another iceboat sailing close by. The rest of the team had been sailing a short distance away. Victor waved and the Eras gave a returning salute. The company continued from the open waters into a narrow river that flowed through the city.

Arriving at the other side in a large pond, both ice ships were greeted by large mages with light blue skin standing on the shoreline. Kneeling down, they placed their hands over the water, which began to freeze until the ice reached and held the vessels that Victor and his friends were on.

"Look how tall our new friends are," cited Sil.

Victor looking at the mages and saw that the smallest among them was three heads taller than he was.

"Let's check on the others," he said.

The other ship docked and they saw Danir come off first. Erastus was limping and one of the ice mages picked up Ophir as he was brought to shore.

"He's barely been conscious," remarked Danir. "He did not stay awake long. He was hit hard by the attack."

"Sil, follow along, find out where they are taking him. The rest of you to me," ordered Victor.

Before those orders could be acted on, northerners approached, barring their passage and quickly returning Sil to the group.

"Well, I was following Ophir like you said, but then was forced back here by some rather large mage-like beings, twice my size and five-times my girth," spoke Sil.

"What do we do now?" asked Danir sounding nervous.

Victor remained silent.

"We fight!" said Sil. "You take the six on the right, I take the one in front, the Eras can tag team the last of them. Victor you find Ophir, food, a boat and a way back. We can meet here and then *sail* home."

"Do you find our situation so amusing?" asked Victor.

"At least *I* have plan and it's one more then Dan has," Sil retorted, trying to cut the tension. "If they wanted to kill us, they would have dumped us in the sea. We have to be of some value to our northern cousins."

One of the north mages spoke to them in their home tongue, paused, and spoke again. While waiting for a response Victor looked at Paulo who shrugged.

"Did you get all that?" asked Sil.

"Will you *stop*, damn it," snapped Victor quietly to Sil.

"Our friend, may we see him," added Victor pointing toward the direction Ophir was taken. The ice mages looked at one another then one responded "du kommer med oss." (You come with us.)

"Well, I think they want us to follow," said Paulo.

The large mages led the team into the city of ice, the heart of their frozen world.

The city's architecture amazed the team. In the distance, mages skied down the mountains, something they had never witnessed before. Gliding overtop frozen ponds with skates made of ice, the team marvelled at the athletic pastimes of the nation. The team's movement completely halted at the sight of an enormous bridge dominating the background, creating a crossing between two large mountains. As if carved from a glacial sized diamond, its immanence sealed itself into the minds of the onlookers. Constantly distracted by these wonders, the team almost forgot their situation.

"Look there!" yelled Paulo. "Under the bridge."

Large rafts made of ice fished the waters. The mages aboard stuck their hands into the water and pulled up fish trapped in thick icicles. As they continued, Sil turned to Victor.

"Is it everything you expected?"

Victor smiled.

Arriving at their destination, the team was seated in a large one room building at the edge of the city.

"Looks like a guest's house," noted Sil.

"Four families could live comfortably in here," added Paulo.

As the others were examining the walls of ice, Victor drew the attention of their host.

"Our friend. Can we see him?"

The strangers looked at one another then back at Victor.

"The other one that was with us," said Victor gesturing.

The blue mages looked at one another then pointed at Victor and motioned for him to follow. When the team began to do the same one of their escorts blocked their way.

"I think that means we stay here," said Sil.

Victor was led into a valley. Ice statues of various sizes littered the landscape. After passing a well, he noticed a structure with no roof that had four entryways and what looked like seats formed within. He stopped, wondering why it was built in this spot.

Is this sacred or just an older, unfinished building?

His guide interrupted his thinking and the travelling continued. Their venture ended in front of a long building that seemed out of place, contrasting the taller architecture. Victor followed his guides inside. Elongated tables of ice arranged in rows filled the interior. Ophir was on one of them. Victor ran to his side, while three other mages stood over, attending to his wounds.

"Ophir! What's happening?"

"I believe they are *healing* me—in their own way," he responded.

"How does it feel?"

"Cold, actually."

His wounds were frozen over, giving them a blue pigmentation. The other mages spoke to the guide, then motioning to Victor, the visit was over and he was brought back to the holding quarters.

"Did you see him?" asked Paulo.

"Yes, he is alright. They're healing him with their medicines," replied Victor.

"Interesting," added Danir. "What is it like?"

"It actually looked *really* cold," responded Victor.

There was an awkward pause and then Sil spoke up.

"Soo… what will they do with us?"

Paulo started first.

"Alright, let's look at what we know. They have not killed us and our friend is being treated, so we can assume certain benevolence on the part of our hosts. We are farther north than we are aware and to return to our home we would need specific abilities which we do not have. Let's also assume we are stuck here for a short while."

"*Also*," added Sil, "we are prisoners confined to a large room made entirely of ice."

Paulo looked over, annoyed.

"Would you let strangers run around your home without supervision? This whole city is built like a fortress; buildings up high for a greater vantage point. A huge sea between it and the land. All the men and even the children look to be trained warriors. If you look carefully at every mage society, you will notice that they adapt to their surroundings."

Paulo paused letting his words have full affect.

"Now, what were those things that attacked us? Did anyone even get a good look at them?" asked Paulo.

The group understood now what he was getting at. Paulo continued with his observation.

"They're bigger than the mages, maybe stronger, but those

things are obviously a threat to their nation. These mages manipulate the environment as necessity demands. *Brothers,* we left light markers to guide our way straight back to the Hold. What is going to stop those things when they reach it?"

A hard silence followed Paulo's grim logic. The entire team, injured and captive, thought of the consequences should those creatures reach the North Hold. Even if they were to somehow warn them ahead of time, would it make any difference?

CHAPTER 31

The large, blue-skinned mages began filling the roofless building Victor had passed on his way to see Ophir. Many of them had dark blue scarring on their bodies, evidence of numerous battles and the prowess of their native healing techniques. Their very being was testimony to an impressive story of the environment they lived in. Beards made almost entirely of frost lined their faces unevenly, giving them a rugged and elderly look. The fact they survived long enough to sit in a position of leadership meant their abilities were unmatched against their brethren. Their age was their honour and strength.

To discuss matters of security, the nobles gathered at the sitting hall outside the city. It avoided the distraction of the city's commotion. The eldest of the council sat farthest from the door. He rose and all present were silenced.

"So, we begin. What is this news from the outlands?" the lord questioned.

A younger mage from the front of the hall stood.

"Our brothers' return always with the same report; the giants are in heavy migration. We have secured all the major food sources and they are no longer attacking the colonies. The defences, even in the new cities, are holding strong."

There was a long pause and then a noble from the front row spoke.

"They should have starved to death by now. There are no other plentiful food supplies and the great lake is completely sealed due to our latest efforts. We control the fishing and the herding. There is nothing left for them feed on. Why have they not made an effort to engage us? What is drawing them so far south to the blank lands?"

A young mage with long blonde hair, standing by the entrance, raised his voice.

"You are correct. By now, they should have been desperate enough to launch an assault. Normally, that is their typical behaviour. However, things have changed. Our scouts from the outlands returned about two days ago. They say that the ancient wall at the other side of the world has been breached."

There was a commotion in the chamber brought on by the last remark.

"After the wall is nothing. It is the edge of the world," one noble affirmed.

"Have the giants been digging there?" asked another from the council.

The arguing continued until the eldest raised his hand, once again calling for silence so that their younger comrade could elaborate.

"No, my lords. It is not the giants who have been digging."

His voice suddenly cut off, as if his next words would sound unbelievable.

"My lords," he continued, "There are others who dug through the old wall and left it with a breach."

Silence...

"What *others* are these?" asked one of the nobles.

"We are not sure," responded the younger warrior. "They seem to be the size of children. We found a small number of them being attacked on a scouting mission and intervened. They are now held in an old store house not far from here."

The head noble spoke again.

"How is it you came to know of a breach in the old wall?"

"A trail was made of glowing rods leading right through the blank lands. We followed it to its source and found the breach in place. On the way back, we noticed the giants' attention had turned to the others that had laid the shinning rods. Due to the equipment and nature of these others, we can say they have no concept of what lies in *our* world. They come from somewhere different entirely and were unprepared for any threats."

"What could be beyond the wall?" asked one from the assembly.

This prompted another explosion of opinions from almost all present. The noble from the lead put his hand to his brow and then raised his voice in protest of the disorder.

"Enough! All of you."

The room's voices stilled as focus was drawn back to the leader.

"You said we have some of them nearby?"

"Yes, my lord," answered the young mage. "There are seven"

"Bring them forward for examination," ordered the noble.

*****

When the team was brought before the council, Danir and the Eras were seated together in one chair. Victor, Silvanus and Paulo were made to sit next to them. The north mages stared at the foreigners in silence.

"I thought there were seven?" asked a noble.

"Yes my lord. One is being treated for heavy wounds. He has not yet been released."

As they continued observing them, Victor leaned over to Sil.

"So, what do you think?"

"Well, these ones are a lot bigger than the ones that captured us."

"Say Ohmm and point upwards," said Paulo joining the conversation.

"That was *one* of my ideas," replied Sil. "Perhaps we could impress them with a glowing rod or melt their domicile with a heat globe. Oh *yeah,* that's right, *someone* lost our supplies."

The two quickly ceased their bickering when they realized that they were being examined. The head noble leaned in and asked one of the mages sitting close by.

"What are these?"

"They are mages, sir," he responded.

The elder mage sat back taking a deep breath in, then impatiently responded.

"They look like children. How is it these half beings breached the ancient wall? Why also were they leaving trails of their travels and what is their reason for being here?"

Again, silence. The noble looked around at the assembly.

"Nothing? Fine. Then tell me, not more than a week ago the giants were set to be starved out of our lands. One final united strike would have ended our ancient conflict. Now, apparently, there is a large hole in a structure that has stood for more than a thousand years, with a glowing trail leading right towards it. What will we do should the jotnar find a new food source and vast lands to replenish their numbers and grow stronger?"

The room remained silent as the noble waited for any who would dare to respond. The noble continued.

"Then through that *same* breach they come for us. These 'mages' are the size of children. Three of them fit in a seat made for one. We cannot expect them to put up much resistance."

Another noble interjected.

"How do we even know what lies beyond the ancient wall?"

"Will you stop?" interrupted the head of the council. "You know our history. We were not spawned out of the ice. We came here a thousand years past. These are obviously mages who remained behind during the battle times."

"How can we even be sure of what these beings are actually doing ..." As one of the ice mages spoke, he was cut off by the head noble, who tired of the debate that had drawn on too long.

"Enough! We will send an elite group to counter the giant migration and if at all possible, to seal the breach and prevent their escape. I will rally one-third of our population and close the gap behind them."

A tomb-like sensation flooded the room after the announcement. It was an immense danger to run against the giants headlong. Even more troubling were the staggering risks associated with trying to flank them at the breach.

"Who would lead this assault and how would they get ahead of the migration before the breach is cleared?" asked one noble.

"I would," spoke the young, long-haired mage standing at the entrance way.

"Me and my crew found the travellers. We will be the ones to reach the wall and prepare a defence."

The head of the assembly rose and approached the younger mage.

"Are you not tired from your work in the blank lands?" questioned the head noble. "It has been months since your leave. Perhaps you would instead like to rest? Maybe pass this task onto another?"

The young mage responded.

"Months, weeks… after this is done, I can rest all I want."

The noble gave a half smile, obviously pleased by his words.

"Very well! In the morning, you and your best warriors will depart from the harbour and sail to the west into the open ocean. From there, make your way south. It should take, maybe, two weeks to navigate the waters and reach the shoreline past the wall. When you land, follow the wall to the breach. From there, prepare fortification and hold your guard. We *will* follow."

Another noble spoke up.

"This effort will take more than two weeks. What if the giants make it through the breach before we are able to surround them?"

"Their migration speed should give us enough time," the younger mage countered. "It is the spring season. They move slower and even though they move in groups, they are not all united. Should some pass, it will not be many. If we act quickly as intended, we should close the gap and surround our enemies."

"What will become of the captured mages?" asked another council member.

All heads turned to the leader.

"They will return with you. After the wall, you will need a guide. Make sure they are fed and well accommodated. It is obvious they pose no threat, so do not restrict them within the city."

This said, the council adjourned their gathering and set out to make preparations for what was to come. The team was escorted out of the chamber and towards a great hall deep within the city. Upon entering, they found a single enormous table covered with enough food to feed a family for a lifetime. The wonderful smells made Victor realize how hungry he was. Already sitting and eating was a rejuvenated Ophir.

CHAPTER 32

They noticed dishes placed close to Ophir. The team quickly took their seats and began to interrogate their reunited compatriot.

"Soo… Ophir… How long have you been eating?" asked Sil jokingly.

"About half an hour. This food is fantastic! I wish we had it on the journey up here," he replied.

"Did they fix you?" asked Danir.

"Ah," he said with food still in his mouth. "Yes, look."

He lifted up his shirt to reveal a sort of blue scarring.

"They actually froze my body and operated. Some of my bones were out of place and now they're cemented back in for healing to take place more effectively, or so I have come to understand."

After hearing the good report from his friend, Victor looked around at the table. Despite the appetizing meal set before them, he felt something amiss. He did not quite understand what it was. After thinking a moment, the realization hit him.

There are no forks or spoons.

Ophir sensed his friend's confusion.

"Just use your hands," he said around a filled mouth.

No further instruction was needed. They all instantly began to consume large portions of the feast immediately.

"What do you suppose this is?" asked Danir.

"Meat, mostly," replied Paulo with his mouth half-full.

"Now *this* is good. This is what every meal should look like," said Silvanus "Era, what do you think?"

Both the Eras looked up at him with full mouths, making no comment.

"Yeah, me too," continued Sil.

"We've got to bring some of this back with us," Silvanus said, making conversation by himself. "We could hold it on these gigantic plates."

He looked at the large dish in front of him.

"You know something, I could fit three Aerial children on this dish. We could trade children for food."

Paulo looked up.

"Why would you trade a child for a meal?"

"Well, I may one day be hungry enough and if trading is done in equal proportion…" he answered.

"You would actually trade a child?" probed Paulo.

"Well," Sil's mouth contorted to adjust to the food he was desperately trying to fill himself with, "Probably not mine. It's good food is all I'm saying."

The team chuckled, most of them trying to contain their laughter for fear of choking. Even when full, they barely cleared the massive table of its contents. They began to drink a warm broth and Paulo raised the first serious question since their reuniting.

"Now that they have fed us, how do we get back home?"

*****

Behind the city, the champion that stood at the door, who was to lead the elite force and the foreign mages over the wide water currents, kept vigil in front of a mage frozen within thick ice. The noble that headed the council arrived and approached quietly.

"You always come here when you're worried," he said.

"I am not worried," responded the young mage.

"You have been gone for months and the plans were made in haste," said the noble. "You need rest. You have proven yourself in the presence of our ancestors and our people. Let another take your place on the wide currents. Stand with me on the attack at the vanguard."

"I knew what I was saying when I spoke. I will sail the currents and stop the giants at the breach. I have fought many times before this," responded the young mage.

The noble looked silently at the mage before him. Both of them stood almost at the same height, but the noble had a greater span and much more scarring. Taking a deep breath in, he turned his attention to the uneven cavern they were standing in.

"Do you know why this area and not others has been used to house the nobles chosen for the frozen sleep?"

The young mage looked intently at his superior.

"According to the legends of our people, these ice mounds are the first waters that became frozen and have been frozen since the beginning of time. Some even speculate that we will lose our abilities should they melt or be disturbed. I do not know if this is true, but for *us*, these mounds are sacred. We do not build close by and we never remove anything contained within. Only nobles have authority to perform the procedure for the long sleep, and only the strongest of us can survive a hundred years under the ice. Here, life began and here, life is sustained."

The noble's words resonated deep within the younger mage's soul. He already knew the history and the meanings, yet hearing these lessons from him was always so much more significant.

"We have lived under threats for the entire duration of our existence. If one threat should prove too much to handle, we have an assurance that life, *our way* of life, will carry on. Your grandfather," he said, gesturing to the frozen silhouette before them, "is one of the chosen.

"I was young when he was to become an immortal living under ice. The whole of the great city was in celebration. My brothers were killed during the battle of the white storm, so I was left alone, barley knowing him, except, of course, from the heroic stories that my mother would tell me. When my time came to join the dreaming brethren like my father had done, I could not do it. I had one son. I chose to remain in the waking world because of my son. I could not leave him to live alone."

He waited silently for a short time prompting the younger mage to ask, "What does this have to do with sailing the currents or ending the threats?"

The noble sighed.

"Even though I resented your grandfather for leaving, as I aged, it became clear that his decision to enter the frozen womb and be born again was necessary, and mine to remain a governing leader and a father also the same. My chance for an extended life cycle is long past. Yours will come in time. With that said, realize you cannot do both. *Also,* when you awake, the world you know now will have changed completely. A good leader knows when to conserve his *strength*. He knew…" gesturing to the frozen column containing their ancestor, "that his strength would be necessary for the future. So he sacrificed his past. If you continue over-exhausting yourself, you may lose both."

The noble's words hung in the air, causing deep reflection and introspection within the young warrior. The noble exited the tomb quietly, leaving the young mage alone with his thoughts. He looked at his grandfather through the layer of ice, knowing that he had been overworking himself. Destroying the giants, bringing glory to the family name and earning his place amongst the great ones had become an overbearing obsession. These next hours were going to be crucial and his choice would have to be the right one.

*****

The team was greeted by a young mage at the eating hall. He led them to sleeping chambers with heavy furs lining beds of ice.

"Remember him?" said Paulo. "He was standing at the doorway when their elders were observing us."

The mage was about to leave when Ophir cried out.

"Wait, what is your name?"

The young mage stood there silently.

"I am Ophir," he said holding his hand to his chest. "Ophir"

The young mage looking down at him responded with one word.

"Vidar."

CHAPTER 33

That morning, before sunrise, the team was roused from sleep by two mages of the north. Even though communication was extremely difficult, the team learned the names of their hosts and were then escorted to the same eating hall where another large feast was prepared.

After eating, they got a tour of the area. Sunrise was just beginning and for the first time, the team saw the city made entirely of ice light up like a marvellous crystal statue. The beauty of frozen architecture captured the sun's rays and spread them from one building to another. For a brief moment, a glowing aura of gold crowned the entire urban apex. Once the sun's position passed and the aura extinguished, the team was urged on by their guides.

The city was even larger than what they had seen on their approach. Buildings and houses were made to accommodate the enormous mages. The largest structures in Nebat were dwarfed by the mountainous dwellings in the north. This nation was unmistakably physical. Everywhere they went, activity encompassed the life-blood of the people. The team observed skiing, skating, fishing and sculpting, as well as construction and maintenance throughout their tour.

The nation's towering inhabitants joyfully greeted the team as they passed by. Curious Northerners would ask questions to the guides. Every so often, a crowd would form around the team, which the guides would gently dismiss.

"We are *popular* little mages," remarked Silvanus.

"Everything is huge! Look at the crafting of these structures," added Danir. "I never would have dreamed a city could be created from ice."

Their tour continued and outside the city towards the west, they saw immense valleys situated between the mountains. Populating the valleys were humungous cow-like creatures. Victor pointed toward them and the guides looked at each other and nodded.

Victor remarked to Paulo, "Well, now we see their food supply: fishing in the river and herding of those beasts. They have a massive land-span devoted only to this."

"Just look at their size," added Ophir. "These mages would probably need significant amounts of food to keep themselves alive."

They came to a stop at what looked like a tunnel leading into the ice. The guides pointed and Victor stepped forward to enter.

"So we have gigantic buildings, a beautiful sunrise, a city populated with giants and now, a hole that leads *down... somewhere...*" Sil stated.

"There are no steps," noticed Victor. "How are we going to pass through?"

The guides looked at each other and then one of them jumped in. Right away, the team ran into the hole and slid toward their destination. The ride was exhilarating. The team was smiling and laughing as they descended. They slid down twenty feet on their backs and landed straight out into a large field filled with the cow-like creatures. The guide, who followed gracefully, emerged from sitting position to his feet as he entered the valley.

Ophir remained on his back while a large, horned beast began smelling his face. Then with a sharp exhalation, the beast turned and began grazing elsewhere.

"I don't think it likes what you're made of," stated Sil, looking over at Ophir.

The valley was expansive and was populated with hundreds of horned beasts. A mage from among a small group of herders came to greet the guides. They exchanged words and the herdsmage welcomed the team. As they talked, Paulo began to survey the landscape.

"We travelled beyond the wall for weeks, we saw none of these," said Paulo.

"Maybe they were hiding," suggested Sil.

"Look, they have rivers for fishing and valleys for herding. The mountains are either entirely artificial or have been added to over the years. This whole society lives in a fortress. Their city is high up and their food supply is walled in. It is one huge military nation. The North Wall," Paulo continued, "was probably an earlier settlement or at least a structure of some kind that kept them safe from enemies."

The guides invited them to pet the head of one of the beasts, interrupting the team's revelatory conversation.

"*Auroch*," said one of the guides.

"Auroch," repeated Victor. "It looks like these things are called auroch."

The team continued to pet the one brought over. They were even offered some of the auroch milk to drink, which none of them declined.

"These things are enormous!" commented Sil. "Bigger than the cattle from the Plains land. One of these could feed a family for two months."

When they finished seeing the valley and interacting with the aurochs, their guides proceeded to accompany them into a large ice cage. Two thick ropes draped from the top of the enclosure. Six aurochs were set with a saddle harnessed to each and the ropes attached to the harness. The team stepped into the cage and the aurochs were driven forward, causing the cage to rise.

"Well," said Ophir, "a pulley system."

"Look at the scenic route." Sil pointed to an unkept stairway that led in the direction they were elevating. The team's next stop was an area of the city with almost no ice at all. It was actually warmer here than anywhere else they had been.

"Boys, look at this," explained Paulo. "This part of the city is actually made of *stone*."

As the tour continued, it became clear where the heat was emanating from. Hundreds of ovens were preparing food for what looked like the entire community.

Carved into the mountainside, a labyrinthine conglomeration of caves and caverns converged together. Wide entrances exposed the fiery hearths within. Smoke rose through a chimney system making the top of the mountain seem like a volcano. The mages worked without pause, preparing auroch, fish, soup and other types of food. Once cooked, the food was placed on trolleys and wheeled to its destination.

"Look how far down it goes," Sil pointed out.

The galley the team was standing in was a three-story chamber with stairways that led outside. Ovens lined the walls on all levels.

"It is like a food factory," added Danir.

"Most probably it is set in the rock so as not to melt the surrounding structures," pondered Paulo logically.

"This whole society is incredibly organized," interjected Ophir. "There is a structure for everything they do, with segments of their city built exclusively for specific tasks."

When the team had sampled some of the food, the tour continued back into the city. As they were walking through the narrow streets, they were guided toward the east. Passing the large pond where their boat had docked, they encountered a large number of the male mages in combat training.

"I have never seen warriors fight like this," Ophir remarked. "With their size, I never dreamed they would be able to move this fast."

They created swords and lances of ice while sparing and even drew blood against each other. One mage formed a shell of ice over his own fist and struck his opponent. Another formed two blades of ice and launched an attack against three mages who surrounded him with ice woven shields.

One of the older mages, who stood by observing, shouted some commands and the fighters broke into two groups. At a second command, they charged each other and created weapons of ice while running. When the two groups struck, it sounded as if thousands of mirrors shattered on the training-ground. The fighting continued seamlessly. Many sustained injuries that would have killed any of Victor's team.

Not far away, groups fashioned lances and launched them at distant targets. Others were broken into teams; one side fought with shields and, against them, the other formed swords. The group toured the battlegrounds with their guides, who appeared to be very pleased to show the prowess of their warriors.

"The ice inborn into them is their weaponry," Ophir commented. "Shields, spears, armour-they have no separate craft for their tools!"

They watched the fighting for over an hour witnessing feats of strength and agility unmatched by any of their own peoples. After viewing the training grounds, they were led back to where they entered the city by the docking pond. Their guides spoke and instructed them with hand gestures to remain where they stood.

"Well, just us again," said Silvanus.

"This is more than remarkable," added Victor. "All of our nations are subjected to the world around us and we adapt according to the conditions we are born in. These mages are exactly the reverse! The entire environment is a product of their design: huge buildings, sailing vessels, weapons, healing - everything comes from their own will and limited only by their ability to control it."

"When you look at their enemies, it is not so surprising," explained Paulo. "This nation may be the most powerful discovered. It's a wonder they did not discover us first."

The team could still hear the warriors training in the distance as they discussed the day's tour. Their guides returned with four others. Among them stood the young warrior Vidar. Three of the ice mages knelt down by the pond and placing their hands over the water, began forming a large mound of ice. When finished, it looked more like a misshapen landmass with walled edges. They gestured for the team to enter. Large skin pelts were given to the visiting mages, which were used to line the floors. They ate a small meal and then broke the edge, setting the berg free to drift.

"Hey Victor, you think we're going home?" asked Sil.

"We are definitely going somewhere," he responded.

"Amazing," added Ophir. "They shape oars of ice to steer with."

"I remember your people being able to manipulate the stone from the earth. How is this amazing to you?" asked Paulo playfully.

"Yes, we are able to *manipulate* the earth, but not *create* it," responded Ophir.

The Eras sat quietly talking in their native tongue and then Sil spoke up.

"So... does anyone actually know where we're going?"

CHAPTER 34

"Well, it looks as if we are returning the way we entered," sighted Paulo.

"An ice mage escort straight into the North Hold!" said Silvanus. "Those Plainswalkers who want to give us more domestic work will have to do another two years of domestic ass kissing as an apology."

Everyone laughed at Sil's jesting. Ophir turned the conversation to a more serious topic. "Danir. you're quiet."

Danir responded. "I can still hardly believe this is happening."

"Well, get used to it. I am going to request a transfer from your station in the North."

Danir looked startled, not knowing what to say.

"We have irrefutable evidence of mage colonies existing in the desert lands," Ophir stated. "However, the territorial beasts have always kept us from deep advancement. The elders will want to establish permanent trade and education with the northerners. When that is done, I think our warlike brethren could be put to use, and I think you should be among us for the next discovery."

Danir nodded, trying to hold back an excited smile.

"Thank you, my lord."

"Enough with that!" snapped Ophir. "We are on the same team, as equals. The only leader is Victor and second to him, Sil. Save the courtesies for our homelands."

"It's nice to see you thinking so far ahead," added Victor. "I do agree. If we can return safely, our new companions might appreciate the challenge."

"Return safely?" asked Sil. "It would be more of a miracle if we were killed on the way."

"You saw their fighting in action," added Paulo. "These mages are a force of nature. We follow the way we came, find the markers and lead ourselves and friends to home."

They continued to discuss the events that would follow and how impressed everyone would be at the discovery of another great mage nation. Also, seeing their families and friends that had been missed in their months abroad would provide a deep consolation. An hour later, Sil noticed something strange.

"So… when will we be landing?" he said pointing to the icy coast.

They looked at him and then noticed the shore. A blanket of silence sprawled itself over the team.

"How long have we been sailing along the shoreline?" asked Paulo.

"A while now," responded Sil.

Victor looked at the ice mages steering vessel and then to Paulo for some explanation.

"We're not docking on the shore."

"What?" Victor exclaimed. "Then where are we supposed to be going?"

"By the looks of it, we will probably be heading towards the ocean," Paulo responded.

The group fell quiet again, as if dumbstruck by Paulo's last words. After a few moments, Ophir spoke up.

"I think I understand. If we use the ocean, we may be able to reach an area closer to the North Hold in faster time. Our burrowing through the mountain has probably caused some trouble for the natives here."

"What trouble could it cause?" asked Sil, "There is nothing between their home and the North Hold. If anything, it brought us closer together."

"No," replied Ophir. "There is a reason why nothing lives beyond the mountain. The herds, the fishing, the entire nation lives behind a barrier of ice and water. After that, to get to the city, it is an uphill climb. They have secured themselves with a tactical advantage. We were out there for almost a month. The flat lands have nothing. I don't even remember seeing any trees. It looks like they have been starving their enemies out, the same way that my people did with the wyrm. Our population and territorial scarcity lead us to encounter our enemies frequently. But they have no such issue. Those giants would have starved to death and been killed off. *We set an opening for them, a path toward food and mages who will be unprepared.*"

The team silently contemplated Ophir's words. A unanimous fear carved into their faces as they realized the danger their friends were in.

"Will we be fast enough?" asked Danir.

"I have never sailed into the deep. You need royal vessels to do that safely. The currents can be powerful and the weather changes frequently," Victor answered. "Let's hope our guides know what they're doing."

CHAPTER 35

"Vidar, the wide currents are just ahead. Make yourself ready."

"Thank you, Olaf," replied Vidar. "Have you ever sailed them for such a long journey?"

"No. The only one here who has sailed this long is Herger," Olaf responded.

Herger, a large bearded northerner, obviously the eldest of the group, was at the back, steering. Vidar asked if he would like to take the head.

"When the currents begin to sway and the sky thunders, I will be more useful at the back end," replied Herger.

With that said, another mage began to give a final spot check and status of the crew and the cargo.

"We have food stored within the vessel, furs on board. All of us are at full strength. The journey should take close to a week *if* the weather is agreeable."

The last comment made some of the crew laugh.

"And the child mages are all accounted for, six of us and seven of them."

"Thank you, Freyr," replied Vidar.

"Brothers," called out Vidar. "We are approaching the open currents. Stay alert and on guard. Prepare for hard nights and an even harder battle. Keep your courage strong. Luck will do the rest."

The North mages gave a shout after the close of Vidar's speech.

"I think we startled the magelings over there," remarked one of the sailors. "Hermod, do you think that any of them know what is going on?"

"I doubt it. They seem to be stunted. I wonder if all the mages beyond the wall are like this. They cannot be very smart if they walk into open terrain without even a single weapon," responded Hermod. "Do you remember when we were younger, the stories of the sea monsters in the open currents? Maybe we could use one of the magelings over there as bait to lure one up."

Both northerners burst into laughter.

"Hermod, Skeld. Enough!" retorted Vidar.

The shoreline's end was in sight. Once past it, they would be entering the open currents. A vast expanse of water with no land and high waves, resulted in strong winds that normally came during the night and storms could last for days. Everyone had to stay sharp.

"Olaf, we're passed now. What do you gather of the weather? Will we have a hard night?" asked Vidar.

"The day is nearly finished. With the winds as they are, most likely it should stay calm," he responded.

"We have to make this trip in good time. I have sailed on the inland rivers, but with the size of our vessel, how close to shore can we stay?" asked Vidar.

"Not close. With our size, we could hit the land hard. Keeping repairs low will allow for faster travel," replied Olaf. "When we arrive, we will have to trek across unknown ground, find the wall's breach, seal it if we can and fight off whatever jotnar threats exist there. You don't think we are a little overworked on this one?"

"A day from now, my father, half the elders, and one third our forces will be marching toward the wall to give us support. If we can hold them at the breach, their size and numbers will count for nothing," said Vidar.

"No one has been behind the wall for over a thousand years since the great migration. What if something happens that we don't expect?" asked Olaf.

"If these magelings could drill through the wall, leave bright rods as a trail and survive in the white fields for almost a month, I think we should cross over safely," Vidar affirmed.

Olaf smiled at his reply.

"It is a wonder there are not more of us for this operation."

"Having two vessels increases the risk of one being destroyed and the other overloaded. Tasks of this kind are best kept small and mobile. This lessens the possibility of high casualties," admitted Vidar.

"You sound so much like your father," said Olaf, smiling.

Vidar let a small smile slip past his somber visage.

"I hope we have the energy for this. I have never ventured through the open currents, or lead a live expedition through them," added Vidar.

"Nor I," said Olaf. "But we have Herger for support. He has sailed the open currents many times and you have some of your best hands aiding the effort. We have fought together since our youth, faced the same challenges on and off the battlefield. This will be no different. You have proven yourself against great opposition. All here stand beside you in victory *or* defeat."

Olaf's reassurance comforted Vidar. He nodded to him, and both returned to their posts. Vidar looked out over the ocean which, at the moment, was serene and calm. Then, looking up at the sky filled with dark clouds, he knew what was at stake. He also knew not to overthink. Staring out into the vast waters, despite his size, the impressive ice craft and the task at hand. Vidar could not help but feel very small floating in the aquatic expanse that seemed to stretch out into eternity.

As the night began, the darkness came in force. Almost within moments, the light dimmed and then was gone. The sounds of water flowing and swaying, along with the calm winds and the fact that seeing was impossible, made their situation almost peaceful.

CHAPTER 36

"Alright. Light them up," the crew member shouted in his native tongue.

Sounds of rhythmic striking came, sparks flew and a torch was lit. Several other torches were kindled from this source.

"The nation of ice bares fire," said Silvanus.

"Why wouldn't they?" asked Paulo.

"I thought they would be allergic or *something*," replied Sil.

The team gave a laugh and with the deep ocean chill setting in, many of them doubled their fur layers. The new lighting made the team feel more secure and, combined with the calm surroundings, many of them fell asleep. A shout from one of the ice mages caused most of them to move from their posts to one side of the vessel. Victor rose with his furs to see what had caught his navigator's attention.

"There, look. We are among the monsters now," said one of them.

What are you saying now? I really wish Paulo could translate…

His thoughts, as well as his body, froze. Sil and the rest of the team were also witnessing the frightful sight. It was in the shape of a giant serpent that never raised its head above the surface, yet the team could see its body curl and twist over. It was very long, wider than the North mages' boat and black in colour. The sea monster spat water into the air like a fountain and then plunged down, raising a tail that was cleft in two like the forked tongue of a snake. It was enormous with each section of the tail being broader than the lone ice ship sailing through the sea.

They saw another monster, and another, and another after that. There appeared to be six or seven. Each behaved as his fellows, curving through the water, spitting a fountain and raising a giant tail split in two. The north mages looked solemn. The sight terrified the team. Paulo actually turned completely white. The northerners found this to be humorous and laughed loudly.

"There are sea monsters!" exclaimed Victor. "Our parents used to tell us stories when we were young of fishermen who sailed too far and had their catch eaten by huge water snakes. We never sail deep for fear of them. I never expected them to be real," said Victor fearfully.

The fact that they were so close to the sea creatures caused some of the team to fall down trembling on deck. As they became distanced from the creatures, Paulo turned to his friends saying.

"No one will ever believe that we saw the sea snakes of the deep."

"Given your record of discovering civilizations in frozen wastes and underworlds, I think you set the standard for what people should believe," responded Sil.

*****

The next day started early for the team. They woke mid-morning while the winds were picking up. The North mages were all rowing at full speed and shouting loudly.

"What's with all the noise?" asked Sil.

"Storm is coming," responded Paulo.

"How far from land are we?" asked Ophir. "I remember being able to see the shore yesterday."

"The winds have picked up, the waves are getting larger," added Victor, noticing the Eras under two layers of heavy furs, shivering from either the cold or fear. As the day progressed, the winds became less aggressive and eventually the ice mages took a rest from their labours.

*****

"I think we moved ahead enough. The storm seems to be staying out of range for now," said Olaf.

"If these winds keep up the way they are, we can expect it to return on top of us," sited Herger.

The mages remained silent, resting and pondering. They were

all worn due to the day's hard rowing.

"Why not just face the storm? We have the combined strength to overcome the waves," said Hermod.

"That is true," answered Vidar, "but the magelings may not and our orders were to bring them beyond the wall *without* injury. We will need them to communicate with the others there."

In the course of their conversation, they decided to divide the crew in half. One group would continue rowing while the other rested in order to beat the storm.

*****

"Does anyone know how long this is going to take?" asked Silvanus. "Being on water is cold and unsteady. My guts are having feelings I don't recognize."

Seeing Sil visibly disoriented, Victor led him to the corner and put him under some furs.

"Need someone to dress you next?" asked Ophir. "Can't you just fly out of here?"

Sil sitting up, looking dazed and slurring slightly, responded.

"It is still too cold. I will freeze."

Ophir continued his harassment of Sil and the other Aerials while Victor moved closer to Paulo.

"How long do you think this will take?

"I have no idea. This is way beyond what I expected," Paulo replied.

"Did you notice the speeds we were reaching when they were rowing?" Victor asked.

"I did. It was hard to keep my footing," answered Paulo. "It looks like they are outrunning the storm."

Victor thought of what might happen if a storm should overtake them this deep in the ocean. He remembered the giant sea monsters and began to cringe at the thought of what else might be lurking within the waters.

"Do you think the storm will catch up?" Victor asked.

"No idea," responded Paulo.

"You never have ideas. You descended from frontiersmen. Normally you're more insightful in matters of natural survival," Victor teased.

"Yes, normally you would be correct, but this is new for me. I have never *naturally* survived in the ocean and even with the current support, doubt I ever could," he replied smiling.

"Our friends seem to know what they're doing," commented Victor. "I really wish we could communicate with them."

"Most likely this is new for them as well," stated Paulo seriously.

Victor looked confused, silently asking for an explanation.

"There are six of them and seven of us. We are apparently trying to intercept those giant creatures that attacked us. A small party, plus us, on a vessel of about forty to fifty feet in length. At the speed we are moving, we'll most likely will do it. However, they sent only a small group, not a large fleet. If they have mastered sailing the ocean, then they should most likely have discovered us first. This is an elite expedition. *These* are elite warriors. The best were sent so the chances of success are greater. When we arrive at the destination, they will need us for direction. Or so I have guessed," concluded Paulo.

Victor thought about it for a while, not comfortable with the idea that this group of mages, he and his friends were forced to rely on, may actually have about as much experience as they do.

"Most probably due to the unpredictable behaviour of the ocean," continued Paulo, "it would be uncommon for them to sail out very deep."

Victor remained silent. Pondering the given information, he felt regret over teasing Paulo. Sil stealthily crawled behind Victor, bundled in furs. His face now as white as his hair, Sil interrupted the conversation.

"So… How long do you think until we reach the shore?"

CHAPTER 37

The winds became turbulent, the temperature dropped to near freezing and the waves grew larger as the end of the day drew nearer. Vidar and his crew frantically rowed, reforming the large thick rowers of ice. Thunder and lightning struck overhead and rain began to fall. The team covered themselves with the heavy skins on board and clung close together.

"This does not look good," said Silvanus.

"I thought we would be out of the storms reach?" asked Victor to Paulo.

"The winds are too fast, even for them," he answered.

One of the crew stumbled over and interrupted the conversation.

"*Make yourselves ready! Hold onto something,*" shouted Freyr to the team.

Despite not knowing what Freyr was actually saying, the meaning came through quite clearly. Staying in one area huddled close, the team resigned themselves to the stewardship of the ice mages. Sil tried contemplating what the ice mage had said in hopes that perhaps his own natural mental prowess would allow for an intuitive understanding. Another command from Vidar and the berg sped up, flinging the Aerial from his seat.

Victor stood up slightly to look over the wall of the iceberg. The waves looked like rolling mountains and he fearfully edged back down to his place beside Paulo and Sil. He noticed the northerners had no heavy clothing of any kind. The cold rain did not negatively affect them as it did his team and him. Instead of grim faces, many of the ice mages were happy and jubilant. They actually seemed to be enjoying the piercing cold winds that assailed them. It was astounding for the team to witness. Despite their momentary awestruck respect, the ocean raged more violently, as if trying to silence the sailors. The team felt the full force of the brine's displeasure, making many of them purge themselves.

*****

"The little ones are blowing their guts," laughed Skeld.

"If we make it out alive, we will have every lady in the high city lining up at our rooms," shouted Hermod.

The laughing continued, undeterred by the turbulence. The cold winds and rain actually gave strength to these mages as they revelled in the onslaught. The waves became larger and it seemed the berg would soon overturn.

Vidar gave the command. "Prepare a shield wall!"

As they rode a wave to its summit, three of the North mages held out their hands. The waters around and beneath the boat began to freeze until the vessel became suspended within it.

"Look! When they freeze the water under us, it aids by bracing our fall over the waves and prevents us from being overturned," said Ophir to Paulo. "When we reach the other side, the additional ice is castoff. Would you ever have thought that such a feat was possible?"

"It seems to tire them, though. Five out of the six are engaging in the wave freeze, one is navigating. I hope they can keep this up," Paulo said in response.

The iceberg, at one point, sailed up a colossal wave. They rose so steeply that many held on for fear of falling off. Reaching its precipice, the moon's light shone through clouds, illuminating their surroundings and provided the team with a full view of their position.

Terrified, they stared at the volume of water threatening to overtake them. Vidar shouted an order and much of the wave's crest became frozen. They hung for what seemed like a long moment, but they dropped down with great speed. The frozen waters sheared off as they descended. The glacier continued through the trough and up another wave height. If threatened by an extreme upturn, the crew froze the waters, letting the vessel sink down the other side through the wave. This carried on until afternoon of the next day when the storm finally abated.

"It's becoming calmer," stated Danir.

"I do not like it here," groaned Silvanus. "I do not want to be here anymore!"

"How many days has it been?" asked Victor.

"Four at least," responded Paulo.

"Any sign of land?" asked Victor.

"None, still just ocean," said Ophir. "Sil maybe you or one of the Eras can attempt an air jump to scout for land?"

"Sure! But instead of freezing to death quickly by taking flight, why not freeze to death slowly by staying here and telling you what I see. To the left, right and below, it looks like water. *Lots* of cold water and when cold is not enough it also becomes angry."

"You Aerials are useless," mocked Ophir. "Air all around you and you can do nothing."

"No stones in your pocket to play with?" retorted Sil. "Nothing to change your skin colour or make a necklace out of? I never expected the burden of the freezing ocean to yield to your sculptures and masonry."

The group laughed while Sil remained discontent. The sailing for the remainder of the day was much smoother. As the day began to wane, the North mages were talking and pointing skyward. Paulo turned to Sil.

"I think I can understand some of their words."

"Really?" asked Sil.

"Yeah, tomorrow… there will be a storm."

"Damn it!" yelled Sil.

The rest of the team laughed at the ruse. That night was calm and allowed for a restful sleep for the team and the off duty crewmembers.

CHAPTER 38

Even though seafaring was foreign to them, the team quickly became accustomed to the ever-changing weather patterns. The crew also began to interact with them. They started eating together rather than in segregated groups and the torches were given to Victor's team as part of their duties. After almost a week of sailing, a thick mist set in preventing the mages from seeing past their outstretched arms. The crew rowed on slowly.

"How long before the mist clears?" asked Silvanus.

"Shh," whispered Victor, silencing Sil.

A bird's chirping brightly cut through the thick vapour. Victor and Sil smiled, realizing land would be close by. Large rock formations began to come into view, narrowly missing the slow moving vessel.

"How far from land are we?" asked Victor to Paulo.

Sil and the Eras looked at each other. Then, raising their hands, they called forth currents of air to brush the mist past. The northerners showed no lack of surprise at the demonstration of the Aerials' abilities.

"Seems like our friends definitely approve," said Ophir.

Now, with a full view of the shoreline, one of the northerners shouted as they prepared for the iceberg to dock.

*****

An abnormal bridge of ice, extending from their glacial vessel, covered a small section of the shore. The team and crew crossed over, finally arriving on land after many days at sea. Sil was the first to complain.

"It's still really cold, damn it."

All of the team members were wrapped in furs, but the cold winds of the shoreline still held their effect. The mist began to clear and the North Wall was sighted in the distance. Ophir and Victor smiled.

"Danir," asked Ophir. "Can you tell where we are?"

"Of course! West shore, no more than four days from the North Hold if we walk without rest."

After surviving all of their ordeals, the way home, though cold and desolate, greeted them as a favourable welcome. The crew were offloading all of the supplies and Vidar held council with Herger and Olaf.

"Do we have enough for at least a week more?" Vidar implored.

"No, four days at the most," responded Olaf. "We used most of the food on the seas."

"Herger, have you learned to speak the language of these children?" asked Vidar.

"Not completely. I barley understand them aside from their names. Victor, however, seems to be the leader."

"I thought you said a week to learn their language would be sufficient," questioned Vidar.

"So did I," Herger responded. "I guess I will need longer."

Vidar made a sort of growling sound of dissatisfaction.

"We need to know which way to move. We are beyond the wall and they know the location of the breach."

"I see no breach by the shore, so it is definitely that way," interjected Freyr, pointing opposite the shoreline.

"Funny," said Vidar, staring seriously at Freyr without amusement. Olaf noticed Paulo approaching the crew.

"Here comes one of them. Herger, deal with this," said Olaf.

Herger advanced toward Paulo, his size and endomorphic build towered over him. Both stared at each other in silence for a short time.

"We need to travel three days, that way," Paulo finally said, pointing in the direction of the North Hold.

He spoke again slowly with less words. Herger stared blankly at him and then walked away toward Vidar and said something discretely. Vidar looked over at Paulo and then shouted loudly.

"Alright! Let's move!"

At this, the ice mages charged towards the team, catching hold of them. Lifting the team members onto their backs, they bolted toward their destination. As the day ended, so did their travels. They set a fire, prepared some food, rested for a short while and then took up the chase again. At night, the team members, on back of the leading crew mages, held torches; this went on until sunrise. They stopped, ate, rested, and then picked up again.

Sil, in the middle of the herd, tapped his chaperone on the shoulder and pointed toward Paulo. The mage nodded and ran up beside him.

"We're making great time," Sil shouted.

"I think they move the same speed as horses," Paulo said.

"I wonder if they will let us breed them when we return," replied Sil causing an eruption of laughter from Paulo.

In a little over two days, they arrived at the breach.

CHAPTER 39

As they approached the opening, the North mages became lighter on their feet. The team followed behind with the same precaution. Staying close to the face of the wall, Vidar held up his hand, issuing an order to halt. Gesturing to others of the crew, he advanced carefully with Herger and Olaf at his side. After a few moments, Olaf emerged giving a sign that all was clear. The rest entered the cave. It was as they had last seen it, except with one difference: large deep footprints littered the ground.

Vidar studied the impressions and looked toward Herger saying '*jotnar*'.

He turned to the others, addressing them in hushed tones.

"Herger, you and Freyr take to the end of the breach. See if there are others. Olaf, take Hermod and Skeld, circle around the outside, look for where the beasts have settled. By the looks of these, there are not many."

With that, everyone was set to their tasks and went about silently surveying the area. Vidar, Victor and the remaining mages exited the cave.

Victor addressed his friends.

"Those things are *here*. We have to get to the hold."

Moving quickly, they arrived at the base and saw that much of the entrance had been destroyed. The hold itself seemed to be divided in half, with one side almost completely ravaged and the other blocked by a thick unnatural wall of stone.

"It seems like some defence was raised," said Ophir.

Examining the wall, Ophir positioned his hand on the surface and the thick solid rock began to crack and eventually gave way, coming apart like flakes of dry sand, creating a small doorway.

Vidar was visibly amazed and examined the new doorway with great interest. They walked in to find many bodies scattered on floor. Danir checked for a pulse on one close by. Finding none, he shook his head and returned to the group. They rounded the halls and large rooms of the hold.

"The walls are reinforced with stone cast," said Ophir. "They must have been under siege."

The team looked at Danir for an explanation.

"It is when you strengthen the existing layer of a structure's wall to endure harsher situations."

Satisfied with his answer, they continued their searching. Many other bodies were found along the way. As they advanced, voices could be heard. Vidar and his crew of ice mages stood ready. Ophir and Danir, recognizing the voices, rushed in.

The western wing of the hold had become an improvised medical ward. Many of the hold's operatives were injured; some on crude crutches, others being administered food. Almost all present had bandaged wounds. When the team entered with Vidar and his compatriots, everyone stopped and stared for a moment. Ophir recognized the base commander who had welcomed them. His head was almost completely swathed with bandages that clearly needed to be changed. Ophir stepped toward him, putting himself in the injured Terran's view.

"Captain, you're alive!"

CHAPTER 40

"When you did not return, we feared the worst. Scouts followed your trail hoping to contact you along the way back. Then some began to go missing. We sent out others to look for the missing ones."

Avi placed his hand on his head, obviously irritated by his injury and then resumed his speech once the pain had passed.

"Thirteen scouts had gone missing in one week. We kept our search teams back until we could figure out what was going on. The guard station beyond the North Wall was found to be deserted and large footprints were discovered when the storm cleared."

Avi paused again due to the pain in his jaw. His breathing became laboured as he continued to recall past events.

"We sent word to the outposts in the south. They told us to evacuate and we initiated a full scale retreat. During sunset, a sound like thunder kept coming closer. The sound, it ..."

"How long ago was this," interrupted Victor.

"Ah, I have not been outdoors for some time. I would say, maybe, two weeks ago. They attacked so fiercely we were forced back into the hold. Eventually, they broke through. We put up as much of a fight as we could, but this is not a military base and most of us are researchers. We set up the wall to keep the rest of us from being killed. It seemed to have worked. There are not many of us left and we are running out of food..." he was cut off by the recurring pain in his head.

"Rest, Avi," said Ophir, leading him back to a table to lie down and catch his breath.

"I'm sorry I could not be of more use, but I have not slept in many hours. There are so few of us left to tend to the injured... So many more are worse than I."

He paused to catch his breath, and sat down on a table. His exhaustion became apparent and looked like he would collapse at any moment. His attention turned to Vidar and his companions.

"It seems you were successful in your undertaking," added the base commander.

"Yes, we were. You get some rest. We will take over from here," responded Ophir.

Danir was aiding his comrades with the help of the Eras when the sound of thunder resounded in the distance. Everyone stopped talking. The ice mages looked immediately in the direction of the noise and Paulo rushed in, as if on cue.

"Need you outside, *now*!"

CHAPTER 41

The reverberations began to increase and become more frequent. Both the ice mages and the team raced outside, following Paulo's lead, and noticed five, giant sentient beings.

"The light has not even settled and they are attacking. The jotnar have no fear of them at all," said Vidar to Olaf. "You and two others follow my flank. I will engage the leader. The rest will follow after."

His last words were directed to the team. Though they still could not understand each other, all of the mages intuitively took their position. The five giants approached. This would be the first time the team members saw the creatures who attacked their camp: Troll-like, gargantuan creatures with tough rock-like skin, reigning six feet taller than the north mages. The biggest of the group, appearing to be the leader, was met by Vidar standing alone and apart from the others. It gave a deafening roar, signalling a challenge to its opponent. Vidar returned with a war cry of his own in return.

"You think they will scream each other to death?" joked Silvanus.

"Only he could joke at a time like this," thought Victor.

Vidar then did something that perplexed the team. He let a small line of saliva fall from his mouth, using his thumb and index finger as a syphon, causing it to freeze. As the giant charged, Vidar threw the small dart, accurately striking its eye. A painful cry erupted as the giant suspended his forward charge.

Taking advantage of the opening, Vidar lunged forward and while in mid-charge, formed a lance of ice. The giant took a wild swipe at him. Vidar rolled beneath the attack and using his momentum, propelled himself into the air, striking his attacker behind the knee. The giant howled once more as its leg went limp. While trying to balance with one hand, the giant instinctively reacted by aimlessly striking with the other. Vidar, anticipating this, ducked the blow and swiftly struck through the back of the giant's neck.

There was a short gurgling from the giant as its life ceased. The other four roared loudly as they rushed at Vidar. Olaf and the rest of the crew launched large ice lances, striking the giants and propelling them backwards with great force. The crew of ice mages then attacked and killed their wounded opponents. With the battle quickly ended, a loud whistle from Skeld drew his comrades' attention.

"We found more!"

Vidar gave a gesture to his crew, prompting Olaf and the others to deal with the disturbance. Freyr approached, running towards Vidar.

"We need you at the breach."

Racing to the North Wall, the team accompanied Vidar, trying desperately to keep pace on foot. Herger was waiting and quickly summoned Vidar to his side.

"Vidar, come listen toward the horizon and towards the west."

The team became silent… Thunder in the distance.

"They're coming and they will arrive in force. It is not enough time to seal away a breach this big," said Herger.

Danir walked out from behind Vidar with a crystal seer and peered into the distance. Paulo was staring at him, wondering if he had it with him through their whole journey.

"I picked it up from the hold," said Danir understanding Paulo's incredulous look. Danir's tool also attracted the attention of the north mages. Taking notice, Danir offered the seer to Vidar, who cautiously accepted and then gave minor visual instructions to bring the stone to Vidar's eye. Vidar slowly looked through and his head suddenly shot back with surprise. Looking through again he could see the giants approaching in the distance.

"Herger, look at this!" Vidar said excitedly.

Herger at first refused. After being ordered sternly, he took the seer to his eye. His surprise became instantly visible.

"Vidar! I can see them, and count their numbers! These children can move mists and see into the distance. They are not completely useless!"

The two north mages quickly recovered from their astonished wonder. Vidar collected himself and began to organize a plan.

"You are right though. They are moving in great numbers. They will beset us in a matter of hours. We do not have the strength to seal the breach or resist their onslaught."

"What do you suggest?" asked Herger.

"We hold out until my father's army reaches the wall."

Just then, Sil glided swiftly between the two warriors, halting their discussion.

"Hey, you guys better come see this."

All present now ran from the breach with the exception of Herger who remained behind. Legions of mechanical carriages and transports approaching from the south met their advance. One cart in the lead stopped as a fully armoured Terran captain emerged with a small retinue of soldiers. They approached the team and the leading Terran spoke.

"Captain Ophir, it is nice to see you safe."

CHAPTER 42

"Sorry we are late, sir," continued the Terran captain. "We have been sent from the council in response to distress letters. We did not think you would make it out. I am Captain Lucius, of the southern colonies."

The team and the North mages began to walk towards the hold behind the perimeter the soldiers were creating.

"How many men do you have?" asked Ophir.

"We have four legions of ground fighters, six teams of heavy weapons and twenty units of iron guard elite. We also have half legions of Plainswalker bowmen and hunters and fifty of the Queen's guard."

"This is a huge force for a simple distress call," responded Ophir.

"The council did not want to take any chances. Those giant beings are the threat I am guessing," gesturing to the corpse of the dead jotnar.

"Yes, they are," replied Ophir.

"And these are?" spoke the captain, looking towards the North mages.

"Friends," answered Ophir.

Lucius smiled. "Successful again. It looks like the politicians will have a harder time getting rid of you and the team."

Ophir grinned and then quickly explained the situation to the captain.

"More of those things are coming. There are thousands of them."

"Is there any way to seal the hole?" asked Lucius.

"There is, but we do not have the time to bring this about fully."

"Do what you can," replied Lucius. "We will finish evacuating the north. My first priority is to see to the safety of the researchers. Take command of the artificers and soldiers. Hold the wall."

Ophir nodded and set to work.

"Victor, gather the team and the Northerners. I will assemble the legions left to me. Also, try to seal the hole with whatever you can. Any advantage would be a good one."

They separated and Victor grabbed Danir by the arm.

"Do you know how to work the drill?"

"Of course," he replied.

Understanding what needed to be done, they raced toward the drill.

"Paulo, Sil, accompany the North mages to the hole. Make sure they are all together at the right auxiliary. Era One and Two, go and aid the messengers to the North Hold. I need you to get word back to the capital that we have a new nation discovered," Ophir commanded.

The team moved forward, fulfilling Ophir's orders. Danir went to work with a small host of Terrans trying to bring about the collapse of the breach. The Terran army mobilized with the heavy weapons pointed directly at the hole, archers in behind and to the right and left, the legions spread, ready to defend their position. Vidar observed the armoured soldiers and the vehicles, seeing the Terran army for the first time.

"The mage children seem to have interesting toys."

Herger was also impressed with his first look at the powers that lay beyond the wall.

"Sir, we have collapsed the tunnel," one soldier informed Ophir.

"Very good. Pull the drill back. We may have use for it later," he ordered.

"Danir," asked Ophir, "how long do you think this will hold?"

"Not long. It will buy us some time to get the injured out and fortify our position."

"Good enough then!" Ophir declared.

Danir made his way over to the team and crew positioned to the right of the hole.

"So, what did the commander-at-arms say?" asked Silvanus.

"We are to hold our positions," answered Danir.

"Since when is Ophir an army commander?" asked Paulo.

"Well, the original commander was probably given strict orders to retrieve the North Hold workers as a priority. Our nation is a military nation and if two captains are present, one may be asked to stand in if necessity requires," responded Danir.

"You sound like a talking contract the politicians write up," added Sil. "So, Ophir is the chosen defender... They had nobody else?"

"Well, Lord Ophir is a proven veteran. He was head scout for Captain Navious. He served most of his life in the legions before becoming part of the envoy for the Terran elders to the uplands," explained Danir.

There was a short silence after Danir finished with the details. The team looked at one another, and then Sil spoke up.

"You guys catch all that?" he asked, speaking to Vidar and his brethren, knowing they could not understand anyone but each other.

"So, now that we are at war again, does anyone know when we get weapons? Last time we fought these things we were surrounded by darkness and had only supplies. *Maybe* something sharp might help this time," Sil said, making most of his friends laugh.

Moments later, the giants began to force their way through the tunnel. The force of their digging seemed to shake the mountain itself. The collapsed ice gave way to the ravenous brutes. Compelled by starvation, the jotnars' senses ran askew, rendering them unable to detect the army of earth and steel standing vigil at the doorway to their realm.

CHAPTER 43

The burrowing from within the collapsed tunnel silenced the legions that lay beyond them. The army waited with valour untested, against a foe never encountered. Sounds of the enemy grew louder and fiercer as they bore through the last layers of broken ice, anticipating their freedom at hand.

Victor stood intently watching with the ice mages close by, waiting for the final moment when two worlds would confront each other. The fallen ice at the caves entrance began to shift. The Terran soldiers stood ready. Ophir noticed the faces of his Terran comrades, many of them youthful.

"Not long now. We hold the line here. Aim all of our heavy weapons at the opening fire by twos, give the others a chance to reload. You have probably seen the group of dead beasts along the way at your arrival. They are larger *and* stronger than us. We are on their territory, so they have the advantage. What's left of the Hold shows their destructive potential. I want every mage aware; there is nowhere to retreat. If they pass us here, we have no force to stop them from overwhelming our allies. You are the only defence for the nations today. Remember your homes, your families; it is for them that you fight. Remember the hardships we faced before the great arrival. These odds are no different! Every battle that our nation fought was with nothing more than what you have now. Stay vigilant. Follow the plan. Good will overcome."

The Terrans verbally saluted as one; the soldiers now standing all the more assured.

Sil looked to Danir. "So, is it normal to just suddenly go into war mode with no real explanation?" he said sarcastically.

"Well, we are a very organized nation, more so than either the Plainswalkers or yours. It is part of our lifestyle. If even one thing goes wrong in a mine or while fighting in close quarters, it has long reaching ramifications," responded Danir.

"You two stay quiet," said Victor.

Spears were passed to the team and to the crew. The ice mages became very much amused at the idea of holding Terran spears. Sil laughed as he watched them hold the weapons. Their hands covered over a third of the spear's shaft.

The final remnants of ice being forced past the caves entrance suddenly interrupted their discussion. Stillness enveloped the entire legion. Slowly, a giant emerged from the cave, followed closely by another. Ophir lifted his hand to control when the artillery would begin their barrage.

The giants were so tall that their heads nearly touched the top of the cave. Many others could be seen from the distance within the cave. The giants looked around, breathing heavily and noticed the crowd of mages waiting. Upon seeing the North mages, they gave a deafening howl. Ophir lowered his hand and two large spears were launched, impaling both with such force it pushed them back into the cave.

Others charged immediately, and in sequence, the heavy artillery fired off two spear bolts at a time. The giants being assailed, caused a barricade and due to the combination of their size and the caves confinement, they became blockaded within.

The firing ceased when enough of the giants had died. A wall of the dead lined the entranceway into the breach. It seemed as if the giants would stop their advance, as being caught in a narrow space with ranged weapons made their numbers and strength less advantageous.

"Not so useless at all," said Herger to Vidar, who agreed with a smiling nod.

The North mages were very impressed with their strategy and the weaponry. "I think they're enjoying this," Sil spoke to Victor.

If we can hold them in this position, maybe we can force a retreat, thought Ophir. *They are susceptible to our heavy weapons. Should they pass through, will our infantry hold against them?*

As he continued his planning, loud sounds from the cave drew his attention.

"Stand ready! Hold your aim," shouted Ophir.

Giants again tried to make an effort to pass through. The artillery released and struck. The giants halted and then pushed onward.

Ophir's eyes widened as he began to comprehend the situation. "They are using the dead as shields. Steady your aiming!"

It was no use. The amount of dead giants provided an almost perfect covering to allow for the live ones to push through. Despite the Terrans firing triple the rounds, the giants pushed through, broke past the opening and into a charge.

Ophir ordered a full-scale bombardment to prevent the escape. Many of the giants were killed, but this only supplied the crowded entranceway with more shielding. A slow advance of jotnar proceeded behind their dead comrades. Eventually, the weaponry needed reloading and because the firing happened all at once, a brief delay in the offensive occurred. This opening created an advantage for the giants who rushed forward, smashing the Terran lines.

The attack happened with such speed that the Terrans almost broke immediately. The positioning of the artillery was too close to the breach, not anticipating the speed at which the targets could traverse. Phalanx soldiers moved in to levy the giants away from the nearly destroyed right flank. More giants poured out from the caves opening, attacking the Terran front line. Thousands of arrows flew through the air, only to be rendered useless by the giant's thick hides.

The heavy weapons were now unmanned and many had been destroyed as the giants fought the Terrans in open combat. Then Vidar joined the combat and threw an ice-lance, impaling two giants standing close together. Its force violently hurled them backwards. The entire battlefield went silent and fighting ceased. A giant gave a loud howl and then charged the North mages, inciting the others to attack as well.

Ophir, seeing an opportunity, called out.

"Regroup! All soldiers fall back, artillery reload and give cover fire."

The remaining artillery units fired at the clusters of giants now turning to attack their prime nemesis. As the injured were pulled from the battlefield, more giants poured out from the wall.

Vidar and the crew drove themselves deep into the giants' front line. As they advanced with weapons of ice and frost, the giants formed a circle around them and began to close in. Victor and the team were drawn into the fighting. But the best they could manage was to dodge the attacks and stay out of the North mages way. Despite being outnumbered, Vidar and his brethren were smiling and laughing as they fought. At one point, Herger and Olaf knelt while the rest engaged the enemy. As the giants closed in, large stalagmite shaped ice shards rose from the ground, impaling their attackers and giving cover for more melee attacks.

The small band continually repelled the giants. Their skewered corpses now formed a shield around the group. Vidar and his crew fought with long spears of ice which allowed for killing at a safe distance. The giants became enraged and began to climb over the skewered bodies, now shielding their enemies. Herger enhanced the stalagmite base, giving the ice a greater reach, forcing greater distance between the mages and their foes. The ice continued to grow, forming a large cone. The sharp ice piercing the already dead giant cascade grew with the improvement. The sounds of flesh tearing and bones breaking intensified as the ice ruptured through their remains.

"You think you overdid it a little?" asked Vidar.

The others laughed. Herger gave a half smile and shrugged as the giants relentlessly beat upon the ice, which began to fracture under the pressure. New lances were forged and as the cone was dismantled, the crew picked off the giants that came into range. A large circle of titanic corpses littered the ground while even more flooded through the breach.

"Iron guard, advance on the front," commanded Ophir.

The well-armoured Terran soldiers lunged into battle. Being smaller than their opponents which allowed for greater versatility. Three iron elite could bring down a giant with two mages stabbing at the legs and one at the neck. They broke the giants' lines into a scattered attempt to pursue the elite soldiers.

"Concentrate your firepower outside the ice mages' position!" directed Ophir.

Ophir's support allowed for a temporary clearing. Bursting through the ice, Vidar led the attack on the wounded. In spite of their efforts, the valley was filling with giants and soon they would be overwhelmed.

"Turn toward the guard! Give them cover for a retreat. We fall back to the Hold!" ordered Ophir.

The Iron guard brought down many of the giants, but as the battle raged and more jotnar entered the valley, the Terran force could not withstand the invasion. Ophir gave the order to fall back and the heavy weapons gave cover as the north mages followed. Herger aided their escape by paving the battlegrounds with a large sheet of ice, making many of the giants lose their footing during the retreat.

The legions regrouped by the hold and began preparing for the expected assault. The crew gathered with them and Ophir instructed them as best he could to ensure that the next Terran attack would go smoothly. The team was drained from the battle. Ophir approached Victor and Paulo who were holding their spears so tightly their arms were shaking.

"Still alive?" asked Ophir.

Paulo looked up and smiled.

"They froze the ground, a lot of those... things are falling over each other," said Paulo breathing heavily.

"You know, you have done this before. Try to look a little more professional," added Ophir.

Victor laughed.

"Yeah, years of politics and diplomatic envoys left us out of shape. We *really* needed this exercise."

"We're going to quake the land," said Ophir.

"Are you crazy?" asked Victor.

"I talked to the ice mages and I believe they understand to hold position. This will work."

"You know what? Go for it. I don't care anymore. Let's just win and go home. Wait… where is Sil?" asked Victor. "Did he return with you?" questioning Paulo.

"I lost track of him during the battle," replied Paulo, now frantically looking around. "...There! Look."

Sil and Danir came running from the battlefield, sliding over the ice. They both stabbed at a giant's legs taking advantage of the giant's weakness over the ice. The two team members slid gracefully toward their friends and regained their footing evenly as they approached.

"Alright, they're destroying the ice," said Sil quickly.

"...What?" asked Victor before getting cut off.

"Yes, smashing it with their fists and feet. They will be here soon," said Danir catching his breath.

"You seem excited," Ophir said quizzically.

"Not tired or frightened enough from the first battle?" asked Victor.

"What? You know we've done this before, *right?* We'll just win like last time," responded Sil light-heartedly.

"Win like last time. Why not?" retorted Paulo under his breath. "And you?" he continued pointing to Danir.

"Me, sir? I have never been in a battle before. This is more than thrilling," said Danir.

"Alright then, enough. You two, behind the lines. We're initiating a quake field," ordered Ophir.

The two settled in their positions and Sil could be heard in the distance asking, "What's a quake field?"

CHAPTER 44

From the North Wall the giants gathered for a collective charge. With the additional outpour, the legions stood outnumbered nine to one. The giants' advance sent tremors through the ground. The area by the North Hold was flat and the legions had little time to set up an adequate defence. Ophir would be leading the soldiers against a larger, stronger force in open combat.

"We can't win this, can we?" asked Victor grimly.

"The odds are definitely not in our favour," answered Ophir.

"Did you talk to our new friends? Do they know what's coming?" adjured Victor.

"I think they know to hold their positions," said Ophir.

The giants advanced cautiously, gaining speed as they approached.

"Iron guard! Stave men, forward," commanded Ophir.

Ten well-armoured soldiers came forward and each knelt down with a small thin rod planted into the ground. The giants gained speed. The sheer size of the jotnar host threatened to march right over the small group of exhausted legionnaires. The injured within the hold felt the earth shake so violently that many struggled to remain stationary on the beds.

"Now!" Ophir commanded to the kneeling troops.

Vidar and his brethren stood ready with lances in hand. Though he thought the Terran behaviour strange, Vidar calmed his men and told them to hold their positions behind the Terran commander. The earth began to vibrate. At first, the giants' stampede made it unnoticeable. It did not take long for the vibrations to become more intense. The mages were within the giant's grasps when the earth struck against them.

Large, irregular protrusions of rock lined a sudden defensive outburst against the giants' charge. The earth vibrated violently as the soldiers struggled to control the power they were unleashing.

Other Iron guard rushed forward to assist them. The earth's shaking was so powerful that the northern mages had trouble keeping their footing.

At once, the land under the giants' feet began to split apart, becoming randomly misshapen. It rose suddenly, as if filled with air and then imploded, taking with it many of the host it previously supported. This broke the giants into two camps and created a large indentation in the earth, making it more difficult for anyone to pass over to where Ophir's legions were stationed. After the quake, the soldiers involved were clearly exhausted and needed assistance to be pulled from the battle.

"Loose!" Ophir shouted.

The legions' bowmen and spear throwers bombarded the injured giants within the crater.

"Our bows do not have much of an effect," said one of the Terrans to Ophir.

"We don't have anything else. Just keep firing," he replied.

The giants that died during the collapse became support for the others still living. They used the dead to aid their escape from the pit. The north mages supported the Terrans, targeting the giants struggling to free themselves from the mixture of corpse and collapsed earth.

Lances of ice pierced giant flesh, preventing escape from the embrasure's tomb. Those that died, becoming stepping points for the living looked as though they had drowned in a deep pool of blood and ice. While this was happening, the bulk of the giant host began to circle the crater and approach Vidar's position.

"Brothers, we have to hold the flank!"

The crew immediately gathered to Vidar and prepared to fight their final battle. The Terran soldiers persisted against the giants now advancing to the crater's summit. The Terrans drove long spears and pikes into the necks, eyes and faces of their opponents. Forcing the jotnars' climb to a halt and using the momentum of their falling bodies to ward off the others attempting to escape the crater.

Even with the strategic advantage, the numbers of the horde

and the opening of the right flank affirmed an immanent fate. Giants continued to arrive through the breach and with the crater almost filled, the last of the living giants made it to the surface. The north mages reformed their lines as the giants renewed their strength.

Vidar and his fellow ice mages stood before the horde like a lone branch against a flood. Forming lances, the northerners awaited the final moment.

"I love honour more than I fear death," Vidar reflected. "This is an ending worthy of our station, brothers. Fight with me once more, this day and then never again!"

Shouting in response they saluted with one voice.

"Shield!" Vidar shouted.

Working as one, the ice mages, wove a large wall of ice, encasing their arms within, the northerners prepared to meet the giant advance. Silence mentally overtook Vidar's senses. He felt the ice forming around his arm; its cold encased his body as a frozen wall materialized before his brethren and him. The ice wall formations merged and jagged shards protruded from its top.

We have been outnumbered before and have stood our ground. We can hold this, Vidar reasoned.

Large fists broke the protrusions as the giants combined bulk smashed the barricade. Vidar was snapped from his deliberation. The ice mages strained to hold their blockade while being forced backwards as they stood.

"Hold ground!" shouted Vidar.

As one, the crew latched themselves to the land. Ice spread quickly from their feet covering their ankles and cementing them to the terrain, halting the acceleration. In anger, the giants began to smash the wall. The assault was so powerful and frequent that the crew could do little but take the hits. Their icy shanks cracked under the pressure. The wall began to give under the thunderous pounding. Once the wall broke, the ice mages, the Terran lines and the team would be completely exposed. Sweat poured from Vidar's brow. Looking to his right he noticed the same condition in all of his friends.

"Too hot for you boys?" Vidar shouted to his crew.

They laughed loudly.

"How are they laughing?" Sil questioned, regarding the carnage from afar. "Are you seeing this? What is wrong with these people?"

Ophir interjected immediately, silencing Sil.

"Aim what large weapons we have left at the right flank!"

"Sir, we cannot target the giants while they are engaged."

"It's not for support. When the giants pass, bring down as many as you can."

Ophir's remark was a frightful reminder of what could soon transpire. The team looked on helpless as their friends' strength failed.

"Push them back! We have fought more than these!"

Vidar's shouts regenerated the men and they advanced slowly, holding the flank with a weakening shield-wall.

"We have to make kills, now!" Vidar expressed to Olaf. "If this wall fails, we won't last long."

The ice mages were beaten back again. The wall began to collapse. The giants, sensing their victory at hand, forced themselves forward. Vidar prepared to call for lances as the wall of ice regenerated itself despite the opposing fury. The crew noticed Herger pouring his strength into their defence.

"Now! Push them back! Find an opening and finish these bastards!" Herger yelled.

"As one!" Vidar commanded.

With renewed vigour, the crew pressed against the giants. The sudden restoration caught the giants by surprise giving the ice mages a serious advantage. The giants fell over each other in the resulting tumult, with many ending up back in the pit created by the Terrans. The battle had turned as the small group of hardened defenders gained ground. Vidar smiled as they steamrolled their adversaries. Soon the ice mages would break the wall and begin the slaughter. Vidar readied himself to give the order to engage when suddenly their momentum came to a halt…

"Push!" commanded Vidar.

"We are," responded Olaf.

...Oh no... thought Vidar, as he tried to brace for what would come next.

The giants rebounded with explosive power. Many of them now charged and punched simultaneously. The shield-wall cracked and broke under the pressure. The crew was propelled backward and an exhausted Herger was swept up in the incursion. The crew lay pinned beneath their own shield-wall as the giants continued their bombardment.

Vidar was being crushed and had no way of defending himself. He could not see anything but the ice planted against the side of his face. Unable to breath, he became light-headed and his thoughts nonsensical. The giants had almost torn the wall as the team looked on in disbelief, unable to fathom how such great warriors were overtaken on the battle field.

"Prepare to fire," Ophir instructed as the giant horde was distracted by the newly felled mages.

Before the order could be executed, a loud horn blast pierced through the pandemonium. The giants, familiar with this, halted and turned, loudly roaring at the appearance of their long-standing enemy. An immeasurable force of ice mages arrived with Vidar's father. The reflection from their lances made them look as if the light itself clothed them.

Without command, the north mages attacked. They broke seamlessly into two groups: one to strike at the bulk, the other to storm the giants in the pit. A row of north mages created long sheets of ice, allowing the front line to slide forward rather than run. They accelerated with great speed and moving smoothly in formation. Using long ice-lances, they struck the giants with powerful force.

The second group stood for a moment at the craters summit. Forming a large spear in his hand, Vidar's father launched it into the crater. Instead of just striking its target, a large residual veil of ice spread over the surrounding area, leaving living and dead giants frozen, and much of the crater lined with a covering of thick ice.

The horde bellowed a war cry of fearless defiance and the

mages charged, many of them jumping into the crater, smashing through the ice formations just created and engaging the giants courageously. The elder stood at the summit while the young men surged forward. Vidar held his lance upward and jumped in with his crew.

"Holy mother of beast!" shouted Sil. "Are you seeing this?!"

The fighting continued and the legion could do nothing but look on in utter amazement.

"I have never known a people who are so at ease when faced with danger," stated Ophir.

*****

Three hours later, the battle finished and Vidar, covered in blood, stood by his father.

"You are late," stated Vidar.

"We caught some trouble on the way; scattered bands following the glowing path," he responded.

Vidar, obviously weary from the hours of battling, paused a moment to catch his breath.

"You should meet our new friends," he said, leading his father and the warrior commanders toward Ophir and the team.

The Northern Nobles and the team just stood silently looking at each other. Ophir whispered to Victor, "You're up."

"Me?" Victor whispered back.

"I led the battle," Ophir asserted.

"Alright then," said Victor, feeling intimidated by the hulking warriors soaked in the blood of their enemies. He stepped forward, said nothing and bowed. The elder returned the gesture and then he looked over at his son who spoke the introductions.

"Victor," he said pointing to him.

A slight smile creased the elder's frost-grown beard and with an open palm touching his chest, he said, "Hodur."

Those first words spoken were a mere introduction that brought to pass another great alliance. Many of the north mages were covered in the blood of giants and laughing loudly. The injured within what remained of the North Hold would soon be transferred to a better facility. The team and the crew were celebrating their victory, an afternoon of battle that brought nations together and eradicating an ancient enemy.

CHAPTER 45

Two years passed and the alliance of the mage nations became stronger. From the north, an exchange for students and ambassadors that would learn the ways of their foreign brethren passed to the capital. Among them was Vidar and his crew. Many from the Terran, Aerial, and Plains nations also took part in the program. The youths in these programs would become emissaries and diplomats who would aid in the trading of resources and services.

Prosperity followed the four nations and Vidar became the official representative for what the Queen's court titled the Kryos Nation. With his title came duties and the responsibility of learning the language, but also of playing the role of envoy to the Plains Nation. This meant long meetings and endless council sessions.

A champion on battleground, a proven mariner, distinguished among his comrades and now — almost dying of boredom listening to the endless legislative chatter. Success had become even more of a test to him than his strongest adversary. After another long meeting, he met up with Olaf outside the Royal Assembly.

"You're back!" said Vidar, opening dialogue in their native speech.

"Yes, and have been for almost three days now. Been inspecting the training grounds. Skeld and Freyr have become very good in their teaching position. You should see it. They're a huge attraction. They have students from every mage nation."

"Well at least they get to battle something. If I knew what lay in wait for me when I was assigned this position, I would have drowned myself in the wild currents," said Vidar bitterly.

"You are representing the nation and one born of your household is more than worthy of such an appointment," said Olaf.

"This whole place is weak. I have not fought a serious battle in almost two years. No sailing, no fishing, no training, just talking: *endless* talking."

Olaf was going to say something encouraging, but Vidar's ranting cut him off.

"They use little circular tokens to trade for everything. This whole place values those trinkets, that have no actual use, as a tool for exchange. They argue for days of how those are to be distributed," Vidar said, becoming more enraged by the moment.

As they spoke, a man passing by stopped, bowing his head slightly.

"Prince Vidar," he addressed before regaining his composure and carrying on. Vidar awkwardly returned the gesture.

"And this prince title. Who would have heard of a place that measures your worth by being born of a certain family? The Queen actually never fought for her position. Do you know how sick that is, to have an untested leader?" said Vidar intensely.

"Well, from home there have been some re-occurrences of the jotnar but the bands were dealt with before my return," said Olaf hoping the good news would cheer his comrade.

"When I took this commission, I thought I would be leading tiny mageling peoples against evil dwarfs. I would have been a hero in both worlds. Is there any word from father as to when I would return?" asked Vidar.

Olaf laughed. "Evil dwarves, really?"

They both laughed at the sentiment, than began walking together.

"Have you heard from Victor and the others?" asked Olaf.

"Yes, actually that's where I have been summoned to next. You should come, too. They would be delighted to see you again," admitted Vidar.

"What project is the team working on now?" Olaf enquired.

"I suppose we should hear of it soon. Victor had Paulo running around in the south with Danir and Ophir. Whatever it is, we will learn when we arrive," claimed Vidar.

*****

In the southeastern end of the palace, huge doors opened and two large Kryos mages entered a large room filled with familiar compatriots.

"Vidar, "shouted more than one of the mages present.

"Brothers, how was your journey?" Vidar asked.

"Long. It seems you learned to speak Plains while I was away," Ophir responded.

"Well, you did teach me, so I assume I can only be as good as you have allowed," he answered back.

"Look at you," interrupted Silvanus. "Have you adjusted to the buildings yet, or do you still have to walk on your knees when you are invited into a house?"

"We live in the palace, as it is the only place that allows for our size," answered Vidar, not realizing Sil was trying to be annoying.

"Alright, that's enough. Everybody take a seat," said Paulo. "Where's Victor?"

"Right here," he said, entering the room. "Sorry, held up by some of the Queen's ministers."

Victor greeted Vidar with a hug and to Olaf he did the same, before taking his seat.

"Alright, now that we all know each other, we can get started," retorted Paulo. "This is a map of the Auren desert." He continued rolling out a large scroll for display at the front of the room. "We have spent the last six months surveying and mapping its borders and studying the beings within it. As you know, our last mission there failed, resulting in many casualties. We know the beings inhabiting this stretch of land are often hostile to our presence, most notably the large semi-sentient creatures that live near the desert's centre. The scouts are calling them ghouls."

Aware that Vidar and Olaf had no knowledge of these events, he went into greater detail.

"Before we engaged in northern exploration, we combed the deserts for almost a year in search of possible mage life. Between the overwhelming heat, lack of water, those *ghouls*, and our artillery sinking in the sands, the mission was a total failure."

"What does this desert have that would make you believe that mages can be living within?" asked Vidar.

"We call it a super-phenomenon, aptly named the 'Sunspire.' It seems an intense luminescence radiates from the core of the desert. We have no idea what causes it or even why it exists, but during the night it can be seen from leagues away. It is almost like a ground level sun. We believe it acts as a barrier protecting anything within it."

"What is inside this ground sun?" asked Vidar.

"Well, we are unsure, as of yet, if there is anything at all. However, that is why we are all here today. As far as discovery is concerned, we are the experts and the questing permits have been issued for a full-scale examination. We will have the use and cooperation of the four nations," said Paulo invigorated by the good news.

"We had that before, remember?" added Sil. "What makes this time so different?"

"The last year and a half, we have been setting up a permanent base in the northern part of the desert. It is now operational and self-sufficient in every way," stated Paulo. "Flowing water supply, advanced defences, food storage and production. It has become a kind of research facility for the Terran nation to study the minerals of the desert land and extract any practical use. We have a headquarters now; no more pitching tents or temporary encampments. We have a strong reinforcement to aid our position."

"How will that matter?" protested Sil. "We still do not have the power to fight *them* with our own weapons, *unless* you've made those work on sand."

"True," admitted Paulo. "Our weaponry is still unable to traverse the dunes, but I think that's where Vidar and his crew would be useful. We need an attack force to engage the enemy."

"Of course we will do this fight for you. Tell us about these ghouls," he said with a thick northern accent that he would let slip when he was excited or angry.

"They're indigenous to the central desert. They inhabit the area closest to the sunspire. They live in territorial segments. Our scouts counted at least a hundred and fifty in the region we would need access to. They do not reside close to one another, so we can take them one at a time.

Here is where it becomes difficult; their speed, size and aggression, combined with their ability to navigate the desert terrain, make them formidable. We cannot engage them with our weaponry and even when we managed to injure them, they would retreat and quickly regenerate, then engage in battle again. We were unable to keep up. When the night came and we froze, the ghouls just picked us apart," said Paulo grim faced.

"When do we strike?" Vidar dauntlessly responded.

"We leave when you're ready. Our first stop will be the base for some desert training and equipment, then onward to the central desert territories," said Paulo showing on the map where their sojourn would embark.

CHAPTER 46

The team had made a special addition to some of the Terran crystal powered carts to accommodate for the Kryos larger stature.

"We should be arriving shortly, only a matter of hours now," said Ophir.

"We have travelled almost a week with no driver. My father will never believe this," said Vidar.

"How do you travel long distances in your homeland?" asked Danir.

"Sometimes we walk, sometimes we ski and sometimes we ride bears," he responded.

"Bears? Really?" curiously replied Danir.

"Like field bears here except bigger and all white, not brown. Not very common though. Only certain families keep them," said Vidar.

"We're here," said Ophir.

Ophir, Danir, and Vidar stepped out of their cart. The other two carts parked close by. The team gathered and took their first view of the Auren desert base. The fort was rectangular, surrounded by a wide ditch. A rampart was built with the earth from the ditch and heavy stones. Four stone gateways allowed entrance from all sides. The mages stared at the fortress for some time before Ophir broke the silence.

"It holds eight hundred men, has a hospital, granaries, barracks, outdoor ovens and a poultry enclosure."

Ophir lead them towards the nearest gate that opened upon their approach. The walls were more than thirty feet high and when they entered, many busy Terrans and Plainswalkers were seen tending to the necessary errands. The structures within the fortress were made of wood and there was a large well near the centre. In the midst of the working cohort, even a few Aerials stood present. As they were being led to the captain's chamber, Ophir began pointing out the fortress's unseen advantages.

"The dunes are not far out. We have set up a vast system of wells and temporary tent sites for resting as we travel. Supplies and food are always available - we will have no shortage this time. Also, an ongoing scouting patrol of the surrounding area is constantly in effect, creating a wide network of surveillance."

Upon entering the captain's chamber, a vast table laden with food was being set out. Ophir gestured to the seats and each mage took his place.

"You will be shown to your sleeping quarters. For the Kryos, we have specially prepared rooms designated for your size. Training begins tomorrow. You will be up early, so rest well."

"Training?" remarked Silvanus. "You do know we are technically hardened soldiers."

"Really?" added Victor. "That's what you think of yourself?"

The others laughed quietly at the joke made at Sil's expense.

"Your military prowess needs no enhancement," said Ophir trying not to break into a smile. "You will have to learn how to ride a dromedary and how to set up tents. Along with that, you will all be fitted for specialized clothing and headgear. We have been doing more than just setting up bases and water wells. The last time we invaded the desert, over one-third of our force was lost, all because we did not understand our environment."

That night they slept in their appointed chambers and early in the morning, as promised, the team was roused for training. Learning to ride the dromedary was, at first, difficult, but they became accustomed to it very quickly. After hours of riding, the team was issued turbans and loose clothing. Everyone had a laugh at how strange the dress code was becoming.

"Shouldn't we have something heavier in case we encounter attackers?" asked Victor.

"No. You have a better chance of dying from exhaustion and heat stroke than from enemies," said Ophir assuredly. "Loose clothing like this will keep the skin from being irritated."

After a light meal, the team went on to learn first aid from Danir.

"In the desert, even the most trivial wound is likely to become infected if not dealt with straight away. Thorns are easily picked up and should be pulled out as soon as possible. Large painful sores develop where skin becomes broken, bandage all cuts, and use the herbal dressings we have provided when needed."

The team learned of heat stroke and heat cramps. They were also instructed to prevent infection by keeping their groin, armpits, and between their toes dry. Their training then turned to setting up tents and beds for sleeping off of the ground and the best times for travel and for resting. After about four days of practice, they headed into the dunes to set up a temporary settlement to adjust to the heat conditions.

CHAPTER 47

After almost two weeks of scouting drills, and riding lessons with strange one humped desert beasts, the team was ready. Setting off on dromback with equipment, supplies, maps and water, they rested at camp sites and safe areas along the way. At their first rest, Victor grabbed Ophir's attention.

"You know, I am amazed at how the Kryos bodies have adjusted to the extreme heat. I thought we would have problems due to their innate composition," sited Victor.

"I had doubts as well, but our eyesight adjusts to the over lands and their bodies adjust to the Auren," said Ophir. "Their predisposition for control of frost and ice has allowed them to also keep cool, even under the high temperatures."

"With all that said, their natural appetite has not reduced. We cannot travel with enough food to consistently feed them," said Victor.

"I know, and we have already planned for that. We will be approaching our encampment bordering the questing region. It is practically another small town and is loaded with food rations. From that point, we enter ghoul territory."

Both mages stood for awhile quietly drinking from canteens, enjoying the endless sight of the golden dunes spread out before them.

*****

"Where is Herger? I have not seen him in some time," asked Skeld to Vidar.

"He was with me at the capital for sometime, but became bored of diplomacy and returned home," replied Vidar.

"I thought he was posted with you?" inquired Freyr. "How did he get permission to return to the homeland?"

"He needs no permission! Even if he was ordered to stay, who would challenge him for returning? He did his job on the currents and now he goes home," said Vidar.

Danir emerged from behind Skeld's massive frame. Vidar half-smiled, laughing internally, having not noticed him before.

"You miss your home much?" asked Danir moments after his appearance.

"Yes, very much. You?" responded Vidar.

"Not really. I have seen my entire nation. I am more eager to help expand the interests of my people up here. We have accomplished a lot in this last year," claimed Danir. He continued turning the conversation to a more serious topic. "Tomorrow we approach ghoul territory."

"Of course. Have you fought with them?" asked Vidar.

"I have never engaged them, but have studied them through observation. These are not an opponent I would want to fight," responded Danir.

"It does not worry me, or any of us. We exist for fighting and warfare; it is our life blessing," said Vidar seriously. "Tomorrow, when we face them, we will do as we have always done."

"Do you *ever* become afraid?" asked Danir.

"No," responded Vidar.

"How can you always be like this? Always unafraid of everything. Don't you ever worry you will die?" Danir enquired.

"Cattle die, kinsmen die, and all mages are mortal. Words of praise will never perish, nor a noble name," recited Vidar.

Silence followed his last words as a cold breeze gave commentary to the night's calmness.

"Alright then," interjected Paulo. "It's time for sleep. Everyone to your rooms."

The cohort broke and each settled into huts made of palm leaves. Inside, mattresses, pillows and blankets provided a simple, but comfortable, sleeping quarter. While the team slept darkness consumed the golden dunes that surrounded the camp. A great distance away, a faint glowing pierced the night's shroud, a sign signaling their journey's end.

CHAPTER 48

The team rose early in the morning, packed food and continued their travels on dromback. It was also decided that part of the camp would come along to test the recently developed bolt thrower: a larger variation of the crossbow, launching a heavy bolt made to pierce ghoul flesh.

"It has never been tested in battle," spoke Danir to Victor. "We believe it would be a major improvement over the original bulk artillery units."

"Why have you not tested it in battle?" asked Victor.

"We did not want to risk confrontation with the ghouls," said Danir. "We can hold position at the base, but in the field, if they give chase most of our shelters are vulnerable to attack. It would be wiser to attack in force against these creatures."

"Has anyone from your unit fought with them at all?" asked Victor.

"No. We primarily do scouting and surveillance," replied Danir.

"Find any weaknesses?" asked Victor.

"At night, they have bad vision. Also, they reproduce on a phenomenally slow level. Their population has probably been consistent for generations due to their long lifespan. We have a chance to wipe them out completely, *that is*, if this works," he added calmly.

"Do you think that our small group can take on a desert full of these beasts?" questioned Victor.

"Probably not. However, if these skirmishes work and we are successful, then we can rally larger numbers, spread out through the Auren and make it safe for travel and study," responded Danir.

"It's nice to see you thought some of this out," Victor stated.

Danir smiled.

The desert was void of any noticeable life. The only consistent noise came from the bellowing and growling of their dromedary companions. The team rode for almost an hour more and the location of their targets became a subject of concern.

"So where are they?" asked Paulo. "The scouts reported that at least one lived in this area."

"Anyone else notice how hot it is?" interjected Sil.

"Do you talk just to hear yourself speak?" Ophir shot back. "I'll send a search for surrounding area. Tell the team and camp members to break for a short while."

Ophir and Paulo busied themselves with the scouting logistics as Danir turned the inquiry to Victor.

"It is possible that if it has eaten, it could be resting underneath the sands," answered Danir.

"What? You mean they burrow?" asked Victor.

"Yes. Actually, it is quite amazing. They need no water but instead gain everything essential from their prey. So once they have consumed a meal, they fall asleep," replied Danir casually.

"So they could be anywhere here, around us?" Victor asked.

"Well, our scouting is quite advanced. If they were around us, I have no doubt we would notice," countered Danir.

At that moment, one of the dunes close by began to lift up. A ghoul emerged from the sands almost directly beneath the team's position, presenting itself to their flank with an ear-splitting roar. Over ten feet tall with large claws, a horned wolf shot upright and immediately attacked Victor. Unprotected and surprised, Victor was made an easy mark. Sand scattered through the air at the beast's sudden movement. A large talon unfolded.

A shining beam suddenly shot forth, narrowly missing the team's stunned leader. The beam struck with such powerful force that the beast was violently propelled from its target. All present turned toward the beam's source and witnessed Vidar preparing again another ice lance.

"It's a ghoul!" yelled one of the Terrans.

With the ghoul fallen, Vidar leaped forward stabbing it again in the leg as it began to rise. Then, with a newly forged shell of ice over his fist, he struck its head, breaking a horn and smashing the beast to the ground. The ghoul fell unmoving and Vidar stood breathing heavily.

"Are you alright?" asked Olaf.

"It took… more… strength then I am used to in ice… forming," replied Vidar, now sweating.

Olaf and Victor brought water to Vidar, who drank deeply, finishing one jug and then moving onto another.

"We had no idea it would be so hard on your bodies to use your strengths out here," said Victor to a semi-exhausted Vidar.

Victor saw that Vidar's eyes widened as he was aiding him. The ghoul arose and was on the offensive. Vidar pushed Victor aside and lunged at the monster shielding his friend. Before the ghoul could strike, a steel bolt struck the ghoul's shoulder, forcing it backwards while it let out an agonizing roar. Vidar wasted no time. Joining with Olaf, they attacked, pulling the bolt from its flesh and striking repeatedly. The hacking went on for minutes. Ghoul blood flowed out over the dune sands, leaving the strong odour of an outdoor slaughterhouse wafting through the air. After their fight ended, Vidar, now sweating profusely and covered in blood, spoke to Victor who was still somewhat shocked from the incident.

"I think…" he said, breathing heavily, "I think we killed it."

They decided to head back to camp for the night and let Vidar rest. At the camp most of the team went straight to sleep. Victor remained awake, while Sil and the Eras controlled cool breezes to calm their cohort. Returning from the stall, Ophir joined Victor, who was sitting by a Terran heating sphere.

"You know they actually decapitated it," he said.

"What?" Victor said surprised.

"Its head came right off, with nothing but a bolt," attested Ophir.

"Did you see how tired he became? This never happened during training," claimed Victor.

"Our training session was not combat related, *only* for desert adaption," Ophir replied.

"One fight and our main attack force is floored," remarked Victor.

"Not exactly. Only Vidar became abnormally exhausted; Olaf joined the assault and he remains unaffected," added Ophir.

"So then, what are you thinking?" asked Victor.

"Arm them with the bolts. They hold them like toys, so it's not really an issue, and continue with the attack as is. I will send for more ammunition during the day. We can stockpile here, clear the ghouls out one at a time and push forward to the sunspire arriving one day late," affirmed Ophir.

"Alright then, we have a plan," said Victor, assured.

CHAPTER 49

The next morning, Vidar rose from his sleep fully regenerated. The plan was explained and the team set off with double the bolts it had previously carried. Travelling through the dunes, they stopped only at a well and then continued onward again into the ghoul territory.

"How is he?" asked Victor to Paulo.

"Healthy, but embarrassed. Normally, that type of fatigue is associated with the younger members of their nation when they start learning how to control the flow of frost," Paulo answered.

"He has not been saying much," Victor adduced.

"I believe it is their custom to redeem themselves after a shameful battle," replied Paulo

"I do remember him winning. What was shameful?" questioned Victor.

"He needed Olaf's help in finishing off his opponent. As the leader, he had to win first," said Paulo.

In the distance, one of the scouts returned in a hurry, yelling as he came.

"They're coming! At least two were behind."

He continued past the front line while the Kryos readied themselves. The ghouls could be seen approaching. They were each about the same height as the ghoul they fought the day before. The Kryos dismounted. Olaf handed the bolt thrower to Vidar who held up his hand to refuse and instead opted for two single bolts of his own.

Vidar charged his attackers. As the gap between them closed, Vidar launched one of the bolts impaling the ghoul's face. The thrust was so violent that when it struck, it sent the ghoul soaring behind its companion. Its companion halted and let loose a defiant roar. Vidar jumped forward, ducking and rolling as a claw narrowly missed its intended target. He came up behind the ghoul in one smooth motion and stabbed the back of its leg. With the ghoul hobbled, Vidar grasped one of its horns, pulled back its head and speared through its neck. The team watched without a word, witnessing the battle like a crowd at a stadium.

Silvanus leaned over to Paulo and whispered. "A *violent* people, aren't they?"

Vidar was welcomed back by the team after his victory.

"We should keep moving, more will be ahead," he spoke in his low northern accent. Then, saying something in his native language, laughter erupted among his brethren. He mounted the dromedary, smiling as they continued their sojourn.

"Redeemed then?" asked Victor.

"I think so," affirmed Paulo.

The team travelled over three weeks through the vast Auren desert with weapons in hand. Whenever they would encounter a ghoul, the Kryos would cut them down. Eventually, it became more like a hunting party rather than an exploration team. Danir led the scouts, armed with bolt throwers, as a support for the Kryos infantry. The rest of the team remained single file, moving toward their destination.

Besides the ghouls, sand storms posed a threat to the team. The Aerials countered them easily, avoiding any slowdowns. Near twilight, the team encamped and set up their temporary tent homes.

"It seems nothing can stop us now," remarked Sil as he took a seat close to his friends.

"These ghouls are getting larger and larger, plus the light is stronger. We are close to the sunspire. One more day and we should be where we need to be," said Paulo.

"When they're fighting," said Victor, turning from the subject, "the Kryos hold the bolts with one hand. Can't we craft swords and weapons for their size?"

"They're doing fine. I think it is apparent, though, that the ghouls will have to be wiped out entirely. The environment itself is hostile enough without fearless monsters attacking us," said Ophir. "I think we should send Danir, half the scouts and half of the Kryos back to the base to await reinforcements, then meet up with them at a central location."

"This will take too long," commented Victor. "We reach the sunspire, set up camp and start hunting parties. They are already proving to be more than adept at fighting these creatures with the limited weapons and resources. In a month we should be able to clear them out."

"Maybe, but the area we have travelled through is populated by the smaller ghouls. The larger are almost three times the size, strength *and* speed. We cannot expect our friends to fight a battle of that magnitude when we could easily call for greater force and crush them with ease," commented Ophir.

There was quiet between the two mages. Paulo, Sil, and the Eras listened on.

"Alright, here," Victor said, "we will ask Vidar. If the Kryos and the scouts think they can handle the ghouls, then we carry on as is. If they decide to await reinforcements, then we retreat back to the camp and when they arrive, we attack full force."

*****

"Ask for help? Is our fighting force not satisfactory?" questioned Vidar.

"We just don't want to take any unnecessary risks," responded Ophir.

"There is no risk. This is a small matter. There is no need to trouble a larger force and waste more time," answered Vidar, who then proceeded to walk away.

Ophir, wanting to understand why his logic was so easily rebutted without any justification, stood for a moment thinking, but was unwilling to approach Vidar again to further explain his reasoning.

Victor came near with a slight smile.

"So how did it go?"

"No reinforcements. We carry on as is," said Ophir.

"They will not change their minds you know," remarked Victor.

"But if we explain the inherent danger..."Ophir was cut off

mid-sentence by Victor finishing his own.

"Because it is a *dishonourable* act to ask for help just because you're scared," said Victor.

It became clear to Ophir, who understood well enough that these mages, above all, pursued honour and glory on the battlefield and would choose death before dishonour.

"Well then," said Ophir thoughtfully, "let's eat some food, get some rest and then go back to war."

"Sounds good," replied Victor.

CHAPTER 50

On a night like any other, a tent site was pitched, fires set to blaze and guards posted. Unlike their usual locations, this site was deep in unconquered ghoul territory. The night progressed as the fires faded. A host of ghouls gathered and surrounded the invaders. Slowly approaching on all fours, the ghouls shadowed the campgrounds. The leader gave a loud cry as the rest attacked the unsuspecting mages in their sleep.

Slashing through the standing guards, their assault left no time for a defensive attempt. The camp was ravaged as the battle quickly turned into a stampede. No shelter was spared as the frenzy continued. With its destruction complete, the ghouls' senses calmed as an auspices realization purged their collective silence.

Suddenly, bolts flew from every side, descending like rain on the attackers. Wind, controlled by the Aerials, threw tent covers at the beasts, which slowed them down and complicated their movements. The trap was a success. The ghouls were killed and the team returned to their *actual* camp site. Sitting around a heating sphere, the team converged and evaluated the day's progress.

"If their sizes keep advancing like this and they begin to group like the smaller ones did, we are going to be in some real crap," said Paulo.

"On the upside, I think we have enough ammunition," said Ophir whimsically. "The fact they're retractable and of high quality Terran make means they're going to see us through to the end of the war; whether we win *or* lose."

"Food supplies are going to be harder to maintain," added Paulo. "If this carries on longer than a month, then we have to start a route and set up resting posts."

"Silvanus," asked Victor. "Where are the Eras?"

"Scouting," he said with a mouth full of food, taking time to chew and swallow before he finished his answer. "They just left for a run about an hour ago."

"Ophir," said Paulo, turning his attention toward another subject. "What of the sunspire? Any new activity?"

"We have been trying to get close. Even with the protective eyewear, this is more than a shining light. It is concentrated and focused in a way that allows no one to approach at a certain distance without incineration. We have been looking for weakness but it seems to be consistent no matter where we advance," responded Ophir.

"Is there any armour or shielding against it?" asked Victor.

"I would need more materials and a larger research group from the base to find out," replied Ophir.

"You sure there is something *alive* there?" asked Olaf.

"I have no doubt," responded Ophir. "The sunspire is shaped like a sphere. It's almost a dome covering."

"It is made of pure light, though?" inquired Sil.

"The North Wall was made entirely of ice," answered Ophir.

"Each mage nation adapts to its environment," recited Sil. "What situation would make a mage have to live in light?"

"Who among us would have believed that mages can create ice, or live on clouds? Something is in there. Too many natural laws have been bent for this to be some sort of archaic phenomena," Ophir explained.

"Alright, enough now," interrupted Victor. "We can deal with the wall later. Right now, what about those large ghouls? What are the chances of these things grouping together?"

An uncomfortable silence fell over the group as the thought of facing off against the more mature ghouls fermented in their minds.

"With the attack force we have now, we cannot face the enemy without losses. It takes three, sometimes four, Kryos warriors to bring down the big ones and we have five. One bad day and we're carrying back more wounded, and possibly more dead, then we can hold," asserted Victor.

"Vidar, what do you think?" Ophir asked.

He thought a moment and then responded.

"The chains for holding the tents before we set up camp: are they strong?"

"Yes, of course. They're Terran made," divulged Ophir.

"We use them. They will help us bring down ghouls," said Vidar with conviction.

"How will these help?" asked Danir.

"Just have them ready for us at morning," replied Vidar.

CHAPTER 51

The sun rose and the Terrans laid out the supply chains. Vidar and the Kryos went to work attaching them to the end of spears to create flail-like armaments. After about an hour of work they loaded their creations onto the back of their dromedary escorts and gave word to set out.

Victor rode close to Ophir.

"What do you think they will use those for?" he asked, lightly gesturing to the recent inventions.

"Not sure. But knowing them, it should be interesting," Ophir replied with a smile.

After many hours of travelling, a cloud of sand approached from the east like a wave. The team and their military aid were overwhelmed. Victor yelled for his friend.

"Sil, come on, stay on top of it."

"I'm on it," responded Silvanus.

The Eras joined in the effort to route the wind's direction. The Aerials forced the winds away from the team, creating an invisible globe, allowing the thick cloud of sand to pass over them without contact. Slowly, it dissipated. While the storm settled, a large figure appeared, previously obscured by the wave of sand. It was so tall that it appeared to block out what remained of the sun through the sand. It made slow progress toward them. As the Aerials routed the sand squall, the ghoul gave a deafening roar.

"Maybe we should have left the storm," asserted Sil.

The Kryos jumped into action, Olaf threw his chain-spear, striking the ghoul in the right shoulder. The ghoul seemed surprised by the attack, regarding it as a sudden annoyance rather than a life-threatening assault. It roared again. The size and intensity of the beast was enough to frighten many of the soldiers. The ghoul moved forward, seemingly unaffected by the lance that protruded from its limb. With the distraction staged, the remaining

Kryos, assisted by a scouting unit, circled behind with long spears and concurrently struck against the shallow depression behind the knees. The ghoul dropped involuntarily onto all fours as its painful crying reverberated through the desert with a deafening pitch.

Visibly irate, it attempted to end their confrontation with a clawed strike at the mages. At that moment, the Kryos spear throwers pulled on the chains, bringing the beast down, exposing the neck as Vidar and Olaf repeatedly plunged their spears into its throat, leading to the ghoul's demise.

"Wow," spoke Sil watching his companions finish off their enemy. "*That* was amazing."

CHAPTER 52

They combed the desert for hours searching for signs of ghoul activity. Finding none, the team decided to stop for rest. The team's leaders gathered in council to discuss a new set of tactics.

"Alright, where is everybody?" began Victor.

"I have kept a body count," replied Danir. "It has been what...? Three weeks? Four? We average about seven kills per day. We dropped just over one hundred and forty."

"We have documented over three hundred ghouls," explained Victor. "Where's the other half?"

"They hold a wide land range," said Danir. "Normally when there is vacancy, others will rush in to expand their territory and eliminate competition. We just cleared the area."

"We have cleared a huge area," conveyed Paulo. "When that is discovered, there will be a flood of ghouls filling this space."

"How long before this happens?" asked Victor.

Danir exhaled heavily, thinking of his reply.

"We have maybe three days."

"Let them come," announced Vidar. "We have held against them. More will make no difference."

"What about the sunspire?" added Victor. "Are we doing anything with that anymore?"

"The fighting has deterred our research, but when the ghoul threat has subsided, we will resume our study," reported Ophir. "Besides, we made no progress with the spire. Here, at least, we advance."

"With this new influx of ghoul activity, will our force be enough for a strong resistance?" asked Paulo.

"We thought of that already," responded Ophir. "We sent out an order for six hundred additional soldiers for reinforcement, along with bolts, chains, bolt throwers, and black shells."

"Black shells?" asked Victor.

"Oh, yes," said Ophir. "They are a projectile weapon we used in our home world. You would have seen them when you first came. The shell, when launched, explodes on contact. We recently found a way to create them on the surface. They're sitting in an armoury. Why let them be wasted?"

Vidar gave him a menacing look.

"Why do we need these others? We have proven more than worthy of fighting the enemy."

"Vidar, listen. We are not here for your personal glory! Bringing results to the council of the sunspire's composition is our priority," admitted Ophir. "When we are finished with the ghouls, then we can resume study of the anomaly."

"How long will it take for the dispatch to arrive?" asked Paulo.

"Three days," said Danir.

"Wonderful," Paulo responded. "They will be fighting the moment they arrive."

"Alright then," interrupted Victor. "Let's head back to camp and get some rest."

The team returned to camp and braced themselves for the approaching storm.

CHAPTER 53

"Any sign of them?" asked Danir.

"Nothing yet," Paulo while staring through a crystal seer replied.

"There is no point standing around," Danir said. "We should head back and see what the others want to do."

They quickly mounted their droms and set back to the base. The desert sun was still bright as the noon's end approached. They entered the base camp as Victor approached, hoping for a good report. Anticipating his friend's inquiry, Paulo simply shook his head as he dismounted with Danir and joined the team's gathering.

"Why have they not arrived?" asked Victor to Danir. "We need these re-enforcements."

A scout, returning from his surveillance, interrupted their dialogue.

"What word from the lookout?" Ophir asked.

"Nothing yet, sir. We have been monitoring the terrain and so far no ghouls have been sighted," answered the scout.

Ophir dismissed him and went back to conversing with Victor.

"Still nothing. This is very odd."

"And fortunate," mentioned Victor. "Vidar and his crew have had time to train the scouts and assemble the weapons. He is a natural teacher and the soldiers really look up to him."

"As they should," Ophir acknowledged. "War has been a lifestyle for his people. It is nice having a second trainer around; allows me to take a break occasionally. I thought you said three days?" turning his attention back to Danir.

"The third day is still happening now. They will be here."

"If we have to engage the ghouls at this rate, we may not have the power to withstand them," said Victor shooting a worried look at Ophir.

An Aerial, racing into the base at wind speed, halted their conversation.

"Era!" shouted Paulo. "What news?"

"They're here!" he yelled on his approach, coming to an immediate stop. "Eight are approaching and dozens more only leagues behind. Large ones are in the lead."

"Give word for the scouts to fall back," Paulo ordered. "Everyone, let's move! On the droms, now!"

Vidar smiled and turned to the young mages standing ready.

"Remember what you learned: stay strong, work together."

The soldiers raced as a unified force, mounted their dromedaries and advanced toward the approaching threat.

"Morale is higher than I expected," spoke Ophir to Vidar as they began their ride. "You really have them excited for battle."

Vidar smiled, not responding. The other Kryos and most of the camp rallied and a shofar blew to signal the attack. The leaders rode closely together. The regiment structure placed scouts, armed with bolt throwers, making up the bulk of artillery along the back. The Kryos and the captains rode in the centre, surrounded by their small armada. As the advance continued, Ophir noted the time.

"We will be hitting darkness in short time. The sunset will begin and the cold will take over. Maybe we should turn around?"

"We will encounter them soon," sighted Vidar. "Let's just win fast."

"Win fast," boasted Sil. "Love the idea! Should've had that plan at the beginning. "

The Kryos shot a scowl at Sil.

Another blast from the horn signified the sighting of ghouls. The army responded in turn by forming ranks and preparing for a charge.

"Danir, signal the artillery to form three lines and two flanks of three rows each. No charging. Support Vidar's attack. Rally around my position!" commanded Ophir.

Danir set to work as Victor yelled to Ophir.

"What's the plan?"

"We win fast," Ophir shouted back.

"I will take scouts forward. We will fight together," Vidar told

Ophir. "You fire first, then we move in. Try to injure the smaller ghouls, so we can deal with the big ones."

They arranged themselves in a way that allowed for the scouts to line between the flanking artillery and the main three lines as to not obstruct the firing cycle. Standing ready with his unit, Vidar begin instruction.

"Throwers, you march out first. When the order for charge happens, scouts follow me. Spread out widely. Aim for the back of the knees. The strongest of you join me and my brethren and grab at the flails. Bring them down. Strike the neck and the eyes. Spill their blood! Bring them death!" he shouted.

"Blood and death!" The group responded.

"Nice," remarked Sil, observing the soldiers.

Ophir smiled at Victor, who was already doing the same.

With the troops ready, a stillness engulfed the brave mages as they awaited their enemy's approach. From behind with the supplies, the braying of the droms could be heard. From the distance, loud howling and ear-splitting roars resounded as the ghouls came into sight.

Three large ghouls drew near; their great size almost distracted the army from the eight smaller ghouls who kept a slight distance behind them. Once the ghouls noticed the army, they initiated their attack.

"Load ready!" commanded Ophir.

The satisfying sounds of artillery being prepped rang through the ranks.

"Face ready! Take your targets!" Ophir continued in his command.

The ghouls were now racing at a fast pace. The eight lesser ghouls took the lead, bearing their teeth and snarling as they charged.

"Fire!"

At that command, hundreds of bolts flew through the air like a swift wind. The lesser ghouls were flung back. Many lost their footing as bolts pierced their bodies.

"Line two, fire!" yelled Ophir.

Two more firing sessions were ordered as the large ghouls came into range.

"Lines, hold!"

The bolts ceased firing.

"Ranks, forward!"

The team's leaders led the troops forward in attack against the ghouls.

"Flails, loose!"

Spear flails struck the large ghouls, allowing Vidar and his unit to use the chains to control the beasts. The army moved swiftly over the sands, breaking into groups and attacking the injured ghouls while the strongest mages aided Vidar in taking down the larger ghouls.

The fighting was fierce on both sides. With the smaller ghouls injured by the bolt storm and preoccupied with half the attack force, the Kryos engineered a clever plan of using the flails to manoeuvre the large ghouls. Dashing beneath the ghoul's legs with the flail ends, the scouts targeted the weak points, forcing the ghouls to trip over each other. As the fighting continued, more ghouls were attracted to the scene. Another dozen arrived and were noticed from a distance.

"Sir, ghouls, from the south-east," reported one of the Terrans with a crystal seer.

"Left flank forward," Ophir quickly ordered to counter the threat.

"Hold! Aim ready."

The ghouls streamed smoothly over the dunes, closing in at great speed.

"Loose!"

A stream of bolts was set off through the air. One line fired as the other reloaded after devastating the ghoul ranks. The barrage was intense, but not enough to land kills. Ophir observed, from a distance, two battles taking place.

The larger ghouls have fallen and the smaller are being dealt with. This has to end soon. We are running out of ammunition and should the sun set the night's cold would be terrible to contend with.

The ghouls were snared within a grid of bolts and flails. The steel web held the ghouls and caused them to halt their forward movement.

We may be able to keep them pinned, hoped Ophir. *If we can hold out a while longer, the Kryos can give support with the main force...*

Without an attack to aid Ophir's bombardment, the ghouls' inborn regeneration allowed for a quick recovery. Now, enraged by the martial resistance, they resumed their offensive with renewed fervour.

"Prepare to engage! As one, blades forward! One flail line forward!" commanded Ophir.

With the sounds of swords unsheathing and bolts equipping as Ophir prompted, the rear guard prepared to engage.

This is bad! If we cannot hold them the team will be exposed.

Glancing over at his friends, Ophir could see there was no chance that the main force would be able to assist them. The ghouls now streamed forward. Ophir raised his hand, then swiftly lowered it, sending forth a wave of flailed bolts to greet their enemies.

"Charge!" he commanded, discarding his defensive position.

If we die... it will be fighting!

CHAPTER 54

What started as an organized conflict became a chaotic collision. Many of the Terrans used the protruding flails to subdue their assailants while the others attacked. Ophir immediately found himself covered in ghoul blood, giving him the impression his men had the advantage. Despite the serious damage done by the flail round, the ghouls' vigour remained undeterred and many of the soldiers began taking serious injuries. Blood from both sides washed over Ophir's brigade and even with greater numbers, the ghouls proved to be too much.

A Terran scout, trying to keep control of a ghoul while his compatriots attacked with spears, was felled by his victim. Ophir leapt forward, interceding for his fallen subordinate, using his sword to brace against the ghoul's claw. Its massive strength pinned Ophir to the ground. Two Plainswalkers struggled against it, trying to keep the ghoul controlled with spears plugged deep within its frame. Ignoring the pain, the ghoul's wolf-like head inched closer to Ophir's face, threatening to devour the Terran. Its breath reeked of infectious decay as its drool slid off its jaws and onto Ophir's chin.

Vidar's men were occupied and fully consumed with the battle at hand. He took notice of the rear guard while strangling a ghoul with a flail. Vidar fell backwards, exposing the ghoul to a hail of spears.

The crowded battlefield blocked Vidar's view of Ophir. Rising to his feet, Vidar began to make his way to the rear, only to be blocked by another ghoul's rampage. Seeing Ophir being overpowered in the distance, the Kryos lord launched forward, hoping to break through the turmoil. His ambitions were crushed by the frenzied ghoul that had now repelled all the surrounding soldiers and attacked an unarmed Vidar. Its momentum forced Vidar to the ground. Vidar held the ghoul's jaws shut while clasping its wrist to keep its talons at bay.

This may be dangerous. But I have no choice.

Forcing ice to form over his thumbs, he pierced the eye and wrist of his attacker. An agonizing wail erupted from the ghoul as Vidar threw the beast into the fray, letting the surrounding carnage overtake it.

Seeing the rear-guard now being crushed, Vidar's heart sank and his cold blood boiled. He was going to signal a dispatch to re-enforce the rear when a shofar blew from afar. The soldiers had arrived in force. They quickly stormed the rear and gave aid to Ophirs forces. Vidar's battle cry sounded violently as he helped finish remaining ghouls and lead the charge to assist his friend.

*****

The battle finished before sunset. Ophir and Vidar gathered next to a ghoul's corpse. Vidar stood partially covered in ghoul blood that was now coalescing with his skin as it dried.

"These ones are about twenty feet tall, like the last one," Ophir said. "We will have to rush back to camp. If we are caught in the open at night, it will be dreadful for us."

"Agreed," admitted Vidar. "The bolts and injured are being gathered. Not long from now we move back."

Ophir noticed the sun was almost half way through its setting.

"Your plan did work. We made it before sunset," claimed Ophir.

"Of course. We win fast," said Vidar, walking off to aid his comrades.

Danir came next with a report.

"It looks like a little more than fifty are seriously injured. Stretchers are being brought out..."

As Danir reiterated his accounting for the day, Freyr passed them by, pulling a stretcher by himself with three injured piled on top of it. The two commanding officers looked at each other and then Danir resumed.

"None dead, sir," he continued. "Over a hundred have sustained minor injuries but should be able to ride. All the scouts have been called back. Should I send for one more sweep of the area?"

"No," Ophir said sharply. "I don't want any needless risks."

"Very good," replied Danir. "It is something of note that almost all of the seriously injured were bolt throwers."

"Where is Victor?" implored Ophir.

"Seeing to the injured with the rest of the team," answered Danir. "We killed twenty-three of them today, sir," he said proudly.

"We should take double tomorrow," Ophir responded confidently.

"How can you predict how many will attack us?" asked Danir.

"Because tomorrow we will begin hunting and attacking them," said Ophir noticing the sun had almost completely set. He ordered Danir to call for torches.

There was some yelling in the ranks to pass on the command and almost immediately, the dark desert filled with hundreds of beacons of flickering light. Raging against the cold, the soldiers rode with weapons bloodied from war and bodies tired from dehydration. Arriving at the camp victorious, mages properly treated the injured, ate, and slept. The next day would come bringing with it new worries *and* more enemies.

CHAPTER 55

Deep into the afternoon, Ophir and Vidar led a group of three hundred scouts close to the sunspire and halted there.

"Are they ready?" asked Ophir.

"Most likely," Vidar replied calmly.

"Ghouls?" questioned Ophir

"No word," said Vidar.

"Where is Sil?" asked Ophir

"With the scouts," answered Vidar.

"How long?" Ophir asked.

"A while now," Vidar said, unsure.

"Victor?" Ophir probed.

"Elsewhere," said Vidar.

"You sure we are where we're supposed to be?" pressed Ophir.

"Should be," returned Vidar.

There was a brief pause as Ophir stared through a crystal seer.

"We are *deep* in their territory. I hope this works," admitted Ophir.

A short while after their discussion, Aerial scouts were seen drifting toward the troop.

"It's them. Make ready," affirmed Vidar.

The Aerials approached with massive speed, leaving a large trail of sand streaming behind them. Sil halted at once in front of Ophir as the huge wave of sand followed. Lifting his hand, he dispelled the wave before it could engulf his friend and immediately gave his report.

"We rounded up as many as we could. They're coming."

"How many?"

"Over fifty," Silvanus shot back.

Before being seen, the ghouls could be heard as they approached with fierce rapidity.

"Every man, face ready!" shouted Ophir.

The bolt throwers were loaded.

"Steady! —Hold... Loose!"

A small wave of bolts flew through the air towards the ghouls. The second wave did the same. The hail of bolts was not enough to slow down their assault, but instead, enraged them into a more frenzied attack.

"I told you it would piss them off," Ophir told Vidar. The Kryos smiled and then raised a shofar and blew a loud blast.

After the horn blew, two hundred soldiers with bolt throwers emerged out of the sand. What was once a hail of bolts became a bombardment. Striking with flail spears from all directions caused great constriction in the ghouls' movements.

Seizing the opportunity, Vidar led the fatal assault against the surrounded and confined ghouls. With so many spears and chains running through their enemies, the Kryos could easily manipulate the ghouls and lead them to slaughter. An hour later, ghoul corpses littered the landscape and the mages were taking back the bolts for further use.

"Fifty-three in this raid. That's more than the last," sighted Danir.

"Sil and the Eras have given word that the southern dunes, before the spire that turns to the west, is cleared. This means half their population is gone," said Victor.

"Didn't see you there. You look a bit dirty," interjected Ophir. "Did you enjoy your wait under the sand?"

Victor smiled proudly and when the clean-up concluded, they marched back to the camp. Sitting around a heating sphere with food and drink, the team held their council.

"Alright then," started Paulo. "We have to begin to take a closer look at the spire."

"I have already sent for equipment. I think my research group can break off from the battle now. We should not be disturbed," said Ophir.

"What of the rest of the ghouls?" asked Vidar.

"They do not look like they will be approaching soon," said Sil. "We covered the desert and found the nearest of them to be leagues away."

"A distant threat is still a threat," sighted Victor.

"If we are going to start research, we should send most of our host home," added Danir. "Many are injured and most cannot take part in the march any more. At the base, they can rest and be cared for properly. They deserve it. This war has taken long enough."

"With the ghouls being as menacing as they were, I am surprised we out-fought them," admitted Paulo. "Last time it was such a disaster. Vidar, we owe you great thanks. Your strategy on the battlefield pulled us through."

"We work together, but you have been exhausting yourselves," discerned Vidar. "I think we should finish this. Let me take our forces and launch a final strike."

"The food supplies would never reach you," informed Paulo. "It's too great of a distance and too harsh of an environment. The last ghouls are into the deep west. We are in the south east. It is too far of a ride without a stop."

"What if Sil leads them to us?" Vidar asked.

"No good," responded Paulo. "The Aerials would die of thirst on the way. We cannot support an excursion so deep without a strong supply of water."

"They're still a threat," insisted Vidar.

"That may be," Paulo said. "But even if we do not consider food and water, almost half the soldiers are injured in ways that deter them from fighting. We are in no shape for a siege."

"Victor, what do you think?" Vidar urged.

Victor sat thinking, looking at his friends, reflecting on all that had been said. "Here is what will happen: Ophir, you begin a full examination of the sunspire. Focus *all* of your attention on that. Vidar, me, Sil and as many capable men as we have are going to cross the desert and finish what we started."

"How will that be possible? You will die of thirst. We do not have the available resources to build more outposts or dig more wells?" protested Ophir.

"Ophir," said Victor sternly. "You leave all this to me."

"If you continue the invasion, you will be placing yourself and whoever comes with you in danger," Ophir maintained.

"Do not worry about me, old friend," assured Victor, "I have a plan. Your work is more important. We cannot risk it being disturbed."

"With what soldiers will you make this attempt?" enquired Ophir.

"We currently have two hundred and eighty five soldiers in good shape. If we send back the injured and take one hundred more from the base, it will give us over three hundred to work with," answered Victor.

"Food, water, settlement, what about *these?*" pressed Ophir.

"We will travel with our tents, food and water," said Victor in response.

"You cannot possibly keep up supply. We have all went over the numbers," repeated Ophir.

"This operation will not take long. We will have enough food and we will have enough water," Victor replied confidently.

"How will any of this be possible?" insisted Ophir.

"I told you, I have a plan. You keep your attention on the sunspire. Let me worry about the ghouls," said Victor. "Let's all get some sleep. We will need to be in top shape for the days coming."

The team broke and as everyone headed to rest, Victor unexpectedly halted Vidar.

"Vidar, I need to see you and Olaf for a moment."

CHAPTER 56

A week later, the soldiers exchanged and Victor prepared to lead the new regiment out into the desert wilderness. On the way, they passed Ophir and the research group, now fully established and running tests. Breaking from the ranks, Ophir joined Victor.

"You sure you want to do this?" he asked.

"Of course. I am leaving Paulo at the base to aid you for scouting and to handle the day-to-day camp operations."

"Fair enough. Good journey, brother," said Ophir.

Victor nodded and silently led the dispatch away, followed by Vidar, Sil, and the Eras. Victor addressed the mages under his command.

"We have to move hard and cover as much ground as we can. There will be very little break between now and nightfall. Do not ration yourselves, drink as much water as you deem necessary. Okay boys, let's move!"

The mages became tired on the way, but pushed onward. With very little rest except to relive themselves, they ate mostly dried, light foods and drank a great deal of their water supply. At night, the tents were set, the scouts returned and guards posted. Victor summoned a group of Terrans, Vidar, and all the Kryos and set to work.

"Let's lay it out," said Victor.

The Terrans brought forward several large, tin vessels, about half a mage's size.

"Vidar, you and the others fill them," spoke Victor.

Vidar nodded and the Kryos took their places by a vessel. They began to focus their energy on creating a mass of ice within the tubs. Seconds later, the tins were filled. Victor inspected the finished work and then questioned Vidar.

"You feel alright? No exhaustion?"

"None," replied Vidar assured.

"So then, in the desert heat, your abilities are a disadvantage, but in the night's cold, you have full use of them. This is good and when all this melts, we will have a full supply of water for tomorrow," Victor said triumphantly.

Leaving the ice to melt, the team members returned to their nightly duties.

"So what do you think, Sil? Making full use of our compatriots' talents or what?" boasted Victor.

"Probably should have made more use of them nearer to the starting of the war. You know, with thirst being an issue and ice melting into water," Sil responded.

"If it was so obvious, why didn't you think of it?" said Victor.

"I'm really not the brains of this outfit," replied Sil with a large grin.

CHAPTER 57

The next day arrived and the caravan's excursion continued. They rode without lack of food or fear of thirst toward their enemy. Minor sandstorms accosted the contingent, but they were driven back by the Aerials. No signs of life were ever seen, only the sunspire shining in the distance.

Victor and Vidar paired alongside one another. Vidar's thoughts were pure, ready for battle. Victors mind was scattered. Many times he looked over at the spire, wondering if there really was some sort of mage-life behind it all.

"Tell them to hold here. We can rest in this valley," he informed Vidar, who gave the command to break.

Vidar, Silvanus and Victor sat close together, eating and drinking from their rations. Victor turned to Sil to ask about the scouting.

"Sil, have you seen any activity of note?"

"If I had, don't you think I would have told you?" he replied.

"We have been travelling for wo days, and we find nothing? They should have picked up on our presence by now," said Victor, slightly angered.

"Actually, there is *one* thing we found," remarked Sil, suddenly filling his mouth with food and taking a drink, causing a longer delay then Victor was willing to wait for.

"Go on," said Victor becoming more then a little annoyed.

"Well, crap is what we found," responded Sil.

"Crap?" questioned Victor.

"Yes," replied Sil.

"Crap, what?" grilled Victor.

"The ghouls leave their waste behind and bury it in the sand. There were some semi-fresh deposits dropped a mile back. They may be running from us or gathering together since they retreated from their documented territory. Either way, we are close," Sil spoke assuredly.

Victor, satisfied by Sil's report, smiled but felt somewhat odd about tracking a mortal enemy by its bathroom habits.

*****

At the sunspire, close to the camp, Ophir's research continued with little result. The mages donned protective masks to keep the light from blinding them. Any material they passed through the wall would either burn up or become melted and twisted.

Ophir and Danir were in full covering and as close to the spire as they could be without being incinerated. They had been working all morning. Ophir pointed toward the cantonment and the mages went in for a break. Removing his mask, Ophir revealed his sweat drenched face.

"Haven't you done this before?" Danir asked. "This is killing us. Between the desert temperature and the sunspire, we need water every thirteen minutes."

Ophir took a long drink just as Danir finished quenching his thirst.

"It's no good. We do not have any substance that can stand being placed through the intense heat," Danir said as he sat down to keep himself from falling.

Ophir, sitting down next to him in the shade of their encampment, took another drink and then began his criticism.

"We brought you here because you are an expert on breaking through walls. Why can't you think of something?"

Danir smiled.

"A wall of ice is solid. Light is insubstantial and it scorches us on our approach. The North Wall was so much more hospitable then the sunspire."

"So," Ophir continued, "you're saying we need an enormous drill?"

They both laughed and then continued their break with some food.

"We could try to work at night," suggested Danir.

"No good. We tried already when we first came. Overheating is followed by suddenly freezing to death in your own sweat," responded Ophir. "Let's rest for now. Hopefully something will come up."

*****

Deep in the western desert, Victor carried on with the expedition. As evening approached, the mages passed over a large hillside. In the valley below, the ghouls had gathered in force. Noticing the approaching mages, they sounded a defensive call that reverberated throughout the lifeless pasture enveloping them.

At first, Victor was frightened. Looking at Vidar he saw no fear at all in his face, only that same stoic expression. Victor always remained amazed at the Kryos. *They have no cause for grief or fear no matter what the situation.*

Noticing, Vidar look slightly towards him.

"You ready?" said Victor smiling.

The contingent moved forward in formation, slowly approaching the enemy.

"We can't let this last past twilight," informed Victor.

"Then we win fast," Vidar returned.

The ghouls began to gather. Soon they would become grouped and then charge as one. Before this could happen, the regiment created a foothold at the bottom of the dune and began arranging their artillery, leaving the dromedaries behind them in the rear position.

"We had the engineers put a little addition onto our lances," Victor said to Vidar and Sil. "They act more like hooks now. When they strike, we attach the flail end to the droms and send them riding, pulling the ghoul ranks apart. This won't last long. Vidar, your group is the strongest. Have them spread out, kill as many as they can and then reinforce our position."

At a loud command from Vidar, the mages marched forward. The ghouls were running in an almost tribal manner: circling around repeatedly, becoming frenzied and more aggressive, roaring and bearing their teeth, sometimes even striking each other.

This went on for a short time and then a large ghoul took the lead. Giving an ear-piercing howl, it stormed toward the mages. Over one hundred ghouls in the assault advanced at incredible speed. The mages, holding their ground, took aim and prepared, waiting for Victor's word.

"Loose!" ordered Victor, sending waves of bolts with long flailed chains into the swarm of oncoming ghouls. After the first wave struck into the moving group, Victor ordered the release of two others. Some ghouls took four bolts before they slowed. The next phase of splitting the ghoul ranks was set to work.

"Drom lines, fall back!"

At Victor's command, the dromedaries were driven away from the battlefield, dragging a great number of the ghouls forward. Victor gestured to Vidar who raised his fist and called out:

"All groups, break off!"

With that, many of the scouts formed into bands and pursued the fallen ghouls, taking advantage of their temporary vulnerability. The remaining scouts charged forward using the flails to bind their opponents. Other mages struck at them with spears through their faces and necks, turning the battle into a barbaric bloodbath. The slaughter went on for more than an hour. The soldiers efficiently carried out their duties and ultimately stood victorious over their adversaries.

Retrieving the bolts and winding the flails became difficult as the modified spearheads serrated the ghouls' flesh. As a result, the soldiers ended up soaked in the blood of their enemies during retrieval.

"What a smell," one Terran complained to a Plainswalker. "I hope I don't get any desert diseases from this."

The Plainswalker laughed as he wound the flails and unknotted them from one another. "You worry too much. If it kills you at least you won't feel this heat."

Both mages and others around them began laughing until Victor interrupted.

"Enough! Keep to your duties. We are still on enemy territory!"

The mages quickly settled and resumed their labour. Victor

gave them a harsh stare as he supervised their progress. Moving through the butchered remains, he met with Vidar to ask about the camp location and tent setup. With the sunset initiated, the cold dark would soon be setting in.

Before he spoke a word, a great roaring was heard in the distance. The team leader immediately jumped to action.

"Ready as many bolt throwers as you can! Call back Sil's scouting units and set lines forward!" shouted Victor.

The soldiers rallied in anticipation of the ghouls' advance. They formed ranks as the first ghouls came into view from the distance, against a setting sun. Moving on the back of the wind, Sil arrived.

"We don't have half the bolts retrieved and the sun is setting," shouted a Plainswalker.

"How many are there?" asked Victor.

"Not sure," said Sil.

"Vidar, ready the scouts. All units assemble!" shouted Victor.

Plainswalkers and Terrans with bolt throwers streamed forward, forming two rows. Scouts assembled behind with small spears. The Kryos stood at their forefront. The ghouls attacked in a scattered formation, making it difficult to use their normal strategy.

"Sir," reported one of the bolt operators to Victor. "We have limited ammunition and no flails."

"Alright then," said Victor not wanting to sound nervous. "Do we have cannonade?"

"Cannon aid?" asked the soldier with an unstrung tone.

"Black shells! Do we have mortars?"

"Ah…Yes! Yes Sir, we do!" The soldier replied assuring his commander.

Victor gave instruction to the surrounding infantry.

"Sunset is approaching. If we get caught in the cold, we're dead. After the first wave, reload and charge behind the scouts and Kryos. Set your targeting ahead of the charge. Strike the ghouls only. Do not let us get caught in the crossfire."

The ghouls' charge increased in speed. As they advanced, their screaming sent a heart-stopping chill into all the mages, except the Kryos.

"Stand ready!" Victor commanded.

More ghouls appeared and joined in the charge. To Victor, it seemed the landscape was overrun by the influx of ghouls rushing over the dunes.

"Loose!" Victor shouted, followed by a command to charge.

Large explosions littered the landscape upon the release of the black shells. The soldiers froze, observing the carnage and if not for Vidar's directive, the charge would have fallen short.

The mages, still covered in ghoul blood, reloaded as they advanced with the Kryos in the lead. The battle raged on fiercely with the desert sun setting into the backdrop as the night's cold readied its strike. For the mages, the war would be decided in the last moments of twilight.

CHAPTER 58

"Dammit, it's getting dark," protested Danir, against the sun's natural course.

"It's not like we're unable to work in the night," said Paulo, who had recently arrived with a fresh supply of water for the research team.

"I am not in the mood to freeze to death," replied Danir.

"So overheating then," suggested Ophir. "A better choice, I'm sure."

"It is really strange that an anomaly named after the sun gives off so little heat. All of the power is focused within the effulgence," said Danir. "You know what this means, right?"

"Effulgence?" questioned Paulo, "No. Actually, I think it means you have a better command of Plains Speak then I do."

"It *means* this thing is artificial. This light is being somehow concentrated. We are closer now than we ever have been to figuring out what it is and why it was created," responded Danir.

"Alright then. Why was it created?" asked Paulo.

Danir breathed out heavily before he answered.

"No idea so far. But we are still close," Danir said assuredly.

Ophir smiled.

"Well, night is coming. Let's get some last minute recordings done."

*****

At the battleground, Vidar and Victor were cleaning blood off the bolts while the soldiers continued with the recovery. The setting sun in the distance gave a faint red glow, illuminating the landscape with the last of strength.

"Not as many as we thought," commented Victor to Vidar. "We will have to make camp close by. Maybe try to get some flat ground, closer to the spire and tell the Terrans to bring bloodstones and fire globes."

Silvanus glided in with the Eras as the clean-up was underway. "Nothing," he said quickly. "Completely blank."

"Good. How far out did you guys go?" question Victor.

"Far," Sil responded.

"Alright. Call back all scouts. Take half the force and set up camp. Me and Vidar will continue the clean-up. Do it quickly."

"Of course," said Sil, rushing off.

Vidar was giving directions to the other officers as the landscape darkened.

"Not long now. We will be finished soon," he informed Victor.

As the clean-up progressed, Vidar and Victor became tired and ordered the mages to finish up with one more sweep. Walking toward the camp Vidar noticed a small cactus.

"I did not know plants could grow in this part of the desert."

"They can, but the ghouls tend to eat them. That's why you see none around," Victor explained.

"They eat those? No wonder why they are always so enraged. They live in a desert and eat those *things*," responded Vidar, making Victor laugh.

"I wonder how many are left?" enquired Victor. "The mortars really pulled us through."

"We are lucky none of our own were injured," said Vidar. "Terran explosives strike too wildly."

Upon entering the camp, both leaders noticed the sunspire's glow kept the area they were staying in to be well lit. The Kryos prepared ice in the large trough like tubs. With carnelian fire globes beneath, the ice melted so water would be available for drinking and washing.

The mages surrounded the troughs almost immediately and began to wash the blood and sweat of war off their bodies. Another trough was set up to feed the dromedaries. Vidar, Victor and Sil gathered in one of the tents when Victor noticed the sunspires colouration began to change.

"Vidar, look," pointed Victor.

The sunspire shifted from its normal golden hew to a deep red and orange mix. The spire itself seemed to vibrate as the colours transposed. Eventually, a full chromatic spectrum brightly illuminated the sky. The mage camp stood in awe while partially shielding their eyes to keep the newly emerging brilliance from blinding them.

*****

Danir, staring at the sunspire in total astonishment, tapped Ophir with his elbow.
"Are you noticing this?"
"Sort of," Ophir responded, with his arm now covering his eyes.
"What did you guys do?" shouted Paulo.
"We don't know," responded the two Terrans together.
The impressive blaze radiated a brilliant mix of all possible colours and seemed to become progressively more intense until an overwhelming white flash exploded forth and then extinguished.
The lights ceased and the mages were left with their eyes needing to adjust. When their vision returned, Danir spoke first.
"The sunspire. It's gone!"

CHAPTER 59

"What just happened?" yelled Ophir rubbing his eyes. "What did you do?"

"Me!" responded Danir. "I thought it was you!"

The entire research team was now staring toward where the sunspire used to be. The darkness settled after their vision returned to focus and night overpowered their dominion. The mages stood silently, not sure of what to do next. Paulo noticed a faint glimmering and ran forward to investigate.

Ophir watched as his friend disappeared into the darkness. In his mind Ophir protested, but the thoughts never formed words. He and the others waited to hear what was happening. Minutes passed. Ophir became impatient and tapped Danir on the arm.

"Let's go."

"Ophir!" Paulo suddenly shouted. "You have to see this!"

Every mage followed Ophir into the darkness. They moved briskly through the cold, gaining speed as they ran. Paulo met them as they came, placing both his hands on Ophir's shoulders to stop him.

"This way," he said. "Look down there."

Paulo lead the mages to a ridge and gazing down, a deep valley filled with shimmering lights appeared. The mages, now even more astonished then with the first light show, stood in awe, looking at what appeared to be stars blanketed over a vast concave surface.

"The sunspire was not a wall—it was a covering," declared Paulo.

The desert night surrounding them became impossible to notice once they set their eyes on the lights spread through the depth of the valley.

"What is it?" asked Danir.

"I think it's a city," said Paulo.

Ophir continued staring at the scintillating paradise, wondering what mages inhabited the visual resplendence. As if his thoughts triggered intended responses, large cylindrical lights were casted towards Ophir and his group.

Arranged like a pathway from the settlement below, the lights illuminated not like torches or Terran bloodstones, but as if a small portion of the afternoon sun was being aimed in their direction. Noticing how absolute the lighting was, many of the mages began standing within the emanated radiance.

"Ophir, stand here!" yelled Danir. "This light emits warmth."

Many of the mages stood directly within its glow and held their arms out to feel the contrast with the desert cold. While they revelled in the spotlights, Ophir took notice of the light's origin.

"This light is a path leading to us," he said sternly.

"Look there!" Paulo added, calling attention to the light's source.

A stream of what looked like stars followed the light and began crossing over the ridge. As the 'stars' approached, their forms became more distinguishable as sentient beings with an encompassing brilliant glow from their bodies. Like a river of pure light, hundreds of them moved effortlessly up the steep side of the ridge. Paulo took out a crystal seer, observed for a moment, then turned to Ophir and whispered.

"Let's make some room."

"Right," said Ophir, "everyone back. Three big steps, give them some room."

When the glowing-light mages arrived at the top of the ridge, they stopped short of crossing its boundary. Now, face to face, the Terrans and Plainswalkers looked as though they were seeing aliens from another planet rather than mages from their home world.

Their glowing was less intense when melded against the path of light that led them. They all had thin bodies and were dressed in long flowing garments of white. An array of coloured embroidery, decorative necklaces, bracelets, and ornaments splayed over their bodies. This, mixed with their natural glow, gave them a sparkling aura. A large crowd had amassed and stood opposite to Ophir and his research party.

"They are *glowing*," whispered Paulo. "I did not ever think mages could glow."

"Our eyes glow," contested Ophir.

"That made sense. You lived in the dark. This is a desert. What's their excuse?" said Paulo. He stopped for a second, realizing his last comment sounded more like Sil.

A light mage with a white, glimmering beard and bald head, clothed in a long white cloak and a sash of jewelled embroidery stepped forward.

"Aftoí eínai oi íroes!" he shouted causing the entire crowd with him to cheer.

"It seems they're happy to see us," Ophir said to Paulo smiling.

The bearded mage offered his hands outstretched at chest level toward Ophir with a big smile. Ophir was unsure as how to respond and raised his arms slowly, only to have them grasped by the joyful mage. The rest of the crowed swamped the contingent. The light mages examined their clothing and their skin, obviously wondering why there was no glowing. After a while, the bearded leader raised his voice and calmed the crowed. He then gave instructions to guide their new companions down into the city below.

CHAPTER 60

The path-light vanished as Ophir and his soldiers were lead to the edge. The steep drop between the ridge and the city had steps fashioned into the rock, making it look like a canyon-sized stadium. The masonry was excellent, with the smallest steps at the ridge's top that became progressively larger as the mages descended.

Ophir and Danir immediately took notice of the stonework. Both Terrans looked at each other with a wordless expression of veneration. Standing ahead of them, their guide continued to give instruction in his native tongue. Paulo was unsure if he were addressing them or the retinue accompanying him. Paulo and Danir looked at each other, somewhat confused, as they carried on down the immense wall of steps.

Arriving at the bottom of the ridge, the beautiful spectrum of lights seen from a distance revealed itself as a myriad of structures made entirely of modified glass. The city's constant brilliance blotted out almost all of the surrounding desert night and gave off natural warmth, creating a comfortable temperature for the inhabitants. As they entered the city, the whole population was there to welcome them. The children gave shy stares and mages of all ages greeted them with smiling faces; some light mages even in tears.

"Do you know what's going on?" Ophir asked Paulo.

"Not *yet*," Paulo replied.

Most of the crowd followed closely behind them as they traversed the new realm. The team immediately noticed the city's diverse architecture. Glass buildings of every size and shape created an edifying presentation of this mage nation's ability. The crystal-like structures not only gave radiance and heat, but also reflected a rainbow spectrum of colour that shone overhead across the municipality. Sparkling wisps floated randomly throughout the city limits adding to the spectacular exposition, flaring up and then burning out, making it seem that even this nation's dust was luminescent.

The first structure that caught Ophir's eye was an immense dome formed into a pentakis dodecahedron. Staring in total amazement, Ophir pointed to it and was directed within the building. Inside the striking building was an unexpected appearance of leafy plants, a variety of vegetable produce, and a gleaming ball of light from the top of spherical chamber, acting as an artificial sun. A series of sprinklers diffused a mist, covering the contained environment and making the entire building cool and moist.

Rows of almost every type of produce, tightly filled the interior, many of which Paulo had never seen. After touring the greenhouse, they were ushered outside and taken through the city.

On the way, a pair of performers caught their attention. With short, shining golden-brown hair and trimmed sparkling brown beards, they dressed in the same white robes but with less decorative coverings.

In front of them, children sat smiling. The two spoke in exaggerated pitches and made wide gestures. As the show continued, the light mages drew out clear marquise-shaped glass shards. With their tools in hand, they produced an array of colours which then formed the image of a large, red-skinned ghoul with two horns. Out of instinct, Ophir immediately grasped his sword. The conjured beast began to walk and move in normal ghoul fashion. However the absence of sound allowed the storytelling to continue.

"They look so real," said Paulo raising his hand to touch the illusion, only to find it pass right through.

The people watching the show listened attentively, entranced by the entertainer's narrative. A second mage standing in the background lifted a glass shard. Instantly, an army of Terran and Plainswalker mages came marching right through the crowd toward the beast.

A fight broke out with the storytellers commentating on the battle and at the end the ghoul fell and dissipated. The soldiers raised their hands in triumph then exploded into a kaleidoscope of colours, making the children laugh with excitement and the older mages smile. After the light show the storytellers addressed the crowd.

"*Ladies and gentlemen, here with us are the real heroes, the ones who defeated the Ifrit.*"

He spoke in a tongue the team could not recognize and pointed at the team members. The entire crowd cheered, exploding into applause not for the storytellers, but for the guests.

"That was amazing," came Silvanus familiar voice. "Paulo, why can't your people do these things?"

"Sil, where are the others?" Paulo asked.

"I sped ahead. They're behind, you know... somewhere," said Sil dubiously.

Shortly afterwords the rest of the team caught up. Many of them were wearing the white robes that were common to the populace.

"Look at you!" exclaimed Ophir. "Getting used to the native culture?"

"Something like that," responded Victor. "We were covered in ghoul blood. They gave us baths and a new set of clothing."

"Look at Vidar's legs, all that icy, light-bluish goodness," interrupted Sil.

Vidar glared at him, not sure what to say, with a slight scowl on his face. The team laughed and re-joined as their tour continued.

CHAPTER 61

"What did you think of the show?" asked Ophir to Victor.

"Saw one just like it on the way over," Victor replied. "It seems to be a popular theme for the occasion."

"Occasion?" questioned Ophir.

"I am certain we wiped out the last of the ghouls and those creatures kept this nation from expanding their society."

The whole city was in celebration. Mages everywhere were seen expressing gratitude toward the team members. Joy seemed to permeate the entire city, culminating in a national festival.

"This is probably the most unique people we have ever come across. How were they not able to fight for themselves?" asked Ophir.

"Look around," said Vidar. "Do you see any warrior class among these mages? Aside from the sunspire, which was employed defensively, I have not seen the resemblance of any soldier or warrior within the city."

As they proceeded, a large, clear building came into view. Square shaped and transparent on all sides, it was filled with children playing and ladies creating spectral illusions for their amusement. They walked along, seeing buildings of all colours and shapes and one in particular stood out. It was taller that the others and had a lateen appearance. Covered mostly with a solid, opaque, light-blue colouring, it had a surrounding outline of clear crystal-like material encasing the entire construction.

Victor and the others greatly admired the super-structure and in unspoken acknowledgement, their guide and many attendants entered the premises. Inside, there were multi-level platforms with winding stairs connecting them, giving the place an open-concept design. Every level was visible from the main floor and no walls existed to separate them. They simply protruded from the side of the interior. Some levels were long and rectangular, others were square and situated in no definite pattern. They were spaced far from one another, creating a disorganized arrangement of thick glass landings leading straight to the building's top.

As if on cue, lights began to shine from all directions and the team saw replicas of themselves. A short time after, a green colouration spread across the main floor and plant life filled the room. Birds flew through the air, horses galloped passed them and large serpentine creatures slithered at their feet. Then, slowly, all the animals and their habitat blurred vanishing from sight, revealing light mages on the upper platforms staring down at them.

The whole building seemed dark after the illusions disappeared. Numerous columns of natural light shone in through small window-sized openings in the structure's frame. As Vidar looked up to see the platforms, he found himself inadvertently bathed in sunlight.

One of the guides, seeing his predicament, acted quickly by raising his hand and repelling the light stream upwards. Vidar watched in amazement at the light, now standing straight up in front of them. The guide's abilities were so proficient that even when he turned his attention away from the light, it remained shining upwards. Vidar continued to stare at the unnaturally reflected light. He even placed his hand within the stream to test the '*sturdiness*' of the illumination.

The guide shouted some orders in his own language and the light mages moved to the platform edges. Holding up their glass fragments, they caused the light to be drawn within. The building emptied of its lighting left it almost entirely blackened. Tiny hints of extravagant shades of orange and red appeared over a skyline. Shortly after, a fiery ball blazed over the horizon.

A great sunrise engulfed their vision. It was so absolute that the entire space they were standing in disappeared. The team stood for minutes transfixed by the rising suns beauty. The revelation of a huge body of water and lightly clouded sky followed. After all this transpired, the colours began to fade and slowly, disappeared.

"I have never seen a sunrise that close," spoke Vidar.

"These people are awesome," Silvanus said enthusiastically.

The platform building slowly returned to its original state and the team's eyes adjusted to the reversion. There was total silence… until, Danir began to clap slowly and the rest of the team joined in. The room quickly filled with applause and appreciative shouts. Exiting the building, the team and the light mages alongside them, were smiling and laughing. Danir walked close to Ophir.

"So, was that an entertainment theatre like the ones in Nebat?" he asked.

"No," interrupted Paulo. "That was a training facility. Did you notice the ages of the mages in there? Even though this city seems strange and chaotic with its architecture, each building has a distinctive purpose. Some for food, day cares, and in this case, training of the younger mages. Victor, I need to talk to you."

Holding Victor's wrist, he lowered his voice to a whisper.

"Did you notice?" he said quietly.

"Notice what?" replied Victor.

"Birds, forest, plant life, horses, animals, the trees?" said Paulo sternly.

"I definitely noticed them," said Victor confused.

"Everything we saw in there besides the sunrise does not exist in the desert *or* this city. Many of those animals are exclusive to *our* homeland."

This stunning realization held Victor silent for a short while, waiting for Paulo to give an explanation.

"What does this mean?" Victor questioned.

"It means they have contact with the outside world."

CHAPTER 62

Leaving the large, lateen-shaped structure, the mages proceeded toward a palace gleaming golden at the centre of the city. As the escort continued, Silvanus stepped off to the side of the road enticed by a group of light mages standing behind small, rectangular tables. On the tables were rows of wine glasses filled with varying amounts of liquid. As the mages used their fingers to circle the rims. Sounds of pitched rhythms surprised him.

Like violins from the Plains Land, the glass seemed to sing in melodic notes. As the concert progressed, colours began to emanate in spectral-like succession. The deeper notes pulsated with red, orange and yellow colours which lead into higher pitched notes of green and blue. As the notes became even higher and more precise, purple and violet colours emerged, completing the colour spectrum. At the end of the performance, the team stood again in awe at the beauty that this world presented. A unanimous applause spread throughout the crowd.

"The glass can sing," said Vidar, totally amazed yet again.

"That was beautiful," Danir asserted. Moving closer to the glass instrument to investigate. "It is like a glass harp. I never would have expected glass to have such properties."

"Really, I thought this was crystal," added Sil.

"No, we could manipulate the properties if that were so," responded Danir. "There is no crystal within this city. It is made completely of an enhanced glass substance."

The multitude of mages continued through the city. More than ever, the population was in an enthusiastic uproar. Taking down the sunspire had become a significant event. Whenever the team passed the light mages would gesture in appreciation by crossing two hands over their chest, raising them to their mouths and then lowering their hands towards the team, as if to blow a kiss.

"Where do you suppose they get the materials for all this?" Victor asked Ophir.

"Glass is made from silica. This material is actually found in sand and I have no doubt that it is in great abundance. As for the thickness and the colour, their natural abilities seem to compensate for extracting the different variations. The same way my people use minerals, stones and ores," Ophir replied.

"Makes sense," agreed Victor.

As the team approached the palace, its golden glow was almost overwhelming, yet it calmed once they reached the base. Now, the team faced a huge stairway that matched the one on the outskirts of the city.

The palace was not as tall as many of the other buildings. Instead, it was much longer than any the team had seen and the brightness pouring from it outmatched all the other structures surrounding it.

The guide called forth some of his attendants and they raised their hands, facing the glowing stronghold. Their actions placated the strength of its brilliance allowing their guests to see clearly. Standing at the top of the stairs, ready to greet them, were three beings that seemed to be of almost pure light.

Their guide quickly ascended the stairway, bowed and then placed his hand in front of the beings' faces. This calmed the power of their natural radiation.

The three beings at the palace entrance were not like those encountered within the city. Light covered their bodies and they glowed in an intensity that out shown the other light mages. The leader wore a square breastplate with twelve glass gems of different colours set into the centre.

These are the elders of this mage society, thought Ophir.

Of the three that stood before them, two were male and one was female. The males had white sparkling beards that glimmered as they walked. Their eyes shone, making whatever they looked at illuminate. Halos emanated from their heads. As they moved, not only was light emitting from them, but was also drawn towards their bodies, causing a field of clear light waves to accompany their motions.

The lady was different; beautiful in every way, her hair was almost solid gold, flowing long past her shoulders. Her blue eyes illuminated all she stared at. Her slender frame's aura permeated a silken single-piece robe and a long necklace of thin glass jewels that dropped down past her chest. All of them had cheerful faces and greeted the new arrivals with a warm countenance. The guide then addressed the audience waiting below.

"In honour of this momentous occasion, a great feast has been prepared. The elders wish you welcome."

"Well, it looks like we're going in," said Danir excitedly.

The group ascended the stairway with a host of the light mages behind them while their guide waited at the top with the three elders. Inside the palace the team encountered anomalous, shining glass walls. Constant mirages floated around, making rooms look bigger or colourful. Sometimes, what seemed like ghosts faded in and out of perception. Colours cascaded through the palace without restriction. Organized chromatic rays merged into a spectral composition that coursed throughout the building. Paulo soon discovered that oftentimes a torrent of colour would disappear the moment he approached.

"Have you noticed," asserted Victor, "none of their buildings have doors."

Before they could dissect any cultural significance from the observation, the conversation was halted by a loud smack.

"Ow, damit!" yelled Sil, after walking into wall.

The guide immediately came to his assistance with a deep look of empathic concern, while the rest of the team laughed.

"This whole place looks like it's shifting!" said Sil in defence of his own stupidity.

"Sil, walk calmly. This is an environment we are not used to," claimed Paulo.

"Yeah, an environment right in my face!" replied the Aerial in an outburst of nonsensical rage.

"You," Sil demanded, pointing to the guide, "come here!"

The guide obliged and Sil grabbed his wrist.

"Now, let's go."

The team laughed again, inciting Sil to respond in his usual way. "What? I don't see him hitting any walls."

They were lead through the palace and presented in front of an assembly of what was obviously the ruling class of elders. It was hard to tell how many of them were present and even harder to tell the layout of the chamber they had entered.

The light flowing from these beings was intense. The whole room filled with a blazing golden-white illumination that made it almost impossible to look directly at them. Even the light mages with them averted their eyes.

Only when the guide and some of the others with him stepped up and repeated the action at the palace entrance did it become tolerable for the team to be in the same area. After the guide used his technique, the elders' light became progressively softer and their appearance perceivable.

All of the light mages bowed before their elders on both knees. The team did the same. The guide gave an introduction and one of the elders rose from his seat. He motioned for the team to rise and then, with a hand gesture, caused the room to fill with replicas of the team members. After a short while, they blurred and became absorbed by the light present in the room.

There was silence. Then the guide said something to Victor while motioning with both his hands to encourage a response. Victor stood looking at Paulo who shrugged.

"I get it," said Vidar. "They want to see what we can do."

The Kryos smiled at his statement and stepped forward ready to impress. Raising both of his hands, he created an ice spear and then, touching it lightly against the ground, froze much of the floor around him. Many of the mages surrounding him were forced to step back or risked being overrun by a surge of ice.

When Vidar finished his demonstration, Sil presented himself and began to float, rising slowly upwards, secretly hoping not to hit an invisible roof hidden by a mirage. He flew around the room and caused a light breeze upon his decent.

Ophir held a jasper stone in his right hand, open for all to see. He closed his hand and focused his efforts on extracting its energy.

Ophir's skin became covered in strong, red armour. He turned to Vidar, who nodded picking up a piece of his creation and smashed it against Ophir; Ophir didn't move. Vidar did this once more, than returned to his position and bowed to the respective authorities. Victor was next in line and all the elders were now staring at him.

"I have no trees to talk to here…" he started saying.

Paulo put Victor's hand on his shoulder to quiet him and stepped forward.

"Ha! No trees here is right," sneered Sil making jest of his friend's awkward situation.

Vidar gave him a light backhand, promptly shutting Sil up. Paulo took from his pouch some soil and placed it on the ground in a pile. Then he took some seeds, displayed them to the elders and planted them within. Paulo held his hands over top and closed his eyes. The court stared intently as small vines began to emerge. They grew rapidly until a shrub blossomed, sprouting berries that ripened moments later. He pulled off one of the larger berries and handed it to an elder. The elder took it, examined its features, and then ate it. He began to smile as his tongue absorbed the berry's sweetness.

"A frontiersmen's technique," said Paulo, retorting Sil's remark.

The elders of the city gave orders in their own language, causing the light mages in the room to rise and escort the guests to a chamber close by, where a thick glass table hosted clear dishes with a feast waiting for the cohort.

CHAPTER 63

The light mages crowded around the large rectangular table, incessantly analyzing the team. The moment any of the team addressed one the glowing mages, they would go silent, as if trying to absorb their guest's intentions through sheer focus. The food was served and after a blessing from the elders, they began to eat. Not long into the meal it was noticed that no meat or animal products were presented.

Danir leaned over to Vidar.

"Looks like this is a vegetarian society."

"Which would mean?" Vidar replied.

"No meat," said Danir.

Vidar looked puzzled for a short while, then responded.

"It's fine. I will just eat more."

Victor ate rapidly. With the day's latest discovery, he had ignored his hunger. As he drank, Paulo disclosed his findings.

"We know that this mage community uses light as a means for adaptation. Their elders are able to actually emit it from their bodies and they could see beyond the spire *even* when it was enclosed around them."

Victor stared at Paulo. Victor's mouth was full of his meal, only partly consumed. He chewed slowly as if not to interrupt his thought process.

"All except the elders use a glass instrument and ornamentation to draw the light in. Even their structures are made of it. Did you happen to see how they make their glass?"

"No. We did see a huge dome used for farming though," responded Paulo.

"There were others like that where we entered. A group of them on the outskirts – exclusively farming," conveyed Victor. "Never saw any glass creation though."

The meal came in stages and every dish prepared was artwork.

Many of the team members deliberately slowed their consumption, feeling slightly bereaved that their hunger could destroy such a beautiful design. The feast went on for hours with the light mages conversing and the team enjoying their food. One of the elders rose, summoning the attention of those seated. His eyes glowed a bright, silver light that gave his gaze a more magnanimous demeanour. He raised his hand to quiet the hall.

A respectful silence engulfed those seated as they fixed their attention on their leader. He called forth an attendant who presented an opaque, marble chest. Paulo wondered how they came across a rock to rare for the desert and assumed that it was made of a thick, coloured glass. The elder opened the chest and within it rested six small glass pyramids. Choosing one, he dismissed the attendant. Placing the pyramid on the table, he lifted his hand and sent a stream of light into it, which caused a prism of colour to flood the room.

The elder returned to his seat as the colours began without any visible manipulation. They transformed the table into the landscape of the Auren Desert. The team looked on, amazed, watching winds cross the dunes, leaving waves in the sand.

Marching figures appeared in rows. At first, it looked as if they were viewed from a distance. As they advanced and the images enlarged, it became clear that they were mages. Eventually, half the desert surface was covered and, from the opposite end, what looked like miniature ghouls began to appear. Both sides stood ready to face each other.

"Herein is the history of our people and conflict with the ifrit, development of our nation and raising of the spectral wall," declared the elder who was standing a moment ago.

"*Ifrit*," mentioned Ophir to Victor. "It's a word I have heard many times. I believe what we call ghouls are actually called *ifrit* by the locals."

A battle between the two sides began. The mages of the desert used what looked like obelisk-shaped glass tools, channelling coloured rays as a means of combating the ifrit menace. The details were so clear and real, it looked as if a little world actually existed before them. Even the glass weapons the mages were using could be seen completely.

Sil reached out to touch the desert landscape. Instead of just passing through or blurring the image as they saw earlier on the street and in the training facility, his hand actually transformed into the desert landscape. His whole arm became the colour and texture of the brown desert sand. The illusion actually began to extend itself onto his body. Sil panicked, jumped back, and pulled his arm free from the table. The Aerial's heart froze, watching the image remain fixed before slowly fading away, leaving his arm as it once was. The others only regarded Sil's antics as a slight distraction, not wanting to divert their attention from the show. Sils' guide gently welcomed him back to his seat.

The fight did not last long with the mages driving back their opponents and then celebrating the victory. A city of glass was abruptly erected. The ifrit attacked again, destroying it. The mages forced them back a second time and a greater city rose, which again came under siege. The light mage defenders defeated the ifrit again The city expanded to over three times its size and the ifrit invaded. This time, the mages weaponry did not have the same effect. The entire community joined their strength, creating a gigantic incinerating blast, exterminating most of the ifrit and killing many of the light mages.

After this battle, mirrors were set along the corners of the city and light was reflected, striking each mirror and creating a web over the city. The beams enhanced until the web became a covering, thus explaining the sunspire.

"So, they had trouble with the ifrit's ability to become stronger after healing from injury," suggested Ophir. "The light mage weapons were unable to repel them in their current form."

The story finished and the table returned to its normal shape and look. The elder returned the pyramid to its former location in the chest. He walked from his seat at the head of the table to the corner where the team and their comrades were seated. Standing across from the team, with a content face, the elder placed his hand on his chest saying: "Apollos," then waited.

Victor, suddenly realizing what was happening stood up, hand at his chest in the same manner, replying, "Victor."

"Victor," said the elder with his unique accent.

The others began to follow his action, introducing themselves as well.

"Vidar," responded the ice mage, who answered with his newly acquired habit of bowing.

"Ophir."

"Paulo."

Signalling to the guide who had brought them, the elder chose those four mages for some unknown purpose. The guide hurried the four mages after the elder, who had already begun his departure from the dining chamber. The four mages were encouraged to follow, with their guide urging them on.

"What is this about?" asked Victor to Ophir.

"Not sure exactly, but it shouldn't be long before we know," he responded.

CHAPTER 64

They walked for longer than Victor expected. Shifting lights created constant illusions that the rooms were smaller then they seemed. Walls would sometimes appear transparent but, upon approach, the lights would shift and it became opaque glass. Without the crowd to guide them, Victor took the lead while the others followed in single file behind Apollos, so as not to strike against any walls that may suddenly appear.

"I get it," declared Paulo. "The walls, the changes, this happens nowhere else in the city. This palace does not absorb light because the elders here manifest so much of it; they cause all of these phenomena to occur."

The team members watched closely. As the elder moved, every slight gesture and careless motion of his arms sent light throughout the room. At first it was hard to notice, but upon carful inspection it became very apparent. These mages were the most advanced in the light mage community. The shining palace they inhabited did not glow because of its construct; The elders within were the source of the splendorous display. Their light was so bright and focused that the structure itself visibly changed as they shone upon its corridors. Visual illusions caused phantasms to randomly appear and in the next instant vanish, as if what was seen had never really been. Their presence distorted reality; for them, there was never darkness and nothing could remain hidden.

Upon entering a chamber of colossal size, the mages saw a clear, round table. A glass sphere protruded from the center of the table. Four feet above the sphere hung an immense instrument shaped like a ram's horn. The entire apparatus was fixed to the wall of the chamber and no matter where the mages stood, the light it reflected made it uncomfortable to stare at it for too long at it. Apollos raised his hand, calming the aura, giving the team a complete view of the chamber, the table and the strange horn-like device.

The horn had uneven ridges throughout its composition, making it look like its construction consisted of fused together individual pieces to complete the development.

"What do you think that's for?" asked Victor.

"To sound the alarm," replied Vidar, in a rare moment of humour.

Realizing that the room had no covering, Paulo pointed to the ceiling. They stood in silence as the elder motioned for them to approach the table. The whole room and the large horn looked to be made of clear crystal.

Apollos touched the small tip of the horn and then lightly moved his hand over the sphere, revealing that it spun independently. As this happened, a small, window-sized image of the light mages gathering water from one of the wells in the city materialized over the table. Apollos settled on this image for a while before a soft turn of the globe shifted the scene.

Light mages working over what seemed like large ovens quickly became apparent as a display for glass production. Light mages diligently worked in a big factory while the team watched over them. Another slight spin of the orb and the camp where Ophir was stationed came into view. Paulo was then hit with a realization.

"This device... it's used for *seeing*," he said surprised. "It's like a seeing-horn."

A stronger downward spin of the sphere and the stars in the night sky became visible within the chamber. The team members became excited and started to laugh. Apollos spun to the left with a slight move of the horn and Vidar's home world came into view.

Vidar's eyes widened as a smile creased his face in an uncommon display of emotional demonstration. Apollos magnified certain locations, giving an in-depth view. The North Wall, the Palace of Nebat, the Aerial Realm, the colonies and a host of other areas were passed through for the team to behold. They even showed them a small dew bug nest on the plains. There was no restriction as to the light mages' capabilities.

"How is this possible?" asked Victor.

"It's light!" responded Paulo. "It draws the light in and with it the images that it carries. Look, we have not seen Ophir's homeland since the sun doesn't shines there. But everywhere else - it draws the images toward it rather than magnifying the visual as a crystal seer would."

The mages stood in awe as the whole world, from the ocean to the skies, was revealed to them. Apollos brought up a visual of the southern wastes where the volcanoes had been erupting. The largest volcano looked almost like an enormous crater with smoke ever-rising from its mouth.

With jade armour, Terrans could enter but never stay long. The intense heat from the lava flow made it too dangerous. The light mages, with their glass artifice and developed technology, could see everything without risk. The exhibition continued under Apollos' control, entering the crater and proceeding into its core.

Deep within, many small, dark, hut-like structures made of volcanic ash became visible. A hidden society was revealed. It was a vast metropolis situated deep under the bedrock and home to mages shaped like sentient flames. Perpetual streams of magma acted as a transport within their community. Their bright red skin gave them the look of fire. Dark embers of burning rock covered their chests and waists, making them look as if they were dressed in coal. This conveyed the appearance of flame and mage merged into a single being.

Another slight wave of his hand and Apollos transferred the image from a small, floating display into a large room-filled presentation. The mage city within the volcano enveloped the elder, Victor, Vidar, Paulo and Ophir. The fire mages went about their familiar activities, unaware of the observers.

Vidar reached out to touch one of the fiery mages only to have his hand pass through. The team stood amazed. This civilization, unlike the others before them, had actually known not only that mage-life existed, but also where to find them and how they functioned. Apollos adjusted the display back as a window over the small table.

"That was amazing!" said Paulo.

"There are mages that live in volcanoes," said Ophir, completely astonished.

"Maybe we should have discovered these ones first?" added Vidar.

"This explains how they saw the horses and birds," said Victor to Paulo.

The light mage elder then manoeuvred the large seeing tool again and in a flash, brought them to the Plains land of the west coast in a bird's eye view. Moving from the shore out into the sea, large waves spread across the tides surface like a flowing mountain range.

 Apollos looked at them, waved his hand and the room filled again, this time with the ocean's presence. Instinctively, Vidar inhaled deeply as they descended into the depths of the sea. A vision of water filled their surroundings. Schools of fish swam past them. Proceeding deeper, they saw creatures never before. The sea monsters encountered on their ice sailing with Vidar were also glimpsed, moving in herds with their young.

Vidar laughed and a grin spread over his face, taking in the sights with a childlike wonder. Giant, tentacled beasts and long, serpentine creatures weaved and glided alongside the team. The creatures of the sea unknowingly held the team in a trance as the mages observed the animals' behaviours and motions. The team became comfortable and started to move around the room, analyzing the underwater life forms. A colourful coral reef made an appearance in their visual expedition as if signalling the ending to the opening of a concert.

Strangely coloured fish, large crabs and other creatures went about their normal activities, oblivious to the surveillance. Past the reef, a school of medium-sized fish was being fed upon by a group of sharks. This made Ophir, who was now more than a little fascinated, almost ask Apollos to slow down and allow him time to further examine this previously unknown world.

Even hundreds of feet below the ocean, there were large fields of vegetation. Incredibly thick plants that looked like pillars extended endlessly upwards. Long silky leaves growing off the stalks of the plants tangled together with their neighbours, creating a dense atmosphere. Apollos slowed their tour down considerably. They continued as fish swam through the forest peacefully. Passing deeper within, the forest became denser. Gradually, in a very compact area, the visual settled. Nothing but the underwater foliage was seen. The mages looked at one another, then around the room.

"Why did he stop?" asked Victor.

"Not sure," responded Paulo.

Parts of the underwater forest began moving as if in answer to their question. From within the silky outgrowth, movements shook the stalks. Three blue-skinned mages with gills slowly emerged from the vegetation.

"They must sleep in the leaves," observed Paulo, a wide smile conveying his amazement.

"Even under the sea," said Ophir, observing the blue mages, who stretched out and in a sudden flash, were gone.

Apollos made a quick adjustment to keep up with the swimming mages. The room briefly spun out of focus. It became clear: they were waking up. Mages under the water lived within the forest and slept in the dense stalks it provided. Like the school of fish viewed previously, a horde of mages swam in patterned spirals, much like how the Aerials fly. Some even rode dolphins. Apollos gently moved the view along, allowing the team to view all of the underwater mages in their natural environment. Thousands of them glided in a spherical formation, expanding outward and then, all at once, bound closer together.

After this, Apollos shifted the view and not too far from the forest, there was another deep reef. Within the reef, corals and stones were arranged like small cabins for mage dwellings. Magnifying the view, it became clear that the entire reef was engineered by the mages of the deep.

Some time for observance passed, then the image returned to its small window size and then finally faded from view, leaving the observing mages silently contemplating what they had witnessed.

CHAPTER 65

"Alright, what do we know?" asked Victor.

"Mages inhabit the southern waste and deep ocean," responded Paulo.

The members of the team present were amazed, almost to the point of being frightened. They watched as Apollos retrieved a small glass obelisk, with pyramid terminations at both ends and handed it out to Victor. He instructed Victor to hold the obelisk by the ends with his index fingers.

Victor felt a little odd, unsure as to what else the luminous sage could possibly show him. Apollos raised his hands over it. A strong flash filled the room as it had before when they were spying on the nations around them. The appearance portrayed was a recording of past moments. The team beheld many of their own excursions, including travelling over the North Wall, battling the giants, celebrating when the Aerial elders walked the surface of the earth, the building of the Terran colonies and even the journey over the ocean with the Kryos.

"They have been watching *us*!" said Paulo.

"Why not," interjected Vidar. "I would. I look good."

"Well said, *Sil*," replied Ophir, joking.

The exhibition ended and Apollos retrieved the ornament. With the presentation finished, the team was taken back to the hall where the others were finished eating and now lightly drinking. Silvanus immediately jumped to his feet.

"So, what happened?" he asked eagerly.

The returning mages just looked at each other, waiting to see who would try to explain the phenomena they just witnessed.

"Soo… what were you doing? I assume lights were involved," said Sil.

"Sil," said Victor in a commanding tone, "Sit down."

The other mages that were sitting with Sil became very attentive to what their leader had to say.

"Our new friends have some interesting abilities and have given us strategic information about remaining mage-life on the planet."

The team listened on. Many were unable to even imagine the fantastic events that occurred only moments ago.

CHAPTER 66

At the end of the day, their hosts directed the team outside to sleeping quarters. The beds were simple enough, all of them much too small for Vidar, who had pushed three together. Many larger buildings were cleared to make room for the hundreds of soldiers that had accompanied the team in the desert. When night fell, most of the city's citizens remained outside, staring in silence at the stars. For hours they watched the night sky as if anticipating a divine omen.

"What do you think that's about?" asked Silvanus, commenting on the strange actions of the desert natives.

"Well, think about it," responded Paulo. "They have been trapped for centuries under the sunspire for their own safety. Seeing the real sky and not some projection of it would be a special event."

Silence overtook the room. The mages began to reflect on how a common night sky would have a special meaning to these people. Ophir and Danir understood their situation more than the others would, having no knowledge of the sky's existence for most of their lives.

Danir spoke up, breaking the moment's calm.

"Many of the injured were given hospitality in the city. Some of them told me the healers used a hand-sized gem to see the bones and organs as they operated on them. They can shine a ray over the subject and it reveals clearly, without pain or discomfort, the inside of the mage."

"That sounds awesome!" Sil said enthusiastically. "I have got to see that in action. Someone, quick, make me injured."

"I'll do it," Vidar replied promptly.

"*Let's* not," said Victor. "We need our sleep. Tomorrow, we return to the base and begin setting up dispatches for trade with the city. They will expect a full report."

"I hate paperwork," whined Sil.

"You won't have to do any. Your writing is impossible to read," sited Ophir who then turned to Victor. "How long do you think they are going to stand out there?"

"Maybe all night," Victor responded.

"So these mages don't sleep?" asked Sil.

"To be fair, this is probably the first night they have had in a long time," Victor said adding to Sil's joke.

"Even in the dark this whole place is still glowing," complained Sil. "We are in clear glass buildings and the light never turns off. I don't think night can ever happen here."

CHAPTER 67

Auron desert field report
Team leader Victor of Miano; on-site narration.

The last three reports have been an exemplification of the powers and abilities of the light mage nation and a description of their natural environment and habitat. Now the attention turns to the system of government and social hierarchy.

We have come to collectively refer to the mage-nation of the Auren desert as the Spectros. They have a society more advanced than anything my team has witnessed so far and their administration is neither caste or generative.

They are organized into unions of glassmakers, teachers, physicians, agriculturalists, caregivers, cooks, charmers, architects, jewellers, tailors and numerous others – I will write a full description on each job and its particulars in a future report.

Of these unions, a certain individual is chosen through nomination and election. Then, for an arranged period, that mage acts as intermediary between the local guild and the ruling administration.

The ruling body that dictates major decisions - city planning, food distribution, special events, celebrations and so forth - all come from among the people, usually as having represented a union for a certain number of years. The mage is nominated and if accepted, is elected to the ruling panel.

Both males and females are allowed to run for any position without discrimination. This is a huge contrast to every other society we have encountered. The Aerials are based on a generative assembly of the oldest and wisest of an exclusively male conclave, the Kryos have a rule of the strong, the Terrans have a stringent caste system, and even our system, though matriarchal, has laws which give preference to an almost exclusively male retinue for political and arbitration roles.

The society's elders are more of a priest class, also made up of males and females. These mages have mastered the ability to bend light to their will, creating illusions and apparitions. Also, like the Terrans, who have a technological aspect of their tradition, the Spectros have incredibly sophisticated tools that allow them to see across the world, within the ocean, out into the stars and even deep into the southern wastes. We have witnessed this many times and can attest for its authenticity.

The Spectros have been observing our behaviour from behind the sunspire for probably hundreds of years. In anticipation of our arrival and in view of our experiences with the other nations, they had a large gathering of the people to discern who would be the first to travel with us as their ambassadors. Two youthful mages, one male and one female, were chosen. Their names are Helios and Kuria. We cannot, as of yet, understand their language, but Paulo is working on lessons with them. Their progress has been substantial. Within the year, they should be ready for a hearing within in the Palace of Nebat.

We have been engaged in setting up a trade route with the natives and Ophir is working on strengthening the outer bases to accommodate for greater numbers. We are also going to be hosting a gathering of leading Spectros at the base for the next week. After the gathering ends, more reports will be issued.

Ophir's reports will be added to my own on the next dispatch.

This report will be transported by the Aerial in service to the Nebatean Messenger Corps, to be delivered to the Queen's hand for immediate reading before the council.

*Victor di Miano, Team Leader of the
Department of Mage Nation Relations.*

CHAPTER 68

A year passed and the two mages of the Spectros nation advanced their learning far beyond what was expected of them. Helios and Kuria learned to read in Terran script and communicate in Plains speak. The two absorbed information in an almost unearthly way. Their thirst for knowledge of the world around them grew into a source of unlimited fascination.

Helios and Kuria quickly cultivated their abilities to clearly communicate with the mages teaching them. They shared information about their home world with the members of the Nebatean council, giving lectures and demonstrations to packed assemblies. Every three months they would return to the Auren desert with Victor and some of the team members to transmit information about the outside world to their kindred. They used visual aids showing images they had captured with their glass gems. The Spectros Nation would gather to hear their discourse and to ask them questions.

After a lengthy dissertation, the two would call for willing youths to go on a student exchange program: Terrans, Aerials, Kryos, and Plainswalkers would temporarily reside in the city and Spectros would move to Nebat, learning each other's customs and languages. The program was a complete success with hundreds of students becoming fluent with each other's culture. Many would stay for a year's term and upon return, teach the youth throughout their nations. It was a great age of discovery in the mage world.

At the end of another term in the City of Lights, Victor received a message from the Terran base.

"Helios, one here from the base," announced Victor. "We have to head over."

"The term is almost finished. Why not wait?" he replied.

"It's from Ophir," said Victor in a serious tone. "He has discovered something."

"Does it say what?" asked Helios.

Victor shook his head, knowing that Helios was unaccustomed to their compatriot's informal ways.

"It says nothing about it, which means we have to leave now. I'll send for the others."

Victor began to write up a summoning to the other team members. Helios, looking over at Victor, tried to comprehend the reason for such a drastic change in plans.

"But the students. There is another session starting on Terran technology. They will need guidance. To tell you the truth, I don't even know much about this subject. Most of it will be me translating what Terran students say," asserted Helios.

"Kuria will handle it," responded Victor, noticing his friend's discomfort in leaving his duties unfinished. "Look, you are a team member now. Your first duty is to *aid* the team. Besides, Ophir will be there and you can learn everything you want to know from him."

Helios needed no further convincing.

CHAPTER 69

The trip was quick. Within three days, they reached the Terran Southern base at the edge of the desert. It had become larger with numerous upgrades and additional constructs, making it more like a small village than a military fortress. Since the demise of the ifrit, Ophir expanded the garrison into a settlement, creating more outposts leading through the desert to the edge of the southern wastes.

Most of the experimentation Ophir was doing involved coping with the conditions of the south. Trying to reach the mages that lived within the volcanic underground was a huge priority. Summoning the team from the reaches of the known territories was a signal that his research was bearing fruit.

Passing through the fortress interior, Victor noticed the changes immediately. Instead of training camps and barracks, several elongated buildings littered the once militant landscape. Most structures had been either replaced or upgraded to suit a more scientific demand.

Ophir emerged from the main building as Victor and Helios approached.

"Friends, you are almost late," he said excitedly.

Ophir greeted Victor with a kindly embrace and then did the same for Helios.

"Have the others arrived yet?" asked Helios.

"Yes!" replied an affable voice from above. "We just flew in now."

"Silvanus," shouted Ophir. "You brought the others with you as well," he continued as the Eras landed beside Sil.

"How have you been? Enjoying the messenger corps?" asked Ophir smiling.

"They made me Division Captain," Sil smiled proudly. "These two are my subordinates," he said pointing a thumb over his shoulder toward the Eras.

"Well, let's go in. There is food and water here," stated Ophir.

They entered the main building. Awaiting them was a long table laden with food. Taking their seats, Victor asked when the other team members would arrive. Ophir began to respond, but was interrupted by Sil.

"Vidar was right behind us, not more than a day's journey," he said, taking a drink. "And he's bringing his boys with him. You know, Olaf and Skeld or Skild and Uthor… or whatever their names are."

Victor gave Sil a frustrated look.

"What?" Sil shot back. "I can't speak freeze mage."

"They are *team* members," Ophir taunted. "After all these years, you still do not know your team brothers?"

The hall erupted at Ophirs criticism of Sil's ineptness. After eating, Ophir accompanied his friends into another chamber filled with maps and illustrations, all portrayals of the southern wastelands. The walls were completely covered, giving the impression that the entire room was actually built of paper and scroll. Ophir wasted no time and began to delve into the subject matter.

"Danir and Paulo are in the south now and we will be converging with them in about two day's time. They have a contingent of mages from all nations working with them. A Terran research team had a significant breakthrough. Armour, created of a refined crystal, withstood the intense heat for up to six hours before overheating became a factor. Also, we can create petrified bridges for travel over the landscape which allows for temporary bases on the southern surface."

The new developments were a clear step forward and impressed Victor very much. He inquired as to how long they have had the knowledge to carry out these operations.

"Almost two years," responded Ophir.

"Two years!" Victor said surprised. Even the rest of the team members looked at Ophir astonished. "Why have we only heard of this now?" Then he thought about the Terrans and nearly swallowed his words. This race of mages who had evolved to rigorously explore and occupy a dense underground world. Now, above ground, without borders the Terran explorative qualities had no hindrance.

"Ah, here, I will show you." Ophir retrieved a small wooden chest that looked as if it were to hold a noblewoman's jewels. Opening it revealed small triangular pieces of glass of spectro making.

"Helios, we need you for this one," stated Ophir, as he handed one of the glass pieces to him.

Helios placed the trinket on a table covered with maps and then emanated some light into the glass. A large display of a fiery wasteland appeared before them. Volcanoes with lava pouring from their mouths created streams that flowed through the arid valleys below. The visual moved, giving a tour, showing the vast expanse of the southern wastes. The ground was black and littered with pools of smoking tar. The rising smoke filled the sky, turning daytime into an eternal dusk.

"Is this the Southern Wastes?" asked Sil.

"Yes," answered Ophir.

"I mean, are we seeing it for real?" Sil probed.

"Ah, no, these are visuals taken not more than a month ago. I have others as well, but they are not as recent," claimed Ophir. "Now, here is where we have the problem."

The visual slowed and focused on one volcano that was erupting. The team watched as it continued discharging lava and smoke with an unyielding vigilance.

"For about six months out of the year it does this. Even with the most powerful armour available, it's impossible to approach. Recently, it has calmed and because of the force it exerted, numerous crevices and small canyons have opened in the ground."

Ophir let them watch for several moments, allowing the observation to set in.

"So, here is the situation. This periodic eruption has left much of the land fissured. Paulo thinks that these fissures lead all the way down to where the mages reside."

Victor took a short while to think about it, watching the landscape and then asked an obvious question.

"How do we even get close to those openings?"

Ophir remained silent and let the visual continue its course and when the rivers of lava were in sight, he began.

"Once those drain out, the region cools significantly and we have found techniques to petrify certain portions of the land to allow for easy access. All we need to do now is make a land bridge over and we can make contact."

Victor, now bewildered, entertained the idea of walking through the Southern Wastes unscathed, but staring at the river of lava made it hard to believe they could just dive in.

"So do they drain entirely?" Victor probed.

"Actually, no. They simply lose about ten feet and the lava remains idle," Ophir replied. "We cannot go down, we will have to draw them up."

"You can do that?" asked Helios, breaking his normal reserve.

Before Ophir could answer, a noise from the hallway distracted the party. What sounded like a rampage came at the door and almost broke it down had one of the Eras not opened it first. The Kryos mages, with Vidar in the lead, stormed the room.

Olaf noticed the maps and the display, then grinned and asked, "So! What did we miss?"

CHAPTER 70

A two-day journey took the team through the desert and into the Southern Wastes. They arrived at another small fortress set up as an entry point for preparation before accessing the volcanic countryside. The fortress in the south was much larger than the base the team came from. It had room for almost four times the populace and it was clear that it made full use of the diversity of the mage nations. It had specific divisions made to accommodate for the natural talents offered by the different peoples.

Terran armour smiths worked to enhance protection; Kryos physicians treated the mages who were unfortunate enough to be burned; Plainswalkers took care of food and water supply. The Spectro scouts had the unique role of capturing images to aid the mapping and investigations, while the Aerials took the information and material requests and delivered them to the surrounding encampments.

The commotion within was intense. Kryos carted injured mages into infirmaries while Aerials constantly arrived and departed. The team immediately spotted some Spectros illuminating displays and discussing their effects through a clear glass structure, training Terrans and Plainswalkers.

In the armoury, hundreds of Terrans laboured over hot furnaces. Trough-like vessels filled with water, where the armour was set to cool, created a sort of perpetual mist that hovered over the area. Ophir led the team through the garrison. As they passed, mages would stop and salute with both arms crossed over their chests and heads down. Danir came forward to meet his captain.

"You made it," Danir opened. "And you brought the rest of us," he said warmly, greeting the others.

"Where is Paulo?" asked Ophir.

"Still with the excursion. He's on his way back soon, though," replied Danir. "We will meet him in the main chamber. We have everything prepared."

At the centre of the base, the main chamber stood as the tallest building, being the only construct within the encampment that had more than one floor. Having a lavishly designed interior made it look like a smaller version of the Nebat palace.

"It's very comfortable living here, for a military operation," stated Vidar.

"This whole garrison is to become a colony when contact is made," disclosed Danir. "We want to give the right impression."

Mages within the building were just as active as those on the outside. Danir proceeded to direct them up a flight of stairs where they arrived at their destination, passing large, ornate wooden doors. They entered a spacious room filled with maps and parchment scattered throughout.

"So, we exchange a small room of paper for a large room of paper," exclaimed Sil.

"These are the latest read-outs since the volcanic activity stopped. This side of the world goes through a sort of cooling after that process. Between our scouting and the Spectros observations, we have put together a plan of engagement," Danir said enthusiastically.

"Ophir mentioned that we are going to try and draw them out," Victor said.

"Yes! That is correct. For that we will be using these," replied Danir, retrieving a small stone container. Within, seven flat rectangular pieces of stone with sharpened points rested. With simple patterned engravings, it seemed unclear what purpose these small markers would serve.

"These are the tools that somehow will bait the mages?" asked Helios. He reached out to grasp hold of one only to have Danir, very quickly, close the container and give stern rebuke.

"Under no circumstances is anyone but me or captain Ophir to handle these. Even in our hands, unless used with absolute caution, they can be dangerous."

Danir paused before continuing his explanation, trying to best describe the potential of his nation's instruments. Helios grabbed some nearby parchment and began to write out his explanation, letting his natural fascination overwhelm him.

"These are *line staves.*' They can only be created by certain clans and are entrusted to elders or clan heads. The earth is filled with magnetic pulses or *'lines.'* The line stave simply manipulates them into a concentrated force," said Danir, not realizing most of the room's inhabitants had no idea what he was talking about.

"What he means," interrupted Ophir, "is it can cause a focused earthquake. We have used them to open new tunnels or parts of the earth we could not pass through easily. Controlling their power is difficult and can be incredibly dangerous. Mishandling, even by non-Terrans, can cause catastrophic results. They are constantly active and need only a slight grounding to engage. Me and Danir must be the only ones to handle them."

A deep silence enveloped the group, as the team members contemplated the power of Terran science. The edifying calm was broken by a knock on the door as a Plainswalker stepped in.

"My lords," he said, "Sir Paulo has returned."

CHAPTER 71

Paulo burst into the room and headed straight to Ophir.

"We are ready. If we leave tomorrow, we can arrive in good time to get started."

"What of the armours and the supplies?" asked Danir. "When I checked, we were behind."

"Our workforce has been in operation day and night. We will arrive with the supplies and support behind us only a day or two at most."

Everyone understood the need for urgency in matters pertaining to discovery. The fact that there was so much commotion within the garrison showed how being a part of the mission mattered to the mages. The entire world awaited the results from this expedition; Paulo was no exception. Silvanus however viewed the not noticing of friends by Paulo to be a poor way to begin an excursion.

"Well! Hello to you, too," said Silvanus, trying to agitate Paulo as much as possible. "Have you figured out a way to swim through lava yet? I saw many burn victims at the Kryos clinic and I hear your forging is behind schedule, so… I'm going to guess not."

"Really? This from a mage who makes his living running paper from one end of the world to the other. Next time you're down, take part in some research or maybe add some value to our developments. If you can't manage something on your own, just keep mindlessly muleing my reports, you silk spun messenger boy!" responded Paulo harshly, surprising Sil.

"You two, enough! Sil, shut up!" yelled Victor, cutting Sil off from retorting. "Paulo, greet your friends properly."

Sil grinned like a child after Victor's affirmation, Paulo rolled his eyes, and the rest of the team smiled, finally re-united for their original purpose. Paulo greeted everyone warmly, including Sil, and then continued with his report.

Paulo finished and the team mobilized. Ophir and the Aerials were going to take a mechanical cart out to the excavation site. Helios followed with parchment and pen, wanting to ask Ophir questions. Three more carts were assigned, one for Victor, Paulo, Danir, and Vidar, another for the remainder of the Kryos, and the last one for the Eras and whatever Kryos could not fit in the second.

Inside Victor's cart, Danir gave an explanation of the site's development and what they would expect.

"All of the paths we are travelling on are petrified flooring. What we used to keep bugs from invading now keeps the searing ground from burning. The site itself is a large, rectangular surface just outside of a lava stream that has now receded."

Danir looked intently at the others.

"This is really important. We have erected walls to keep the winds from blowing hot ash and embers at us and also to keep hot tar from randomly bursting to the surface. Just because we have armour and walls does not make us safe. This whole land is treacherous. The air you breathe will tire you out. Stay close together and follow commands."

Victor thought for a moment and then asked. "How are you certain of this as an entry point for contact with the fire mages?"

Danir smiled, almost anticipating the question.

"We have been able to pinpoint a safe approach for us and a safe opening point for them. We have been working closely with the Spectros elders, between the exchange program and the Aerial messengers. Those staves we are going to be using, they're no joke; if they fall accidentally, something bad could happen. Only Ophir and the captains waiting at the site can operate them."

Vidar interjected, enquiring about the Terran artifice. "What do these staves actually do?"

"In short," replied Danir, "they cause earthquakes. Elders can control them perfectly, but for our purposes, the captains should suffice. You saw a lesser form when we battled the giants at the North Hold. We are going to open a small canyon straight down into the fire mages' home world, *without* harming the inhabitants. Hopefully, they will become curious and decide to come up."

It had taken almost one year to find a location that complimented both the surface approach and the subterranean entry. The team's coordination with the Spectros elders allowed for casual observation of the volcanic underworld. A lot of pain and sweat had gone into this. Hopefully the mage natives from the heart of the earth would correctly interpret a violent breach into their domain.

CHAPTER 72

Arriving at the site was uneventful. All the commotion and hustle of the garrison was exchanged for a dreary flat piece of land, surrounded by arranged stand alone walls formed from Terran skill. The heavy, soot-filled air made it hard to breathe. Tar pits bubbled and belched, adding a ceaseless putrid stink to the atmosphere. Smoke emanated from every opening in the ground causing an unhealthy mist to form.

Standing on the petrified land, Victor scanned the area. Many Terran and Plainswalkers huddled in groups by the walls, while Aerials used their abilities to keep the smoke from overwhelming the operation. Small huts of rock stood in the background served as lodging for the mages on-site. The other carts arrived and the team assembled in full force. The usual welcome of salutes and cheers was replaced with tired soldiers and lifeless landscape. At first, they silently analyzed their surroundings, then Silvanus spoke up.

"Sooo... you have armourers from the Terran nation, observation from the Spectros, nourishment from the Plainswalkers, medical assistance from the Kryos and the ability to *breathe* from my people. All of that together leads to a large piece of flat land with incomplete walls... we have come *so* far."

Helios, having seen the site many times from his homeland, continued to speak to Ophir about the properties of different stones found within the Terran arsenal.

"You were explaining Onyx?" Helios asked Ophir.

"Yes, Onyx makes the user blend with shadows. It can, like many of the stones, be used as a point for wall building, but is not very stable and deteriorates quickly. Lapis is a special stone, blue in colour and makes the awareness of the user rise substantially. Jasper is used in healing after childbirth, but red jasper is used for creating temporary armour. The gemstones have multiple effects and take a long time to master. The metals have more permanent effects related to the armour, weapons, or tools used."

"Ophir, where is everyone?" Victor asked, interrupting the conversation.

Ophir looked around, noticing the small group of mages occupying the site.

"We were running behind," he started. "Reinforcements and supplies should be following us soon."

As Ophir concluded his statement, a heavily armoured Terran soldier approached.

"Sir, we are almost ready. If you would put on your armour, we can take you to the stream."

Ophir turned to Victor.

"I had our body armour placed on top of the carts for storage."

The team unloaded their equipment; the large, stiff, crystal coverings were bulky and difficult to fasten. Each of the team member's armaments had been crafted for their particular composition. The Aerials had trouble adjusting to a heavy piece of crystal enclosed around their faces. After some trial and error, they all managed to fit themselves into their appropriate equipment. The guides directed them towards the lava stream where they would break though into a new world.

"So," enquired Sil, "why this place now?"

Even standing twenty feet away from the flow, the heat was sweltering. Many of the team members began to sweat and had to move further away or risk becoming nauseous.

"Well," Danir answered, "we needed a part of the earth already loosened so the force we exert could be tempered. It also needed to be close enough to the underground home world to get their attention, but not so close as to destroy their living space. Along with that, it is accessible to us. This place has it all."

Sil looked up at Danir, satisfied with his reply.

"Well said. So, are we breaking through now?"

"Soon," interjected Ophir. "The other captains are behind us. They will arrive shortly."

Examining the inhospitable landscape, Victor secretly hoped

that the mages they were discovering would not be as malicious as their environment. As he drifted into deep thought, an over-large caravan arrived. Danir gave a loud yell, drawing everyone's attention, as Victor mentally prepared himself for contact with a nation that lived within a sea of fire.

CHAPTER 73

The garrison arrived in force. With it came armoured mages, the captains needed for the use of the staves and supplies. Almost two hundred in number, the soldiers, mostly Terrans, took their places as the captains approached Ophir.

"We are ready to proceed if you could bring forth the staves," said one of the captains addressing Ophir.

"Paulo!" called Ophir. "Victor, you too."

Victor took his place with the Terran authorities and Ophir continued his discourse.

"Victor, you and the team will stand in the center. The soldiers will be situated around the back. Keep about fifteen feet away and under no circumstances approach without being asked to. We will open the land to form a companionway for the fire mages to ascend.

"Danir," Ophir commanded.

"Sir."

"Make ready the water. We will need refreshment if the process becomes extended."

"Yes sir."

Ophir instructed the corps about what could go wrong and to wait for orders before doing anything. The team stood in the center ground. To their backs were armoured soldiers, and in the frontline, close to the searing crevice, stood ten Terran captains. It became apparent that, if they should make a mistake in using the staves causing earth to move in an uncontrollable way, the river below would claim their lives. For the mages of flame, their world would soon change and the reclusive nation would become a part of a global community.

"Captains. Stand ready!" commanded Ophir.

The heavily armoured captains marched forward in Terran fashion: Standing far apart from one another, facing the fiery stream before them.

"Stave keeper! Come forth!"

Answering Ophir's order, Paulo slowly approached the captain to the furthest right and halted immediately behind him. All the captains then raised their left hand, palm up as if to accept alms.

"Keeper! Hand the staves."

Paulo carefully withdrew a stave and placed it in the hand of the awaiting captain, then slowly moved onto the next, until all of the captains were equipped.

"Stave keeper. Step away!" adjured Ophir, as a final charge to his friend.

"Captains, move in!"

The Terrans stepped forward about nine paces and then halted.

"Captains ready!" They shouted.

The captains' tightly clenched fists grasped the staves with the sharp end down, lowered onto their right knees and held the staves out in front of them. They then slowly brought the staves down and gently planted them into the earth. Closing their eyes, each let out a deep humming causing a light vibration to pass through the earth around the platform.

Ophir could feel the earth responding. The mages atop the site remained unmoving as the scenery surrounding them began to waver.

"Soo… why does our land not move?" asked Sil.

"Shhh," said Danir gently. "They need focus. The land under us is petrified; it will be more resistant to any disturbance."

Just as he said that, the light vibrations became significantly more violent. Many of the team members had to steady themselves forcefully to stay afoot. The land began to convulse all around their platform. The earth shifted and broke apart sending smoke into the air that created a blinding fog throughout the area. The team members clung to one another for support until the Aerials dispelled the fumes.

Victor's eyes watered as he choked, many of his comrades suffered the same. After a fit of coughing, Vidar helped Victor to his feet and looking out, the team leader could see the havoc wrought by the Terran powers.

Massive shifts overturned the volcanic morass creating unbridled devastation. The sight of it caused Victor to freeze up with fear. Even though the land under them was not breaking apart, it was definitely being displaced. Most of the mages were now huddled together on the ground. Smoke rose in the distance. Ash and flaming rock shot into the air causing a spectacular sight. The land from beneath the lava flow suddenly thrust upward creating a series of bulging hills that almost filled the river. The quake around them began to calm while the arched hills started cracking and as quickly as they were displaced, the hills collapsed within themselves, sinking into a deep, newly formed canyon.

The captains, now sweating profusely, collapsed from exhaustion. Danir gave an order in Terran speak and armoured soldiers from the corps rushed in with Paulo alongside them. First, they collected the staves and returned them to their container. With the staves secured, Paulo made a point of showing the team how the staves continued to vibrate and randomly bounce before softly shutting the lid. The team turned their attention to the captains, who were being stripped of their armour, given water, and wrapped in blankets. The exhausted Terran captains were taken to the far end of the platform, away from the recently made canyon. Sil decided to step forward and take a look.

"It looks deep," he stated. "Still hot, too."

The rest of the team gazed downward. The river had become a very deep, narrow chasm. Magma blanketed its depth and the heat was even more intense than before.

"Do you think they see it?" asked Vidar.

"They definitely should," responded Helios. "This area is well within their range. Not far down is a small colony of the fire mages. Hopefully they respond positively to our forced entry."

"So… now what?" questioned Sil.

"Now, we wait…" answered Victor.

CHAPTER 74

Hours passed and nothing happened. Eventually, Ophir, wrapped in a blanket and supported by Danir, was lead back to the team. Visibly weakened and pale, he sat next to Victor, leaning on one of the walls.

"Nothing yet then, eh?" asked Ophir.

"No, nothing yet," replied Victor.

Over a day passed and no activity from the canyon emerged. Smog from the volcanic bloodlines below spewed out continuously. The Aerials in camp kept an invisible barrier erected, forcing the smoke to rise like giant pillars. This caused ash to rain down upon the camp, while the haze blocked out the sun. The sky turned a deep grey, making it look like a sinister canopy supported by monstrous columns of malodorous smoke.

CHAPTER 75

The day after the dreadful showing was followed by an almost equally uninteresting stillness. The team took turns standing watch during the night. Spectros used their abilities to illuminate the darkness while the Aerials continued to keep the smog at bay.

Dawn broke as Paulo stood staring at the new chasm. He would have wanted to be next to the opening, but the high radiant temperature made it incredibly uncomfortable. Helios awoke and approached the site. On his way, he relieved the other Spectros handling the lights. Silently, he stood behind Paulo, not wanting to disturb his tranquil state.

"Can you see into it?" asked Paulo.

Helios, surprised at being noticed after moving so silently, collected his thoughts.

"No, only our elders have the abilities to scope over distances."

Paulo was quiet. Helios, not sure what to say, awkwardly broke the silence.

"We watched you discovering other nations for years. The elders would put the display up throughout the city. All of our buildings are made so they can be used to transmit what the elders are observing. Sometimes, one from the palace would give lectures on what we theorized was happening. When you finally made it our way, it was one of the most exciting moments in our history."

"Why did you not just develop weapons?" asked Paulo. "How did such an advanced civilization not devise a way to attack your oppressors?"

"Well, to control the light in a focused manner for martial purposes takes years of stringent training, without which causes more harm to the mage then the enemy. We are advanced in that we are resourceful. We can control light, but need to use glass that has to be created specifically for those purposes. Glass is not strong like rock or metal. If you look closely, you find we have a rather one-sided growth. We have always had immense difficulty fighting, since only elders and the advanced elite can control the light flows perfectly and even then, victory is not certain," explained Helios.

Paulo contemplated this as they stood before the gorge. Silvanus presented himself, interrupting the moment.

"Soo… what are you guys talking about? Paulo are you still up? Get some sleep or eat something."

Paulo rolled his eyes, ignoring Sil's usual behaviour.

"Sil," interjected Helios. "Paulo is only concerned for the success of the operation."

"Yeah, I bet he is and I am sure his focus will make them arrive sooner," Sil responded. "Do you think these mages will have the same problem as the Terrans did? You know, if their eyes can't handle the sun," enquired Sil.

"No, we researched their behaviour. Because they live around magma and flame, they should be able to adjust to the brightness from the surface," explained Paulo.

"Here then, eat something," Sil added before handing them both some spiced bread.

At noon the team gathered, discussed past events and talked with other soldiers. Ophir had recovered and was standing with them. Many of the younger mages questioned them about their different adventures that led to the uniting of their nations. Vidar and Sil each gave spectacular accounts, keeping them entertained for hours.

Another day passed. The lights were activated and the watches posted. The team and the captains ate together, letting the younger mages hold the watch.

"Do you know how long it will take?" one of the captains asked Ophir.

"No, they must act now. We cannot proceed within," he responded.

"Is there anything else we can do to encourage their arrival?" asked another captain.

"The chasm we created is probably over two thousand feet

deep. They know we are here. It's only a matter of time now," assured Ophir.

"Two thousand feet?" exclaimed Helios. "That is amazing."

"Well," Danir threw in, "We have been softening the land for eight months using the staves; we just culminated our efforts recently. Much preparation went into this. Hopefully, we did enough."

That night, the team and captains took leave from the watch. When morning came they resumed their positions and continued the vigil.

CHAPTER 76

On the third day, afternoon came and Paulo walked back from his shift to eat with Victor.

"Maybe we missed something," Paulo opened.

"Over a year of planning went into this," Victor replied. "Most of our expeditions end with accidentally contacting another nation. This time the accident is more…… in their hands."

"With all this planning, things should happen faster," said Paulo.

The team ate a meal and then took an hour's rest. During this time, two Terrans and a female Plainswalker stood the watch. Two were talking with one another, while the lady gazed blankly at the chasm, letting her mind drift. She was in such a deep reflection that she did not immediately notice the sound of rocks falling from within the fissure.

When the noise broke her train of thought, it prompted a slow advance for her to investigate further. At first, she saw nothing, but could still hear the noises. She continued to scan for its source. This drew the attention of the two men.

"Hey, you see something?"

"Shhh," she retorted.

They hurried over to the canyon and immediately felt the strength of the rising heat. Now, all three were looking down and could hear the noise.

"What do you suppose that is?" asked one.

The trio probed and began noticing red figures blending into the rock-side of the canyon. Something was climbing up.

"My lords! I think you should see this!" called out the Plainswalker.

CHAPTER 77

The team rushed over to the site to look into the canyon, despite the heat and strong glow from the magma. They witnessed sentient-shaped flames scaling towards them. Victor sprang into action quickly.

"Assemble the captains! Get everyone ready!"

All the mages gathered in their respective positions, as it was before. The soldiers took up the back, while the team stood with the captains in the forefront. Those present made themselves ready for what would emerge from the fires beneath.

A serene calm wrapped the ranks as they awaited the arrival of the sixth mage race. Victor stood focused, thinking of what the next move would be and trying to decide how best to communicate with them when they reached the surface. Though unsure about many things, he was thankful that they did not have to fight hordes of giants or some other monstrous enemy. Standing and waiting was much preferred to battling to the death.

As the wait continued, Silvanus broke the silence. Approaching Victor, he tapped his arm and whispered.

"How many did you see?"

Victor without turning to Sil replied.

"A lot."

"Like a hundred a lot or a lot a lot?" Sil persisted.

This time Victor turned to face his friend. "They filled the canyon side."

Satisfied by the response, Sil returned to his place. Not long after, fiery hands emerged, gipping the edge of the cliff. Initially, only a few arose. After quickly scanning the area, one of the fire mages spoke, obviously signalling the others.

Seeing these mages up close was different from observing them in their native environment. The flames given off by their bodies coated most of their features and made it hard to perceive them without being irritated. Large pyre-like mages began to dominate the area. Their presence quickly became overbearing. The team leaders were relieved as their fiery coverings died down the longer they stayed above ground. With the adjustment, clearly formed mages stood before the team and their comrades.

Most of the fire mages stood at the same height as Victor and had a thin to medium build. They wore charred rock over their torsos, leaving their heads, arms, and legs exposed, giving a strange ash-black with at times red tinges contrasting their bright red skin. Dreadlocked hair exuded like fiery serpents from their skulls.

The emerging mages took immediate notice of the layer of fire extinguishing from their beings. After a moment of adjusting, one of them took to the front to examine the group of beings that had caused this rift that lead into their territory.

Confronting the fire mages created an unnerving environment. Their eyes flashed like swaying candles. Their faces were grim and almost seemed to be perpetually angered. Unlike the other mage races whose people came in many shapes and sizes, they all adhered to a biological conformity that made telling them apart only possible by the thickness of their dreadlocked hair.

As the fire mages approached, their bodies gave off a high temperature that made it uncomfortable to be close to them. Along with their collective heat came a trait that frightened even Victor. Each step they took left an imprint of fire behind. The mages following from behind would unconsciously absorb the flames their brethren would discharge. This created a carpet of flame that connected the newly exposed nation.

The team and their retinue watched in silence as countless mages continued to come up through the crevice. After an extended wait, the fire mages crowded the scene and outnumbered the garrison at least nine to one. Positioned together, these mages radiated a visible heat wave. Most of them stood off the petrified ground in the tar pits, over geysers and areas that none of the team could approach without harming themselves. This created an intimidating situation that allowed the fire mages to almost completely surround the site.

Sil moved in behind Victor, who remained silent at the overpowering presence in front of them.

"Sooo," Sil started. "It looks like they outnumber us."

"Yes, that is true," Victor replied.

"They also are able to walk over the burning ground."

"Yeah, I noticed," spoke Victor, affirming his statement.

"Plus, they look *really* pissed off," Sil added.

"It does seem that way," replied Victor, now starting to get worried.

After a moment of silence, Sil put all of it together before he presented a summary that would make Victor feel more uncomfortable then he already was.

"Sooo… we are outnumbered, they have a territorial advantage and are angry we broke into their home. Next time, we discover the water world first."

"Well done, Sil. I'll bring it up with the council," responded Victor, nervously trying to anticipate what would happen while absorbing Sil's wit.

Ophir stared at Victor who nodded. The two of them then slowly walked forward. From behind, Vidar followed closely with the rest of the team. The captains kept their position along with the soldiers; none dared to make a sound. All stood together, unsure what to expect from the immanent convergence that was about to befall them.

"Hail, I am Ophir of the Terran nation. We have come on a goodwill mission from the Council of Mage Nations to bring about a coalition of your peoples with our own."

Taking a small step back after delivering his speech, he waited for a response. Victor stared at him, not sure how that could possibly be the introduction to the newly emerged mages.

"Really?" Victor remarked. "Their first meeting with us and that's what they get to hear."

"You have something else in mind?" countered Ophir. "They probably did not understand it anyway. I am just trying to make contact. We should have made more effort to think further ahead."

"I will remember that for next time," said Victor, wondering if there would ever be a next time. These mages may have been born of fire, but their expressions were pure stone.

From among the fire mages, one came forward. His hair was thick and knotted inordinately. He spoke quickly, and sounded as irate as he looked. He paused to let his words have full effect before continuing, this time with hand gestures. The Victor and Ophir looked at one another, not comprehending what would happen next. Ophir gestured to Vidar and in a low toned speech, requested Sil. The Aerial glided towards him, leaned close to hear his orders, and then sped through the ranks with unknown intent.

Ophir continued to try to show a docile approach, which seemed only to aggravate the fire mages. Sil returned quickly and handed something to Ophir, who in turn presented it to the infuriated mage.

His head turned on an angle, not sure what to make of the gesture. Anyone witnessing this event would have sworn these beings were from different planets rather than distant neighbours. Ophir put some in his mouth, indicating what the gift was. The other mage, now understanding, slowly did the same.

Almost immediately, a smile materialized on his face. Though not very evident in expression, the mage's eyes lightened after tasting the sample. At once, he began passing the food along and many of the mages rushed in to try some of the offering.

"Feeding them is what you came up with?" asked Victor relieved by the result.

"I actually thought you would have thought of it first," asserted Ophir.

Though simple an act, this first sharing of food became recounted as the *Southern Feast* that joined the nation from the flaming heart of the planet with the rest of the world's body.

CHAPTER 78

With the first meeting a success, the fire mages became acquainted with the team. Content with the food and impressed with the mechanical creations, their interest turned to their counterparts very quickly. However, their behaviour was unlike any of the other previous nations. If something was done that surprised them, or if caught off guard by an approaching Aerial, they turned hostile and when one became agitated, the others followed suit. It made for awkward situations because of what appeared to the other mages as constant phenomena.

Eventually, Ophir and Victor gathered everyone together and gave demonstrations from each mage nation to accustom the fire mages to their surroundings.

Captivated by the display of the nations, the newly discovered mages' mood turned and they became more relaxed. After the demonstration of their hosts, many stepped forward to do likewise. A group of twenty began by creating fire in their palms and then extending it to engulf their bodies. Under their control, the fire spread to cover the crowd. The flames grew and covered the entire host from the garrison. It never actually burned anyone; however, it did warm the mages significantly. Every mage involved was awestruck. Having their bodies bathed in flame and not consumed by the heat created a mixture of fear and wonderment.

The team examined the new mages, observing their conduct. After two days of working with them, the team became exhausted and set in for some sleep.

CHAPTER 79

Victor awoke to find Paulo and Ophir already working at communicating with their guests. The whole site had become a sort of circus where mages from the volcanic underground brought their children to see a Spectros light show. Victor rose and woke the others. He met Paulo who was giving orders to some Terrans. After dismissing them, he greeted Victor.

"How long was I out?" Victor asked.

"Half the night and most of the morning. You feeling alright?" replied Paulo.

"Yeah, of course. What's going on? Where is everyone going?" Victor questioned.

Paulo looked around and gestured to Ophir, who began to approach the pair.

"We are leaving. There is nothing else we can do here. Food is running low, the Aerials are overworked and we are making no progress," Paulo said with his usual serious demeanour.

Ophir stepped into the conversation, looking at Victor, assuming he had already heard the news.

"We have figured out nothing about this people. No evidence of hierarchy or social structure. This whole excavation has become a festival. The more of them that keep adding to their already significant horde increases the temperature of the entire area. Many from our camp are having heat illness and some have even collapsed. We are moving back to the Southern Base. The captains have already left with half our forces, the rest of us are following. Make yourself ready."

They waved to their newly discovered friends and gradually evacuated the site. The team members stared at one another silently, not sure what to make of the situation.

"Soo…" Silvanus started, "We search for mage nation, we spend a year digging for mage nation, we find mage nation and *now* we leave mage nation. I know I'm not the most intelligent, but *maybe* we're breaking protocol on this one."

Ophir responded to Sil's criticism.

"We will not be leaving long. We just need to find a way to make contact with them without being overwhelmed by heat. We also have to find a way to get some of them to accompany us to the council."

Back at the Southern Base, most of the conversation was of the fire mages and their abilities. Ophir called a meeting of the team and captains to try to figure out a solution to the problem.

They debated for hours, trying to find a method of approach. Such a tightly wound people was difficult enough with the language barrier, but with physical contact being a problem, the whole strategy to integrate the new nation would have to be re-thought.

Night fell and the lights were activated. Most of the mages went to sleep, but within the commander's quarters, deliberation was still active and showed no signs of letting up.

"We have to report something to the council," said a Terran captain. "The investment into this mission actually amounts to more than the last two combined! How do we explain that after making contact, we just walked away?"

"We are not walking away. Tomorrow we should have enough information for a small contact team to make progress," responded Ophir.

A nervous Plainswalker ran through the door unannounced. His entrance silenced everyone. He took a while to catch his breath and then rose an alarm.

"My lords! You must come see, outside!"

The team arose with the captains and proceeded onto the walls of the fort, where a frightening and surprising portent laid waiting. Thousands of fire mages had walked a great distance and now stood outside the fortress. They made no noise, not even to talk to each other. They simply stared at the stronghold. Their bodies gave off a light similar to a burning torch. Night's shadow staggered under their swaying glow. Their arrival solved the imperative problem with little effort.

"Soo…" Sil started. "Should we let them in?"

CHAPTER 80

"We cannot let all of those in," Danir began. "We may suffocate most of the barracks."

Victor and Ophir quickly left their positions and opened the gates, rushing out to greet their guests. The presence of the fire mages loosed upon the environment an oppressive humidity. Both Victor and Ophir started to sweat under their fiery emissions.

The fire mages gathered were not like the others they had met. This group was organized. At their head stood what looked like aged males; one even had a cane constructed from charred rock.

"Ophir," Victor whispered, "these are elders... I'll start."

Victor stepped forward and bowed deeply. The elder turned his head slightly, indicating confusion, but then returned the gesture. Victor then did something that he knew he would regret; stepping forward, he extended his hand to make contact. Now perplexed by the strange behaviour the elder reflected on his actions, then realizing what the actions conveyed, did the same. Victor grabbed on. His flesh began to burn. Smoke rose from his hand and he let out a yell. The startled elder tried to release, but Victor held strong. Ophir looked horrified at the display and shouted for Victor to let go.

Eventually, Victor broke the bond and fell to his knees. The elder remained completely confused, not sure what to make of the situation. He only stared at his hand and at Victor. Even many of his retinue were frightened at what was happening and unsure how to react.

Ophir helped Victor to his feet. Victor held his hand, now burned and red from the encounter. The elder studied his limb and immediately comprehended the situation. He shouted orders in his language and two younger mages emerged from their ranks and presented themselves to the team leaders.

"Now we can let them in," stated the seriously injured team

leader.

As they entered, the team and a host of mages crowded the entranceway. Paulo spoke up first.

"What the hell was that about?"

"Vidar!" shouted Victor. "Summon one of your people. I need a healer." Turning to Paulo, Victor responded to the previous statement.

"Now they know: we cannot get too close to them. Look."

Three fire mages followed the team. They were escorted to the large room within the main chamber. For the three, the team brought forth Terran stone chairs rather than the normal wooden ones. Food was set out and torches lit. Seeing flames moving individually, caused great discomfort for the visitors, making them forcefully absorb all the flames in the room into themselves. The Spectros corrected the problem by creating light using their abilities.

Introductions were first: Ophir placed both hands on his chest saying his name, everyone else followed suit. The elder was much a faster learner then his brethren. He stood and said. "Farsad," and then introduced the other two with him as, 'Delshad,' and 'Jahan.'

With the introductions complete, everything went smoothly. Food was ordered to be brought to the fire mages outside the fortress and the mages of the garrison ate with them. Many of the fire mages also tried water and wine for the first time and contrary to an almost unanimous belief, none of them were poisoned by the liquids. The meeting was not very long, but at one point the elder stood, obviously pleased with what had transpired. He addressed the younger mages accompanying him, then did the same with Ophir, using words and hand gestures. The message was clear: the boys would stay here. Upon finishing speaking, he promptly exited the building, leaving the team moderately confused by his foreign behaviour.

"Alright," Victor requested as he entered. "What just happened? Did I miss something?"

"Victor, we did it," Ophir announced.

"Wow, that was much faster than expected," noted Helios.

The two young fire mages stood as if they were military trainees being scrutinized by a superior. Victor stepped forward and invited them to sit, then called over Danir.

"Have bed chambers prepared. Make sure you use stone instead of wood. The last thing we need is a fire in the base," whispered Victor.

Victor looked at the two young fire mages and made them repeat their names, then shared his again and the names of the rest of the team. Eventually, the reception finished and the two were shown to their rooms. Silvanus jumped at the chance to make himself useful.

"No worries, I got this one. Boys, if you would follow me," he said placing his arms around their backs.

"Aaaaow," he shouted, not remembering that fire burns, as did these mages. The two looked rather apologetic about the situation.

"Danir, why don't you do this," said Victor, as the rest of the team laughed.

With contact made, the education would get underway. Victor was pleased with how well this was going. He checked with the watch and confirmed that the fire mages had vacated the area. With the land clear, the doors were ordered closed. Tomorrow would bring with it new opportunities and even greater accomplishments.

CHAPTER 81

During the next three months the team trained the new mages and the name 'Pyros' was given for their nation. Lessons began immediately, mainly in Plains Speak. Every week, an elder would return with a small group of Pyros to investigate their progress.

After six months, the two boys could communicate with the team and translate for their elders. They informed the team of their people's history and culture. The Pyros nation had a select group of caste clans. Leaders would be replaced by their eldest born males, constantly passing the title from father to son for generations.

"These clan names are Karen, Mihran and Suren," said young Delshad.

The Pyros paused after his statement to allow Helios time to write down what he was saying. The team endeavoured to learn as much about the Pyros nation as the two young mages had been taught of theirs. The information would then be sent to the council for analysis.

"Well, actually, there are technically seven ruling clans but they all are ruled by the top three," Delshad specified.

"Are you from any of these?" asked Ophir.

"No! Me and Jahan are from lesser clans," he said, looking toward Jahan "It would be considered lowly if any from those clans would be sent here. Their place is with the nation."

Ophir waited a short time before proceeding.

"Are either of you from any of the high standing clans?" he said pointing to Jahan, indicating he was to respond.

"No," he answered. "Our clan is Avtalion and falls in the domain of the Suren. The elder that introduced us was from that clan."

Ophir took the opportunity to ask if there was any resentment toward the ruling class for the lack of opportunity to advance from one's position.

"Oh, no," said Delshad. "Nothing like that. All the ruling clans are kind to their people."

Jahan then interjected.

"They are descendants of the great warriors who lead us to victory in the past. Just like with candles, when two flames are placed together they form a perfect joining - so it is also with our people. If one is in a higher placement, then his position exists only to protect the others."

Ophir delayed his next question to give Helios some time to catch up.

"You spoke of an enemy. What would that be?" he asked.

"The djinn." Both answered simultaneously. They looked at each other, smiling and laughing softly.

"Do these *djinn* exist today?" Ophir enquired.

"No, they were blanked out hundreds of years ago," responded Delshad.

Ophir corrected the young Pyros, stating that *'wiped out'* was the proper term, not *'blanked'*. Then nodding to Helios, ensuring he finished recording, decided to end the questioning. Ophir told the boys they would carry on tomorrow and for now to go get something to eat from the dining hall. Both Pyros jumped up, visibly delighted to oblige. Ophir then turned to Helios.

"Are you coming with us?"

"In a moment. I have to get these transcribed. The council has been asking for reports and I am behind," he responded.

"That makes two of us," stated Ophir. "Well, I'll meet you in the dining hall."

Helios affirmed this while he organized his writings and headed to the scribes quarters. Ophir left the learning room and started back to the main chamber where the dining hall was located. Passing the barracks on his way, Paulo waved him down and ran towards him.

"You going to eat?" he asked.

"Of course," replied Ophir

"Hey, Victor," Paulo shouted. "Going with Ophir to get food. Meet me inside."

They began walking together and Ophir enquired how the

conversion was going. Paulo informed him that within three days everything would be complete. The Southern Garrison was very quickly becoming a dormitory. Upon entering the dining hall, food was served to them. Delshad and Jahan were already sitting, using their left hands to eat and their right hands clasped together. The awkward custom encouraged Paulo to question Ophir.

"They have a special connection. Not just with each other, but with their entire race. Feelings and even nutrition can be passed between two or more of them during contact. It really is a marvellous quality. I have never heard of any other mage race having the ability to actually join with their environment and with one another," Ophir replied.

Just then, Helios walked in and was served a plate. Paulo pointed out the boys who were laughing and eating merrily. Paulo invited Helios' opinion on the discussion.

"Yes, I have asked them about it. Their natural composition allows them to become synchronized to one another, like two flames being pressed together. If one is sick, another who is healthy can heal. They mentioned it as a customary activity, where they sit in large circles and hold hands. They are a people almost completely fused with their surroundings."

"That's what Ophir was saying," said Paulo. "Another thing, if you have been teaching them about our customs, what's with the barehanded eating?"

"They never use utensils where they are from," replied Helios. "I actually once saw Delshad take a piece of raw meat, cook it in his hand and eat it."

Paulo smiled after hearing this and then continued eating. The others did the same and the table was silent. The Pyros could be heard giggling and eating while reciting stories in a mixed dialectic of Plains speak and their native Flame tongue. Victor arrived and the Pyros immediately gave a loud shout welcoming the team leader. Victor tapped Paulo on the shoulder, getting his attention after sitting down.

"Thanks for your help today," Victor expressed. "We have been short staffed since the recall."

Paulo waved it off, telling him not to worry.

"We would have been done sooner," Victor continued, "but the delegates coming to see the Pyros just left yesterday. Everything is set."

Arrangements to take Jahan and Delshad on a tour of the Mage World territories after a year's time. Their desire to see the rest of the world was so strong that within the year, they became proficient in Plains tongue while also able translate the Flame speak clearly.

The tour would commence the second level of their education. It was agreed that each stop would be a three-month duration. First, the City of Lights, then to the Terran homeland, from there to Nebat and finally to the North Hold. After a year of touring, the Pyros would return to the south, acting as their nation's ambassadors and aid the training of their kindred.

"Their progress shows they are more than worthy of this," sighted Helios.

"Another something to keep in mind: when they leave, so do we," said Victor casually. "I heard from some of our friends back home that there are plans for our relocation."

They all looked intently at Victor wondering where they would end up next. Their stay at the garrison had been stretched beyond necessity. All the mages assembled were well aware of one nation still left to uncover.

"Paulo, do you remember when you were teasing Sil about being useless when we arrived at the Garrison? It turns out he may have taken it to heart. Over two months back, we sent Vidar and his crew, along with all our Aerials, to the council to deliver the first letters of progress. I don't know what happened, but between the two of them, they have apparently figured some means of approach to our underwater friends."

Victor stopped a moment to collect his thoughts. Now aware of all the team members being incredibly focused on what he would say next, he took a deep breath and continued.

"We will not be staying the rest of the year, so make yourselves ready. A legion of teachers and scholars from every nation will be arriving to greet the wave of fire children and complete Delshad's and Jahan's training."

Ophir suddenly spoke up.

"What of the trading?"

"It will be under different supervision, but the garrison will maintain support," answered Victor.

After they could communicate with the Pyros nation, Paulo and Ophir set up a mercantile relationship with them. Obsidian, prevalent in volcanic regions, and volcanic soil, rich in nutrients, was traded for Plainswalkers food. Since the food itself could not be stored, the site became a marketplace where Pyro families would come to indulge in the different delicacies not previously available to them. The larger clans exported tons of obsidian and soil, and in turn, made sure that all their people could enjoy the result. The base doubled as housing for students and storage for product.

The meal concluded. They summoned the young Pyros, telling them of the situation. Though they did not want to see their teachers leave, the boys were equally excited about the tour being offered early. Giving them the rest of the day off, Victor and the team caught up on lost time with their reports. The team knew they would be called upon, once again, to venture into the mysterious deep.

CHAPTER 82

The scholars arrived a week early, relieving the team of their command. After one last feast and many goodbyes, their journey back to the capital began. They slept most of the way, making brief stops at other bases and outposts for food, water and bathroom breaks. Victor and Paulo showed visible enthusiasm upon their return to their homeland. Passing through the countryside, hearing the birds and seeing the plains after years of absence, brought them great comfort.

"Well, we're home," sighed Paulo.

"Does anyone know what we will be doing?" asked Danir. "We were called away much faster than anticipated."

Nobody actually understood the reason for such a quick move. It normally took the council months to make a decision and about as long to enact it. Entering the city became an enlivening endeavour; what once was a constricting domain became a comforting scene. They travelled along the Queen's road, which united most of the known world. The mid-afternoon sun shone brightly and the endless fields surrounding the capital created a serene backdrop.

Finally, arriving within, the carts stopped in front of the palace. Victor and the team took leave of the cart. Many important diplomats emerged to greet them and almost immediately after they were escorted into the palace. One of the diplomats apologized for the absence of other political figures. Victor said he understood, but in reality, did not actually care.

"I assume you heard your teammates have been busy?" asked the diplomat.

"I have," responded Victor.

They entered a chamber and like the ones previously housing them, it was full of maps, readouts and technical information. Writings were strewn over the walls and covered the tables completely. The peaceful welcoming was replaced by an immediate situation.

"Over the last year, while you were in the south, Silvanus and Prince Vidar have been engaged in a sort of special project. They have apparently found a way to make contact with the mage nation that dwells within the ocean," expounded the diplomat. "Now, we have no idea what this technique is. Between the lack of description and misinformation, we have had to rely on Aerial messengers. Most of which arrive, make a report, and then disappear again for months."

Paulo actually held back from laughing knowing that Sil could speak the language but not write while Vidar could hardly write and barely speak.

"We made an attempt to send mages into the field for assistance with documentation and support." The diplomat paused a moment, looking at the team. "And every one of them was sent back."

"Sent back?" queried Victor. "But why?"

"It seems," the diplomat paused and started speaking slower, "that most of them were afraid of venturing into the deep."

A quiet spell overshadowed the mages until Paulo started to laugh, causing a chain reaction, eventually filling the room. Thinking of a situation where Vidar had to deal with some soft bureaucrat made the team wish they were there, just to see it happen.

The laughter died out almost as quickly as the team considered the dignity of their surroundings. Satisfied with the resumed quiet, the diplomat continued.

"After the first wave returned and reported, none have volunteered and even the ones we force instantly resign. What we need are mages with experience who are also competent with writing and reporting."

He finished his sentence, staring at the team intently, silently telling them that the only mages with this exposure were in the room.

"Well," responded Victor, looking for any protests among his friends. "It is what we do."

"Excellent!" said the diplomat, clapping his hands together and ordering his attendants to bring some food for the heroes.

"When do we leave?" asked Paulo.

"Three hours," he responded.

Without time to rest, they were loaded with supplies and given a royal transport, replacing the Terran one with a horse drawn carriage. The three hours passed quickly and the team set out toward the Western Ocean and from there, into another world.

CHAPTER 83

Travelling to the west was more peaceful then coming from the south. Many of the familiar rivers and farmsteads remained unchanged. Victor and Paulo both recognized everything as they began recounting stories of their youth and their early travels with the Aerials. Even though to Ophir, Danir and Helios, all of the landscape seemed flat and had no particular appeal, Victor and Paulo always found some sort of historical reference to specific areas. The entire journey became a narrative between the two.

Both Paulo and Victor went silent as they passed Miano, their hometown. Their families would be getting ready to eat a final meal for the day. The trees were lined endlessly in the distance creating a forest wall that bordered their town. Both also knew the harvest would be ready in the months to come.

To a Plainswalker, the family was the center of almost all culture and tradition, and it had been years since they had been back to see them. The team was the only qualified unit to truly face the hardships that discovery brought with it. The time had passed so quickly and with it, festivals, holy days and naming day celebrations. Both Paulo and Victor, now so close, could see smoke rising from one of the homestead's chimney.

Victor made himself a silent promise: after finding this world and establishing contact, the first place he and his team would go was to his home. It was not enough to make up for lost time, but it would be a start.

The team arrived at the harbour days later. Tents were sprawled out along the shore, making it seem like a small circus was set up. The carriage pulled in and the team stepped out. Their arrival went unnoticed, receiving very little welcome. No one greeted them, or gave them hospitality. Victor gestured to the team to follow him into the campsite.

Most of the mages present were using crystal seers to peer toward the ocean. They remained concentrated on their task. Their conduct became contagious, and other team members began speaking in hushed tones. Danir whispered to Victor, asking what they were looking for. Victor shrugged, figuring it was only a matter of time before they found out.

Twilight arrived and they still found nothing. As hope was beginning to fade, icebergs were seen coming from the horizon and Aerials flew in, with Silvanus in the lead. Landing at the shoreline, the team was reunited, but instead of rushing off to eat with the rest, they stood together and awaited the arrival of their Kryos brothers.

CHAPTER 84

Vidar and his crew, along with other Kryos the team had never met before, landed and stepped off the berg. After a cheerful welcoming, they gathered and sat to eat. Victor moved close to Silvanus and Vidar as the meal began and everyone was introduced. Ophir opened with the question on everyone's mind:
"Tell us, how are we to make contact?"
Vidar and Sil looked at one another as Sil responded.
"To keep it short, I draw air tightly around myself creating a sphere, so when I dive into the water, I have a supply to draw from. As it depletes, I rise back to the top for more. We are getting pretty deep and if the coordinates from the Spectro elders are correct, we should be able to make contact soon."
Ophir marveled at how brilliantly simple their approach had developed and was more than a little surprised that Sil had thought it up. Vidar continued the topic and explained the situation.
"We have many Kryos here. In summertime, the ice melts fast so we need their additional strength to keep this from happening."
His plains speak had degenerated slightly due to his constant coordination with his people. Victor mapped out the position mentally, trying to get a grasp on the methodology.
So, each managed a different part of the excursion: The Kryos maintained the transport and the Aerials formed the diving teams.
 The morning came and the team jumped into action. The Kryos forged three floating barges of ice. The Aerials and the team boarded. After setting off, it took more than a half-hour to reach the predetermined location. The weather was agreeable and the waters were calm. Sil explained that the extra Aerials were used to ensure no storms interrupted the expedition. Both Kryos and Aerials communicated in their native languages, which confused the others.
"Why this location?" asked Helios, eager for a deeper understanding of the expedition.

"This is the area coordinated with your elders," replied Sil. "We have been diving for months. Even though we cannot get low enough to view their homeland, we have seen them."

This caused a sudden disruption in focus among the team. All eyes turned to Sil to hear what he would say next.

"You saw them?" questioned Paulo. "What were they like?"

"Fast," he answered. "Very, very, fast. I think we have figured them out, though. Most of the ocean's predators stay clear of the areas these mages dwell and we are certain they herd schools of fish at specific times of the year. One of those schools is close by and about this time, they come for food."

They all stared in amazement, thinking of the last nation yet to join the fold.

"What will you do to make contact?" Danir probed. "Can you speak underwater? Or draw their attention?"

"No," responded Sil. "We're going to have to catch one."

He went on to explain how they would position themselves in a way that allowed them to close in and snatch their target from their environment. A call from one of the Kryos sent the rest of the mages into motion. They rowed fiercely until each berg reached specific bearings. Vidar yelled a command, instructing the Kryos to hold their vessels.

The bergs were spaced widely from one another, with two adjacent and one apart, creating a triangle formation. Vidar pointed to the waters and the team immediately noticed the horde of fish swimming in unison.

"Make yourselves ready!" shouted Sil, as he and numerous Aerials began floating into the air, drawing the currents around them.

The team and crew watched on as the Aerials drifted over the water's surface. They surrounded the cloud of fish and then gently descended into the ocean causing only a light disturbance. With the Aerials gone and the suspense calmed, the Kryos kept the icebergs steady. No one dared make a sound. All of the mages on the oceans exterior stood silently watching the waters, trying to discern what was happening. In calm tones, Paulo asked Vidar, "Now what?"

"It rests on them now," he responded.

Beneath the surface of the water, the Aerials moved slowly, spreading far apart so as not to hinder each other. They continued to descend, following the large swarms of fish that had gathered. Signals to one another were the only form of communication, so each needed to stay constantly aware. After some time, Sil began to notice some strange figures quickly moving in a predatory fashion. He calmed himself and signaled to the others to slow their motions. The figures were dark and it was hard to see until one approached. A group of large sharks coursed through the waters, their streamlined bodies reflecting the light as they moved. Sil quickly signalled for a halt. The sharks swam by them slowly. Seeing the sharks up close was even more frightening then seeing their shadows from afar. With lidless eyes, the large fish seemed to be staring right through the Aerials as they glided by. Thin jaws sprawled forth from their mouths as they lunged into the horde. Sil signalled to the other Aerials, knowing that this breed fed only on smaller fish and that soon more would approach.

An hour later the air around them started running low. Sil gave a sign by tapping his wrist and holding up two fingers indicating they would have to surface soon. This signal passed throughout the ranks: what one did, all did.

The sharks feeding rapidly escalated into a frenzy. Watching for any sign of approach, Sil evaluated the situation:

So, *over an hour and no show. This is normally the right time. Did we scare them off? Is it that easy to scare them off? The depth is right. The time is the same as always with few differences. I wish Paulo were here. He could probably track them for us... I hope he didn't hear me think that. Time is running low, signal for the surface, quick rest and then return.*

As he signalled, the Aerials began to lift from the waters. Sil always stayed back to ensure everyone made it safely. The exit was never all at once but in sequence of four mages at a time. With all of them gone, Sil and the last three began to make a start for resurfacing. At that moment, a water mage sped past. It seemed more so to be flying through the water then actually swimming.

This time, though, it was different. These mages were not hunting the small fish; they were hunting the sharks. They had long bright spears. In packs of three, they attacked while the sharks fed on the schools of fish. Three water mages would spear the shark through the gills, the stomach and the back. The sharks struggled violently as the hunters withdrew with their prey.

Seeing one of the hunters focussed on dragging its victim, Sil made a drastic move. Lunging forward, he wrapped his arms around him and made a break for the surface.

The mage struggled and the others perused. They would have caught him but Sil held his breath and strengthened the shield of air preventing the mages from being able to stop him. Rising faster now, he breached the surface, soaring through the air and landing hard on the ice with his new companion falling beside him.

Sil gasping for air pointed to their new guest, who also was gasping and struggling. Sil prostrated on the ice, breathing heavily and wet from the dive.

"What's wrong with him?" Danir inquired.

Vidar looked down at the water mage, obviously male. He had blue skin similar to the Kryos but with a darker tinge. Not sure what to say, Paulo jumped in.

"He cannot breathe and look at his body-he's freezing. These mages are not used to this environment."

"So, what do we do?" shouted Sil.

"It's your game. You tell me!?" Paulo shot back.

"We didn't think this far ahead. I don't know!" retorted Sil.

They quickly wrapped the young mage in heavy blankets as his body turned purple. His gills struggled against the environment, trying to pull in oxygen.

"We have to throw him back," stated Victor.

"It took us almost a year to catch him," Sil protested.

"He will be dead soon!" replied Victor.

Sil thought for a moment, then at once sprang into action. He grabbed the water mage's head and tilted it back. He lined up mouth to mouth with the mage. This move caused unanimous surprise among everyone present.

Sil breathed into the mages mouth, visibly inflating the lungs. With every breath, the water mage's stomach would expand. After half a dozen breaths, the water mages body calmed. He sat up looking around in surprise and breathing on his own. What once was a threatening hunter was now a confused and frightened hostage. He took deeper breaths, testing his new ability to breathe out of water.

"How did you know to do that?" asked Victor.

"Well, the Terrans couldn't see when they first came up, so I hoped breathing would be the same for... whoever these are," Sil answered.

The young mage was helped to his feet. He was breathing steadily now. Paulo asked what they planned to do. Again, Sil had not thought that far ahead. Vidar turned everyone's attention to the waters where the mage's brethren were swarming underneath the berg and suggested they bring the water mage to the shore. The young mage from the deep curled into a fetal position in a state of shock. He listened without understanding while his comrades circled below, unsure what to make of his current circumstances.

CHAPTER 85

Upon reaching the shore, the team escorted the water mage to land. The scenery overwhelmed the water mage's senses. Everything fascinated him. Wrapped in the blanket and shaking from the shock, the team guided him to the camp. Silvanus watched him, remembering his first time along these shores and how frightening and captivating his surroundings had been.

They sat him down within one of the tents and to make sure he was not intimidated, only Victor, Vidar, Sil and Paulo entered with him. For long moments, they just stared at each other. Now, within the tent, true fear coated the young mage's face. Victor stared, analyzing his features: he noticed the gills on his neck and the webbed hands and toes, the small fins that protruded from his arms and calves, thin, dark green hair smothered his head like seaweed, and a light blue hue covered his body, while dark, obsidian eyes contributed to a terrified look fixed on his face.

"Sooo... what do we do now?" asked Sil.

"I thought you figured that one?" replied Vidar.

They both stared at the mage they had kidnapped from the sea. As they were thinking of a solution, Victor interrupted.

"You mean, you have not even thought about what to do when you caught one?"

"Well, it took up all our time to *actually* catch him. Never really thought about speaking to him," Sil admitted.

Their argument lasted a short while before Victor silenced them.

"Maybe we should try feeding him?" Paulo asked.

The team brought forth a variety of berries and fruits to present to the young mage. He stared at them for some time and then looked up at his kidnappers, confused. Vidar, not able to resist, took from the plate and started to eat. Sil shot a menacing look at him, while the large Kryos, with his mouth full, defended his actions.

"What? I'm hungry."

"You may be from a part of the world where being barbaric is a way of life, but even *you* must have some esteem for what we are trying to accomplish," Sil shot back.

"Barbaric? How is it barbaric to eat something?" retorted Vidar around his half-full mouth of food.

As they started to feud, the water mage looked closely at the plate, reached for a small melon and then, after examination, took a bite. The two arguing mages ceased their bickering. Both watched as their hostage ate and then began sampling more of the food until all of it was gone.

Another plate was brought and gradually, the water mage's fear subsided and he was introduced to his captors. Trying to pronounce their names became a serious problem. His manner of speech was made up of vibrations and drawn out guttural expressions. He sounded more as if he was chanting or singing, a rising scale.

Night came fast and the water mage, standing on the beach, looked out to the sea as the sun was setting. Sil understood what was happening, seeing the sadness in his eyes. The Aerial silently wished he could communicate with him. Sil pointed to the sea, enunciated slowly.

"H-Oh-Mm-E"

The water mage did the same.

"*Huuuuuummmmm.*"

His voice seemed to propel the sound rather than vocalize words. His vibratory articulation made Sil's skin shiver. Sil stood with goosebumps running from his head to his feet. He decided it would be best to let the language lessons settle for the day.

As the two continued to enjoy the water mage's first sunset, Sil announced, "You know what? I think we will call you Blue."

He led the homesick mage to his quarters where he would sleep. Watches were taken: team members would check on him to make sure he was secure. The next day's actions would determine the final step to a reunified world.

CHAPTER 86

Morning came and as the sun was rising, the team began preparations for the day. *'Blue'* also awoke and walked out to the shore. There he saw the Aerials flying overhead and the Kryos preparing large ice barges for transport. His eyes widened in complete wonderment as he observed the activity on the shoreline. Seeing Blue, Silvanus waved while shouting a loud greeting. The water mage kept his distance, but returned the gesture. Victor walked up to Sil and asked if he wanted Blue to be included in the preparations.

"No," responded Sil. "He won't understand anything anyway and whenever he speaks, it causes tremors in my body."

Victor thought about yesterday when they were introducing themselves to him to ease his anxiety. Blue's voice seemed to puncture holes in everyone's thoughts. With the preparations complete and the water mage summoned, the team ate a light meal and then set off. They sailed out to the location where they had abducted Blue and almost immediately, the presence of Blue's kindred became noticeable. Blue smiled when he saw their shapes darting around. The iceberg steadied and the water mages surrounded the vessel, ceaselessly swimming in circles, much like the sharks Sil had witnessed.

"Well, you wanted to draw them," stated Paulo.

Sil stood silently staring at the mages, noticing that many of the water mages were armed with the same spears they had used yesterday. Blue was given some sweet food and told he could go back to his home. Victor affirmed this visually, hoping that when Blue returned, their kindness would have some effect on Blue's report to his people.

The team members waved to Blue and indicated that he was free to go. He looked nervous, but after a short while, smiled and slipped back into the water. His departure was seamless. He simply walked off into the ocean causing almost no disturbance to the water. Within the ocean, all of the attention went from surrounding the Kryos transport to the area where Blue had descended. Vidar looked off the edge of the berg.

"What do you think?" he asked.

"It's on them now. We have to wait for a response," replied Victor.

Several moments passed in silence and then a sudden jolt shook the iceberg, catching everyone completely by surprise. Helios's arms waved wildly as he tried to retain his balance near the edge of the berg. His body tipped towards the water where an unknown number of armed mages lay in wait. He shouted an unintelligible cry for help just as Vidar caught hold of his collar. There was stillness for a moment and then an even more ferocious shock struck the vessel.

"Sil!" yelled Ophir. "What's happening?"

"They're pissed off!" he responded.

The iceberg began moving, gaining speed as they travelled. The Kryos tried to halt the cruising but their oars were snatched from below. The water mages had pierced the underside of the berg with their spears and were now propelling it toward some unknown destination.

Moving at an uncomfortable speed, they cleared the view of the shoreline. No one knew how far they were or what was going to happen. Their ride halted abruptly, sending most of the mages to the floor. Released from their forceful propulsion, the team found themselves stranded. The team members began helping one another to their feet. Surrounded by the ocean, the waves cascaded gently and the iceberg remained in a free float.

After what seemed like an eternity of silence, Sil spoke up.

"Well, look at all that sea."

"Why are we here?" asked Paulo.

"You didn't hear the pissed off part I threw in back there?" retorted Sil.

"They could have easily overturned the ship with their power and then outfought us underwater," stated Paulo. "Why all this?"

As if on cue, the ocean began to answer Paulo's question.

"Sil, calm the winds?" requested Ophir.

"There's no wind involved. The water is moving on its own," Sil replied.

Knowing what was coming, Victor and Ophir looked at one another.

"Everyone hold strong!" shouted Victor.

The waves increased in size. The sky remained clear and even birds flew overhead, but the waters raged. Eventually, the force built up and a huge monolith of water emerged in front of them, towering over the barge. The horrifying force accumulated, looking to overwhelm them at any moment. The current flowed upwards, continuously maintaining an unnatural column of water. The waves around the iceberg calmed while the pillar remained. The team looked on, waiting for what would occur next. They all knew that they were completely at the mercy of this new found mage nation.

Vidar moved as close to the column as possible. Then, reaching out, he felt the water moving. Sentient forms swimming within caught him off-guard. Hundreds of mages had ascended within the column and more continued rise. Vibrations from the water mages could be felt from where the team stood. The liquid obelisk moved closer to their ship, slowly advancing until the front half of the berg was engulfed within the water.

"Shouldn't we be overturned?" asked Danir to Vidar.

"No, the water is moving gently," he replied. "This… is their power!"

The water ceased its advance and one mage stepped forward from within. He was obviously male, larger and more muscular than Blue. He had a head of long, bright red, stringy hair and was lightly clothed in green seaweed. As the new water mage stepped out of the water and onto the barge, the team stood staring, not sure how to approach.

The water mage began to speak. Everyone on board covered their ears, as the water mage's vernacular overwhelmed their senses. Many of them, unable to stand, fell trembling into fatal position. Their hearts began beating faster and their bodies trembled under the pressure the mage's voice released. Noticing their discomfort, the mage pointed to his mouth and then gestured outwardly. The team stared, totally unsure as to what this could mean. He did it again and this time pointed to them at the end of his silent instruction. Still, no one knew exactly what to do. The mage then turned to the wave and stuck his head in, held it for a moment then came out.

Sil was the first to understand: Jumping to his feet, he ran to the mage, grasped his head between his hands and forced air into his mouth. Sil's friends looked on with horror and moderate amusement. Sil continued with the process and after seven breaths, the mage held Sil by the shoulders to stop him. Then, looking up and breathing in deeply, the mage smiled and signalled to the others. Sil, being the only Aerial, found himself working for hours, opening the lungs of all the water mages. By the end of the day, Sil was exhausted. The water mages apprehended his condition and swam them back to shore. With the last nation drawn forth, the mages now stood on the beach, at the edge of the world, finally unified as one creation.

CHAPTER 87

It took many months to understand and coherently learn to speak with Blue and his kindred. The team invested great effort to train the water mages to communicate in a way that would not have such adverse effects on their environment. Their nation was named the Aqueous, using the root term for water in scholar's tongue from the Plainswalkers.

At first, trying to keep them from exploring was a huge difficulty. Because of the painful consequences of listening to them speak, it was nerve wracking to think of the blue mages speaking with others. Eventually, an elder of the Aqueous stepped forth and order was given.

Everyday many of the young Aqueous would line up and be 'treated' by the Aerials, so they, too, could breathe outside of their watery homeland.

After this, most were confined to the beach. A few selected from their society attended classes, of which Blue was among them. It was here that eventually their voices calmed and they developed the ability to understand Plains tongue.

It took over a year and the Nebatean diplomats were not allowed to visit until the Aqueous were fully trained. They exchanged knowledge of cultures and had weekly celebrations where food from both peoples was shared. History was made when the elders of the Aqueous society ate their first cooked meal. The Aqueous mage students, including Blue, showed enough progress to answer the questions of the team, who were eager to learn of their society. Helios was placed in charge of chronicling the discourse.

"Would you tell us more of your nation and its government?" Helios prompted.

"We are ruled by mostly an eldership that is chosen by trial. That involves the testing of the strength, will power, and courage. This test has been in our civilization for generations. Only the worthy may leads us."

"Do many die in these trials?" asked Helios.

"Sometimes, but most of them die after the test," responded Blue.

This answer surprised Helios, who enquired further.

"They pass through first, the long way where there is no cover and many... uh, predators. It takes many days, and so they normally do so without sleep. When the larger predators approach, they must be slain and parts of their bodies brought back for examination. This shows courage.

"For will power, they must pass through the pillars of heat on the world's floor, endure the pain it causes and remain standing the whole time. If they fall, the heat will destroy their faces and cause them death.

"Then, for strength, they must swim into the void. My people say it is the deepest part of the world; no predators or animals live there. The pressure is so intense that it is like having all the world's weight pressed upon them. The one who does this is taught special words...... vibrations that create a barrier of protection around him and allow for him to survive, so long as he is vigilant with the practice. He touches the bottom and then returns to the top."

Blue deliberated about how he would continue his explanation, hoping his inelegance did not cause his friend annoyance.

"This is how our leaders are chosen. The ones who survive are assembled and one of the current elders brings a large, hallow clamshell. Inside are different coloured corals, recently placed within. All of the chosen reach in at once and pull out either a red or a green coral. The red ones are directed to lay with many ready females and are then sacrificed, as our tradition demands."

*****

Helios transcribed all of their conversations and compiled a report:

To the council, explaining the nature of the Aqueous as dictated by Blue. I have taken the liberty to use a more correct Plains Speak in the report. Oftentimes, Blue has difficulty talking clearly and, for the purposes of transmitting the message, I have given you a redacted explanation. Also included are the originals for comparison:

Here we have a most astonishing society surviving beneath the deepest waters. We have observed them for many years, and even though we have seen most of their activities, we have never learned of their history. According to Blue, they originated from the surface and were a much larger people. A great war took place and forced their enemies into the ocean. Fearful that their adversaries would gain strength and return for vengeance, a large group pursued them into the deep.

The war continued for decades and after adapting themselves to the conditions underwater, they could no longer return to the surface. It was, believed by their nation, however, that the mages that remained on the land would someday come for them. At the time of our arrival, this belief had been replaced with the misconception that the dry land had all been swept under the ocean and land no longer existed at all.

No one could even attempt to rise out of the water due to the inability to breathe. Therefore, there were no ventures into shallow water and drifting on the top currents was dangerous, due to the presence of predators.

This ends my formal report. There are a number of facts I left in the initial writings. Please be sure those are read alongside this text.

CHAPTER 88

Helios took his seat and waited. There was no base or outpost set up. Instead, a small temporary village of tents was installed to house the Aqueous and the other mages, led by the team, for the duration of the study. Blue burst in speedily.

"Sorry for the lateness," he exclaimed. Helios smiled, telling him not to worry.

Blue sat down and recounted a meeting with some of the locals from the villages nearby. Some had been from Victor's family and Blue and his brethren were introduced. After Blue's tale, both took a drink of water and Helios, taking ink and pen, opened with a question.

"I wanted to ask you about your living spaces under the ocean. We have observed your people from afar for many years and have no clear understanding of how mages survive against the amount of predatory competitors. Your coral home is a source of shelter and defence. Can you share some information as to its development?"

Blue responded.

"Yes, home is in the long plants which you are calling kelp. Most of the large groups reside in the forest. All of those plants are grown by our people."

This statement surprised Helios, who had thought that they had just naturally adapted to their environment.

"We created the dense forest so that predators could not sneak up on us without causing some disturbance. There are special quarters for children and elders. Other quarters for males and females of certain ages and, as you grow, you move out from one place to make room for the next portion of younger ones. In the hierarchy, the young ones are taught by stewards appointed by the elders.

"The females live in a similar structure with some differences. Pregnant females live in the centre of the forest. Close to them are the children. Mothers only care for them for the six years and then the children are watched by the stewards; it is like a school. Females are taught by females and males teach males."

Helios wrote all of this down word-for-word ceaselessly. Blue paused to allow him to finish, then he went on.

"There are other groups also who live outside our society. The creatures that you call sea monsters and what the Kryos call whales and orcas herd with them. They stay in family groups and have a different society then we do. Their society is more tribal and ours more social."

"Do you get along with these tribal Aqueous?" asked Helios.

"Of course! We have no problem with them. We actually hunt together during special times of the year. Normally, the forest provides our clothing and food comes from seaweeds and plants that we grow. But at certain times, we bring home…uh, hard food. These are special celebration times."

CHAPTER 89

Report number 19-3: Languages and Speech

{In the previous dispatch, there was mention of different specimens of the deep. I realize that half way it cuts out due to an editing failure on my part. The remainder of that report is issued with this one.}

As for the language of the Aqueous, it is relatively simple as compared to our tongues. In all of the mage nations, I have never seen anything like this. The transcript attached could not be copied so I have taken the liberty to summarize its intent.

All the systems of communication throughout our world depend on phonetic sounds emanating from the throat to produce word combinations that allow peoples to understand one another.

With the Aqueous, this is not at all true. Their underwater breathing prevents the use of sound in any conventional way, so words can never be formed. Instead, they use a system of vibrations that not only allows for communication, but also perception. Sending out waves of sound can warn of potential dangers, prey, or even the location of other mages. As they advance in age and experience, the vibrations can be used as a shield in harsh depths and as a defence against predators or larger aquatic life.

As one reaches maturity, the vibrations can actually control the flow of water, allowing one to not only constrict or expand its composure, but also propel a mage through the depths at alarming rates. If the mages vibrate in unison, they increase their powers immensely.

Since mathematics, cosmology, and advanced engineering were unnecessary contrasting in every other nation, the in-depth complexity of the language remained non-existent. However, because of its compact efficiency, a great many concepts can be communicated with simple instruction and as such, they have developed their soci-

ety around these ideas.

For instance, they live in specific regions that separate age groups, genders, and leadership roles. When the issue to call children, women, or elders, it is usually addressed to the whole segment rather than the individual. Nothing is ever done in solitary.

As a result, these mages can feel the language itself. Their names are partly a resonance of sound and an imprinted sensation within the mages nature. Words and concepts are replaced by feelings and emotions expressed through varied frequencies.

It is impossible to truly put to paper their units of language, since I would have to not only describe the sounds, but the feeling it evokes.

There are seven main vibrations that I have been able to record and they serve as the foundation for the Aqueous communication. These sounds are spoken slowly. They oscillate in frequency from high to low, or lower to higher pitches. I have made a phonetic recording as close as possible to the original seven vibrational tones. They are as follows:

LAM
VAM
RAM
YAM
HAM
AUM
NG

Normally a vibration is drawn out and would sound something like this:

LLLAAAAMMMmmmmm

Each one can be used for different results – which are, of course, going to be outlined in my appendix, currently being produced.

These vibrations are introduced to the community in stages: LAM, VAM are given to youth, RAM, YAM to the middle aged, HAM, AUM to the mature, and NG to the elder class.

These sound patterns are given as tools to expand their abilities and better cope with the world around them. The above-mentioned *techniques are not merely taught to their people, but rather are introduced to them as a sort of therapy. The sound first imbues the body and is then released by the mage. Therefore, the need for a tightly bound society is essential for development.*

This will conclude my report and the appendix will follow shortly.

If there are any questions, please hold off as I am sure the appendix will solve most enquiries.

CHAPTER 90

The year passed with the entire team working toward the advancement of the Aqueous nation. The inevitability of their progress was realized within the appointed time. Half of the students went on to teach their brethren, while the others became trained as ambassadors. Among them, Blue was selected to join the team and journey to the North Hold to meet with Delshad and Jahan, who were completing their training with the Kryos.

The team prepared for the excursion, and with little delay, they loaded the carriages and made ready to set off in three days' time. Within one of the larger tents at the centre of the camp site, Paulo and Silvanus discussed the final preparations. The waves on the beach set a peaceful tone during their final twilight by the shoreline. As they enjoyed wide cups of herbal tea, their leader made his entrance.

"So, there he is!" exclaimed Sil. "The mage who pulled it all together."

"You should look happier," sighted Paulo. "All of our nations are as one. Our mission is almost fully accomplished."

"Annnd, we managed to pack in record time," added Sil. "Right when we become really efficient, we run out of nations to discover."

Victor looked at them both silently. Then, half smiling, quietly announced, "He is afraid of going."

The two mages looked at one another, confused by the report. Victor continued with an explanation and a larger smile.

"He believes that if he stays away from his home for too long, he may never be able to breathe underwater again."

"Did you explain to him that all mages who left their homes for long periods of time experienced no problem returning?" Paulo asked.

"Yes, but he has never done this before," explained Victor.

Sil quickly intruded.

"But he's still coming, right?"

"Of course he is," Paulo affirmed. "We have invested too much time into him. Even if he says no, we will kidnap him out of principle."

Victor smiled.

"We make ready for tomorrow. We leave at sun up."

Sil asked Victor why the early rise; Victor responded that they would be taking a short detour. Both Paulo and Sil understood immediately and with silent enthusiasm, left for their sleeping quarters knowing that they would be returning to where the team's history first began.

CHAPTER 91

Sunlight still stretched out over the horizon as they departed. With the horses hitched up and the carriages loaded, most team members slept during their travels. Victor remained awake and alert, watching the sunrise as they rode. Silvanus silently kept vigil next to him. During mid-morning, the shining sun roused the rest of the team. Blue looked out at the scenery in utter fascination. The hills, the birds, and the wheat fields were like nothing he had ever seen before.

The team smiled, noticing their new comrade's interest in their surroundings. Blue marvelled at everything, pointing and laughing as they passed different sights. As the world kept him amused, Vidar spoke to Victor.

"When do we stop for food?"

"Soon," Victor replied. "We're going to a special place today."

After some time, the convoy veered off the road and entered a pathway leading to a fenced property. It was wide open and filled with trees that walked about by themselves. Some trees in the distance were being herded, dropping fruit into baskets below. As the team continued, trees of all sizes could be seen and many Plainswalkers began toward the unexpected visitors.

Victor ordered a halt to the drivers.

"We are here" he said assuredly.

"Where is this?" asked Helios.

"Home," he replied frankly.

The team emerged and were greeted by large trees and their caretakers. In the distance, smoke vented from a homestead. Victor smiled and shouted to the inhabitants of the area. Upon realizing who he was, the tree herdsmen rushed to meet their wayward kinsman, welcoming him with hugs, kisses and cheerful outcries. Paulo and Sil were immediately recognized and soon after, enveloped in the wave of hospitality that overcame the team, who stood standing quietly in the background.

"Who are these people?" asked Danir to Ophir.

"This is Victor's family."

After all the excitement calmed, Victor introduced his friends, inviting them to the homestead.

"Is Mom up at this end?" Victor asked a nearby relative.

"She is preparing the first day's meal. She will be so thankful to see you."

Victor and his retinue stayed at the door as one of his cousins entered, smiling. They heard talking—then yelling. The sudden outburst, common among country born Plainswalkers, startled even Victor. Eventually, the cousin opened the door, revealing the prodigal son standing with a group of strange looking mages.

Victor's mother's face went into a blush. She immediately rushed over and embraced Victor and all of his friends. Vidar was too tall to enter the doorway and had to deeply hunch over to pass through and into the house. With the meal served, everyone swamped Victor and his team with questions, endlessly imploring of the distant lands and the different cultures. Victor relayed everything to them; every detail of their struggles and their successes brought joyful animation to his family's faces. Victor's mother had an unending delight in seeing her son again and hearing of his escapades.

Sil also interjected with humorous comments, enlivening the situation further. For Blue, the concept of a family unit was foreign and Helios found himself at odds explaining the situation.

After the meal, they took a tour of the lands, tasted the berries and fruits, met the trees and then ended up back at the carriages. Victor and his mother said their goodbyes. She packed up loads of food for the ride and as they left, the whole family waited at the edge of the property, seeing them off.

*****

"She was so happy to see you," stated Paulo.

Victor smiled, nodding.

"I write when I can, but work keeps us busy. Now however, that's changed. I think I will make sure to return more often, at least for the festivals."

They rode for hours, eating the food packed by Victor's mother. Blue asked about the place they were headed to.

"We are going to the North Hold to meet up with Delshad and Jahan, the Pyros who will be completing their tour. From there, we rest a short while and then return to Nebat for a gathering before the council," Helios replied to him.

After a week of dedicated travelling, they unloaded the furs as the cold set in and the signs of snow and frost began to take shape. Though summer was in full sway, the night's cold was countered by Ophir's heating stones.

*****

Terrans and Plainswalkers greeted the team at their arrival. The team entered the familiar building only to be overtaken by Delshad and Jahan. They both began talking at the same time, telling Victor what they had been learning and seeing. Simultaneously, they took notice of Blue, staring at the new mage while silently analyzing his features. Then, as one, they scrambled over and hugged their new brother. They both overloaded him with questions, gleefully asking him about everything they could possibly think of. Blue, bewildered, just stared, not sure how to handle the overwhelming onslaught of enthusiasm.

Victor silenced everyone and introduced Blue to the Pyros. Vidar was the first to notice how the fire mages were able to make contact without burning them. One of the mages from the Hold stated that their bodies had adjusted to the north by cooling down. The greetings ceased and a meeting was immediately called to order.

Victor settled at the head of the table as refreshments were provided. The Pyros asked questions about the Aqueous nation. The talk went on for hours. Both Blue and the boys engaged in numerous discourses on a variety of topics, showing what they had learned and sharing their experiences in the different parts of the world.

"This is excellent to see such progress," announced Victor. "When we return to the council, they will know it was our combined efforts that united all the nations. Our primary responsibility will be to ensure that the knowledge we have gathered is passed on. The arrangements at the capital for…"

A Terran entered unannounced, interrupting Victor's lecture and whispered in his ear. Victor stood up and signalled for Ophir to rise with him and left the room abruptly. The rest of the mages sat in silence, wondering what could be happening.

"Do you know what's going on?" asked Sil.

Paulo shrugged, awaiting their friends' return. Not long afterwards, they re-entered the room and called for Vidar. The Kryos rose and with him, the rest of the team proceeded outside and were met by a group of Vidar's brethren riding on large, white bears. For most of the team, this was shocking. The bears were huge and fearsome looking. None dared approach, except Vidar, who warmly hailed the riders. One dismounted and began speaking quickly in Vidar's native tongue. After talking for a short time, he returned to Victor.

"I have a slight problem," he began. "My grandfather is going to be released from the cold sleep. As a leading member of the family and of my people, I must be there to attend."

"Cold sleep?" asked Blue.

"It's what happens to old mages who get bored from living in the coldest part of the world," replied Sil, who instantly took a backhand from Vidar.

Ophir explained to Blue that some of the elders of the Kryos nation would be chosen to sleep under thick ice, so they could be thawed out at certain times to ensure the survival of their people.

"Tell them you cannot!" asserted Victor. "You have responsibilities here."

Vidar shook his head.

"They may try to take me by force."

"They can't do that!" exclaimed Sil. "I thought you were *'Prince*

Vidar,' lord of the snows, slayer of giants and sailor of ice. Don't let this crap slide. Tell them you're staying here and that they should respect your authority."

Vidar laughed upon hearing his friends' concerns.

"You don't understand. Someone with greater authority then me sent them."

"We need you at the gathering. The people know you and you know the language better than any of the other Kryos under your command," declared Victor. "Can you reason with them?"

Vidar laughed even louder at Victor's remark, shaking his head. "That's not how this works."

"Alright then, we fight," said Sil loud enough to make everyone uncomfortable. "Can we win?"

"Yes. But most of you would die," responded Vidar seriously.

Victor tried speaking to the riders with Vidar translating to no avail. Vidar talked a while longer then walked over to Victor.

"I must go, but he will not stop you all from coming with me."

"What the hell are you saying?" asked Ophir.

"No outsider has ever seen an awakening. Want to come along?" he asked casually.

"Vidar, we have the council to report to. The royal court will be gathering and with them, representatives from *every* nation. We can't just skip this," explained Victor.

"If you come to this, you will be able to bring back with you a Kryos elder who has lived for over a hundred years. This will be useful, I think," stated Vidar.

Upon thinking about it, the opportunity was almost too good to pass up. Victor looked over at Ophir who shrugged, smiling, knowing what was about to happen.

"Well, where one of us is, all of us go. Send a letter to the Aerials closest to here. Tell them we have been detoured and give them the reason for it. Helios, find ink and take down what I say."

The Pyros boys and Blue were both visibly excited and the rest of the team began to prepare for a return beyond the North Wall.

CHAPTER 92

The note was dispatched and the team made ready to journey north. They quickly loaded what provisions they needed. The young Pyros were eager to see the bears up close. One of the Kryos riders dismounted and happily introduced the youngsters. Under the instruction of the Kryos rider, both mages began to stroke behind the bear's ear, causing a gratifying purr in response.

When the team had finished gathering their belongings, they stood out in front of the North Hold with Vidar. He remained silent as the Kryos riders consorted with one another.

"Sooo, do we get to pick the beast we ride, or does the beast choose the rider?" asked Silvanus whimsically.

Helios held back a laugh, but the Pyros boys now smiled ever more brightly at the suggestion. Vidar held a finger up to his lips. The Kryos riders then began using their powers. Ice was formed into a great mass that took the shape of a large sunken oval supported by almost a dozen long flat skis. Two bears were then connected to the apparatus.

"Let's go," commanded Vidar. "We sit in that."

The team climbed in. The riders took their mounts and without any command or warning, they were off. The bears pulled the icy carriage with ease and after a sudden acceleration, gained momentum as they picked up speed. The other riders followed closely and formed into a single file as they passed through the tunnel leading into the northern realm.

Emerging on the other side, more riders joined the convoy. They moved at a speed that surprised the team. Delshad and Jahan who were normally easily excitable and always in a delightful mood, were now reviling with joy. Their laughter brought smiles to the faces of their team members.

"Do you have rides like this back home?" asked Ophir to Delshad.

"We have the streaming flow that moves us between places, but nothing this fast or like *this*," he responded.

Ophir looked to Helios, confused about what he just heard.

"The streaming flow is a concentration of magma which flows freely around Pyros society. It is commonly used as transportation."

The ride continued for hours with no stops or breaks. The North Wall was so far behind them it could hardly be seen.

"How long until we reach the city?" Victor asked Vidar.

"Three days and a bit if we keep speed" he responded.

"Really? I wish we had these on our first trip."

Vidar burst into laughter at Victor's remark.

They rested briefly, stopping only to eat and relieve themselves. Sleeping happened while mobile, but the Kryos conditioning allowed the ice mages to sleep little and remain constantly moving.

After the third day, they saw mountains in the distance and a large river of which they all were familiar. Stopping at the shore, many of the flanking riders dismounted and in unison, began forming a platform with which to cross. This task was flawlessly completed and right away they charged over and began to drift across.

They were following a tight path between the mountains when the architecture of the great nation of the north became clearly visible. Seeing the enormous buildings glisten in the sunlight, the young Pyros took in their surroundings with a deep admiration. Blue had no idea that water could freeze, so he had endless questions which he unloaded onto Helios who was more than willing to answer.

Vidar took the lead. Behind him, the team and the riders followed closely. Inside the city, everyone was busy and more than a few Kryos stared, curiously noticing the foreign mages. Vidar was greeted with traditional salutes almost everywhere they went.

Eventually, they entered a main square. If it had been a normal city in the Plainswalker nation, this area would have had trees and a park, but instead, there was a block of ice supported by piles of large stones. Close by a controlled fire was used for heating up flat stones, which were placed on the block of ice to slowly melt it. It looked as if all the population was gathered for the event.

As the ice melted, a shadowy form could be seen resting within. It went on for an hour. Stones would be heated and exchanged with the ones that were cooling. The process repeated several times. Light talking spread throughout the crowd until, as if by surprise, they noticed something that silenced them.

None of the team members knew exactly what had happened, but stared intently at the melting coffin of ice. The stones were removed and from within, movement. A large form thrust up a hand, which was grasped by the Kryos who had been heating the stones. Gently pulling the elder up, another Kryos came to assist, supporting the recently thawed mage by both arms.

This was the thickest and largest mage Victor had ever seen. Even though weakened by his current state, his naked body displayed many scars healed by crude Kryos methods. The entire nation dropped to their left knee with their right arm down for support, heads bowed in reverence for their recently resurrected leader. Vidar rose and approached his grandfather, taking the place of the aids and escorted him to a nearby building. When the elder was out of sight, the Kryos stood up.

Not long after, the elder emerged, this time clothed in light skins. His large white beard and white hair were groomed so the ice was completely removed. Surprisingly, he could already stand on his own and move in small steps. The crowd cheered loudly and a celebration began. A large feast was prepared and the entire nation was ordered to attend.

All of the elders sat at one end of the feast, with their recently thawed compatriot elevated slightly above the rest of those gathered. The team was given a special placement close by and everyone ate a meal where the food portions were larger than the mages eating it.

As per Kryos custom, there were many loud shouts of praise and tales of glory, fists pounding on the table accompanied by laughter and even joyous singing. The Kryos were the loudest of mages when excited.

"I cannot believe he has recovered so quickly," yelled Victor to Vidar.

"No, he hasn't. He cannot even see. Three days from now he will be back, with the right foods and much water." Vidar replied.

Victor noticed that the elder silently drank deeply from his cup that all those close by took turns to refill. After eating all he could, Victor exited the hall with Sil and Ophir. The outside was just as boisterous.

"So how long does all this last?" asked Victor.

"From what I have determined, this is a three day event," responded Ophir. "They use loud noises to symbolically 'wake up' their sleeping leader."

"I heard his motor functions are not working. This all comes back in three days?" Victor asked.

"Yes, that is true," affirmed Ophir.

"How do you know so much about this?" asked Sil.

"I had a contingent of Kryos healers under my command in the south. I learned the language to communicate better with them," Ophir stated.

"If it takes three days to regain sight and three to return to the Hold, plus another two weeks to reach Nebat, we are going to be late for the gathering" Victor reasoned.

They silently thought of their duty to their nations. Ophir spoke up first.

"We should talk to Vidar."

"Yeah, tell him to speed up! This whole one hundred years of sleep is no excuse for laziness. Seriously, he should be fully rested by now, right?" Sil jokingly interjected.

*****

Getting to Vidar proved more difficult than they were used to. Since he was an established leader and related to the main reason for the ceremony, a large concentration of the Kryos leadership crowded the area and made it impossible to pass by, or get the attention of their comrade.

The party continued throughout the night. The Pyros were both dancing on the table with Blue while Helios kept an eye on them. Most of the team had moved outside the hall and sat together eating lightly and drinking in the main square. Paulo drifted from the conversation and noticed Vidar approaching.

"So the prince returns to his friends," stated Paulo to the others.

"Been a little busy?" asked Victor, smiling.

Without wasting time or breaking composure, Vidar spoke.

"We leave tomorrow."

"Alright then," said Victor, not completely understanding what was going on.

"He is looking to see the rest of the new world. He demands to be taken on a tour and given hospitality by your rulers," said Vidar.

"Ahh, yes of course," said Victor. "That would be more than possible. Will he be alright physically?"

"He will recover along the way. The other elders insisted he stay. He thinks this would be better and him, they won't refuse. We make ready at sunrise," declared Vidar.

Victor stood, somewhat confounded, but also thankful at the same time. Vidar turned to leave as Victor called out.

"How did you convince him?

Vidar looked back, shooting him a sly half-smile as he continued back into the hall.

"Well, he came through for us," Sil said happily.

Paulo rose quickly.

"I will gather the young ones and the others. We will need our rest."

Finding a resting place during a nationwide celebration was next to impossible and asking for one brought nothing but laughter in response. Eventually, they were led to a room. Getting to sleep was even more beyond the bounds of possibility. The Kryos mages were not known for their reserved behaviour and giving them a reason to celebrate enhanced their extroverted mannerisms exponentially.

After almost an hour, Sil yelled, "I'm done" as he jumped out of bed.

"Sil, you need rest. Tomorrow we leave," Paulo informed.

"Is the celebration too loud?" asked Victor.

Sil stood for a moment looked around and said, "Well there is that and I am for some reason, hungry again. I'm going to eat. Who wants to come with me?" he shouted.

The Pyros immediately jumped out of bed, and then looked at Victor for approval.

Victor sighed.

"Alright, but remember be ready for sunrise," he ordered sternly.

The trio joyfully ran back towards the party. It would be a while before Victor fell asleep, but the right mix of exhaustion and comfort sent him into a pleasant dream state.

CHAPTER 93

Sunrise seemed to come too quickly and with abrupt orders, the team was up. Very quickly, they were taken outside toward the edge of the city with Victor stumbling along from the lack of sleep. Reaching the river where an ice barge was already forged, everyone stepped on and as they floated across, Victor remembered Silvanus and the boys.

"Ophir, where is Sil?" he questioned frantically.

Ophir looked around, now fully awake, with a startled expression. As he became instantly infuriated, Paulo offset his anger.

"They will be here soon. I sent for them as we were approaching."

Paulo's discretion caused an immediate halt to the rage that would probably have shaved at least a year off Victor's life. Reaching the other side of the river, they found that the Kryos were at work creating transports similar to the ones that pulled them into the north.

Almost a hundred Kryos mages would be accompanying them back to Nebat as an escort to the elder. Vidar guided his grandfather to a recently completed transport, seated him and then boarded alongside him with another of his clan. Sil and the boys showed up cheerfully and were greeting everyone.

"How was your sleeping?" Sil asked, half-grinning.

Victor made no reply and the team boarded onto an icy conveyance. The Kryos made ready as the bears were strapped up and they took off. The acceleration caused all aboard to be driven back forcefully. The painful start made everyone uncomfortable, except the Pyros boys who giggled joyfully. Even though Victor was extremely tired, the laughter of the younger mages made him smile.

"You really are enjoying this," he stated.

"Of course! We have nothing like this at home," replied Delshad.

"You are not weary from your long night?" asked Ophir playfully.

Jahan spoke up in response.

"There are so many great things happening. We will not sleep at all on this trip."

*****

After three hours into the trip, the group showed no signs of slowing. All of the bear drawn carriages moved in a set formation, keeping the elder in the middle. Ophir looked over at the Pyros boys, who now leaned on each other for support as they slept. Delshad was drooling slightly, the fluid from his mouth simmered as it flowed passed his chin. Ophir pointed this out to Sil who laughed quietly.

They pressed forward with very little rest, coming to an abrupt stop near nightfall. Many of the Kryos dismounted and set up camp. Structures of ice were created for the team. The bears were taken to one side of the camp while Vidar helped his grandfather down. Once the camp was settled food was prepared. As the elder passed by, the Kryos would completely stop their work with right hands raised to their chests and heads bowed reverently. Vidar seated his grandfather near what was to be a temporary fire-pit and hearth that would cook the meal.

Even though he was in a weakened state, this old lord of the Kryos with his impressive stature, held a silent dignity that commanded respect. After he sat, Vidar aided the others with their tasks. The Pyros boys looked at each other and grinned, now seeing their chance to be useful. Walking towards where the elder sat, they set ablaze the hearth.

The Kryos operating the pit leaped backwards as intense flames engulfed the area. The flames receded, leaving the Pyros boys beaming with pride in their natural abilities.

"Delshad, Jahan… my grandfather would like to meet you."

The elder stared intently at them.

"Can he see us?" Jahan whispered to Vidar.

"Yes," Vidar answered. "His eyesight is not at full strength, but it has improved much."

The elder spoke to the boys in North Speech, his powerful voice epitomized his authoritarian presence. The boys looked toward Vidar for translation.

"He asks your names."

Both were given. The elder leaned forward, placing his hand on his chest.

"Buri."

Delshad and Jahan smiled and repeated it with their Pyronian accents, causing the elder to smile. The Pyros gave a demonstration of their powers by engulfing their bodies in flame and then tossing flames back and forth to one another.

"Looks like our boys are becoming popular," expressed Ophir.

"You should have seen them last night," Sil threw in. "Those fire boys are more like burning beasts. Just endless balls of energy."

"You were supposed to be watching them," uttered Victor.

"What? I was. If not for me, they would have melted the city," Sil affirmed.

With their display at an end, the boys bowed and were applauded by the Kryos who had gathered to watch. Vidar moved closer to Victor.

"We should have them perform more often," he declared.

"Long time no talk," Victor said, greeting the prince.

"Food will be ready soon," Vidar informed the team.

As they conversed, one of the Kryos from the hearth called everyone over for the meal.

"We are making excellent time and should be at the Hold early on the third day," Vidar said, as they walked towards the bonfire.

When they took their seats, Sil stepped in with a question.

"It's taking us three days, but your army took almost three weeks. Why didn't you guys strap up the bears and head for the hold when you pursued the giants?"

Vidar thought for a moment and informed his friend about the logistics of war.

"The bears are raised by a select group of families. They were once all over these areas and were as much a danger as the giants.

Eventually, we hunted them to near extinction. Some of the cubs were taken and as time went on, they became… how you call…… tame. They only respond to their trainers, so if in battle their master dies, they are likely to turn on anything they deem a threat. They take almost triple the food and we do not have enough of them to move groups much larger than ours. Their breeding is tightly controlled."

Sil took some time to think and after taking a bite out of his provisions and with a full mouth, replied.

"Makes sense."

Following the meal, the mages went to sleep and rested. At sunrise the next day, all were roused. They ate a light meal and then set off. At night, the same process repeated and on the third day, the North Wall came into sight. As they approached, a loud horn signaled their arrival. The Kryos at the base emerged to greet them.

Stopping at the other side of the Wall in front of the North Hold, Buri was the first to dismount. His sight, strength, and senses were now fully restored. All of the Kryos at the base kneeled before him and he began to speak in North speech to his people. The bear riders turned away and retreated towards their home. The Kryos rose to their feet and the rest of the party dismounted. They entered the North Hold and a large feast was prepared.

The team sat close to Vidar during the meal, who then opened conversation:

"Victor, listen. When we reach Nebat, you must inform the council that all questions to my grandfather must be directed to me. Our people, especially those of his generation are not used to the manners of… everywhere else."

Victor, looking back at Buri eating and conversing, understood without having to be told. This was a people of war. Heavy tribulations and intense hardships formed their entire being. Meeting with others who had a more pleasant lifestyle would be best with a buffer.

"Not a problem. The council will understand," Victor said, assuring his friend.

"Hey," Sil said getting Vidar's attention. "Why did the bears get sent away?"

Vidar scratched his nose before responding.

"It is not a good idea to expose creatures from our environment to things from here. It could become unpredictable."

Sil thought about it for a while and as per usual, Vidar's short explanation allowed for internal comprehension of the listener to come to the conclusion by himself.

As the banquet ended, Helios rose from his place and stood before Buri. He pulled a small crystal from a hidden pocket and held it out towards him. Suddenly, the room filled with images of vegetation and trees growing. A small river ran through the centre of the room and birds flew through the air. The elder was stunned. His ancient visage, for the first time since he could see, showed a level of surprise never experienced before. The images slowly faded and with the same crystals, Helios made a stream of light very quickly burst forth, engulfing Buri's body and seconds later, disappear.

Buri quickly inspected himself for what impact the light would have left on him. Finding none, he starred back at Helios, puzzled. Helios then used that same ray of light to project an image of the elder. Buri immediately jumped to his feet, leaning closer to observe this latest phenomenon. The image moved like him and looked like him, but made no sound. Buri reached out to make contact, only to find his hand pass right through. This caused a wide smile to cross his face. Helios then let the illusion fade and bowed before the elder. Buri spoke to his grandson who relayed the message.

"He is more than amazed. He never dreamed powers like this existed beyond the Wall."

Helios took his leave, while the smiling elder continued to praise the recent display with his kindred.

Two weeks passed quickly. They had eased their travelling and pressed on calmly. Every night they would break for food and camping. Helios would put on a show and the Pyros boys would juggle flames.

One night, the caravan settled beside a deep stream. As the

mages refreshed themselves, Blue vibrated over the waters and began to cross over without sinking. Even more impressive was when he invited Buri to do the same.

"I did not know he could do that," stated Sil to the cohort.

They finally arrived at the palace and were welcomed by the council. Buri was introduced and everyone proceed inside. One of the council mages approached Victor.

"We would have had a special welcoming had you been here on time. You are over a week late! We have elders from every society wanting to see the result of our progress."

"My apologies. There were circumstances beyond my control," Victor replied.

"Be that as it may, tomorrow all of your findings and your team will be presented to the assembly. These delays have run on long enough," he said ardently.

"We will be ready," Victor assured.

"And one other thing," the councillor threw in. "Games and demonstrations have been requested by all nations present to show the world the diversity of the mage prowess. Have your team ready to participate."

Victor thought for a moment. The demonstration he could understand. But...

"These games? Will they be competitive in nature?"

"Some of them, yes."

"I was not informed of this. The nature of some of these peoples can be more extreme than others which may cause conflict. This must be delayed until me and Ophir examine these activities."

"You should have thought of that before arriving late."

With that, the councillor departed and left Victor to find his way to his friends. Following his ears towards the loudest noise in the palace, he found Sil and Ophir at its source.

"They have the iceberg set up for questioning. Vidar is in there with him," Sil declared.

Victor was silent for a short while, looking at them, still thinking of what had occurred.

"What's with you?" demanded Sil.

Victor looked back at him seriously. "We may have a problem."

CHAPTER 94

"I still don't see how this is so bad," declared Silvanus.

"Not saying it is bad, just saying there could be issues," replied Victor.

Both took turns arguing about the possibility of predicaments that might ensue. Ophir eventually stepped in.

"How can you even know this? There is nothing we can do for today. Let's just go to sleep and see how things end up in the morning."

The mages agreed and headed off to assigned rooms within the palace. Victor did not feel like sleeping, but when he saw the warm bed and large room, he realized how much he missed the home comforts of his nation. Getting into bed, he noticed fresh fruit in a bowl on the dresser nearby. Tasting it brought a smile to his face. It was a midnight pear, grown only in summer times. It aided the eater by helping induce a deep sleep and he remembered his mother giving it to him: good for children with too much energy, mages with the coughing sickness and Victor, who had too much on his mind. That night, sleep came easy.

During the early morning, an attendant went around to all the rooms where elders and delegates were sleeping and roused Victor. The team ate together and Victor watched Sil enjoying some berries and asked where all the elders were.

"Other wing of the palace," Sil responded while shoving his face full of berries and other food as he continued to speak in an unintelligible manner. Paulo picked up where Sil's gorging left off.

"The elders and the council have already decided the games and demonstrations to be used today."

Sil nodded, approving of the message relayed by Paulo. Vidar walked in, sat with his friends, picked up a plate, and began to eat.

"Last night, they had to push two beds specially made for Kryos mages together for my grandfather," he said and started eating.

The rest of the team silently thought of the odd opening. Sil started laughing with his mouth still full of food. His laughter spread through the whole table.

"Does anyone know what time everything begins?" Victor asked calming the mood.

"They will send someone to gather us," Paulo replied.

Vidar noticed that some of their compatriots were missing.

"Blue, Delshad, Jahan are they coming?"

"They're with their people," Ophir confirmed.

Helios and Danir suddenly entered the room.

"Sorry for the lateness," Danir expressed.

"We were held up translating for a group of governors and aided some of the elders. Sil, you might want to dress appropriately as your elders arrived last night," added Helios.

"Crap, yeah," he responded shoving more food in his mouth as he stood up. "Be right back. Don't eat all the berries."

Ophir then asked Danir how everything was going to start.

"At the stadium, there will be demonstrations from the elders. After that, there will be speeches from us, so be ready."

"I was not aware of this," said Victor.

"We only heard a few hours ago," Helios explained.

A palace attendant entered the room and interrupting their discussion requested their presence in the main chambers where they would be escorted to the stadium. They finished eating and then rose from the table.

Outside of the stadium, an enormous crowd had gathered. In the previous week, a great festival had been ordained and the celebrations would culminate at the event happening on this day. The queen and her advisers, as well as the governors, would enter the arena, alongside the team and many of the highest-ranking elders from the surrounding nations.

The team's arrival brought about cheers from everyone present. The stadium was huge. It was the second largest building in the city next to the palace; dome shaped with an open roof, the colossal structure was filled to the brim with mages from all nations.

Even though the team and head elders sat in booths close to the queen, the rest of the arena was divided into sections. Each nation had a special portion reserved and the seats had been constructed to accommodate for the unique body structures of each nation present.

Larger seats were built for the Kryos, ones made of a carnelian stone that could absorb heat for the Pyros and the Aqueous had moistened fabrics that would allow for comfortable sitting. The queen's booth was located opposite from the entrance and high above everyone else. The team sat just below the queen's position and the mage elders were assigned with their respective nations.

There was much commotion and the anticipation of great events kept everyone excited. Victor, impressed with the fantastic turnout, nudged Ophir. "Where is Sil? He should be seeing this."

"On his way, I'm sure," Ophir said.

Paulo, observing the crowd, leaned over to Helios and asked when the events would be starting.

"Soon. It looks like the Aerial elders are running behind."

Sil then flew in over top of the stadium and landed in his seat next to Victor. He was dressed in a long dark coat, similar to the one he had when he landed years ago. This one was obviously crafted by Plainswalkers with materials native to the surface land.

"Am I a beast of gorgeousness or what?" he stated with absolute confidence.

"Well, a *beast* maybe," Paulo retorted softly. Lifting a small pair of crystal seers, then remarked at what he saw.

"Sil, it's one of yours."

Silvanus looking out toward the arena, noticed his elders flying in, their large wings drawing a short-lived silence as they approached and landed within the stadium grounds.

"How come you don't have wings?" asked Vidar.

"My parents had them removed when I was young," he promptly shot back.

"What he *means* is," Helios corrected, "only elders of their nation grow wings."

The Aerials in the crowd flew forward producing an amazing display. Sil jumped in with them to greet their leader. The whole stadium launched into an uproar at the arrival; many of the crowd having only now seen an Aerial elder for the first time. Sil returned to his place and the Aerials flew back to their seats.

Everyone was now joyfully cheering and from the Kryos quarter, a war chant that involved a unison stomping and clapping swept through the amphitheatre and caught every mage in a wave of celebration.

A governor from the Nebat council stepped forward and raised his hand, causing a slow calm to fall over the audience. Once all attention was on the governor, his speech began. He welcomed everyone and conferred great praise on the work done in unifying the world by the team, prompting other cheers.

"We have today," he went on, "for your edification, a demonstration of the hidden powers that govern our world. Hidden powers of frost and fire, powers to command the winds and even powers that dictate the perception of reality around you. Today, for the first time in our history, elders and masters from all of the nations will exhibit the full strength of their abilities for all to see."

Cheers abounded loudly before being silenced by the governor's raised hands.

"This very arena where we are gathered shall become the cradle of our coalition. In the name of the Queen of our Plains Nation and all nations of the Mage-World, the age of unification begins now!" he shouted, raising his arms, invoking a blaring response.

The crowds continued their appraisal as a group of Kryos elders emerged from their section of the stadium and stepped onto the grounds. Their large, light-blue, scarred bodies gave off a slight glow in the sunlight. All eyes focused on them. As one, they slowly raised their hands and concentrated. Immediately, moisture particles began to freeze around their bodies and soon after, actual ice began to surround them. The field of ice grew, covering the entire stadium floor, spreading to the walls and lightly travelling up the aisles until the entire arena was almost completely covered with thick ice.

Cold took hold of the mages present. Even the elders themselves were covered, making it seem to the mages unfamiliar with their nature that something had gone wrong. Silence traversed the assembly, only to be broken by bursts of flame shooting into the air. At first, no one could see the source of the fireworks, but upon closer inspection, the crowd began to cheer as they noticed Pyros elders shooting bursts of fire into the sky. The flames would explode far above the stadium creating a hail of sparks. A rapid firing over-clouded the arena with fire particles.

Large flames continued to shred into a scorching rain that threatened to cover the entire stadium. Before the fire could touch down, all of the small flames drew together, creating a sea of fire above the arena and within the aisles. The flames coursed over many mages, yet none were harmed. Before long, everyone went from being frightened to captivated.

The great canopy of fire caused the ice to melt, which then brought about a large warm stream of water flowing into the center of the area. The flames died down and began to rescind. As the stream continued its course, a loud reverberation pulsed through the building, affecting all present with a slight imbalance and equilibrium loss. The Aqueous elders stood at all the entrances to the arena floor. Their voices sounded a unified resonance, sending tremors through the skin of all those gathered. The flowing waters began to cascade together into four thin columns, each apart and parallel to one another in a squared formation. They rose high, absorbing all of the water until they towered over the colosseum.

Then, from the Aerial section, winged mages took off and flew around the pillars. As they passed over the stands, a great gust of wind followed. This continued until they began to swirl closer to the centre point between the pillars of water. The twirling drew in the currents of air, creating a huge vacuum. Mages had to hold onto their seats for fear of being sucked in. Eventually, an all-out tornado was happening within the stadium. No one could speak as terror swept over the faces of all present. The winds were so strong that it drew in the four pillars of water, and sprayed the crowd with an omnipresent mist, refreshing the mages and calming their nerves.

After this marvellous spectacle, some Spectros raised small

pieces of worked glass and reflected light through the droplets of water creating three ground level rainbows which encompassed the whole amphitheatre.

The crowd was astounded, rising to their feet, cheering and shouting praise in their native tongues. Those that sat at the border between the sections all turned to each other excitedly. Even though most mages did not understand one another, they still impulsively spoke energetically, as if somehow their sheer enthusiasm would be enough to ensure communication. The exhilarated crowd began to calm as the Plains governor stood with hands raised, ready to announce the next performance.

"Sealed beneath the surface of the earth, the Terran nation has thrived. With the use of metals, stones and minerals, they carved their lives out of the rock. Creatures of this underworld constantly threatened their existence. Shielding the people from annihilation were the greatest of the subterranean legions, skilled in deadly martial sciences that have been developed by centuries of training. Here, today, the masters of these arts will provide a live demonstration. I give you the captains of the Legion Elite!"

The crowed rose with loud cheers as over one hundred fully armoured Terran mages marched out onto the grounds. They assembled in a semi-circular formation. The soldiers of the inner area held long spears, while heavy pikes were carried by the Terrans on the outer area. They started as one with a barrage of sequential strikes, their uniform movements displayed their prowess perfectly, which impressed the crowd instantly. Even the Kryos found themselves astounded by their martial skill.

At one point, the group spread out, covering the stadium grounds: one-half began to use their abilities to conjure targets and the other engaged in destroying them, showing off the Terran proficiency. Crossbows, small swords, and pikes were used with great proficiency. After all this, the Terrans began sparring with one another, showing off special weapons like halberds, maces and an assortment of chain weapons. The exposition ended and the crowd gave a very loud standing ovation.

Delshad and Jahan emerged in the arena. The crowds recognized them as members of the team and gave a forceful applause. They bowed to the queen and then to the crowd, then to each other.

"There they are!" exclaimed Sil. "If they're down there, how are they going to see this part of the show?"

His semi-witty remark generated minimal laughter from the team, as they all watched on in eager anticipation of what was to come.

At first, they set themselves ablaze. Next, they began juggling fireballs. That went higher and higher until they were twenty feet in the sky. As the Pyros did this, they slowly moved apart from one another, spun, and began tossing the fire back and forth. The flames grew larger as they hurled it back and forth until eventually, one large flame passed between the two of them. Jahan caught the flame and threw it up into the air where it exploded, sending a bright display of sparks falling. The crowd applauded generously and cheers abounded throughout the stadium.

Some of the falling sparks were harvested by the boys and made into numerous birds that flew around the stadium and close to the crowd causing a nervous, but exhilarated, reaction. As they flew, more and more birds were created and they filled the entire arena sky, threatening to engulf the building and the mages within. Then, spiralling together as one, the birds dove, crashing into the boys, covering them completely with a fiery explosion. The crowd gasped in horror as the two youngest team members stood engulfed in fire. Moments later, the fire calmed and the boys took their bows, well received by a grateful audience.

Next the elders of the Spectros nation presented themselves. Their white garbs and shiny ornamentation was a stark contrast to the rest of their neighbours. With long, white, sparkling beards glistening in the sunlight, they held up small, finely cut glass pyramids in their hands and waited.

The governor stepped aside for Helios to give the introduction:

"These are the elders of the Spectros nation. For centuries, they have watched the world become what it is today. From our desert enclosure, we have seen great historical events and have kept records of our observation. For the first time, these recordings will be open to the public on this momentous occasion. Today, great history will not just be made, it will be seen."

Edified silence and clapping filled the stadium as Helios sat down.

The elders stood for a moment with the crystals raised. It seemed as if nothing was going to happen, then light began to syphon into their artifice. Almost at once, a flurry of images spread through the arena, then slowly came into focus. First, they showed the Aerial Realm and the entire stadium was totally taken over by the scene. None but Aerial natives could lay eyes on the air mages' home in the sky. All mages present were astonished by the presentation as they witnessed everyday life with Aerial children and school, as well as the repairs made daily to the foundation of their sky homeland. It turned dark and they beheld a rare sight for any, other than Aerials. The last flight of an elder, who mature in years, flew off to the resting place of his ancestors.

Next, the Spectros elders showed the first Terrans' meeting with the Queen. Some of the elders, actually present in the audience, gave a cheerful shout of appreciation.

Scene after scene mesmerized the crowd: The battle of the North Hold, the first sailing of Vidar and the team, the desert battles with the ifrit.

The Pyros kingdom was toured briefly and so was the underwater forest dwelling of the Aqueous.

The Spectros' manifestations ended with the awakening of the North elder from his hundred-year sleep, showing the team by Vidar's side and the feast that followed.

The illusions slowly dissipated, leaving everyone speechless. A moment passed. The crowed launched into tremendous applause. The elders bowed and took their leave.

Lastly, the Aerials, prompted by the excessive happiness, began flying around and lifting other mages alongside them. A group of the air mages surrounded the Pyros section and with a concentration of air underneath their bodies, lifted many of them out of their seats. The whole of the stadium was in an overly joyous mood. Mages held up their hands, allowing the Aerials to snatch them, sharing their unique experience of flight.

After over an hour of mirthful behaviour, many of the governors also took to the air. Soon after, the feast was declared and the crowd departed from the stadium. The deluge of joy spilled out into the streets and flooded the city.

CHAPTER 95

The second day dawned and the games were declared. The world was once again exuberant in anticipation of the festive display that the stadium would offer.

All manner of games were chosen and the best mages were selected to represent their nations. It was not so much a competition, but an analysis of the temperaments, strengths and weaknesses mages have developed over the thousand years apart from one another. Most of the challenges would be simple: running, jumping, lifting, the tossing of heavy, round projectiles, throwing javelins and an assortment of other games that combined different elements from each other.

The team gathered in the same booth and as before. Silvanus and Paulo were already present as Victor walked in.

"This is good so far," said Ophir to Victor.

"It still does not feel right," stated Victor.

"You are over-thinking, as usual," Sil paused as he took a drink. "You need to relax. If things get out of hand, we have all of the world's leaders here. Who else better to solve problems?"

His statements are actually making sense for once, Victor thought to himself. Helios and Danir showed up late with Delshad and Jahan.

"Fire boys!" shouted Sil. "Nicely done out there. You were great yesterday."

The rest of the team nodded and with welcoming approval from their mentors, the boys entered the room and took their seats. The games opened with a moving speech. As the first event was being revealed, Blue stepped into the room taking his place beside the boys, who gave half-hugged greetings from their seats.

Next, a vocal description of the game was given and then mages from among the crowd would be chosen by their elders to participate. This went on for hours and if a mage participated in one event and did well, he would later be called to do it again. Players' names were taken down and champions recorded for advancement.

The world seemed to revel in this newfound entertainment. As the athletes were narrowed by extensive competition, Plainswalkers began placing bets on who would be victorious in the later rounds of the contest.

The team sat in their booth, cheering for their nations and admiring the winners. Since they were diplomats, they thought it wise not to engage in athletic competition as it may prove a conflict of interest. As the event progressed, an Aerial messenger flew up and addressed 'Lord' Victor.

"Sir, a complaint has arisen from many of the people," he said sternly.

"What's going wrong?" responded Victor.

"Many of the mages in the stands are claiming the referees are making poor judgements," replied the Aerial.

"Ugh..."

Victor, not expecting to handle such a mundane situation and unsure what to say, thought for a moment.

Paulo then interrupted.

"We will handle this from here. Return to your post."

The messenger saluted and flew off. Victor sat down looking at Paulo.

"I know you have more on your mind," Victor stated, waiting for a response.

"I do not think you should take this lightly. I have been watching the games closely. Those judges down there work here at the arena normally," Paulo informed.

Victor sat in stunned embarrassment that he did not notice it before. Coming to his senses, he thought up a solution.

"Make sure the judges enrolled are mages from all nations. If we saturate them enough, they won't be able to operate. Do this now!" Victor commanded sternly.

Paulo got up, gesturing for Danir and Helios to follow.

"What does all this mean?" asked Sil.

"The normal function of this stadium is to provide entertainment and leisure expositions that, often enough, are events like this. Sometimes, gladiator matches and even horse races are held, but all of them are set up, so winners and losers are predetermined." He paused a moment to let everything sink in.

"The main revenue this stadium generates is through gambling on these contests. The nobles who control this ensure that the victory is predetermined, so they bribe officials and pay players to fall. In *this* case, most of the nations at hand have no use for currency, so the judges that have been posted have most likely been compromised."

Sil remained speechless as he let all of the information process, then asked why they would want to damage their own tournament. Victor thought about how to answer his friend as the Aerials and many of the other more elemental nations had no concept of greed. The Terrans, to an extent, could understand, but Victor had no easy way to alleviate his friend's curiosity.

At that moment, Paulo and the others walked in.

"It's done," he said sternly. "The judges have been scattered. Kuria is one of them, so this should work out."

The team sat back down, comforted from the recent report. Sil still looked uneasy, not sure what to make of the incident. The games continued unhindered after that minor delay. The stadium was packed with mages. With the stands overcrowding and the competition becoming heated, it set the stage for what was to come next.

"Where did all these extra mages come from?" asked Danir. "I thought there would be limited seating?"

Victor looked nervously at Paulo who, understanding the urban mentality as well, answered the question.

"Men are making extra coin by letting people in to see the games. We call them scalpers."

"This is a diplomatic gathering!" Ophir snarled. "Damn it, there are elders from other nations down there. This cannot be allowed. Silvanus!"

"Yessir!" Sil responded, half comically.

"Summon a contingent from the Aerial corps. I want those

scalpers cleared out and order restored. Also, ensure that the sections devoted to specific nations remain for those nations. The last thing we need is misinterpreted bullshit to start conflict."

All this was done with quick efficiency as Aerial and Terran forces escorted all onlookers outside of the stadium. This created a sort of protest group of urban Nebateans, which, instead of overcrowding the arena, now began making trouble outside.

Ophir himself went out with Danir and Paulo to aid the security forces against what could potentially turn into a riot.

"Why are they not dispersing?" Ophir asked Paulo.

"They seemed to have paid money to get in. Without a refund they will not leave," he responded coldly.

Paulo summoned Danir to him.

"Find all arena security personnel and inform them they are to leave the premises immediately. They are to be replaced with the Queen's Guard or any of our people..."

"Captain," said Danir hesitantly, "on what grounds do we have the right to do this?"

"Tell anyone who resists that they will be arrested for breaking the Queen's peace," Ophir said, reassuring his comrade.

Within the stadium, a Plainswalker arena official and a Kryos judge gave rating on a long jump contest between a Pyros and a Terran champion. The Plainswalker gave order for victory by the Pyros and the Kryos showed a resolve for the latter. The large Kryos judge confronted his counterpart and in a broken Plains speak, began to contest his discernment.

"Why you make call like this? Burning mage won by short leap. You do this many times already. Is not right," he said with an angry tone of voice.

"Listen, things are done differently here. Let this go, it's nothing," the worker replied. "At the end of this, I'll split the difference with you."

The Kryos judge was adamant about his position. The Plainswalker leaned closer, grabbing him by the arm to talk secretly. The Kryos immediately thought this a challenge and sent the other judge flying across the field. The entire arena went silent. Buri marched onto the field and demanded an explanation.

"It is alright. He challenged me first. He is brave, but not smart," replied the young mage.

"These are our traditions. They have no such practice here," Buri insisted, assuming a misunderstanding.

"He was calling falsely. I spoke against him. He struck first."

This made the elder visibly angry. He shouted commands and all of the Kryos emptied their section and rallied behind him.

Victor looked on with horror.

Of all the races to be angered, it had to be the most war loving mages in existence!

"Sil, take me down there. When we land, find Ophir."

They quickly flew down. Victor immediately engaged the elder.

"Buri, what is this about?"

The elder spoke in his native tongue while Vidar, standing next to him with a worried expression, translated.

"Your games are made to humiliate us. One of your people was cheating."

Victor kept a straight face, knowing that the Kryos prized straightforwardness in all their dealings. If he showed any emotion that could be interpreted unfavourably, all credibility would be lost.

"Buri, you are mistaken," said Victor with an unnatural calm. "This mage will be taken from the trials. Let us have a drink, I will watch the games beside you."

The apology worked. The Kryos prepared to head back to their seats.

"So, that's how it is then? You take a foreigner's side over your own," said the judge, being helped to his feet. "He nearly broke my back, he did."

Victor turned, controlling his rage. "Go take a seat and recover. Food will be brought to you. Take the rest of the day off."

"I will not!" he protested. "I work here, *Queen's* man. I am a Nebat citizen, and I do not take orders from any tree dweller."

A group of arena workers formed behind him and one foolish mage from among them threw a handful of gravel wildly at Victor.

It seemed as if the world slowed. Victor watched as the crushed rock sailed passed him and struck Buri in the arm. His calm demeanour changed instantly. The arena judges finally understood that this nation played by very different rules, that Nebat was not the centre of the universe, and that this learning had come too late.

Oh, crap, thought Victor. *Oh crap! What now? Vidar, please do something.*

Victor's face had become seized with rage and fear all at once. Buri had been insulted by a mage of lesser stature. He roared, raising his arms, summoning the power of frost and ice to strike at everything around him.

"Run!" Vidar shouted.

The Kryos launched a disorganized attack against the native judges; all of the mages in the stadium were terrified. The elders of the Pyros nation were shouting for order, while the Aerials took to flight. Victor ran toward the nearest exit, wishing that the workers were not following him so closely. The Pyros marched forward to help settle the dispute only to be blocked by a large wall of ice. Victor emerged outside and waiting for him were Aerial corps members, as well as Terran security forces armed with crossbows and short blades, accompanied by the Queen's Guard.

The Kryos marched out, ready to face them. Victor stopped and turned, not moving, while the arena workers fled behind their protectors.

"Do something," Victor said to Vidar, who had an extremely troubled expression from the chin up.

Vidar responded by marching ahead of his grandfather and turning full circle, arms held up, head bowed down. A sign of submission.

"Bestefar huld!" he said penitently.

Buri responded in North speak.

"Are you turning on your own? Have you been away from your people so long that you forget your brethren!?"

"Buri, you know us," said Victor with Vidar translating instantly. "These actions have been carried out by a group of boys. Treat them as such. They will be dealt with, I promise."

Buri calmed at Victor's word. Victor then gestured for the soldiers to lower their weapons.

"There must be no more dishonourable behaviour," he stated through Vidar.

"Even if I were not able to silence it, your display just now would have," responded Victor.

Buri and other Kryos, within hearing distance, smiled at the comment.

"Please let's go back in..." Victor was cut off by what he saw next.

Smoke began rising from the stadium. Loud shouting and flashing lights could be seen from the outside. Aerials circled overhead. Out of breath, Sil landed.

"It started between the Terrans and Pyros blaming one another for the problems." He panted, his brow drenched with sweat, his face awash with worry. "Words turned into threats, others tried to intervene. You have to get back in there."

"Buri, rally your people. We need to stop this fighting." He paused a moment remembering who he was talking to. "Please, help us."

Buri nodded and gave an order. Vidar followed him back inside while Victor and Ophir led the security forces alongside them. Already mages were stampeding through the exits; a huge riot was in full swing.

They fought in the stands, on the grounds, and in the aisles. It was impossible to determine who was against whom. The entire stadium was in chaos. Fire had engulfed one section of the building. The Aerials flew to higher ground, crowding around their elders. The Kryos started breaking up fights, with the Queen's Guard trying to form barriers between groups that were fighting. Aerials from the corps were lifting aggressive mages out of the warpath and placing them far from one another, making the crowd control easier.

As one fight quietened, another broke out in an even fiercer uprising. The arena workers began fighting with contestants. Since almost all of the security was at one side of the stadium, the fighting erupted like an intense disaster. Many of the mages that had taken refuge from the onslaught were now fleeing the animosity through the nearest exit.

A huge wave of mages poured through the passageway, completely filling the corridor and making it difficult to move easily. The fighting from behind propelled them forward. Everyone thinking the same thing led to overcrowding and a slowed escape.

There was a loud scream... silence... crying and shouts for help in different languages. The unthinkable had happened. An Aqueous elder directed his people in a unified vibration, causing all within the arena to lose their equilibrium. The security forces came to their senses the quickest and forced the remaining mages into a pseudo-peace.

Victor, in great anger, rounded up the arena workers to be dealt with later. The Queen's Guard assisted. Sil sped forward, his face pale, sweating as he had been before, but this time, more emotion swept through his features.

"Victor, you have to come. It's bad!"

CHAPTER 96

"How could all this happen!?" demanded the Queen.

Within her chamber, the entire team, with Victor at its head, stood before her. What was once a proud group with great accomplishments was now broken by a single day's infraction. Their faces sank with disgrace and embarrassment.

The Queen, realizing the situation, stood up.

"From which nation were they from?"

"Both Aqueous," responded Victor. "A mother and her child."

"Do we know who is responsible?" the Queen enquired.

"It happened in an overcrowded exit-way and they were trampled. How do we punish over a hundred fleeing mages?" responded Victor.

The Queen took a while to think.

"Where are they now?"

"All have returned to their lodgings and the Aqueous mourn their loss," Victor answered. "Their elders demand restitution and that something be done."

"Summon the elders from all nations at once," instructed the Queen.

The elders soon entered. All were silent, each one waiting for the other to speak first. They sat silently, waiting to see what the others would do. Blue stepped forward, knelt before the Queen and then spoke.

"As stated by Victor before, your Highness, what will be done about our nation's loss?"

"Rest assured, not only do you have the deepest sympathies of the Plains nation, but an investigation is being conducted as to who started the riot that led to this disaster."

Blue translated for his elder, vibrating softly so as not to disrupt the other mages present. The elder replied back to Blue, with justifiably angry tones. Blue listened and relayed the message.

"This is unacceptable. Until you find those responsible and punish them, we will not stay here."

The Queen, saddened by their decision, was unable to do anything but comply.

"Very well. Full accommodations will be made. Set up the carts and carriages and ensure they make it home safely," she commanded.

Towards the evening, the Queen watched as the Terran carts drove off with a wounded people. The Aqueous mages came as guests to a banquet and left as mourners attending a funeral. The whole company of elders and delegates, as well as the team and even the Queen herself, stood the vigil.

Upon re-entry, the team summoned an audience, where Vidar spoke first.

"My grandfather has decreed that we are to take our exit tomorrow. Seeing the lack of control and weakness of this people makes them unworthy of alliance. In the morning, we depart. All Kryos are to return to their homeland and the North Wall is to be sealed, lest some of our brethren should re-enter this land and be contaminated by its defect."

What he had to say visibly saddened Vidar and the team even more so. Jahan and Delshad stepped up next.

"Your Highness," they both said at the same time.

Delshad gently placed his hand on the shoulder of his friend implying that he would deliver the message.

"Our leaders have given orders to leave the city and return to the home world. They say that after seeing such a slow response for a crime against a foreigner, it shows that even our people are in danger. In the interest of safety, we are withdrawing all of our nation's members and returning home."

Jahan being younger, started to cry at the end of Delshad's report. Kuria came forward and placed her arms around him to comfort him. She escorted the Pyros boys away from the throne allowing Silvanus to step forward.

"Your majesty," he said half-heartedly, giving a quarter bow with both hands outstretched to his sides.

"Well, since the day has been filled with such a consistent stream of reports, why break pattern now. My elders have in their infallible wisdom decided to, for the time being, suspend their membership to the alliance. They say that, in the future, perhaps they would re-consider, but with so many nations deserting, it would be pointless to remain. We will be leaving before nightfall. The Aerials that are members of the corps and ambassadors to the throne are discharged. Soo... well, that includes me."

Not able to make eye contact with the Queen, the mage who started it all moved back to his place, embraced his team brothers and left the chamber.

No one could sleep that night. Most of the mages prepared to leave early in the morning and almost all of them pleaded with their elders to reconsider. All was to no avail. In the morning Victor, Paulo and Ophir gave a heartfelt, depressing farewell to their friends. For most, it would be the last time they saw each other.

The Pyros boys shed tears as they joined their people's retreat. They marched single file and were taken back to the fiery wastes where none could follow.

Vidar delayed as long as he could, but with his place at the head, he wasted few words. He knew that as long as his grandfather was alive, this decision would not be reversed. His people would head back to their secluded realm in the north and see the plains, deserts, wastes, and oceans no more.

Sil flew with his nation. Light tears fell as he followed his brethren. They flew in tight formation, lifted by currents propelled by their elders. Looking behind him, all he could see were other Aerials. In a swift blinding sweep, the gale force brought them home as one: the elders, the mages, Silvanus and his memories.

By noon the city was deserted. Street venders closed and the stadium, half destroyed by the riot, remained as a silent testament to yesterday's failure. The Queen occupied her chamber alone and took no visitors or food. Victor stood by himself watching all of it disappear, remembering the venture it took to bring all of it together.

Paulo and Ophir approached silently and Helios brought food, which was refused. They drank on his insistence. This silent city, for a brief moment, had been a shining beacon, drawing the entire world together and now, even the strong noon sun could not replace the light lost. Victor stood for hours wondering what all their work was for. Eventually, they moved indoors and Ophir sat next to him.

"So," Victor began speaking quietly. "What will your people do?"

"Well, since I am captain of everything above ground and even though the situation is upsetting, I think it is in our best interest to stay," Ophir said.

Victor smiled softly.

"Helios, what say the Spectros?"

"We have spent centuries in a prison of our own making. To go back would be foolish," he responded, smiling, trying to cheer his friend.

"The alliance lives," Helios went on. "If we hold strong to what we believe, maybe some luck will make others do the same."

CHAPTER 97

A week later, evidence was presented to the Queen's justice and four very wealthy noblemen were charged with breaking the Queen's peace. The penalty was the first death sentence in almost four hundred years.

The stadium was shut down and the workers relocated. This was relayed to the Aqueous that still frequented the land and spoke with the Plainswalkers of the area. It made little difference to their situation. As time healed their wounds, many returned to the surface and visited during festivals; this included Blue who remained loyal to the ideas of a global unification all the rest of his days. None, though, ever returned to the city.

In the fiery heart of the planet, two young boys would become the greatest storytellers of their generation, speaking of worlds beyond and of adventures with the mages who lived there. They would inspire their people to colonize the surface of the southern wastes and create the first above-ground Pyros metropolis. The Pyros never reopened trade with the alliance, but for over a century afterwards, the stories of Delshad and Jahan were told to the children of the burning nation.

In the frozen north, Vidar surpassed all expectations of becoming a great leader of his people. He married a lady worthy of his station and they had seven children. The time came and he was offered a chance to pass into the hall of the immortals. Even though he had longed for that moment, his thoughts turned to his children growing up alone. Since the wars had passed, he stayed with the living, surrounded by a loving family and a loyal people.

He passed onto his children all the arts and practices he had been taught, with one addition, about a huge mountain across the frozen desert that only seemed like a mountain. In truth, it was a doorway to another world and that one day their people would pass through.

Silvanus would return periodically for festivals and berries. His elders had withdrawn from the alliance but had not forbidden their people from stepping on solid ground. They allowed free passage periodically. He and Victor would remain close friends throughout their days. Victor's attitude toward the team ideals changed and one dark afternoon, Ophir discovered a letter left in his quarters.

> *It has come to my attention, in light of the recent events, that our endeavours have been permanently sidetracked. I have given this decision a great deal of thought and have decided to resign as team leader. I declare that after the opening of this note which you will read aloud in front of Her Majesty's council, that my position is forfeit and my title surrendered.*
>
> *In my place, I appoint Helios, for there is no other who understands the history of our world better than this mage.*
>
> *I will make clear that our efforts were not for nothing. My resignation is due to the verifiable reality that we cannot achieve our long-term goal of unification.*
>
> *The new aim will be better served by a more capable leader, with talents that lean toward this form of service. Therefore, with little regret and great hope, I leave my post expectant of a future time when all nations will rejoin and our world will be as one.*

Ophir finished reading the letter to the Queen and her council, as instructed. The Queen, saddened by the news, waited in silence and then gave instruction that Helios was to replace Victor. Helios would be given all powers and privileges that came with his position.

Ophir and Helios met in the royal courtyard where they sat at a table to talk over the day's events; Kuria joined them soon after.

"So, this is it," stated Helios. "I become leader of a broken department and a failed objective. What's left to build on?"

"Also, remember: Paulo was offered the job first," Ophir added, teasing his comrade. "He turned it down."

"You are starting to sound like Sil," Helios said smiling.

"I guess someone has to," Ophir responded. "Our base in the Southern Wastes was destroyed. We did not have enough mages to keep it together and the Pyros felt it too close to their domain. They burnt it down after we left."

Ophir looked saddened at his own report. Danir arrived and sat with them, immediately congratulating Helios.

"Orders were given yesterday to abandon the North Hold as the Kryos sealed the wall completely. Even the false hole that lead to the deep crevasse," Danir announced. "They really know how to stick it to us. Any word from Victor?"

"He left yesterday - Paulo too, actually," Ophir declared. "We will be visiting him during the festival though and from what I hear, Sil will be coming along."

The mages all smiled after hearing this and Ophir set the tone that would define their duties.

"So, what is our first order of business?" Ophir asked.

Helios, now realizing the situation he was in, thought for a few moments and then set out a plan for restructuring the department.

"Kuria, hence forth you are chief ambassador from our nation. I cannot fulfil my duties and lead the team. As for our mission, we will no longer be involved in expeditions. Our new goal will be to publish all of our findings. In our time, we failed to secure an alliance with our neighbours. Nevertheless, future generations must not be denied their chance. With all of our resources, we will compile a course of study that details the full diversity of our mage world and spread it throughout the nations of the alliance, so that one day, perhaps within our own time, other heroes will arise that may rekindle the unity we had hoped for."

CHAPTER 98

Victor travelled back to the deep plains on a beautiful summer day. He walked most of the way. The Terran carriages took him as close as the roads would allow. He slept many nights outside under the trees, eating what he could find from the bush and anyone who saw him greeted him with great respect.

As he neared his home, he recognized where, as children, many of his friends and family members would celebrate the holy days. It had been years, but everything was just as he had left. Then he came to the tree fields – he saw them moving using their roots to grasp the newly turned soil. Smoke rose from the chimney.

Someone is cooking, he thought as he walked towards the house.

No one noticed him and no one was there to notice. Victor moved slowly, savouring his childhood home, remembering where he played with his cousins and worked with his father during harvest.

Back in Nebat and the surrounding cities, things were always changing. The team would make contact with a new nation and different technologies or advancements brought about a sudden upgrade to the surroundings. But not here, the traditions and routine had been the same for almost a thousand years.

He stopped at the doorway. He could smell the food from within and knew his mother and her sisters were cooking and preparing for when the men returned. Even with all of the adventures and great accomplishments that had a profound effect on the entire world, at his home, it seemed he had done nothing at all.

About the Author

Matti Silver is the creative, right side of the brain among his friends.

His forte is intricate world-building and the shooting down of logical, sound ideas. While the rest of the world makes 1-screen indie retro games, Matti releases an MMO that has its own language so every nationality is equally burdened by it. A lover of film, comic books, fantasy and anime, he takes it upon himself to combine all the best ideas and present them to the world, like a master curator of fine taste and limitless free time.

Besides his endless energy and eclectic taste in everything, Matti loves nothing more than reading everything except speed limit signs and expiry dates on his government documents.

To see more

If you enjoyed reading this, we would love it if you could leave a review. Reviews are the lifeblood of our authors and allow them to keep producing quality content.

Thanks again for reading and make sure to check out **www.evwpress.com** for more works from the publisher

CPSIA information can be obtained
at www.ICGtesting.com
Printed in the USA
LVOW08s1449111116
512625LV00001B/81/P